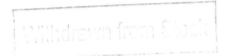

M
IS FOR
MUMMY

M

IS FOR

MUMMY

KATY COX

CORVUS

Published in hardback in Great Britain in 2022 by Corvus, an imprint of Atlantic Books Ltd.

10 9 8 7 6 5 4 3 2 1

A CIP catalogue record for this book is available from the British Library.

Hardback ISBN: 978 1 83895 313 3
Trade paperback ISBN: 978 1 83895 314 0
E-book ISBN: 978 1 83895 315 7

Design and typesetting benstudios.co.uk
Printed in Great Britain by TJ Books Ltd

Corvus
An imprint of Atlantic Books Ltd
Ormond House
26–27 Boswell Street
London
WC1N 3JZ

www.corvus-books.co.uk

For J-boy, Jimmy and Mr Belafonte.
In the words of Michael Bublé,
'You're my everything.'

Prologue

It started with a fart. Not any ordinary fart, but a fart with purpose. A fart that was to change our lives forever.

It was 6.30 a.m. and Ed had already left for work, as he had to be there early for hair and make-up. He was going to be playing live on *Good Morning Britain*, strumming his guitar behind Josh Groban, whilst I was stuck at home, cutting a banana into identical semicircles, hoping that they'd pass Stanley's thorough inspection. But then came the fart, and with it came a gush of fluid which exploded all over the floor with the force of a burst water main.

There was no time to process what had just happened because Stanley had already appeared in the doorway.

'Excuse me, but where is W?' he said as he walked in clutching a letter V in one hand and a Y in the other. 'I need it. I need it. Need it. Need it,' he chanted four times because he was four years old and, in his mind, every demand *had* to be made exactly four times.

'Stan, Mummy is having a bit of a problem here. Can you wait a second?'

But of course, he couldn't.

'Need! Need!' he continued, the hysteria in his voice rapidly escalating. 'Need! NEED!'

There was little choice but to ransack the flat looking for the letter W to complete his treasured alphabet puzzle. So, whilst the floor became saturated with the birth waters of his unborn brother, I tore the living room apart and, eventually, I found it wedged between the sofa cushions. A crisis was thankfully averted.

With Stanley entertained lining up his letters in the lounge, I threw a towel down on the wet kitchen floor, stuffed a pad in my pants and grabbed my phone to call Ed. As usual, he didn't answer, so next on the 'in case of emergency' list was my best friend, Charlie.

'Charls. It's me. My waters have gone. Ed is at ITV and I'm alone here. Can you come?'

A simple but shrill 'Fuck' flew out of her mouth and, after pausing briefly to collect herself, she said, 'Okay. Let me just stick on a bra, cancel my gig and call in the cavalry. I'll be over in ten.'

'Haul ass!' I said. 'Promise you won't faff about?'

'I won't! I *won't*.'

But she would, and she did.

After checking that Stanley was still happily engrossed in his puzzle, I hurried to the bathroom to remove nine months' worth of body hair in preparation for my impending showcase of nakedness. I hadn't actually seen my fanny since conception and I was determined that, this time, she was going to look her best (unlike when I gave birth to Stanley and wound up in hospital with a seventies Disco *Bush*-ferno grooving out of my pants).

Climbing carefully into the bath tub, I set to work with Ed's razor in one hand and a magnifying mirror in the other, but it very quickly became too much. My back was on the verge of spasm, I had pins and needles in the most delicate of places and my contorted wrist felt like it was about to snap. So, after two minutes, I gave up.

Au naturel would have to do.

I heard the key in the lock at around 7 a.m. Charlie had arrived and was dashing down the hall calling out my name along with a mixture of colourful expletives. She threw open the bathroom door and found me totally naked, one leg up on the toilet seat, frantically spritzing every inch of my body with Marc Jacobs's Daisy.

'Luce!' she gasped. 'You okay? Sorry I took so lo—' She paused abruptly and the panic in her tone instantly dispersed when she clocked the bottle in my hand. 'Ooh, Marc Jacobs?'

'It sure is, my friend.' I winked. 'It may not look that pretty down there, but at least it smells divine.'

'Good call.' She nodded in approval. 'Hand it over, will you?' She snatched the bottle out of my hand and gave her cleavage a healthy spritz whilst I reached for a towel to cover myself up.

'Right, so, I've nailed it,' she said. 'Jen and Will are on their way. She'll stay here with Stan, and Will and I are driving you to hospital. And don't panic, I've already left several strongly worded messages on Ed's voicemail telling him to meet us there.'

'God, I love you, Charls,' I gushed and threw my arms around her.

'I know. I'm, like, fucking incredible.' She patted me gently on the back of my head, then withdrew from my arms. 'So, what now? Want me to rub your back or get you a shot of vodka or something?'

'Zero rubbing required, pal. Or vodka for that matter.'

She looked disappointed. 'But doesn't it hurt?'

'Hardly at all – I'd say it's only a two right now. But when it hits a ten and I'm begging to be put down, you've *got* to promise me that you'll do whatever it takes to get me *all* of the drugs.'

She flexed her muscles and planted both hands firmly on her hips. '*That* I can do, my friend.'

I sent her in to the lounge to hang out with Stanley, then threw on some comfy clothes and called the hospital. I was expecting to be told to take a paracetamol and wait at home for two days to writhe around in agony on a yoga ball. But no.

'Mrs Wright, if you're thirty-six weeks then you're not quite full term and must come in immediately to be examined,' said the midwife with a tone of urgency.

Anxiety levels were suddenly cranked up a few extra gears, but when I turned around and caught a glimpse of my hideous reflection in the bedroom mirror, all I could hear were my mother's words: 'You need a wee bit of lipstick there, love.' Since my early teens, I'd been trained to apply a 'wee bit of lipstick' at *all* times – family parties, weddings, trips to the dentist and for routine smear tests – and in my mum's mind, giving birth would certainly be an occasion that warranted a splash of colour across my lips. So, I dug out my make-up bag and got stuck in just to make her proud.

As I was smearing an extra thick layer of foundation across my cheeks, Stan wandered into the room wearing nothing but his Thomas the Tank Engine slippers.

'Excuse me. Excuse me.'

'Stan, where are your pyjamas?'

'But I want my shapes puzzle.'

'It's on the big table in the living room. Go and ask Auntie Charlie to find your pyjamas, please.'

He stood totally still, staring at the floor, so I tried again in a way that I knew he would comprehend. 'Stan. I need you to do *four* things. Number one, go to the living room;

number two, ask Auntie Charlie to put on your pyjamas; number three, get your shapes puzzle off the big table; number four, play. Okay?'

He nodded stiffly then left the room in silence.

The buzzer sounded, marking the arrival of Jen and Will; the rest of the cavalry had arrived.

'Whatever you do, Luce, do *not* give birth all over Will's new car,' Charlie called out from the other end of the flat. 'He's only had it a few days and Jen said he's really precious about it.'

Before I could respond, Jen came bounding up the stairs and into the bedroom with her arms fixed wide open and tears streaming down her cheeks. She pounced on me, nearly knocking me clean off my feet.

'I can't believe it, Lucy!' she sobbed into my earlobe. 'We're going to have another baby!'

In followed her boyfriend, Will, who hovered awkwardly in the doorway with his eyes glued to his phone.

'All right, pull it together, Jen!' said Charlie firmly as she pushed past him. 'There's no time for hysteria. And don't you freak out either, Will. You *can* look – there are no heads hanging out just yet,' she said reassuringly as she ushered him over to join in the group hug.

Then, BOOM! I was smacked in the guts by an invisible cricket bat and dropped to the floor in agony. Just as I began to clamber up, another hideous blow came to the uterus, then came another: thick and fast, like being repeatedly pounded in the guts by a sledgehammer.

'Ten! Charls, I'm a ten!'

Sobbing followed, then the swearing: ugly words that I'd only ever heard spewing from the lips of Charlie when she'd overdone it on the Stella Artois.

Stanley wandered into the room. 'Excuse me,' he said, oblivious to the fact that my insides were rupturing directly in front of his eyes.

'Call me "Mummy", Stan, not "excuse me" – *Mummy*. What. Is. Iiiiiit?'

'Excuse me, *Mummy*. Excuse me, but did you know that a dodecahedron has twelve sides?'

'Yes, yes. Go and put on your pyjam—'

'A nonagon has nine sides ...' he continued as the tears rolled down my face and hit his slippers.

'Fuck! Get the car, Will! She's a ten!' yelled Charlie frantically as she pulled me off the floor.

Within minutes, I was mooing on the driveway on all fours like a heartbroken cow as Will screeched to a halt in his fourteen-year-old Fiat Panda. He emerged from a thick black cloud of exhaust fumes looking as proud as punch, then he promptly stuffed my suitcase in the boot. Using Charlie's arm as a crutch, I pulled myself up and leant down to kiss Stanley, who was standing on the drive, still wearing nothing but his slippers.

'Goodbye, my darling, I'll be back home soon with your baby brother.' I smiled. 'Auntie Jen will take good care of you and Daddy will be back later.'

'Excuse me,' he said, looking directly into my eyes for the first time in weeks.

'Yes, my darling?'

'But what does "fuck" mean?'

1

The Flabalanche

My day starts the way that every other day has for the last six months: at 5.01 a.m. with Stanley's foot wedged under my chin, Jack hysterical and demanding milk, and Ed snoring like a jackhammer smashing through tarmac. The man doesn't flinch, even when in a moment of rage I push Stan's foot away from my jugular, then lift Jack and press his screaming mouth up to Ed's ear to jolt him into action. It's *his* turn to feed him, after all.

Ed wasn't this useless when Stanley was born. I remember him being pretty crap to start with, but by the end of the first year, I'd transformed him into Mary Poppins with a penis – a Gary Poppins, if you will. Under my rigorous guidance, we tag-teamed the night feeds, passing Stanley back and forth through the night to each other like he was a baton in a relentless relay race. We shared the explosive nappy changes, spurred each other on through the milky vomit attacks and embraced the crippling exhaustion together.

But now that Jack has come along, the novelty has totally worn off. Ed has developed a 'been there, done that' attitude, and since becoming busier at work, his enthusiasm for burping a baby in the middle of the night has waned significantly. This time around, he doesn't hear Jack cry at all. A marching band of topless trombone-blowing models could parade through our bedroom and he probably still wouldn't stir.

When I can take no more, I attack him repeatedly with a feather pillow until he falls out of the bed onto all fours like a startled cat.

'Okay. I'm up. I'm up!'

'It's *your* turn,' I say, seething. 'Take the baby. His bottle is there ready. I need to get Stan his breakfast.'

'Just give me a sec,' he says, before disappearing for one of his epic twenty-five-minute-long sessions on the toilet seat, as he does every single morning like clockwork.

I am perhaps less patient with him than usual because today isn't a regular day, but an important one: I am officially going back to work. Miguel, my agent, has been in touch with the offer of a gig and finally, for the first time since last July, I'll get to leave the flat with just a cello on my back.

A gig for Miguel is *exactly* the sort of gig that I need to gently ease me back in to playing the cello again. He exclusively books what we in the music industry call 'background gigs', which typically involve bashing out tunes to shitfaced business men at their fancy company dinners. Such gigs aren't exactly artistically satisfying, but they're an easy source of income for most musicians and they're essential if you want to keep the bailiffs from breaking down your door.

On a background gig, our job is solely to create a sophisticated ambience – to be *seen*, not heard. Easy-fecking-peasy! There will be no TV cameras zooming up my nostrils, no picky audiences, no brutal critics or fiendishly difficult music to prepare. And what's more, I'll probably squeeze a free glass of champers out of one of the waiters if I play my cards right. This particular gig will be a goodie because

Charlie and Jen have been booked on violin. The 'A Team', as Miguel calls us, will be reunited at last and I simply cannot wait!

These past few months, I have been cooped up inside with two small kids, wading through an endless tunnel of soiled babygros, mucus showers and 2 a.m. wake-up calls. This has been taxing enough, but I've also had to cope with Stanley's explosions every time I serve him his dinner with my right hand and not my left. In short, I'm ready to get back out there and remind my fingers that they're not just skilled in smearing Sudocrem on a tiny bumhole, but they are also capable of playing some Mozart in the dark corner of a chandelier-filled ballroom.

The main concern that has kept me awake most of the night: I don't have anything to wear. Two kids later and my formerly upstanding boobs now hang down over my belly button like a pair of deflated balloons, and my nipples are the size of helicopter landing pads.

My gut is even more troubling. An avalanche of flab (a 'flabalanche', as I've christened it) has descended over the top of my high-waisted pants, the flimsy elastic straining under the force of it. After stuffing down a three-course Christmas dinner and an entire box of Celebrations last month, I ended up in tears when I caught sight of it smiling back at me in the bathroom mirror. All saggy and misshapen, my gut has developed a wicked grimace that strongly resembles the Grinch, only not green.

In Miguel's email, he stated in block capitals that we have to wear 'SHORT BLACK DRESSES' for this gig – a most unusual request, as full-length ballgowns are the norm for black-tie events. I'd banked on throwing on my trusty black maternity gown, but with that no longer being an option, I spend most of the morning wading through my wardrobe in a blind panic trying to find something suitable.

'Ed, what does this look like?' I say, twirling around in a tight jewelled dress that has been gathering dust in the wardrobe for the best part of three years since I last wore it. He is engrossed in an episode of *Thunderbirds* and doesn't look up.

'Ed!' I snap. 'I said, what does this dress look like?'

'What do you mean?'

'I *mean* my dress! What does it look like?'

'It's fine.'

'But do I look fat in it? Be honest.'

'Um,' he pauses, 'a bit.'

'No need to be *so* honest. Damn, taking a bullet to the heart would be less painful!'

'What? You said be honest.'

I sigh heavily, then squeeze my flabalanche into several more sparkly garments like some sort of amateur contortionist. Puffing, panting and fearing that I may have cracked a few ribs, I return to the lounge to seek his approval once again.

'You looked the thinnest in that one,' he says, pointing to an off-black beach dress that cost four pounds in Primark a few years earlier. It's a casual cotton slip designed to go over a bikini and has clearly been tumble-dried over a hundred times, given that it's greyish and has small fuzzy balls stuck all over it.

'But that's a beach dress. Is it posh enough?'

'Yep.'

'But do I look nice in it?'

'Yep.'

All other options have been exhausted. I don't have the patience to compete with Lady Penelope for his attention, so I chuck it in a bag along with my stilettos and devote the rest of the day to preparing to leave the flat.

This solitary gig has caused me to lie awake several nights in a row in an anxious mess, thinking about everything that needs to be done before leaving the kids for just a few hours. I put Jack's nappies, wipes and bum cream in a neat pile on the changing table. I lay out clean pyjamas for both of them, then sterilise bottles and dummies and type out Stan's meticulous routine in bullet points so that it's easy to follow. Then, most importantly, I double check that all the pieces to Stan's new Russian alphabet puzzle are in place and put it safely on the kitchen counter so he can find it with ease. Only when all of this is done can I even consider setting foot out of the door.

What has fuelled my anxiety the most about working tonight is the thought of leaving the boys with Ed's mother, Judith, who is due at 5 p.m. From experience, I just know that I'll get home from work and have to spend the whole night rocking Jack back to sleep after the woman has ignored all of my instructions. It's a definite that she won't do what I've asked because she'll be too busy rummaging through our cupboards, searching for more evidence to justify why her beloved son should never have married me.

Last year, she stumbled upon my Rampant Rabbit in the drawer of my bedside table and couldn't look me in the eye for weeks after. Thankfully, when she snooped into Ed's drawer on her next visit and found the leopard-print thong and pink fluffy handcuffs that I'd bought him as a joke for his birthday, I felt an explosion of joy within.

I'd gone down, but I'd dragged him along with me, all the way to the gutter.

2

The Model Mother

Ed leaves for work at 4.30 p.m. He lifts his guitar, opens the door and walks out of it. Just like that.

Judith arrives a few minutes later and, against every natural instinct that I have for self-preservation, I buzz her up to the flat.

'Hi, Judith. Thanks so much for this. You're really saving me,' I say with the most enthusiastic tone that I can muster.

'Hello, Lucy.' She strides into the hall and dumps a large box on the floor, which misses my toes by millimetres. 'I've had a big clean-out of the garage.'

Stepping backwards, she slowly scans my body from top to bottom, then opens her skinny arms and leans in to give me a brief, stiff hug. 'Lost a few pounds, I see.' She smiles wryly.

As usual, I have no words. I simply shake my head and fake a slight smile.

She pats me on the arm. 'Well, keep at it, Lucy. I've read that it's harder to lose the weight the second time around, which is why I stuck to having just the one.'

I quickly steer the conversation towards something else before I give in to the temptation to headbutt her. 'So, what's in the box?'

'Books mainly. Most of Edward's schoolbooks, his drawings and his collection of *Spiderman* comics. Oh, and wait till you see this.' She delves into the box and pulls a painting out of a plastic wallet. 'He did that when he was Stan's age!'

'Wow,' I say, staring down at an immaculate picture of an aeroplane that was blatantly drawn by a teenage Ed … perhaps even Leonardo da Vinci.

'It's such a shame that it's been in the garage for thirty-odd years. I thought you might like to hang it somewhere?' A squeaky giggle escapes her lips before she slips it back in to the box. 'Anyway, here. Take it all. It's for you to enjoy now. My new exercise bike is arriving next week and I need the extra space in the garage for it.'

'No problem, I'll find somewhere for it,' is all I say. I lift the box and dump it in the corner of the hall where it will no doubt stay for the next year.

'Anyway, Judith, thanks again for tonight. I really appreciate it. I just need to quickly run through the routine with you before I head off.' I hand her a list detailing exactly what she needs to do to ensure that her evening runs smoothly.

She nods. 'Yes, yes. I *do* know how to look after children, Lucy. I did raise your husband, don't forget.'

'But Stan is *very* particular. You have to stick to the list or else he will get upset and make your evening a misery.'

She rolls her eyes dramatically, then folds up my list and puts it in the back pocket of her burgundy cords before heading to the kitchen to survey the inside of the cupboards. 'So, what's for supper?'

'Jack is having one of his pouches and a yoghurt,' I say, 'and he'll need an 8-ounce bottle at around 7.30 p.m. before bed. Stan is having fish fingers and waffles, but make sure you cut them into equal-sized rectangles or he won't touch them.'

'And what about vegetables?'

'Nope. I've tried everything, Judith, trust me. He won't go near them. He gags.'

'Gags? Lucy, you *really* should—' I stand back and brace myself for one of her lectures but something more distressing catches her eye. 'Whose is *this*?' She pulls a chicken and mushroom Pot Noodle out of the cupboard and holds it up in the air as if it's a dead rat.

I jump in first. 'It's Ed's.'

'It isn't!' She tuts and then pushes it to the back of the cupboard where she doesn't have to look at it.

I know now that my list will not leave her pocket. She is going to spend her evening researching the carcinogenic effects of Pot Noodle, and Stanley won't eat a morsel of his dinner because she will not serve it in the shape required.

Despite the bitterly cold January frost, I skid up to the venue in a sweaty mess after lugging my cello for the best part of a mile across the icy pavements from Old Street station. My recently straightened hair is now a ball of frizz. Sweat is running down my back and my foundation has melted into globules in the creases around my eyes – classic side effects from transporting such a large instrument during rush hour on the tube.

From the exterior, the venue in Hoxton looks like an abandoned warehouse, but when I've dragged all of my stuff through the graffitied wooden door, I discover that it's actually slick and impressively high-spec on the inside.

Standing behind the bar are beautiful shirtless men wearing tight tuxedos, the jackets of which are gaping open just enough to expose their waxed, muscular torsos. Several waiters are dotted around the place, carefully laying out plates of baby-pink cupcakes on tables draped in black velvet cloth. Down the centre of the full length of the room is what looks like a stage, with chairs laid out on either side of it, and directly in front of it stands a short woman, wearing a chunky headset.

'You! I need more candles here. Stage left is too dark,' she snaps, 'and get Jules over here to sort the orchid display. It's patchy! Patchy ... Jason, I said PATCHY! We've only got half an hour, people. Let's pull it together. Come on, now!'

It's only when I look to the back of the stage and notice a gathering of tall, flat-chested girls and muscular men in skin-tight leggings that I realise where I am.

It's not a stage, but a runway.

I've brought my flabalanche, my frizzy ball of hair and my four-pound beach dress to play in a fucking fashion show!

Charlie strides over, all dolled up in her strapless black dress and her Jimmy Choo-esque stilettos (which are actually convincing copies from eBay). Her long, glossy dark hair hangs in thick ringlets down her bare back, her lips are a piercing red and her complexion radiant. As always, she looks stunning and exactly as pictured in our publicity photos on Miguel's website. Our act – the Vixen Trio – is marketed on the site as 'Three glamorous and highly talented ladies who play for some of the world's most esteemed artists on TV and stage'. We're supposed to be young and sexy – a 'must have' for your exclusive event – but now the Vixen Trio is missing a sultry fox and has acquired a hippo instead, which isn't quite what the client booked.

'Luce! You're here. Fuck me, what's with the 'fro?' Charlie teases. 'Rough trip was it?' She hugs me tightly.

'Charls … What. The. Fu—'

'What the fuck, what?' she interjects.

'What kind of gig is this? I thought it was just background shizzle.Tell me it's not a—'

'Duh! It's a fashion show, baby. Hot men wearing next to nothing … and there's loads of free gin. Cushdy one, eh?'

'Well, it's the first I've heard of it. If I'd known I would've turned it down. I've got a shit dress here and about eighteen extra kilos of flab under this coat. I'll look like a whale.'

'Calm down. Let's get some GHDs on that head, pronto, and maybe stick a pair of suck-in pants on you and you'll be back to your beautiful self,' she says. Then, after lifting my cello, she takes me by the elbow and drags me backstage to hair and make-up.

In truth, I'd rather have been dragged off for a smear test.

'Babe, what's going on with your eyebrows?'

There's nothing more demoralising in life than having to sit next to a bunch of supermodels and explain why I look like I've been yanked out of a ditch. Zoe, the freelance make-up artist, is taking no prisoners. She doesn't have time for pleasantries, having made it clear that she has to be at the O2 arena within the hour.

'Um, I don't know,' I reply sheepishly. 'I haven't really thought much about them lately.'

'Well, trust me, you *need* to, babe,' she says, her face a mixture of horror and pity. She leans in so close to my face that I clock a whiff of her fruity chewing gum. Running her manicured fingers slowly over my eyebrows, she yanks out a few errant hairs then sighs heavily, blasting me in the face with a hot burst of Hubba Bubba air. 'Look, I haven't got time to really get stuck in. I've got to do Ronan at eight forty-five. He's on at nine thirty, so time's tight.'

'What, Ronan Keating? Wow!' I say, my eyes still watering from the brief assault. 'My sister would go nuts to meet him. Is he a nice guy?'

'Gawd!' she interjects, pulling back abruptly. 'Your bags are so dark! Tell me, babe, what product do you normally put on them?'

A hot rush of blood hits my cheeks when the entire row of models sitting next to me turns to have a gander at my baggage. I briefly consider diving under the table for cover, but instead squeeze out an 'Um' and follow it with an awkward chuckle.

'Right,' continues Zoe, 'well, I haven't got my full kit here to sort it, so I'll have a go with the Touche Éclat, babe. It's good stuff but there's only so much it can do, if you know what I mean.'

The woman tries her best but she's right: all the luxurious concealer in the world isn't going to cover my dark circles, which look like they've been scrawled on with a black Sharpie. She slathers all sorts of lotions and potions across my face, tutting at regular intervals as she interrogates me about my skincare regime. Telling her that I moisturise with E45 and use Jack's Sudocrem on my zits isn't going to go down well with this woman, so I keep schtum and let her get on with it.

'These roots!' she exclaims loudly when she moves on to my hair. 'When did you last get these done, babe?'

Before I have a chance to invent an elaborate excuse as to why I have totally let myself go, Charlie pops her head around the door with a much-welcome treat in hand.

'Gin, Luce?' she chirps. 'Got you a double.'

I'm not breastfeeding, and even if I was, Jack is on the other side of London and my useless boobs are here, flatpacked in a cheap beach dress that is at least two sizes too small.

'Hand it over and grab me a straw, will you?' I say, just as Zoe scrapes a brush through my fringe, pulls it back off my forehead and twists it up to form a towering bubble.

Jen arrives shortly after and is sat at the end of the dressing table wincing in pain as Zoe's assistant drags a comb through her tight blonde curls. An entire can of hairspray is being offloaded onto her lumpy bubble when I glance behind her and clock a massive unopened multipack of crisps sitting on the table. The only benefit of working with supermodels that I've seen so far is that they survive solely on a diet of electric cigarettes and sparkling water, so the crisps are up for grabs.

Three packets of crisps each and two double gins later, the Vixen Trio are ready for showtime. Reeking of vinegar and gin and caked in thick, dramatic black eyeliner, we clamber past the queue of svelte supermodels with our instruments and take our seats at the top of the runway.

Miming expressions of sophistication, we serenade lines of beautiful people with Mozart trios as they glide up and down the stage like swans draped in chiffon. Photographers flash their cameras and the audience claps gently in that upper-class we-are-so-rich kind of way as they sip elegantly on their complimentary gins. When the show is over, we immediately dismount from our stilettos, stick on our trainers and head straight to the bar to sedate ourselves from the pain of blistered feet with as many free gins as possible. Not surprisingly, the trays of cupcakes, like the crisps, are totally untouched, so we stuff down a few of those too.

Once Charlie has eaten her fill, she disappears to the loo and returns with a full bottle of Molton Brown soap and a bog roll stuffed in her tiny bag.

'Charls! You can't take those.'

'Nah, Luce. They shouldn't leave this stuff lying around if they don't want us to take it,' she garbles as she shoves another cupcake into her mouth. 'There's another one in there if you want me to get it for you?'

'No way. I'm *not* going to prison for a bottle of pretentious soap. I've got kids to raise now. A slab of soap from the pound shop will do me just fine, thanks.'

'Your loss,' she says, then wraps up another two cakes in a serviette and squashes them into her already bulging handbag.

Pert, scantily clad models stand around networking with agents; beautiful and flawless, they look as though they've been airbrushed, and the hot barmen flock around them like dogs on heat. It doesn't take long for one to come sniffing around Charlie and Jen.

'Move on, mate. It's a girls-only table tonight,' Charlie says playfully, 'but we'll get some more drinks if you're pouring?'

And off the man scampers to the bar, returning moments later with a tray full of drinks and his phone number scribbled on a pink napkin for Charlie.

I'm invisible: *totally* invisible in a crowd of stunning people. My gut, my big forehead, my tired baggy eyes, the mono-boob: I have nothing worth looking at, nothing to say, nothing to contribute at all and, honestly, I just want to go home. So, I make a lame excuse and leave my friends behind to drink the free bar dry.

One hour and three tube journeys later, I drag my cello down the full length of Windsor Road, my cheeks sore and my teeth chattering percussively from the vicious sting of the icy wind. Within arm's reach of my front door and mere seconds away from collapsing onto my cosy bed, I'm suddenly accosted by my annoying neighbour Alan, who – clothed in a tartan dressing-gown and matching slippers – is standing on his driveway organising his recycling bins. Naturally, I have to stand and listen to the man rant about the 'ghastly hooligans' that have been speeding down our street, then to shut him up, I agree to sign a petition to persuade the council to lay speed bumps before one of us gets 'mowed down in our prime'.

After aging the best part of ten years, I eventually escape and head upstairs to discover, to my utter delight, that Judith has left. Stanley is fast asleep in our bed clutching his Russian puzzle, which suggests that he's had another bout of nocturnal anxiety. I gently kiss his forehead and lay his puzzle down on the bedside table, then wander through to the lounge to find Ed snoozing in the recliner with Jack in his arms, his tiny hand resting on his daddy's hairy chest.

It's beautiful.

Not supermodel beautiful, but a beauty that far transcends anything one would ever see on a runway.

3

Starfucks

My body confidence is low, and working alongside models with waists barely wider than the circumference of a toilet roll has done nothing to help it.

The flabalanche is officially out of control, and if I'm ever going to get out of my maternity jeans and back into regular ones, then drastic action needs to be taken! No more sneaking packets of crisps at 4 a.m. as I feed Jack. No more double dinners where I scoff Stan's leftovers and then make my and Ed's proper dinner two hours later. I *have* to control myself, and must stop giving in to the squeaky voices of the double-stuff Oreos that call out to me all day long from the cupboard. *Pick me! And me! Screw it, pick us ALL!*

Although I don't want a ribcage that can grate cheddar, it would be nice to shave my bikini line without having to lift my gut up with one hand to reach it first. I've done the maths and I estimate that my current body mass is composed of 40% Stan's leftovers, 20% Big Macs, 20% cake and 20% crisps, and if my blood was ever analysed, the lab would probably report the results as being 10% plasma, 50% instant coffee and 40% Pinot Grigio. These figures are shameful and need *addressing* if I want a figure that's worth *undressing*.

Therefore, the day after my encounter with London's most-emaciated, I put myself on a strict diet and I have been slowly starving to death ever since.

At the start of the week, I did pretty well.

Monday
Breakfast: Fat-free natural yoghurt with granola
and berries
Lunch: Chicken and beetroot salad
Dinner: Steamed salmon and fresh vegetables
Dessert: A bottle of wine, two packets of Cheetos, a
Snickers bar and four rounds of toast with *real* butter

Tuesday
Breakfast: Fat-free natural yoghurt with just the
berries
Lunch: A remorseful salad
Dinner: Overcooked chicken seasoned with an
abundance of misery
Dessert: Two packets of Cheetos, three double gins
(but with slimline tonic) and only two rounds of
toast with real butter (progress?)

Wednesday
Breakfast: Three cups of coffee and a bowl of air
Lunch: A McDonald's salad, Diet Coke, six fries and
a lingering sniff of Stanley's hamburger
Dinner: A boiled egg and dry toast ... followed
by the remainder of Stan's fish fingers, three
'BURNT!' Smiley Faces, seven double-stuff Oreos
and a long hard look in the mirror
Dessert: An early night where I dreamt of Hugh
Jackman force-feeding me jam doughnuts – he
was wearing nothing but a leather thong

I carried on in pretty much the same pathetic way until Friday when I summoned the courage to weigh myself. Before breakfast and just after my morning poo, I stripped naked, removed all jewellery and hair accessories then climbed on to the scales with hope in my heart. The crushingly disappointing result? I hadn't lost a gram; not a single one. So ...

Friday
Breakfast: Yoghurt – *not* with berries or granola,
    but with salty tears
Lunch: Tuna salad with water (whilst watching
    some guy icing a three-tiered cake on the *Great
    British Bake Off*)
Dinner: Vegetable chilli and a pot of Jack's pureed
    cauliflower that he threw at me.

By the end of the day, I was starving but genuinely felt thinner, more energetic and positively vibrant. I even contemplated trying on my pre-baby jeans but decided to hold off until Monday when they would undoubtedly fit.

But it all went to shit when Ed came home with a box of beer and a twenty-pound note in his wallet. 'It's Friday' was all he had to say. So ...

Dinner number 2: Chinese! Half a duck with hoisin
    sauce and pancakes. Fried noodles – *large*!
    Chips – *extra large*! Some unidentifiable fried
    meat slathered in a chemically enhanced spicy
    sauce that will probably give me cancer. All of
    this was washed down with beer: bottles upon
    bottles of delicious, icy-cold, thirst-quenching

beer. Then out came the imitation Baileys from Lidl that had been gathering dust in the cupboard since Christmas and we drank the lot between us.

Come Sunday, I've gained two pounds and am forced to switch from wearing maternity jeans to maternity leggings to give myself a little extra breathing room.

I call Charlie and whinge about my week of shameful behaviour.

'Don't be ridiculous. You're not fat, you're fucking beautiful!' she says emphatically.

'I am, Charls. Be honest. None of my clothes fit, my tits are swinging under my pits and I haven't seen my fanny in months. I am totally un-shaggable! Ed hasn't gone near me in ages and, let's face it, who can blame him?'

'Well, I'd do you – but that's not really what you want to hear, is it?'

'Not really. You're not exactly my type.'

'Fair enough. I'm not to everyone's taste, I admit.' She laughs. 'Okay. I've got a plan. I'm free tomorrow and so is Jen. Let's hit the shops and kit you out in a new sexy bra and pants. Lift the tits, lift the spirits, I say!'

'Sounds good. Although, right now, I'd prefer to lift the tits and *drink* the spirits.'

I'm forty-five minutes late to meet my friends for our sexy-underwear shopping trip. Leaving a house with a baby comes with plenty of stress as standard, but trying to get Stanley out of the front door on time causes heart palpitations resembling a Beethoven-esque timpani roll.

First, I have to change his socks twice before I find a pair that feels 'right'. Then, he kicks off when I put the 'wrong' T-shirt on him. It's the same brand and colour of polo shirt as the one he wears *every* single day, but he can tell that this particular one isn't the exact original. The child has some super sixth sense for this kind of thing, and it is only when I pull the original shirt out of the dirty laundry basket and put it on him that he agrees to leave. I must make my peace with the fact that he is going to wander the streets with a large orange juice stain all down his front. But some battles, I've learnt, just aren't worth having.

It's early February, it's icy cold and the heavens are emptying with the sort of harsh, spiky rain that threatens to slice straight through my skin. Standing on the driveway, I wrestle for ages with the cover on the pram, trying my best to keep my language clean. Soaked to the bone, I then grab Stan by the hand and try to make a run for it down Windsor Road, but he stops dead every few steps to tell me the make of every car on the street. Staying dry is not a priority for him, but pointing out every single Saab and Alfa Romeo is. Once he has positioned himself ankle deep in a muddy puddle, he starts telling me the number plates of the cars parked further up the road.

'Excuse me, but we will be getting to BT20 NXZ soon,' he says, and once we've skidded around the corner on to Oxford Road, there it is, just like he said.

'That's incredible, Stan! How do you know that? Who taught you about cars?'

'Daddy teached me,' he replies.

I recall a day a few weeks back when I caught Ed and Stan lining up dozens of Matchbox cars across the kitchen floor just as I was about to start cooking dinner. I snapped at them and told them to move, then poor Ed ended up flat on his arse after he was taken down by a rogue Honda that had slipped out from under the dishwasher. Come to think of it, he still has a yellow bruise there, even now.

Twelve number plates later, we arrive at Starbucks to find Charlie and Jen outside, huddled under a tiny umbrella. The pile of cigarette butts on the floor next to Charlie's foot indicates that she is on edge.

'It's rammed inside: batshit crazy toddlers, stressed mums and the usual laptop loners. I say we ditch it and go somewhere else,' she says. 'I don't know why you even suggested Starfucks in the first place, Jen.'

A steamed-up coffee shop filled with 'batshit crazy toddlers' doesn't sound remotely appealing. Not only had I fed Jack four times in the night, but I'd also been up for ages trying to calm Stanley down after he had a nightmare in which he was being chased by a 'giant kicking K'.

'Sod this. We're going to the pub,' Charlie declares, taking the reins.

I am weak – physically worn down, emotionally drained and totally soaked – so I don't even try to object.

En route to the nearest pub, The Grove, we bump into Marsha and her well-adjusted son, Hugo, because sometimes life can be *that* cruel.

'Lucy! Hi, Lucy!' She waves from across the road. She glides over the zebra crossing in her Cath Kidston floral raincoat and matching umbrella, with Hugo trotting alongside her like the Cruft's Best in Show winner. 'How are you all, ladies?' She leans in and kisses me on both cheeks and I play along, inhaling the thick fumes of her sickly perfume as I try to avoid getting clocked over the head with her umbrella. 'Awful weather isn't it?'

'Yep,' I say as a thick raindrop drips off the edge of my nose onto the pavement.

'Hello, Stanley,' says Hugo sweetly.

Stanley looks straight down at the floor and doesn't say a word.

'Stanley is going to Ealing Primary in September too, Hugo,' chirps Marsha. 'You might even be in the same class.'

Hugo proudly thrusts a Spiderman figure up to Stanley's face to show it off, but it sparks no reaction. Stan doesn't even look up, but shuffles in behind me and buries his head under my coat. Rejected, Hugo backs away and reaches for his mother's hand and I see her lips shrivel up tightly in disapproval.

'What is it that you have there, Stanley? The alphabet?' she says as her tinted eyebrows disappear into her hairline.

Stan is still lurking under my coat, feigning mutism, so I am forced to answer for him as usual. 'Yes,' I say, 'it's his favourite puzzle that he takes everywhere.'

'Oh. How *unusual*! Well, we like Lego in our house and Spiderman ... as you can see.' She reaches down and ruffles Hugo's hair. 'Speaking of which, did I tell you that Richard renewed our annual passes for Legoland, Lucy? The new season is starting next month.'

'No, I don't think so,' I say, even though she had on several tedious occasions just like this. I stand back and wait for the 'P' word, which I know is coming next.

'Well, he bought us the *premium* ones as an impromptu gift, so we can just pop down whenever we like. It's so fab!'

'Great,' I say, 'we'll have to check it out.'

More P's fly out of her mouth like a shower of bullets. 'I mean, it is *pricey* – especially if you haven't got the *perks* included with the *premium* passes,' she continues, 'but if you bring a packed lunch then you won't get stung too badly.'

Silence falls on the group. We are all drenched, Stanley is pulling on the back of my jeans and Charlie is executing her 'let's go before I stab someone' glare.

Marsha finally breaks the silence. 'Anyway, we'd better go. We're off to meet the new school mums and their kiddies at Starbucks, then we're heading into town together to see the new dinosaur exhibition in Kensington.'

Her dagger strikes me straight through the chest.

'Well, *we* are going to the pub,' Charlie says pointedly. She links her arm through mine and pulls me towards her.

'The pub? Gosh! I haven't stepped foot in a pub in years,' says Marsha, her mouth shrivelling once again.

'Excuse me, but I want to go!' Stanley says bluntly. 'I want to go, I want to go, I want to go, I want to *go!*' he yells four times, as standard. His volume knob is turning itself up rapidly and it won't be long until he reaches maximum decibels.

'You'd better get him into that pub quickly, Lucy!' Marsha chuckles before bidding us farewell and gliding off up the high street with Hugo cantering along beside her.

'God, that woman is a dick,' says Charlie when Marsha is still within earshot.

'The biggest dick,' agrees Jen.

'The *ultimate* dick!' I conclude.

We arrive at The Grove, and as I force the bulky pram through the tiny door, I immediately clap eyes on a group of mums breastfeeding in the far corner. I smile and give them my best wave of admiration – a sort of Jennifer Lawrenceesque, *Hunger Games*-style salute to acknowledge my fellow pub-going warriors of motherhood.

'What are you *doing*?' says Charlie, glaring in confusion at my dramatically extended arm.

'What?' I shrug my shoulders. 'I'm doing a Katniss Everdeen, obviously.'

'No, Luce – it's more like a Hitler.'

I elbow her sharply in the arm. 'What are you trying to say? That I need to bleach my moustache?'

'Yep,' she sniggers, 'and maybe refrain from doing any elaborate arm extensions until you do.'

Noticing that these mums are drinking coffee, I ask Charlie to order a Diet Coke for me and a smooth orange juice for Stan whilst I look for a suitable table.

'Diet Coke?' Charlie is disgusted. Taking a bullet would be less painful to her than hearing these two ugly words said out loud in a respectable beer-serving establishment. 'What's happened to you? First this, next you'll be asking for a tap water with a slice of fresh lemon.'

'Leave her alone, Charlie,' says Jen, jumping in to defend me.

'I will *not*!' she retorts. 'This is *our* day of fun. This woman needs a beer. Look at her – she is positively miserable and only a delicious pint can fix her.'

'Okay, okay, Charls. I give up. Get me a half, but we've *got* to sit out of the way, maybe down the back where no one can see. And don't forget an orange juice for Stan. *No* bits.'

The unfortunate run-in with Marsha has chinked my armour, so bottle-feeding Jack with a beer in hand, in full view of the breast-feeders, is the last thing I need. I've already experienced glares of disapproval every time I pull a bottle out amongst the 'breast is best' brigade down at the baby clinic, and I don't particularly want to be on the receiving end of any judgemental daggers from this pack of women. This day is about rebuilding self-esteem, not shredding what is left of it. And so, tucked away at the back of the pub, with a half of lager on the table and a bottle of formula in hand, our afternoon of blissful girly fun begins.

Whilst I pace back and forth trying to burp Jack, who bursts into tears every time I try to sit down, Jen and I discover the ground-breaking news that Charlie, the eternal singleton, is seeing someone. She is sketchy on the details, claiming that she doesn't want to jinx it, so we're only told that his name is Tom, he is thirty-six and a doctor, and that she met him at a gig. 'All I can say is that he's smoking hot, *highly* energetic and has unlimited access to an abundance of free lube … *not* that we need it. And that's all I'm saying for now.'

Jen is stunned, as am I.

A hot doctor? Free lube?!

Even Jack is shocked into silence, so much so that he allows me to sit down for nearly a whole minute to digest the news. Of course, the bliss of being in a seated position comes to an abrupt end ten seconds later when Stanley takes a sip of his orange juice.

'Bits. Bits. Bits. BITS!' he screams as he spits it out, darts to the centre of the pub then throws himself down on the floor and convulses like a paralytic starfish. Hysterical tears ensue, and even after Jen dashes to the bar and returns with a smooth orange juice, I just cannot calm him down. His Oscar-worthy display of emotion captures the undivided attention of every person in the pub, in particular the pack of mums in the corner. I can actively feel them marking my child-calming techniques out of ten like the panel from

Strictly Come Dancing, and I'm expecting them to hold up their score cards to reveal a pitiful result.

One out of ten.

It's minus two from me.

Zero – poor performance. Poor!

When I can take no more, I lift Stanley and put him into Jack's pram, taking several vicious kicks to the chest in the process. I then secure Jack into the harness that I've packed for emergencies such as this and scramble to the door, leaving my friends and a room full of aurally traumatised punters behind me.

My blissful afternoon of girly fun lasted a measly twenty-five minutes. Bra shopping is officially on hold, and my boobs, for the time being, are going to remain deflated.

Much like my spirits.

4

Dr Google

By the time Ed arrives home from his gig at 6.30 p.m., Stanley has already fallen asleep on top of his duvet, still fully clothed with his arms wrapped loosely around his favourite alphabet puzzle. The poor child is totally wiped out from crying most of the afternoon, and I'm hanging on by a thread myself. I lay a blanket over him and gently kiss his forehead, then head to the kitchen to rustle up something for dinner, leaving Ed in charge of getting Jack ready for bed.

Three hours later, I'm still sitting on the sofa trying to rock Jack to sleep as Ed sips a beer and spoon-feeds me stone-cold tuna pasta bake. In between the chewing, shushing, swallowing, sighing and cursing, I manage to fill him in on the day's events, including the orange juice ordeal.

'But did you ask Charlie to order the juice without the bits?'

'No, Ed.' I roll my eyes. 'I told her to make them throw in as many as humanly possible – just for shits and giggles.'

'*What?*'

'*Joking*, Ed. I'm joking. Of course she asked for smooth.'

'Well, it's all *their* fault! They shouldn't have given her the bits,' he huffs angrily. 'If she asked for smooth, then they should have given her smooth.'

'I know, but they didn't.'

'But she asked for no bits!'

'Yes, Ed! Stop saying "bits", for God's sake. Life doesn't always go to plan and Stan will have to learn to deal with that. And at some point, so will *you* – hopefully before you hit fifty.'

He tuts, takes a gulp of his beer and then stabs several bits of pasta on to the fork. 'I don't like bits either,' he mumbles before stuffing it in his mouth.

'Hey! That's *my* dinner, punk. You've had yours. Cough it up!'

He sits in silence staring at the TV, an intense frown on his face.

'By the way, did you know that Stan can name all the number plates of the cars on the street from memory? He did it today and it was, like, incredible.'

'Yeah. I know. I used to know all the cars when I was two or three,' Ed says quietly, clearly still in a grump about the thought of an incompetent barman poisoning our child's drink with orange pulp.

'Forget it, love. I'm sorry I mentioned it.' I sigh and briefly rub his leg. 'It was just a bad day.'

I don't sleep at all well. Jack waking for several feeds is nothing new, but once he's finally drunk himself unconscious, I still can't settle.

'Bits! Bits! Bits! BITS!'

Stanley has had a rough day, his first in a while, and after such days, I'm always drawn to the internet to find reasons for his explosive behaviour. As Ed snores next to me in bed, I lie with my phone and type questions into Google, the same ones that I've typed in many times over the last couple of years. Skimming through the same old articles, I reread the same answers to the same questions, somehow hoping that this time I'll get different answers.

But I don't.

Three words appear on my screen – words that weren't part of my vocabulary nearly two years ago but are now safely stored in the depths of my mind, waiting for the day that I might be told that I need to use them: *Autism Spectrum Disorder*.

Just after Stanley turned three, I took him to the doctor because I was concerned about his speech. Although he would blather on about pentagons, count into the hundreds and quote dialogue from his favourite YouTube videos, he struggled to answer simple questions and would wind himself up into a state when trying to express what he wanted. Naturally, I sought the advice of Dr Google and learnt that many kids struggle with making decisions and having spontaneous conversations. Our doctor referred him to a speech therapist, but six months later, an appointment came through to see a paediatrician. At the time, it wasn't clear why he'd been given such an appointment, but I took him along anyway.

Not much happened when he met Dr Collins. All the man did was measure Stan's head, prod his belly, check his joints and then scribble on a thick file in silence. When I asked what he was looking for, he wouldn't give me a clear answer but instead bombarded me with medical terms and acronyms that I didn't understand. However, one of the acronyms that slipped out as a 'possibility' was 'ASD', short for Autism Spectrum Disorder, and it has stuck with me ever since.

That appointment was months ago, and until Stan's next one in September, I still have no idea what's going on. For now, I've only got Dr Google to guide me.

I try not to dwell on the difficult days because there have been so many good ones – remarkable ones, even. I've lost count of the number of times that Stanley has said or done something truly incredible – things far advanced for a kid of his age – and when that happens, I still can't sleep.

After one of his amazing days, I'll still lie awake till all hours, blocking out Ed's insufferable snoring as I trawl the internet looking for information, but Google will direct me towards web pages of a very different nature. Articles about two-year-olds with IQs higher than Einstein will load onto my screen. Then stories will follow of five-year-olds who have taught themselves Mandarin, ten-year-olds who are doing maths degrees at university and babies – still in nappies – who are counting to over a hundred. I'll click on links that lead to pages filled with checklists and questionnaires, then fill them out as honestly as I can.

And once I've clicked Enter, Dr Google will always present me with a totally conflicting diagnosis: *Genius*.

It was just before Stan's fourth birthday when I started filling out these kinds of quizzes – after a particularly amazing day when he opened *The Very Hungry Caterpillar* and read it from cover to cover. Around the same time, I discovered he could write the alphabet, not just in English, but in Spanish and Russian. He'd taught himself to do it using an app that Ed had downloaded for him on the iPad and soaked it all up in a matter of days, instantly thirsty for more.

A while later, Ed had mentioned that Stanley recited the alphabet backwards on the way to nursery. At first, I assumed he was exaggerating, but when Stanley came home, I said, 'Stan, Z, Y, X ...' and he rattled it all off without pausing to breathe.

There's no denying that our son has gifts – exceptional natural talents that many people would consider to be the qualities of a genius. But, on bad days like today, when the juice has bits in it and all hell breaks loose, the three words that I've stored in the back of my mind resurface and I find myself running through the checklist once again.

Signs of Autism in Children
Difficulties with social interaction ✓
Avoids eye contact [*Sometimes yes, but sometimes no*]
Prefers to be alone [*Again, sometimes yes and sometimes no*]
Lines up toys or other objects ✓
Obsessive interests ✓ [*But don't all kids have these?*]
Lacks empathy [*No!*]
Repetitive behaviours and need for structure ✓
Speech delay ✓

I'm not convinced by the word 'autistic', and much as I would like to believe it, my gut tells me that 'genius' isn't right either. But when it comes to loving, kind, sweet, funny, sensitive, incredible and adorable, I have no doubts at all.

These words are a perfect fit because Stanley is all of them.

And so much more.

5

Fond Mammaries

Ed has the day off – his first in over a week – so I've seized the opportunity to leave the flat without the kids and attempt bra shopping with my pals.

Round two. Ding! Ding!

The icy-cold February rain is still falling thick and fast, but I don't care. As I wander up to the Broadway, I pull my hood back and let it thrash against my face, taking immense pleasure in the fact that, for the first time in forever, I am free. No work, no kids, I don't have to worry about anything or anyone. I don't have to clock watch, adhere to feeding schedules or think about where the nearest nappy-changing facilities are. I don't have to lug a heavy bag crammed with half the contents of my kitchen, or make time to stop and have the number plate of every car on the street recited in my face. And best of all, I don't have to spend the afternoon on tenterhooks, worrying if bits of orange pulp are going to wreck my day.

Walking into the swanky new bra establishment, I find Charlie and Jen parked on a purple velvet sofa at the back of the shop with coffees in hand.

'It's about time!' Charlie says. 'I'm gasping for a beer here. Let's get this show on the road.'

The shop is filled with hundreds of fancy-looking, industrial-strength cup-holders: cotton, silk, lace, balconette, push-up, pull-down and halter-neck. Every type of bra in every colour imaginable is available, waiting to help women of all shapes and sizes manage their chest flesh effectively. If I can't find the bra of my dreams here, then it's safe to say that I'm not going to find it anywhere.

Bra shopping used to be a breeze. As a teenager, it was always such a low-key affair. Back then, I had 'boobies', and a quick trip to Tammy Girl with my mum to buy two tiny triangular slivers of white cotton to decorate them was all it took. Those 28AA days sure were simpler times. As I grew older, the 'ie' fell off and I became the proud owner of a fully formed set of boobs. This meant that I was now qualified to enter the lacy/satin bra sections of H&M and New Look, where my main goal was to pump up, decorate and exaggerate what I had so that I could dress to impress. And at the time, it worked. My 32C years were, well, bags of fun.

Since having kids, however, my 'boobs' are no more. Now, they are just 'breasts' – or 'mammaries' (according to medical textbooks). They are the udders that failed to feed my babies so they've become the plump cushions on which they rest their tiny sleeping heads instead. They've been squeezed, prodded and poked, and not just by my kids, but by midwives, doctors and health visitors. Because of this, they've become floor-facing members of society. Having lost their fight against gravity, they now hang their sad faces in defeat.

The bras of New Look and H&M aren't going to cut it any more. I need a piece of sophisticated attire, a solid structure of mechanical marvellousness that will lift the spirits of my depressed chest. Given the situation, Charlie suggested this place, which caters for women who are in possession of more than a handful. And that, most certainly, is me.

We are sent downstairs to wait for the fitting specialist and set up camp on another velvet sofa just outside the changing cubicles. I'm expecting to meet a middle-aged, soft-handed lady with a tape measure – a kind, warm soul like Angela Lansbury, a woman who can empathise with what my chest has been through and offer it support. But I don't get an Angela. Not even close. Down the stairs comes a nineteen-year-old girl dressed in a skin-tight black top which perfectly exaggerates her firm, upstanding rack. Gravity, it seems, is still her friend.

And there is *no* tape measure.

'I don't need to measure you,' she says casually. 'Just show me what you've got and I can determine your size by looking at them.'

Charlie nods, obviously impressed by the girl's skill.

'I'll show you mine if you show me yours.' I wink, but she doesn't flinch. There is no messing about. I walk into the cubicle and, without waiting for an invitation, she follows me inside. She then stands there in silence with her hands planted firmly on her tiny hips, eyeballing my chest until I am forced to strip and expose myself.

'Right,' she says as her eyes survey the damage, 'so, you've been wearing this, have you?' She suspends my off-white, over-tumbled maternity bra in the air and the corners of her mouth curl downwards in disapproval. 'Well, this *can't* be doing much for you,' she says pointedly. She glares at my reflection in the full-length mirror, then tosses my bra on the stool and proceeds to grade my chest further and further down the alphabet, away from the AA classification of my youth. 'Right, let me see what I can do. There's a robe there if you want to cover yourself up,' she says cuttingly before disappearing out of the cubicle.

The girl returns ten minutes later with several bras hanging off her arm like it's a clothes rail. 'Okay. Have a try of this one first,' she says. She hands over a black lacy number with a small pink bow on each strap and backs out of the cubicle. 'It's pretty, high-quality lace and one of our most popular styles.'

I pull the curtain over and wedge my handbag against it to seal it fully closed, then try it on.

The girl is right. It is pretty, but it's also pointless. One tit goes left and the other goes right, like they're attempting to do the Macarena. I lose sight of my knees in an instant (which is quite important when one takes the safety of escalator-riding with a pram into consideration).

The curtain is yanked back, and the girl ushers me out of the cubicle. She flips me around like a piece of meat on a barbecue and starts adjusting the straps.

'Nope,' Charlie intervenes, 'I don't like it. She doesn't want to decorate them. She just wants to lift them up a bit, y' know, make them look smaller. Firmer.'

The girl nods and pulls another bra off her arm. 'Okay. So, this one offers more support. It doubles up as a sports bra too, so it's perfect for running and intense cardio workouts if that's your thing?'

A roaring belly-laugh escapes Charlie's mouth and Jen swiftly elbows her in the ribs to shut her up. Backing into the cubicle, I redraw the curtain and put it on. Surprisingly, this bra feels great. It's a slick, minimising number that squeezes and flattens, magically making my bosoms vanish from centre stage. They're totally out of sight and almost out of mind.

I admire my firm, petite chest in the mirror for a good few minutes – mere seconds away from asking if they stock this style in different colours – but then I turn around and catch a glimpse of myself in the mirror from behind.

Jesus! My tits are on my back!

Charlie yanks the curtain open. 'What's taking so long, Luce? Any good?'

'No!' gasps the girl before I can answer. 'I think you need something with more of a lift.'

'No shit!' Charlie blurts out. 'That's *not* a good look, Luce.'

The girl starts to lose patience, made crystal clear when she glances up at the clock on the wall and exhales loudly. 'Here,' she says. She virtually throws the next bra at me. 'It's a balconette with extra padding. Again, an extremely popular style, et cetera.'

Before I can retreat to the cubicle, she slips in behind me and undoes the sports bra and I feel my boobs swing back around to their regular position at the front of my body. She then scoops them up, along with my stomach and most of my back fat, in her hands and balances them on top of the polka-dotted balconette bra.

I achieve a size zero waist and a comfortable chin rest instantly.

'Jesus!' squeals Charlie. 'Ed will have a fit if he sees you in that!'

I turn to face the mirror. My neck is no longer visible, and I can literally count my ribs. 'Yeah, maybe he will,' I say, 'but I'm not sure my car insurance company will pay out in the event of an accident if my vision is compromised.'

'But, on the plus side, you'll have your very own built-in airbags!' Jen chuckles.

For the sake of road safety, the balconette is dismissed, and I ask to try a plainer white cotton bra that I see dangling off the girl's arm.

I throw it on in front of my audience, the need for privacy having totally vanished, then turn once again to face the mirror. It's by far the worst of all! The cups overflow to the degree that I have two extra boobs spilling out under my armpits and a further two hanging down under the wire. I'm no mathematician, but I count six in total, and although I'm an avid fan of a six-pack of lager and a six-pack of muscles on a man's torso, a six-pack of tits is less than desirable.

'Nope, lose it,' says Charlie firmly and the girl releases yet another, even heavier sigh.

A further twenty minutes of tucking, lifting, squeezing, contorting and debating later, we finally find a bra capable of standing up to the challenge. A 34F! Charlie admits that she's jealous, but she has no idea how hard it is to navigate your way through life with a pair of 34Fs dragging you down. Given the choice, I would trade mine in for a set of bee-stings like hers any day.

We leave the shop laden with not-so-fun bags filled to the brim with black cotton cup-holders (and a leopard-print silk thong that Charlie insisted I buy). At the very least, the new bras have underwires, which, all things considered, is an absolute triumph. This is worth celebrating, so off to the pub we go for a beer, where we toast the departure of my 32C boobs.

6

The 'Keys to My Clutch'

Valentine's Day has arrived: the one day in the year when most husbands feel intense pressure to execute the perfect romantic performance and, in our home, that pressure is *very* real.

Ed and I have always had a rule when it comes to Valentine's Day: no roses, no presents and no posh restaurants, *maybe* a blow job (if the moon is in alignment with Jupiter, Mars and Saturn, that is) – but what's most important and absolutely essential is we *must* write each other a poem.

The tradition was born two or so years into our relationship, at a time when we were both going through a dry patch with work, and it was such a success that it stuck. There's been some fabulous poems over the years: some soppy ones that have made me howl with tears and others so funny that I've laughed to the point of accidental urination. I've never been the sort of woman who places any value on being given bouquets of overpriced roses that die within four days, and I've never expected Ed to express his love with extravagant gifts. For me, it's all about the poem. It's the ultimate expression of love for those on a budget.

Ed has a gig tonight, but he has been so well-trained that he's left a card for me by the bed. Whilst he is out serenading loved-up couples at a Valentine's ball at the Savoy, I am home chilling with our lovely little men and a very cool Chinese number puzzle that arrived this morning to Stan's total delight.

Once they are both out for the count, I open a bottle of Pinot and dig out my memory box to reminisce about our lives before kids and Chinese numbers. I find the very first card that Ed gave me a couple of years into our relationship – a fuzzy felt one, with two people stuck to the front of it holding hands.

Inside is a list because Ed is nothing if not a fan of writing lists.

The Reasons I Love You Can Be Expressed in
    Alphabetical Order:

Your AROMA is AROUSING
Your BODY is BEAUTIFUL
Your CELLO PLAYING is CHAMPION
Your DANCING is DIVINE
Your EYES are ENCHANTING
Your FEET are FABULOUS
Your GRIN is GROOVY
Your HAIR is full of HAPPINESS
Your INTELLECT is INSPIRED
Your JUGS are JUICY
Your KISSES are KOSMIC
Your LIPS are LUSCIOUS
Your MOUTH is MESMERISING
Your NECK I love to NIBBLE
Your OCTAVE SCALES are OUTSTANDING!
Your PIES are PERFECT

Your QUESTIONS are QUINTESSENTIAL
Your RHYTHM makes me RANDY [Weirdo!]
Your SMILE is SENSUAL
Your TEETH are TERRIFIC
Your UNDERSTANDING nature is UNIQUE
Your VAGINA is VERY VERY nice
Your WICKED sense of humour is WONDERFUL
Your X-RAYS are XCELLENT!!
Your YING is my YANG!
Your ZANG is my ZING, ZING-a-ZING!

The message at the bottom reads:

To my gorgeous, beautiful girlfriend,
HAPPY VALENTINE'S DAY!
I love you so much. Here's to many more years
    together,
Ed xxxxxxx

At the time, it made me cry both from laughter and from feeling tremendously loved, and although there were weak points in his effort, it was still wildly romantic. I then open the card that he left for me this morning.

Nine years, one marriage and two kids later, the poem that he has written for me on this Valentine's Day says:

I love you so much
You're lovely to touch
You're the keys to my clutch
I'm glad you're not Dutch
Let's celebrate soon, my darling wife! xxxx

This profound message of love is scribbled on a tacky card that he'd blatantly picked up from a petrol station on his way back from work last night at 2 a.m. I detect the faint stench of tuna-and-sweetcorn sandwich wafting off the envelope, and I could be wrong, but there appears to be a salty fingerprint of crisp residue on the inside of the card. My nostrils tell me that it's a beef Hula Hoop stain, or possibly the mark of a BBQ Dorito.

Oh, how far the man has slipped over the years!

Back in the day, Ed was the most romantic man on the planet, if you can believe it. While most of my friends were being sent dick pics on seedy online dating sites or being groped by drunk losers in nightclubs, I was one of the lucky ones. We'd met at a TV gig, playing behind some B-list pop star on a cheesy chat show, and after the broadcast, all of the musicians had piled into the pub across the street from the studio.

We didn't speak all night. He was at one end of the table talking shop with the rhythm-section lads, and I was at the other end with the string girls. But after last orders, I popped to the loo, and when I came out, there he was waiting for me right outside the door.

'I think you're really beautiful,' he said, 'and I'd like to get your number and take you out for dinner some time. Fancy it?'

In my twenty-four years on the planet, a man had never asked me for my number – literally *never*. This man had guts. He was direct, honest and courageous and, in my mind, his approach was as romantic as it gets. I was knocked clean off my size eight feet.

Our first date was dinner in a pub, where we talked for hours about music and movies as we drank the bar dry.

The night ended with a raunchy snog around the back of Tottenham Court Road station and throbbing cheeks from smiling so much. The next day, he was straight on the phone to arrange another date, and he invited me to Ronnie Scott's to watch him play some jazz. Of course, I dragged Charlie and Jen along to scrutinise him accordingly, and the moment I saw him in action, I didn't care what they thought because I was instantly besotted. The man was mesmerising on-stage, an absolute musical genius, and I was left hopelessly giddy after he stared across at me through the crowd during his entire performance, as if there was no one else in the room.

'I think I'm gonna marry this guy,' I said to Charlie, and I meant it.

'Calm down, woman! Maybe wait until you see him naked first,' she replied. 'He might have a minuscule dick or fifteen nipples or something.'

But, thankfully, he didn't.

Ed was never one to buy fancy gifts, but he expressed his feelings by doing things for me instead. Nothing was too much trouble for him. Even though we lived on opposite sides of London, he would meet me at the station after work just to carry my cello five minutes up the road to my front door in the dark. He would insist on driving me to my cello lessons, which were all the way out in Windsor, because I didn't have a car. He would plan our dates weeks in advance and take me to places that he knew I would love. He would put me on the guest list to watch his gigs, then show me off to his friends and colleagues at the backstage parties afterwards.

He wasn't like any of the other men (total jackasses) that I'd dated before. If he said he would call, he always did. And if I texted him, his reply would come straight away. If I cancelled a date, he would become wildly upset, which may seem stifling to some, but it made me feel desired.

His heart was always on his sleeve, and just four weeks after we met, the L-word popped out of his mouth. I was sat on the toilet, my pants around my ankles, at my friend's New Year's Eve party when he said it, and I remember being quite taken aback.

'How can you say that you love me when you hardly know me?' I said.

'Because, for the first time in my life, I feel totally comfortable to be myself with you,' was his answer.

If it wasn't for the obscure setting (and the sound of someone puking just outside the door), I would have said that it was like a scene from a romantic Hollywood movie.

If any problems arose between us, he would go above and beyond to fix them. One day, after casually mentioning that his snoring had kept me up all night, he reacted by shelling out eight hundred quid on Chinese herbal remedies to cure himself. A man on a mission, he religiously boiled bags of potent green herbs from scratch day after day and forced the smelly potion down his gullet without complaining. He was so committed that for two months our entire dating schedule revolved around the sodding herbs. 'You'll have to stay at mine tonight. I need to do my herbs,' he'd say, or, 'I'm going to be a bit late – I'm just waiting for my herbs to cool down.'

When the herbs didn't work and the guttural snoring persisted, he went to more extreme lengths to prove his love. On one memorable occasion, he was lying on the acupuncture table with needles poking out all over his body when I called him in tears. I'd received a rejection letter from an audition that I'd worked really hard for and was devastated. 'I wish you were here' was all I said and, without hesitating, he yanked the needles out and boarded three different trains and a bus to the other side of London, just to give me a hug.

But now, nine years down the line, I sit holding a tuna-sweetcorn-beefy-crisp-stained poem – the only romantic gesture he has made in months.

Ladies and gentlemen of the court, in the palm of my hand is solid proof of what having kids does to the romance in a relationship.

In short, it kills it! DEAD!

And, to reinforce my findings, I ask the court to glance into my bedside drawer where they will find a bumper box of condoms that has sat there, totally untouched, for nearly a year.

In fact, the way things are right now, I'm certain that our box of johnnies will probably still be there after condoms become extinct. Historians may discover them long after we are dead and will display them in glass boxes in museums for future generations to marvel at.

Still, at least he has made an effort of sorts. And, if nothing else, it's reassuring to know that, despite all the nit-picking arguments we've had lately, I am still the 'keys to his clutch' … whatever that even means.

7

Dirty Talk

Charlie called this morning to 'check up' on me, but two minutes into our conversation, it became clear that she only wanted to divulge all the juicy details of her exciting sex life with Tom and to announce that, as of Valentine's Day, they're officially an item. The woman has been getting up to all sorts in the three weeks since I last saw her, and to be frank, I could have done with being spared some of the sordid details.

'We did a *Fatal Attraction* last night and shagged over his kitchen sink,' she said. 'I ripped the tap clean off so we're going to Wickes to get a new one later.'

By comparison, my sex life is totally non-existent. Aside from Ed giving me his shitty 'Keys to my clutch' poem a couple of weeks ago, nothing even vaguely romantic has happened since. We don't kiss any more, cuddles are rare and I haven't seen him naked other than when bursting in on him in the shower to pick his dirty pants off the floor. My washing machine is getting stuffed more regularly than I am, and that's the sad truth.

Deep down, I'm starting to worry that we're drifting apart. I'm not expecting to be thrown over the sink in the heat of passion, nor does tap shopping in Wickes sound appealing, but I'd like a little bit of intimacy – just enough to keep things ticking over until we're out of the woods with Jack and his nocturnal feeding frenzies.

Since becoming parents, everything revolves around the kids – our thoughts, schedules and conversations – so it's no wonder that the flames of desire have struggled to stay alight. And now that we have Jack, our tenacious little sleep thief, the tension in our relationship has been cranked up to blistering levels.

Lately, I find myself ripping Ed to shreds at every given opportunity. When he strolls in late from a gig and launches into a game of 'Thunderbirds are GO!' just after I've finally settled Stanley for the night, I exhale fire. Every time he forgets to empty the nappy bin or escapes to the bedroom when Stanley is acting up, I spit neat acid. And when I send him to the shops to buy emergency nappies and formula, but he returns with just formula and beer, the veins in my brain start to rupture.

Just a few days ago, we had a ridiculous row after I caught him layering up a stack of eight baby wipes when preparing to change Jack's nappy.

'Eight! For a tiny poo? Are you serious?' I tutted. 'The likes of Greta Thunberg would rip you to shreds for that, Ed.'

'This is how I do it,' came his retort, 'four for a wee, eight for a poo.'

'And multiply that by ten nappies a day by 365 days for three years and you'll have killed off half the creatures in the ocean. Good one.'

I'd like to report that this heated row was resolved with a raunchy shag over the kitchen sink, but sadly not. I ended up taking over the task, and in doing so, a minuscule piece of the environment was saved but my marriage was plunged further into the 'at risk of extinction' category.

It's pathetic, but arguments of this nature have driven a wedge between us – a wedge that needs removing. Tonight, we are celebrating Valentine's Day, a full two weeks after the actual event, and I'm determined to make it special. Tonight will *not* be about our kids, but about us. I want to feel close to him again, I *need* to feel close to him, and the filthy banter with Charlie earlier has inspired me to jump back on the horse (or rather to climb *carefully* and with *great* caution back on the horse).

'To quote the well-known slogan, "Just do it",' Charlie said on the phone. 'Or rather, "Just do *him*".'

With my boobs underwired up to the rafters in my new bra, my legs shaved and my lady jungle pruned, I've decided to make my move and get our marriage back on track.

Ed slumps through the door at 9.30 p.m. after spending the day recording a TV show for the BBC celebrating eighties music. He finds me in the kitchen, dolled up to the nines, frying steaks with a glass of Prosecco in hand.

'Hi, love,' he says, his tone deflated.

I look up to see that all of his discernible features have disappeared under a thick mask of liquid foundation. 'Jesus! What's happened to you? You look like you've been Tangoed!'

Gold glittery stars are painted across his cheeks and there's a film of glue peeling off the top of his bald head. It's a sight that might seem strange to most wives, but it's pretty standard when you're married to a man who works in show business.

'They made me up,' he says, 'and they glued on a silver wig and even ripped my nose hair out. With tweezers!'

'Damn. Harsh!' I wince. 'Mind you, I'm on board with the nasal hair removal. It's a shame they didn't sort your ear hair out while they were at it.'

'They made me wear a tight jumpsuit too and a pair of high-heeled boots. I think my toes might be broken.'

'And I thought my day was traumatic!' I can't help but laugh. 'Want a wipe to de-orange yourself?'

'Nah. Just fill up a glass for me, will you?'

With both kids settled in a deep but temporary sleep, I sit with my orange husband at the dining table for the first time in months and we share a bottle of Prosecco with our steaks. No phones, no Netflix, no Facebook: I'm determined to have a night without distractions.

'So, how was the show?'

'What do you mean?' he says vacantly, which he follows with a long pause. 'It was … good.'

'Well, go on. Elaborate.'

'What do you mean?' he says again, his fingers drumming on the table.

'Uh, what do you *think* I mean, Ed?'

He picks up his knife, which has fallen on the floor, disappears to the kitchen and returns with a KitKat and a clean knife in hand.

'Did the producer like what you did?' I say. 'Did you see any famous people in the canteen? You know, did *anything* interesting happen at all?'

The same four words slip out of his mouth for the third time – 'What do you mean?' – and I'm close to throttling him. It feels like a week passes before I manage to squeeze some decent information out of him. The big news: he saw Jonathan Ross eating a sandwich.

'Ooh! Exciting! Did you talk to him?'

'Nope' is all he says.

He snaps the fingers of his KitKat apart, then realigns them perfectly before chopping them into eight identical pieces with the clean knife.

'Was he short or tall? Friendly or a total jackass? Did he rack up a load of cocaine across the table or, I don't know, rip off all of his clothes and randomly cartwheel across the canteen singing "I Feel Pretty"?'

'No. He was just eating. He had a sandwich. And crisps … cheese and onion, I think.'

He lifts two bits of his KitKat, puts them in his mouth, then readjusts the remaining pieces to make a symmetrical pattern on the plate.

'Ed!' I snap. 'I've literally been waiting all day to chat to a grown-up. Please, say *something*. Or better still, why don't you try asking me how my day was for a change?'

He stares at the table for a few moments, then says, 'How was your day?'

'It was really boring, but thanks for asking,' I reply pointedly.

'I'm sorry. I just want to chill. I'm very tired is all, love.'

I stop myself from flying into the same old rage about who is more tired. It's a battle that he's never going to win, and as we are celebrating Valentine's Day, and I've gone to a huge effort to shave every square inch of my body, I must keep my eyes on the prize.

'I'm tired too, but I could do with a little exercise, if you're willing?' I wink.

'Oh. You mean—' His left eyebrow curls upwards. 'Right now? Can I just finish my KitKat first?'

'Stuff it down and strip, baby!'

He shoves four pieces of the chocolate into his mouth

in one go and grabs the remainder off the plate, frantically munching away to make room for them.

'Actually, Ed, let's just have a quick tidy-up first. I don't want to wake up to a shithole.'

I send him in to the kitchen, his cheeks stuffed with chocolate and his arms laden with a stack of dirty plates, then dash to the bathroom to douse myself in perfume and stuff two condoms in my back pocket. My loins are throbbing with anticipation as I head back into the dimly lit kitchen to find him in his boxers and socks, bent over in a rather compromising position.

'Are you sure you want to put *that* there?' I whisper seductively.

'Yes … it's dirty. It needs to go in. Right now.'

'But it's so *big*!'

'I know it is – big and very, *very* dirty.' He lifts a large pan that he used to fry bacon at breakfast time and places it on the bottom shelf of the dishwasher.

'But what about these?' I say, pointing to a pile of heavily soiled plates stacked on top of the counter, queueing for a clean.

'No. I'll do my big pan first. It's really filthy.'

'But they're even filthier!' I moan. 'They're not going to fit if you put your massive pan in there.'

He ignores me and starts lining up the cutlery in order of size on the top shelf.

'Just get on with it. Shove them in!' I plead. 'But don't overstuff the top rack!'

'I am *not* overstuffing it; it can take it!' He throws his buttocks against the machine, forcing the top shelf closed.

'Look, why don't I just hand-wash your pan – then you can fit the plates in?'

'No! It takes far more water to hand-wash my pan than to put it in the dishwasher.'

'No, it doesn't,' I reply passionately.

'Yes. Yes it does!' he retorts, slamming both hands down on the counter.

'No, no, nuhh-no!' I continue, my heartbeat quickening.

'Yes, yes! I know it does,' he repeats over and over as beads of sweat start to gather on his forehead.

The more I disagree, the more riled up he gets, his orange make-up rapidly melting away to reveal a bright-red complexion underneath. Then, without warning, he explodes. 'Well, *you* do it then!' He storms out of the kitchen, stomps down the hall and slams the bedroom door closed. I hear the thump of the headboard slamming against the wall as he collapses onto the bed.

A few minutes later, I pop my head around the door to discover that he is already fast asleep, clearly exhausted from the flurry of passionate activity. I, just like old times, am left to clean up the mess whilst he snores away on his back, with both arms tucked behind his head. And that was it. Our first night of marital passion in months:

Passionate. Dirty. Explosive.

My fanny breathes a sigh of relief as I switch on the dishwasher and lift a screaming Jack for his next feed.

8

The Predator

My attempt to seduce Ed was a disaster. Honestly, I don't know why I even pushed myself to try because, deep down, I'm just not ready. Aside from being perpetually exhausted, I don't feel sexy in the slightest, and the thought of letting anyone or any*thing* near my fanny right now is too horrifying to contemplate.

I was left in quite a mess after having Jack – far, *far* worse than the aftermath of Stanley's birth. As much as I've tried to block out the trauma, I can't seem to shake it off. Most days, I think about the ordeal and shudder. I think about the two midwives who delivered him: a buxom woman by the name of Mary and a timid, wide-eyed student called Esther who looked no more than fifteen.

Mary was terrifying. Her approach involved barking orders at both Esther and myself with the tone of a military drill sergeant.

'Up on the bed!' 'Pants off. OFF!' 'Legs down, put 'em down!' 'Esther, hold this!' 'Esther, hold that!'

I was bawling, thrashing around in agony and mooing like a deranged cow, but instead of offering words of comfort, Mary persistently bossed me about and slapped the insides of my thighs, intent on forcing me to unclench.

Then, without warning, she went up *there*. In fact, what felt like her whole arm went up … *there!*

After Mary finally withdrew, she declared that I was 8 centimetres dilated, then for the sake of Esther's invaluable hands-on education, she ushered her over to have a turn. Thankfully, her examination was less harrowing. She had the slim and elegant hands of a concert pianist, unlike Mary, who was sporting mitts that could have knocked out the Incredible Hulk with one punch.

Two hours and twenty or so mitts-up-my-insides later, Mary announced that I was fully dilated and ready to start pushing. Both Ed and Charlie were in the room, but Ed had slipped into some sort of temporary paralysis and was absolutely useless. He stood, totally mute and white as a sheet, gawping at the floor, so Charlie ended up having to take control. She slapped my back and chanted like a crazed cheerleader as she tugged on my gas and air at regular intervals.

'Go on, go. Go. Go! You can do it! Push! Fucking *push*! Go, Luce. You've got this!'

As much as I wanted to punch her in the face, I was so grateful that she didn't abandon me to pop out for a fag. To this day, it's the longest I've ever known her to abstain from nicotine.

The pain rapidly escalated from excruciating to absolutely unbearable and I begged desperately for an epidural, but Mary wasn't having it. 'No! Not possible. It's too late for that. It's time to push. You gotta push! Push! Put your legs DOWN!'

The woman wasn't messing around and not even Charlie was brave enough to take her on. I had no choice but to do as I was told, so I snatched the gas thingy out of Charlie's hand and tugged on it as hard as I could, then pushed. Mary slapped my thighs down, then barked at me again, so I took a deep breath and pushed a little harder. She slapped my thighs once more, and I mooed. I meowed. I neighed. I performed my entire repertoire of farmyard-animal noises, in fact, and then I pushed some more.

And … I shat myself.

'Esther!' Mary bellowed. 'Scoop the poop. Quickly! The baby is in distress!' And poor Esther ran to my aid and filled up more poo bags than a professional dog walker.

Suddenly, Mary slammed her meaty hand on the emergency button and a team of doctors dashed through the door. Before I knew it, I had a room full of strangers with their eyes and hands up my hospital gown, poking at my privates. Had I known that there would have been such an audience, I would have sold tickets. At the very least, I could have made some cash from this one-woman show of utter humiliation.

Jack arrived safe and sound moments later, bursting through a ring of fire into this world, on to a table where his own mother's excrement lay just seconds earlier. The moment I held him in my arms, I wept tears; not just tears of joy, but of relief, fear, embarrassment and shock. Ed had a little cry too, and even Charlie squeezed out a few salty drops before darting outside for a cigarette to recover from the trauma.

The worst part was over and our beautiful son was in my arms at last.

'Okay. You have second-degree tears and need stitches,' declared Mary as she pulled off her gloves and reached for the soap dispenser.

My eyes widened in fear and my heart pounded so intensely that I thought it would burst through my ribcage.

But then she briskly rubbed my arm, muttered some words that sounded like 'well done' and left the room abruptly. The relief was immediate for many reasons, but mainly because I wasn't overly confident that a woman with such cumbersome mitts would be much of an accomplished seamstress. But when I clocked eyes on the obstetrician strolling through the door, all I wanted to do was scream for her to come back.

My obstetrician was a man – a discovery that, in itself, was bad enough to digest, but there was more. He wasn't your typical middle-aged bald guy with hairy nostrils and a slight pot belly, but a six-foot-tall hunk of a man who wouldn't have looked out of place in a Dolce and Gabbana advert.

I dealt with the embarrassment the only way I knew how: through the art of jokey banter.

'Please tell me you have GCSE Textiles at the very least?' I said as he brandished his needle and thread around my lady parts. 'And whilst you're down there, chuck in a few extra stitches, will you? We'll call it an early Christmas present.'

Oh God!

Once the hunky doctor was finished, he swiftly informed me that the midwife would come to the flat to check my sutures after I was discharged, then bolted out the door without looking back.

A few days later, in the comfort of my own bathroom, curiosity got the better of me. After everything that my body had been through, I had to examine the damage with my own eyes before I could even consider allowing another stranger to have a gander at my undercarriage. So, in a fleeting moment of foolishness, I hoisted my leg up on the toilet seat and whipped out a magnifying mirror to have a good look.

BIG MISTAKE! My fanny was the Predator.

Although it's one of Ed's favourite Schwarzenegger films, I instantly knew that neither of us would ever sit through it again (at least not without sedating ourselves with a litre of absinthe first). I should *never* have looked because, months down the line, the face of this monster still haunts me every time I close my eyes. It will take years, if not decades, to undo the damage caused by that one glance in the mirror.

But it's not all bad news. Lately, I've started to feel marginally better about the situation downstairs thanks to an explicit feed that I stumbled across on a parenting forum online. I've salvaged some comfort in learning that I'm not the only woman who's been left in this state. One lady, a northerner by the name of Donna, commented that hers looks like a 'ripped out fireplace', and another girl, from Scotland – Michelle – said that hers resembles a 'yawning hippo'. Some women might cringe at Donna and Michelle's honesty, but their graphic use of adjectives – although disturbing – has brought me great relief. Thanks to their oversharing, I've been much more motivated to do my pelvic floor exercises, and now I'll clench at every possible opportunity (when chopping veg for dinner or when I'm on the phone, whilst queueing at the Tesco checkouts or when in gridlock traffic on the M25, when stuck on hold with the bank listening to floaty panpipe ballads or when being subjected to my neighbour Alan's tedious monologues about speed bumps and recycling bins. Hell, I'm even doing them right now!).

The truth is hard to hear, let alone see in the mirror, and part of me wishes that someone had given me a little heads up as to what was in store. Too many women are tight-lipped about their loose lips, so I've vowed that if Jen or Charlie ever decides to have kids, I will make it my personal mission to be honest so they can manage their expectations.

And the honest truth is if you deliver a baby the natural way, the chances are that your postnatal fanny will end up somewhere on the **FANNY-O-METER**.

The myth that C-sections cause less long-term damage also needs to be knocked firmly on the head. My sister Rachel had one, and although she escaped the perils of the Fanny-O-Meter, she felt like she'd been robbed of a natural birth and was utterly bereft about it at the time. Mentally, she managed to move on from the trauma, but she has yet to make peace with the gruesome overhang of skin on her belly that still remains. We have christened it 'the shelf' – it's essentially a wide flap of scar tissue from her incision that hangs ominously over the top of her pants. My nephew George has just turned seven and her shelf hasn't budged one bit. And eating carrot batons by the ton and drinking beetroot smoothies by the gallon have done absolutely nothing to shift it.

No woman escapes labour unscathed, and although I've been left feeling totally sexually desensitised, in my heart, I know that it was worth it. If I have to walk around with the Predator in my pants for the rest of my life, then so be it; my beautiful boys are worth *all* of it, a million times over and more. And if I continue to take Donna and Michelle's advice and commit to the pelvic floor exercises, then maybe I'll work my way down the meter from Predator to Wizard's sleeve at some point, and my mojo might well return.

In the meantime, Ed is either going to have to go without sex or summon the courage to face the Predator.

It is one of his favourite films after all.

9

The Geek
Done Good

'Excuse me. Give me two numbers. Two numbers!'

'Call me *Mummy*, Stan. *Mummy*,' I say for the hundredth time this week.

'Excuse me, *Mummy*' – he pauses briefly – 'but give me two numbers. Two!'

A long heavy sigh slides out of my mouth. 'Okay, what is, um, 4,328 by 753?' I say, as I continue to wade through the mountain of washing that has taken over the entire sofa.

'Wait.' He fiddles with the calculator, then announces: 'It is three millions, two hundred and fifty-eight thousands, nine hundreds and eighty-four.'

'Hooray!' I shriek, feigning enthusiasm, as he jumps up and down on the spot, flapping his hands in excitement.

'Another, another, another, ANOTHER!'

'Okay. Um. Um. What is 690 plus 4,573?'

'Wait …'

And so the whole cycle starts all over again.

This is how it has been every few seconds since 5.30 a.m. Realising that I am on the verge of prising the calculator out of his tiny hands and crushing it to bits with my foot, I decide to opt for the less aggressive cure for my inner torment by getting Ed's ass out of bed to share in the mathematical misery. I secure Jack in his highchair, hit Play on the remote then march down the corridor as Stan follows me with the fecking calculator in hand.

I throw the bedroom door open to find Ed … *not* asleep, *not* sat on the en suite toilet, but standing in his pants, carefully putting a tiny pair of boots on one of his Action Man toys which are laid out across the bed.

'What are you *doing?*' I say.

'What do you mean?' He jumps, dropping the boots on the floor. 'I'm, um, I'm just tidying my figures away.'

'Your dolls, you mean?'

He scrambles to pick up the fallen boots. 'They are *not* dolls, they're figures – vintage figures. How many times do I have to tell you?'

'About 4,328 by 753 times, I'd say, and the answer will still not make a blind bit of difference. You've been in here for God knows how long playing with your *dolls*, and I've been subjected to nearly four hours of calculator torture!'

'Excuse me,' Stan interjects, 'give me two numbers. Two numbers.'

'It's *Daddy*, Stan,' I say calmly, then I turn to Ed and spit: 'It's *your* turn! Put the dolls down and get your butt in there and share the load. I need a shower.'

'Okay, okay!' he mutters defensively. 'Let me just quickly wash my hands and put my figures away first.'

'Two numbers!'

'Yes, Stan, wait a sec,' says Ed. 'Um, how about seven plus three?'

'Excuse me, but you have to say *what* is seven plus three.'

'*What* is seven plus three?' Ed repeats curtly.

Content with the correct wording of his father's question, Stanley gives the answer and repeatedly demands another, which propels Ed into a fluster – a mere ten seconds into his shift. 'Okay, Stan, uh, I can't, uh, I can't think right now. Shall I just download a new numbers puzzle on my iPad instead?'

Stanley stops chanting, puts the calculator on the floor and nods assertively.

'Good, go to the living room and wait for me there,' Ed says. 'Daddy just needs to do something important first.'

I stand in the doorway of the en suite with my hands on my hips, glaring at Ed as he washes his hands to remove any 'destructive oils' from his fingertips. Then, without a care in the world, he wanders back to the bed and carefully lifts each one of his immaculately dressed dolls and places them back in their pristine boxes. Once satisfied that they're safely stored inside the wardrobe, he slumps down on the pile of dirty clothes on the armchair in the corner, with the iPad in hand, and begins searching for number puzzles while I make the bed.

'So we've done Spanish, got the Russian one. Maybe a Chinese one?' he mutters to himself as I huff around the room, plucking dirty pants and socks off the floor, which I toss in a pile at his feet.

I re-hook the fitted sheet around the corners of the mattress, then virtually snap my back in half pulling the king-size duvet across the mattress. With a more vigorous technique than usual, I plump up the pillows and grab my sparkly cushions off the floor before returning them to their home at the head of the bed. With order restored, I lift the laptop that is lying open on top of the dresser and flop down onto the bed to catch my breath and check my email. My fingers slam down on the keys, then wiggle impatiently across the track pad to try and get the computer to jolt to life.

'Stop! Stop! *Don't!*' Ed yells. Knocking the iPad off his lap onto the hard laminate floor, he dives across the bed and pushes the laptop out of my reach.

'What?'

In that split second, my heart stops dead in my chest.

What's happening here? What's he hiding? An affair? Is this why we're not having sex? Is my entire life about to come crashing down because he's been bonking a firm-boobed, tight-fannied blonde woman?

The answer is revealed seconds later. 'What is this?' I snap, my eyes glaring in disgust at the screen.

'Okay, okay. I can explain, I promise. I can!'

'A plastic sailor? Ed, why? You're a grown man! Why don't you just perve on slutty big-titted women online – y'know, like an ordinary hot-blooded man?'

'I'm *not* buying. I'm selling. And it's not *just* a sailor – it's a 1971 vintage Action Man sailor … in the *original* box. The bid is closing in one minute so *don't* touch the computer.'

People might think it strange that I would prefer my husband to be having an online affair than looking at toys on eBay, but if they were in my shoes they'd understand. Over the years, Ed has haemorrhaged money on his Action Man collection, so catching him on eBay, when our cash supply is at an all-time low is far more damaging to our marriage than any slapper with a 34GG set of hooters.

'Three, two, one … sold! Oh, my, *God!*' His mouth drops open as he stares down at the laptop in utter disbelief.

'What. *What?*'

'It's sold for,' he pauses, 'wait for it … *five hundred and eighty-six quid!*'

'Sweet Lord! For a shitty plastic sailor?' I pounce on him and shower his bald head with kisses.

'Plus twelve quid postage! We're loaded!'

I forgive him in an instant for all of the hours that he's wasted dressing and lining up his Action Man collection across the bed, hours that should have been spent helping out with the kids. I forgive him for the hundreds of pounds that he's blown on teeny pairs of goggles and flippers to complete their outfits, and for the countless occasions that he's snapped at me for touching them without washing my hands first. Most of all, I forgive him for every time that he's abandoned me in the middle of bath or dinner-time, claiming that he has to 'make an important call', but really he's just 'tidying up' his toys.

Five hundred and eighty-six quid is nothing to scoff at, especially given our current dire financial situation. Aside from the fashion-show gig, I've earned zilch since having Jack, and Ed's agents, as usual, are yet to cough up the cash for work that he did way back in December.

'Steak tonight?' I say. 'And wine – *not* a bottle with a screw top, but one with an actual cork?'

My man – the geek – has done good.

And I can say with full confidence that he has an extremely high chance of getting his own cork popped tonight.

10

The Six-Month Check

J ack is seven and a half months old, so the health visitor is arriving at 10.30 a.m. for the routine six-month check. Better late than never, I suppose.

I have, of course, been up since 5 a.m. cleaning. The last time she came was when Jack was just two days old. She rolled up an hour early to find Ed still out cold and me wearing stained pyjamas and eating crisps for breakfast. Stan was buck naked, playing with his number puzzle amongst twenty binbags of my nephew's old baby clothes that were clogging up every inch of floor space. Dirty nappies were stuffed in carrier bags on the dining table, and there was a smell of old farts – perhaps even a dead carcass – wafting around the kitchen. I discovered only after she'd left that the source of the stench was actually a rancid lump of broccoli that had been festering in the kitchen fruit bowl for the best part of two weeks.

Needless to say, we didn't make the best first impression.

She arrives on time and walks into our immaculate flat that is fragranced with fresh daffodils and four Glade Plugins that are cranked up to the max. Jack is dressed in his finest babygro: sparkling clean, fluffy and super cute. Stan is fully clothed for a change and playing with the calculator. And I have clean hair, a supported chest and even a thick layer of foundation spread across my cheeks

'So, Mum, how's it been going?' she says as she sits down and pulls out a thick ring binder and a pen. She is a plump woman in her fifties and is dressed in a cheap navy suit, the jacket of which is fighting to stay closed over her large drooping breasts, which must constitute at least 75 per cent of her full body weight.

'All great, thanks.'

'Right, good. And how is the breastfeeding going?' she says.

'He's bottle fed now,' I say bravely then sip my tea, sit back in my seat and wait for the onslaught.

She doesn't even try to hide her disappointment. 'Oh! And why is that, can I ask?'

'I tried it for a while,' I lied, 'but it didn't work out in the end.'

She releases a deliberate sigh that hangs over my head like a black cloud. 'Don't you think you should keep at it? Perhaps just a bit longer? The benefits *far* outweigh formula – there is a reason why they say "breast is best".'

'I know,' I say firmly. I stare directly into her eyes. 'But he is seven months old and I'm all dried up. I dried up months ago, in fact.'

The woman hasn't heard a word of what I've just said. 'I fed my twins until they were five,' she continues, 'and it was the *best* thing that I could have done for them.' She smiles dreamily and I can actively feel her mind wander back to the day when she had two five-year-olds sucking on her boobs as she watched *Coronation Street* with a cup of Ovaltine. 'Okay. Um. Well, I suppose I should make a note of it.' She shakes her head, jots something down in her file and continues her interrogation. 'And how about weaning? Is *that* at least going well?'

'Yes, we started at five and a half months and he's been trying a wide selection of things.'

Jars of carrot (but not a real carrot), jars of spaghetti bolognese (but not my home-made version), £4,000 worth of Ella's Kitchen pouches, Cheetos, Quavers, half the hair on my head, the remote control, his left hand, oh, and an abundance of wood chippings from the floor of Walpole Park ... quite a variety of things, as it happens.

'Wonderful, wonderful. If you're stuck for ideas, Ella's Kitchen have an Instagram page and they've also got a few recipe books out that I hear are good.'

'Oh yes. I have a couple of those books.'

And I have a freezer full of their cheesy cauliflower and sweetcorn purée that will undoubtedly be rejected in favour of a Petit Filous and some fries from my Big Mac meal.

'Well, he certainly looks fit and healthy, Mum. I'll weigh him in a minute. And how about you? Are you feeling well?'

'Yes, great. Feeling really good, thanks ...'

And fecking knackered, morbidly obese, wildly unattractive, frustrated, on the verge of murdering my lazy husband, lonely, bored, unappreciated, anxious, penniless, brainless and generally pretty negative about the future of my marriage, my career and my pelvic floor muscles. But thanks for asking.

'And have you been getting out and about with baby? There's a wonderful baby yoga class down at St Mary's. It's 10 a.m. every Monday and Wednesday.'

'Oh yes, I'll check it out,' I lie in the most jovial tone I can manage.

She picks Jack up to weigh him. 'Ah! He is such a bonny boy!'

'Bonny'? No, he's only the cutest, most adorable baby in the world ever! 'Bonny' doesn't nearly cut it!

'Excuse me,' Stan interjects, clearly oblivious to the fact that we have a guest, 'give me two numbers.'

'Stan, I am speaking to the lady right now.'

'Give me TWO NUMBERS!'

'Okay. *Okay!* What's 4,309 plus 3,998?'

'It's … eight thousands, three hundreds and seven.'

'Gosh! What a clever little boy you are. How old are you?' the health visitor gushes.

Stan totally blanks her and continues as if she isn't in the room. 'Two more. Two more!'

'He's four,' I reply, 'very nearly five,' and then I give him another random sum.

'Goodness me. That's remarkable! What a bright boy you are, Stanley.'

His total disregard for her compliment makes her visibly uncomfortable, so she turns her attention back to Jack and places him down on her weighing scales.

'Ah. Nine point one kilos. A great weight.'

That'll be down to the copious amounts of demonic formula. And the Cheetos.

'Right, wonderful. Now, before I go, do you have any questions?'

Yes, have they invented a drug to get babies to sleep through the night yet? Or is there an amazing new device on the market that makes dummies stay in for longer than forty seconds? Will I ever have a size-ten waist again? Or boobs that don't hang down around my sides like saddle bags on a work horse? And will I ever have a proper career again now that we have two kids to raise? Will I ever stop worrying that something bad is going to happen to my kids? Will I ever be able to eat an entire hot meal in a seated position? Or have a shit or a shower alone?

'No, I'm all good. Thanks so much for coming.'

'Nine thousands, six hundreds and fourteen,' comes Stan's answer.

'My goodness!' She gasps. 'You should call Mensa. Your son is a genius. I've never seen anything quite like it!'

Genius? Doubtful. Autistic? Possibly. Awesome? Definitely.

I nod and just say, 'Maybe I should.'

As I am showing her out, she glances at the highchair and clocks the polka-dotted latex sucking device that Jack is trying to pick up off the tray. She stops in her tracks, lays her hand on my forearm and squeezes it briefly. 'You really should wean him off that dummy. They're *very* bad for children's teeth. Research shows that he may develop an overbite.'

I spend the rest of the day panicking about Jack's addiction to jarred food, salty snacks and rubber suckers. If I don't get the Cheetos and dummy situation under control, then the future could be bleak for him.

And it will be all my fault.

11

Body Parts

'Excuse me! But there are three things you should know. Number one, my favourite colour is not green any more, it is red. Number two, I think Jack has done a poo because it smells very not nice in here. Number three, letters and numbers and shapes aren't my favourite any more. I like body parts the best now.'

I roll over and glance at the clock. It is 4.07 a.m. 'Stan, go back to bed! It's still night-time and we all need to rest our brains.'

He drags the covers down to the foot of the bed, climbs up and slides in between Ed and Jack, who are both fast asleep. I lean down and pull the covers back up over the four of us, then sink into the pillow and brace myself for one of his nocturnal monologues.

'I like body parts now.'

'Uh-huh.'

'Because they all have different shapes and because lots of them are red. And red is my new favourite colour.'

'That's, uh, nice.'

'The heart is an upside-down cone. The kidneys are in the shape of baked beans. The stomach is like a letter J. The lungs are like a wonky triangle. And the intestinines are curly-wurly.'

'It's "intestines", Stan, not "intestinines". Now, go to sleep, love, it's sleepy time.'

'*Intestines.* And did you know that there are two hundreds and six bones in a body? Jack has two hundreds and seventy bones because he is a baby, but you have two hundreds and six bones because you are a grown up.'

'Uh-huh.'

'And did you know that ...'

This is all I hear before I pass out.

It is only after downing three extra-strong coffees at breakfast time that I'm able to process that I hadn't dreamt our conversation. 'Stan, did you tell me that you like body parts now?' I say as he opens his mouth and waits for me to place a spoon of yoghurt into it.

'Yes. I like the heart best because it is red, and red is my—'

'Oh. That's right,' I interrupt. 'So, how did you learn about them?'

'Mrs Kinsella told me. I now like body parts more than I like letters, numbers and shapes.'

'No way! I don't believe you!' I say, smiling. 'You can't possibly love them *more* than your letters?'

'I do. I do!' he yells defensively. 'I do, I DO!'

'Shhh, Stan. *Indoor* voice,' I whisper on autopilot.

His volume halves and he continues, thankfully at a more aurally manageable level. 'Did you know that the heart is like an upside-down cone?'

'Yes, I did, Stan. And did *you* know that the heart pumps blood around your body so that all of your body parts can get oxygen?' I reply, rather impressed that I can remember the basics of human anatomy on virtually no sleep.

'And did you know that the kidneys look like baked beans?' he continues.

'I know, Stan. You told me already.'

'Red is my new favourite col—'

'So,' I interrupt, 'does this mean that you don't like letters at all?'

'No! No! I still like letters, but I like body parts more! The heart is my favourite because red is—'

I mouth the words *indoor voice* once more then shove a spoon of yoghurt in his mouth and take a deep gulp of cold coffee.

And so it goes again; there's a new obsession in town. The alphabet is out, and body parts are in. Call the press!

Last year, Stan dabbled with Thomas the Tank Engine for a few months, then out of nowhere, he switched to monkeys, then fire alarms. The fire-alarm fixation was the most taxing, as a simple trip to Marks and Spencer always resulted in having to walk through all three floors of the shop so he could point out where they all were. Popping in for a pint of milk and a bag of Percy Pigs became more traumatic than a colon cleanse.

Experience has taught me that no matter how passionate he becomes about such things, they will be no more than a brief but intense affair. His letters and numbers are like a childhood sweetheart that is never forgotten, and they hold the number-one place in his affections. I know in my bones that they'll be back in favour at some point, but in the meantime, I must do my best to welcome 'intestinines' into our home as a temporary guest.

After spoon-feeding Stan his entire breakfast, I help him button up his favourite polo shirt, which I managed to tumble dry overnight. I quickly throw on some clothes, strap Jack to my torso and hurry out the door to nursery in the usual flap, inwardly relieved that this is the last time I'll have to do this before the Easter holidays kick in. A break from this daily ordeal is long overdue.

By the time we make it to nursery, the other parents are queueing all the way down the street, waiting for Mrs Kinsella to come and open the door. I take my place at the back of the line with Stan and listen to him rattle off a list of body parts as he clutches my hand tightly.

'A is for arm, B is for bladder, C is for chin, D is for ...' he chants.

'Stan, why don't you go and have a quick play in the yard with the boys and girls before you go in?'

'E is for ear, F is for finger, G is for ghoul-bladder,' he continues as he swings off my arm, nearly pulling it out of its socket.

Spring has fully sprung; the sun is out at last and the majority of Stan's little classmates are making the most of it. Coats and cardigans have been discarded in a large pile and the kids run about the yard like wild monkeys. They swing off the railings, jump over wooden logs and roll around on the small patch of grass in the far corner, laughing, shouting and squealing. Some parents are gassing away to whoever is standing next to them in the line, others avoid eye contact by burying their heads in their phones, and a few are scraping toothpaste stains off their kids' faces and fixing ponytails that have already fallen down.

'That little boy is playing on the alphabet yard, Stan. Why don't you ask him if you can play too?'

'H is for heart, I is for eyes, J is for ...'

'And that little girl over there in the red dress is standing by herself. She looks a bit sad. Maybe you should say hello.'

He reaches 'N is for nipples' when the door finally opens and Mrs Kinsella welcomes the children in.

I wait for the crowd to disperse before I mouth, 'Can I have a quick word?'

'Miss Caffrey, can you settle all the children whilst I speak to Mrs Wright, please?' she says before ushering me in to the cloakroom. 'Stanley, take off your coat, put it on your peg and go and sit on the carpet next to Emmanuel, please.' She smiles warmly and Stan does exactly as she tells him.

Once he is out of sight, I am granted the opportunity to speak freely. 'Stan has been speaking about anatomy all night. I just wondered if you'd noticed this too?'

'Oh, yes, Mrs Wright. We did a colouring activity last week called "My Body". It was very basic – just hands, eyes, ears and feet – but he loved it so much that I gave him a more detailed book to read. To be honest, it's been difficult to get him to do anything else since.'

'Well, you certainly have fuelled his passion. He's now talking about "intestinines" and "ghoul-bladders".'

'Gosh!' She chuckles. 'He is such a little star – and so clever!'

'I know. He definitely doesn't get it from me. Anyway, I just wanted to find out if he's been getting on any better with the other kids.'

'Definitely,' she says without hesitating. 'There's a little girl called Holly who always makes sure she sits next to him, but …' her volume drops significantly and she leans in closer to my face, 'she is a touch on the, um, bossy side.'

Say no more. I hear you. She's a dominatrix in the making. Not Stan's cup of tea and definitely not daughter-in-law material.

'Okay,' I say out loud.

'I'm encouraging a friendship between him and Emmanuel. They are both very quiet and enjoy learning, so I think they suit each other better.'

So he's a loveable little brainiac too? Perfect!

'Emmanuel, you say?'

'Yes. He's a sweet little boy, but very shy as he's new and still settling in. His parents have just moved to the area, so he's only been with us a couple of weeks.'

'Can you point him out to me?' I say.

'Um, sure,' she replies hesitantly, presumably because she's worried that I'm planning to abduct him. She opens the door to the classroom and subtly points to a cute little boy wearing thick black glasses who is sat next to Stanley on the carpet. He is fidgeting with the Velcro strap on his shoe and Stanley is gawping at the alphabet poster on the wall.

'And who picks him up at the end of the session?' I enquire.

'Um ...' She shifts uncomfortably, then folds her arms around her waist.

'Don't worry. I'm not planning on abducting him,' I say reassuringly. 'I was actually thinking it would be nice if one of Stanley's nursery friends came for a playdate over the Easter holidays.'

'Phew!' She exhales and chuckles sweetly as she brushes the back of her hand across her forehead. 'Well, it's usually his sister who picks him up, but today I think it's his mum. I'll point her out to you at the end of the session.'

'Brilliant, thanks so much for your time. I'll head off now and leave you to it.' I edge towards the door, but she stops me.

'Oh, Mrs Wright, before you go, there was a woman here yesterday from the Ealing Green Children's Centre. She stayed about an hour and observed Stanley, but I didn't get a chance to speak to her before she left.'

'Oh, brilliant. Thanks for letting me know.'

I head home with a spring in my step. Some action is finally being taken by the Children's Centre and Emmanuel is a little darling. He's the perfect candidate to fill the role of Stan's best friend, a position that has been vacant since, well, forever.

Once home, I put Jack down for a nap and set up camp on the sofa with a cup of scorching-hot coffee, ready to embark on a mammoth eBay shopping session. If Stanley is changing his fixation from letters to body parts, then I need to stock up on some new supplies. Two coffees, a Twix and four custard creams later, my shopping basket is loaded to the brim with treats for our budding little anatomist: a Squishy Human Body 3-D puzzle (which comes complete with nine mini removable organs, twelve bones and a detailed educational book), a *My Human Body* sticker book and a lift-the-flap body book. I'm all kitted out and ready to go!

With a celebratory bonus custard cream in hand, I lie back on the sofa and glance across the room at the rows of letters and numbers lined up immaculately across the floor. Perhaps Stan's new fixation will mean that he'll finally let me put them away and we'll get our floor space back?

I shudder.

Rows of rubber body parts lined up across my rug isn't exactly a more desirable option. But whether I like it or not, 'Fish Stan's rubber pancreas out of the hoover' is soon to be added to my already long list of daily chores.

If he's passionate about it then Ed and I, as always, will embrace his passion as if it's our own.

12

The Hunt

We had made big plans for the Easter holidays. Ed had kept the week free and we were going to jump in the car and drive to Wales to hang out with my family. My mum was going to cook one of her famous roasts, Ed and my dad were going to sit on the sofa drinking beer all weekend, and my sister and I were going to throw together an egg hunt in my parents' huge back garden for the kids. A weekend of stuffing our faces, raiding my dad's Scotch collection and suffering his midnight bagpipe recitals was on the cards and I couldn't wait.

But, sadly, the gods had other plans.

Three days into the holidays, everyone came down with a cold. Stanley started off with a runny nose and a temperature, then it spread through the flat like wildfire, claiming Ed as its final victim. He was convinced that the 'virus' must have mutated before it entered his system because his symptoms were far more severe than those the rest of us were experiencing. He was rendered immobile and spent five straight days in bed in order to 'contain the disease' whilst praying for his life. I would have called a priest to perform the last rites but, firstly, we're not Catholic and, secondly, I had no time to organise it because I too was battling the same 'disease' and attending to the needs of a sick young boy and baby to boot.

It's now 10.45 p.m. and Easter Sunday is just hours away.

With my third glass of wine in hand, I'm sat on the rug in a blind panic trying to throw an Easter egg hunt together for Stanley to enjoy come morning. The pressing issue? I have no eggs. Not a single one.

'Hi, love.'

Ed is hovering in the doorway, a sight painful to my eyes because he's wearing his bright-red Spiderman dressing-gown and matching slipper socks that Stanley chose for Father's Day last year. With thick, wiry stubble sprouting all over his cheeks and dark, heavy bags hanging under his eyes, he doesn't exactly look well-rested considering he hasn't left our room for days.

'Wow! It's a miracle!' I snip. 'He. Is. Risen!'

'I'm feeling a bit better, love,' he mumbles weakly, 'think I'm through the worst of it.'

'Well, thank God, Ed, because we missed our life insurance payment last month and I was panicking about how to pay for your funeral.'

'What's all this?' he says, staring down at the rug where I've emptied the entire contents of the kitchen's junk-food cupboard. 'Chocolate Fingers and Jammie Dodgers?'

'Yep. That's right.'

'But where's the eggs?'

'We're not doing eggs this year, Ed. We're doing Fingers, Dodgers and Cheetos.'

'Uh … does the Easter bunny bring Cheetos? Is that a thing now?'

'No, Ed. She doesn't generally bring Cheetos but *she*,' I slam my index finger into my chest, 'couldn't get near a shop to buy any eggs, because *someone*,' I point the same finger at him, 'was dying in bed all week with a measly cold and has been no help whatsoever. So, *she*,' the finger is back on me, 'is using what she has at her disposal because the shops are closed and Stan will be up for Easter in six hours.'

'Is the Easter bunny female then? In my head he's always been male.'

'Of course she's female! In one day, she hides eggs for millions of kids across the globe and probably still makes it back on time to get dinner on and sort the kids out for bed. She's a champion multitasker, Ed. *Definitely* a she!'

He shrugs his shoulders and wanders out of the room and returns with a beer. 'What about that body-parts thing that came yesterday?'

'His puzzle? What, it came?'

'Yeah. It arrived when you were cleaning the shower. We could open it up and hide body parts all over the place with clues. He'll love it.'

'Um,' I frown, 'is that not a bit serial-killery? Sending our kid on a hunt for body parts?'

'Nope, more police-detectivey, I think. He doesn't like eggs anyway. We've still got chocolate Santas in the fridge and Halloween sweets in the cupboard lying untouched. He'll like this loads more.'

It's a weirdly brilliant idea, and at this point, it's all we've got. I decide to roll with it and hope that our actions won't encourage our child to pursue a career that involves handling human organs in a psychotic way. Together, we sink a bottle of wine, listen to music and compose quirky clues to accompany the mini organs that we've dotted about all over the flat. By the time our heads hit the pillow, we have an incredible (if a little twisted) hunt lined up ready for our son come morning.

'She has been. She has been!'

It's 5.36 a.m. and a bony little finger is prodding my chest. I endure the assault for a few minutes, but realising that it's not going to stop, I redirect the attacker to a victim more deserving. 'Go and poke Daddy, Stan. Get him up, then we can all start the hunt together.'

He totters over to the other side of the bed and resumes poking, only now Ed's bald head is on the receiving end of it.

Ed caves within seconds – 'I'm up! I'm up!' – and sits bolt upright, his eyes still stuck together with the thick crust of deep sleep.

'The bunny has put a letter on my bed.'

'Read it to Daddy, Stan. I need to change Jack's nappy.'

'Okay. Okay. "I look like beans and I come as two, you can find me where you wee and …"'

'Wee and … Stan? What rhymes with "two" and is the opposite of wee?'

'POO!' He flaps his hands and bounces up and down on the spot. 'It's the toilet!'

'Well, go on then. Go to the toilet and see if you're right!'

He scampers down the hallway and Ed follows, dragging himself across the floor like an extra from *The Walking Dead*.

'It's kidneys! I have two kidneys!' he shrieks excitedly from the bathroom at the other end of the flat. 'And there's another letter!'

'Read it, Stan,' I call out from the bedroom as I secure Jack's clean nappy closed. 'What does it say?'

'"I look like a cone and I go tick-tock, I beat all day, just like a …"' he pauses for a second, 'CLOCK!' He dashes to the bookshelf in the living room – 'HEART! I have a heart! And excuse me, but there's *another* letter.'

'Go on, read it.'

He bellows, "'I'm curly-wurly and long and wet, A, B, C, I'm by your alpha ... BET!'"

All nine organs and twelve bones are found within ten minutes, each one getting an even bigger shriek of joy than the last, and when Stan finds the final prize, he's practically hyperventilating from the thrill of it all. 'It's the body! It's the body! Now I can put all of the parts inside of it!'

The rest of Easter Sunday is spent exactly as expected. Stan stays in his room for hours lining up his treasured set of new rubber organs, and Ed vegs out on the sofa watching Spiderman cartoons. He persistently complains that he still doesn't feel right and threatens to hunt down whoever was responsible for giving him this debilitating disease and make them pay. Jack – a teenage girl trapped in a baby's body – fluctuates between crying and laughing for no fathomable reason, and as for me, well, most of my afternoon is spent trying to rustle up a special meal from an empty fridge freezer so we can celebrate the resurrection of Jesus.

Chicken Dippers, Potato Waffles and Alphabetti Spaghetti is served at 5 p.m. and we all take our usual seats at the dining table, except for poor Ed who is forced to give up his place at the top to accommodate our new family members: lungs, heart, kidneys, 'die-fram' and an incredibly special, *very* curly-wurly set of 'intestinines'.

13

A Visit to McDonald's Makes You Wail

'Let's all go out for lunch,' announces Ed.

The second week of the holidays has been totally Ed-less, so the least he can do is take us out for a slap-up family meal before Stanley goes back to nursery tomorrow. I'd hoped that after spending the first week quarantined in the flat, Ed might want to go on a few nice outings with me and the kids this week, but no. The guitarist on *Chicago* in the West End came down with a brutal bout of gastroenteritis and Ed ended up stepping in to cover him. So, my Easter holidays have mostly been spent watching the same cartoon of a googly-eyed singing gall-bladder on YouTube, and any conversation that I've had has revolved around pancreatic ducts and bile storage.

'Lunch?' My ears prick up. 'A table for four at the Ivy it is then. Just give me a sec to find my tiara.'

'Or McDonald's?' he says.

'Oh, monsieur, wiz zis Big Mac you are really spoiling us!' I say in the sexiest French accent that I have in my repertoire.

'Well, I just thought that, one, it'll be nice to do something to mark the end of the holidays and, two, we're out of bread and I can't face shopping right now, and three, it's Stan's favourite. Shall we just throw a Happy Meal at the problem?'

'So we can sit in McDonald's and have a conversation in numbered points there instead of here for a change?' I say.

'It'll be rammed 'cos all the kids are still off school. What about a drive-thru?'

'This is London, love. Everything is rammed *all* of the time. You should know that by now. Besides, if we drive to the one in Brentford, we'll lose our parking space outside.'

I can almost hear the cogs in Ed's brain turning as he weighs up which of the two options is less hideous: having to eat in a busy public place amongst other humans or being forced to park the car a fifteen-minute walk from our front door after losing our regular spot by the bins.

'Okay, you're right. You're right. We'll eat in at the one on the Broadway, but only if you queue for the food.'

'Deal. But what about the toy, Ed? Can you really face it if it all goes to shit?'

'Nope, it's Sunday and the new one is out,' he says confidently. 'I asked them last time and they definitely said Sunday.'

'Okay. McDonald's it is. I'll dust the cobwebs off my tiara another day, I guess.'

As predicted, the McDonalds on the Broadway is packed full of parents who had the same genius idea as us. Every table is occupied, and every inch of floor space is clogged up with highchairs, prams and H&M shopping bags. Tables are stacked high with torn Happy Meal boxes, cups and opened tubs of ketchup; fries and paper straws are scattered all over the floor; and the air is thick with the sound of crying babies and gossiping teenagers.

'Fuck's sake,' says Ed. 'I told you. Rammed!' He's already turning purple and on the verge of having a brain bleed.

'Indoor voice!' I snap. 'Just take Stan over there to look at the toys and I'll sort out the rest.'

Hand in hand, they duck and dodge their way through the assault course to stare at the Happy Meal toys in the display cabinet, and while they're distracted, I wait with Jack for our usual table to become available. Thankfully, an elderly couple are drinking coffee in our seats – the easiest of prey. They leave within two minutes after I hover over them with a whingeing Jack in my arms, flashing my finest and most intimidating stare.

'Ed, come! Sit. I'll get the food – you get the balloon. Deal?'

He gives me a thumbs up and makes his way back to the table, then takes Jack in his arms and starts scanning the room in search of the balloon distributor.

'What drink do you want, Stan?' I say as I help him take off his jacket and get him settled.

'Orange.'

'I'd like orange, *please*.'

'Week number one is milk. Week number two is orange. It is week number two, so I want orange with *no* bits.'

'I would like some orange without bits, *please*, Mummy,' I say and he repeats my words, in the exact same tone as prompted.

I join the queue and practise the order in my head like an actress waiting behind the curtain just before she heads out on-stage. There's no room for error: a plain burger, two tubs of ketchup on the side, some small fries with *no* salt in a separate bag that's *not* ripped, and a bottle of orange juice, NO BITS, and a straw. The only potential issue is the toy, but Ed seems pretty sure that it will be okay.

When I return to the table ten minutes later, I'm relieved to see Stanley holding his red balloon. So far, so good. I hand him his Happy Meal, then, with my heart in my throat, I wait for him to open it and examine the contents. He carefully pulls the strip around the middle of the box, takes off the lid and, with bated breath, Ed and I watch as he carefully lines up the items across the table for inspection.

'I have this one! I have this one!' comes the piercing screech two seconds later. The toy is thrown with force on to the floor and he follows it, knocking all the fries off the table as he goes down. I flash Ed a look of venom before reaching under the table to pull Stanley back up on the bench.

'*Fuck's sake!*' Ed explodes. 'They said the new ones were out today. Bastards!'

'Not helpful, Ed. It's *not* helpful for me if you lose it too. Calm yourself. You're a grown man. Just calm yourself!'

'All right!' he snaps. 'I'll go and ask for a different one.'

'Don't be rude to them – promise you won't shout,' I call out as I watch him strut towards the counter like a boxer heading to the ring.

He returns several minutes later – flaming red in the face – holding the same toy. 'I'm sorry, Stan. They don't have the new one yet. But don't worry, Daddy will get you the next one on the list. I promise.'

Stan is back under the table within a flash, screaming even louder than before, and as I try to pick him up, his elbow clocks me across the face and I topple backwards on to the pile of fallen fries.

'The new one! New! New! New!' he howls as every eye in both the seating area and the queue looks down on him disapprovingly.

'Let's just go. Ed, bag up the food and grab Jack. I'll wait for you outside.'

Taking several punches to the guts, I pull Stanley off the floor once again and manage to make it out on to the high street before I'm forced to stop and lie him down on my lap. He continues to thrash around wildly, slamming his fists into anything that is in his way, and I follow the instructions I'd read online and make sure that I support his head so he doesn't knock himself out on the pavement. Shoppers stop in their tracks to stare and cars slow down to gawp at the chaos, and although plenty of people make the effort to tut, not a single one offers to help.

Ed eventually comes out with Jack in his arms and what's left of the food balanced on top of the pram – wide eyed, sweaty and traumatised.

'Hello, excuse me,' I plead to anyone who will listen, 'can you please hold our baby for a second so we can get our son in the pram?'

Of all the people walking past – mums with shopping bags, dads pushing prams, able-bodied middle-aged men with Starbucks cups in hand – the only person to stop is a skinny long-haired teenager wearing a black hoodie and a faded Guns N' Roses T-shirt. The most unlikely of heroes.

'Is he all right?' he says, tucking his straggly hair back behind his ears with both hands.

'Could you hold the baby?' Ed pants and, without waiting for an answer, he plonks Jack in the young man's arms. The teenager stands there visibly uncomfortable – like he's just been handed a ticking bomb.

Together, Ed and I lift Stanley off the pavement and push his little body into the pram, and with great effort we manage to fasten the straps around him.

'Get him home quick!' I order Ed and he immediately launches into a mild sprint up the road. 'God, I love you! Thank you so much,' I say as I pull Jack from the young man's arms. 'You're the only decent human being around here.'

His spotty face flushes pink instantly. He pulls his hood up and holds it tightly around his face and, without meeting my eyes, he says, 'No, uh, big deal. My little brother is autistic, so I'm kind of used to it.'

No words come from my mouth. Instead, I wrap my free arm around the boy and hug him.

'Uh, best of luck, yeah. I hope he's okay.' He pulls away awkwardly, and before I can apologise and reassure him that I'm not some kind of weird stranger-hugging lunatic, he slips back into the steady stream of shoppers.

Hurrying along the Broadway with Jack in my arms, I notice every person turning to stare at Stanley up ahead as he screams with the shrillness of an ambulance siren, and I can still hear him wailing after Ed has skidded around the corner on to Windsor Road. Once home, I lug Jack up to the flat, strap him into his highchair, then dash back down to the driveway to help Ed. We carry Stanley up together, toss the sofa cushions on the floor and lie him down where he can thrash around safely.

'I'll go and get your toy now, Stan,' Ed says urgently, wiping the sweat from his forehead.

'Leave it, Ed. Remember, we agreed that he *has* to learn that life isn't always going to go his way.'

'No, I'm going. He won't stop until he's got it. I'll be as quick as I can,' he says, and with that, he grabs the car keys off the coffee table and dashes out the door before I have a chance to talk him out of it. Nearly two full hours of heart-wrenching hysteria pass by and, despite my best efforts, nothing I do or say will calm Stanley down. Ed was right, and when he finally comes running back into the room with the toy in hand, I'm ready to dive on him and shower his face with kisses.

'Here, little man, here! I've got it,' he says, excitedly. 'The new one. I've got it!'

He pulls a small plastic bag out of his pocket and tears it open. Inside, there's a one-eyed Minion holding an acoustic guitar and, more importantly, the sacred bit of paper which lists all of the Minions available to collect over the coming weeks.

Stan is lying on the floor rocking back and forth rhythmically, as he has been for the entire time that Ed was out. I place the Minion in his hand and the rocking stops. He studies it for a few seconds, then gets up and disappears to his room, presumably to line it up along the window sill with the rest of his collection. He returns almost immediately – his eyes puffy and bloodshot, his hair soaked in tears – with the paper insert from the bag in his hand.

'Next week, I need the one with the fart blaster gun,' he says quietly.

'We'll try, Stan,' Ed says, 'but if they don't have it, I'll have to look on eBay – okay?'

Stan doesn't answer and wanders off back to his room. I sigh, then put Ed's quarter pounder in the microwave and crack open a beer to calm my nerves. 'How many McDonald's did you go to this time, love?'

'Five,' Ed replies wearily. 'Brentford, Hanwell, Acton, Southall and Hounslow. And I lost our space! I've had to park all the way down the very end of Florence Road.'

I reach out to hug him. 'Well done, my hero.'

'Give me one of those beers, will you?'

'Sure. Have twenty. You deserve it.'

He kicks off his trainers and slumps down into his reclining chair.

'So, how long do you think it will be until we can take him to the Ivy for lunch?' I say.

'I *can't* believe they didn't have the new toy. How incompetent are those people? They said Sunday – today is Sunday. I mean, how fucking hard is it to stick to a plan?'

'Don't dwell on it, Ed. I've told you before, not everyone in this life sticks to the rules.'

'Well, they *should*. They said Sunday, and it's Sunday.'

'I know. The jackasses! The wankers! I shall torch all their houses! Bring them to justice for their heinous crimes!'

'I'm going to see the manager tomorrow. I'm going to,' he mutters.

'Enough – what's done is done. Let's forget it. Come on, humour me – how long until we can take Stan to the Ivy?'

He swigs his beer and lays his head back in the chair. 'Right now? I'd say probably never.'

'Even if they start serving their filet mignon with a side of Minions?'

'What, like a filet *Minion*?' He smiles cheekily.

And we both laugh. Very, very hard.

14

The Cyborg

'Stanley Wright. Room Nine. Stanley Wright.'

I take Stanley by the hand and lead him through the waiting room and down the long white corridor towards the speech therapy room. The thick smell of disinfectant catches the lump at the back of my throat that's been there since I entered the building: the lump of dread.

Here we go again.

The therapist is propping the door open as we approach, flicking through a thick wad of sheets threatening to burst free from her clipboard. She's a different therapist to the last one we saw. She's older, perhaps in her late fifties, and her natural resting expression is that of a slight frown, which doesn't instil me with much confidence. Her complexion is ghostly white, and every strand of her dark-grey hair has been scraped back off her face to form a thin, limp ponytail that trickles over her right shoulder. In the words of my mother, this is a woman who is crying out for a 'wee bit of lipstick'.

'Stanley Wright?' she says in a high-pitched, deliberately slow tone. 'Come on through.'

He heads in first and automatically takes his usual seat by the table on which lies the dreaded bag of plastic animals, and I sit against the far wall out of the way.

'And how are you, young man?' says the woman. She takes a seat opposite him, her eyes still focused on her notes. 'I'm Sandra.'

He says nothing, so I take the lead. 'You're very good, aren't you, Stan? You have a new passion. You like body parts now, don't you?'

Still nothing.

'Tell Sandra about the new puzzle that the Easter bunny brought you?'

He presses the palms of his hands over his ears then nosedives off his chair under the table. I'm straight up on my feet to lure him out, but Sandra doesn't move a muscle and just jots something down on her clipboard

'Come on, love. Come up here and sit on my knee.' I hold out my hand and, thankfully, he accepts it and crawls out willingly. After taking a seat on the tiny blue chair, I say a little prayer that it won't collapse as my arse spills over its edges, then pull him up onto my lap. 'Tell the lady about all the funny body parts that your new puzzle has.'

He cups one hand around my ear, then whispers, 'Bladder, brain, die-fram, heart, intestinines, kidneys, liver and lungs. That's the order.'

'Stan, don't tell me because I already know. Tell Sandra because I think that she likes body parts too,' I say, and to my surprise, he repeats the same sentence audibly. 'And tell her what else the bunny brought you?'

'A body book with stickers,' he whispers, but I gently pull his hand away from my ear and he repeats it out loud.

'Okay,' Sandra says distractedly – too engrossed in skimming through her notes to pay proper attention. With the clock ticking, she doesn't make time for chit-chat and just dives right in. 'Mum, I have here that his last batch of sessions was four months ago. Is that correct?'

'Yes.'

'And the other therapist has noted that he did "What's in the Bag?"'

'Yes, quite a few times,' I say, staring down at the wretched bag of animals on the table.

And he pulled the same monkey and the same tiger out of the sodding bag five straight weeks in a row. He identified them as 'monkey' and 'tiger' and even told you what species they were, so please, for the love of God, let's move on, woman!

'Well, I think that we should do some flash cards today.'

Amen!

She lays her clipboard down on the table, and before I can sneak a peek at her notes, she lifts a leather briefcase from under the table and dumps it on top. Out comes an A4-sized folder full of tatty picture cards, with illustrations that look like something from a Ladybird book from the fifties.

'Stanley, I am going to show you some pictures,' she says slowly, her pitch rising and falling dramatically, 'and I would like *you* to tell me what you see.'

She puts the first one down on the table. 'What do you see in this picture?'

'A girl,' he mumbles eventually.

She nods, her pen hovering over her clipboard ready to scribble. 'And what is she sitting on?'

'A gluteus maximus.'

'Stan!' I smirk. 'How do you know those big words?'

'From my videos.'

Sandra nods without meeting my eyes, briefly scribbles something down, then pulls out another card. 'Okay. And what do you see in this one?'

This time, he doesn't hesitate. 'A boy.'

A painfully long silence follows, one where I can only hear the squeaking shoes of strangers walking down the corridor outside.

'And what is the boy doing?' Sandra asks.

He pauses and with a look of confusion says, 'Excuse me, but why is your nose so big?'

'Stan!' I snap, horrified. 'I'm so sorry, he really doesn't mean to—'

'What do you see here?' she interrupts.

'Do you breathe in lots more oxygen if your nose is bigger?'

My face is on fire. I'm desperate to crack open a window and make a run for it, but Sandra continues relentlessly, totally unfazed by his observation. Her lack of reaction coupled with her total inability to find any humour in the situation leads me to suspect that she might be a cyborg. 'What is the boy doing, Stanley?'

Before he has a chance to drop another bomb, I quickly step in. 'Stan, answer the question, love. The faster you answer, the faster we can go for ice cream.'

'The boy puts a apple into a mouth, and it is going down a oesophagus to a stomach and acid will melt it.'

'Right,' she says. The scribbling persists and her head bobs metronomically.

This woman is clueless. She's no more than a perpetual nodder and an overpaid form-filler with a laminated name badge pinned to her tunic. I want to wrench the clipboard out of her hands, clock her over the head with it and scream, *Talk to him! Look at him! Engage with him! How do you stand a chance of helping him if you won't do any of these things? He is an individual, a human being, not a fucking lab rat!*

Not to blow my own trumpet, but I'm certain that any progress Stanley has made up until now has been solely down to me. When he was a toddler, I used his passion for colours to teach him how to say simple sentences, make choices and interpret basic instructions. It was hardly rocket science, but I would say things like, 'Stan, would you like a YELLOW banana or a GREEN apple for a SNACK?' Because he was familiar with yellow and green, he eventually learnt the words banana, apple and snack, and over time, his vocabulary and understanding, plus his ability to express his needs, improved significantly.

It wasn't all that long ago that he referred to windows and doors as 'rectangles'. Cups and straws were 'cylinders' and Mini Cheddars and his nipples were 'circles'. He now knows the correct names for most things, but it's still very much a work in progress – work that I expected a qualified therapist to do with him. But clearly not.

One tedious hour of flash cards later, I thank Sandra and ask her opinion as to how Stanley did. With a blank expression, she says that she will send a report to our GP at the end of the block of sessions. Based on last time, I know that when this report arrives, months from now, it will just be a standard string of sentences that she has cut and pasted from a chart stating where Stanley's language skills are in comparison to other kids his age.

'Stanley Wright cannot blah blah blah.'

There will be absolutely no information on how to help him improve, and in all likelihood, I'll remain in a trapped state of abject frustration for the foreseeable future.

Hand in hand, Stan and I escape the building and head down to our favourite place for ice cream: McDonald's. Here we sit, in our usual seats with McFlurrys in hand, playing our newest game: *Would you rather?*

'Stan,' I say animatedly, 'would you rather eat a burger with ketchup or eat a burger *without* ketchup?'

He doesn't answer at first, so I rest my hand on his and then repeat the question. One word eventually escapes from his lips: 'Ketchup.'

'Ooh. Me too. Can you tell me why?' I say. 'It's because ...'

'It's because ketchup is ... RED!' he eventually blurts out. 'And red is my favourite colour.'

'I like red too, but do you know what? I think that yellow is *my* favourite,' I say, 'because yellow is the colour of the sun and I love it when it's sunny outside.'

He sits quietly for some time, picking the bits of cookies out of his ice cream with his fingers then piling them up on a napkin that he has laid on the table.

'Now, it's your turn, Stan. Do you want to ask me a question?'

After a gentle nudge, he comes out with, 'Excuse me, but would you rather have a really big nose or a really big gluteus maximus?'

'Um, I think that I would rather have a big nose,' I say, swallowing my laughter. 'Do you want to know why?'

He nods, his eyes still focused on his McFlurry.

'Because if my gluteus maximus gets any bigger, then it won't fit into my trousers.' The laughter escapes and once it starts, there's no stopping it.

He looks up at my face, studies it intensely and then starts laughing too.

It's a glorious moment. He has answered a question, made a choice and given a reason for his choice, and after slight encouragement, he has expressed an interest in my opinion too. He's even squeezed out a laugh!

Simple, effective and ground-breaking.

I realise that I don't need a degree, a clipboard and a name badge to help him. I'll leave that to the professionals and focus on what I do best: I am his mummy, and this is the only qualification that I need, because I know how his little brain works better than anyone.

15

Bread and Butter

'And how were your Easter holidays, Benjamin?'

It's 10.30 a.m. and I'm in my teaching room in one of the poshest private schools in London. I've worked at this fancy-ass place two days a week for nearly eight years, teaching cello to the sons of millionaires. Technically, I'm still on maternity leave and shouldn't be back here until September, but Nikki – the cellist who has been covering me – texted yesterday to ask if I could come in for just the one day.

Ordinarily, I would have flat out said no. The effort of putting on my cheap suit and dragging my arse across London through rush-hour traffic seemed like too much of an ordeal. But then the anxiety started to creep in. What if my students have fallen hopelessly in love with Nikki? What if they've forgotten all about me and want her to teach them forever? And what if I end up with a 'your services are no longer required from September' email? It may sound dramatic, but the job isn't contracted, so the school could quite easily ditch me at any given moment. I figured that if I planned on hanging on to my job, then it was in my interest to remind them of how irreplaceable I am, and with Ed free to look after the kids, this was the perfect opportunity to do it.

'Did you go away anywhere nice?' I continue.

'We had to stay in London this time, miss,' Benjamin replies politely. 'I had my Bar-Mitzvah on the weekend.'

'Wow! That's pretty amazing. And how did it go?'

The boy doesn't have much to say about the ceremony itself, but he's full of beans when relaying every single detail of the extravagant party which followed – a fancy affair in the ballroom of the Mandarin Oriental in Knightsbridge, where over four hundred of his friends and family gathered. The dinner was eight courses and it was followed by a magic show, then a live band (some girl group who are currently number four in the UK charts) and the finale was an elaborate fireworks display that apparently cost over fifteen grand to execute.

'I got forty-nine thousand pounds in cheques,' he says matter-of-factly. 'Papa is putting it in an account for when I'm eighteen so I can get a flat in Oxford for university.'

When working in a thirty-five grand a year private school, it's pretty normal to be hit in the guts with this kind of information. It's not exactly great for one's morale to learn that your thirteen-year-old student has raked in more cash in one afternoon than you have in two years – especially when you're wearing a suit that you bought on sale in Sainsbury's six years ago. But I'm getting used to it. Sort of.

The school campus is set on a gazillion acres of manicured lawns in the countryside north of London. The boys talk like miniature investment bankers and dress in pinstripe suits, and walking through the playground is like strolling down Wall Street during rush hour. Although most of them are yet to hit puberty, they've already experienced more than I ever will. Rishabh, my first student of the day, told me in a casual manner that he'd 'popped over' to Dubai during the Easter holidays, and while Tommy Belfort sawed his way through a painfully inaccurate rendition of Gershwin's 'Summertime', he mentioned that he'd been on a cruise around the Bahamas. Then, just before morning break, Louis Robertson-Wade announced that he'd spent a few days in his dad's castle in Scotland. That's right, a fucking castle.

'Okay, so let's hear your G major scale, Benjamin. Your Grade Two is three weeks away and Miss Feaver told me that your pieces are good, but your scales need some work,' I say.

'Papa said he'll buy me an Oculus VR headset if I get a distinction, miss.'

'Well, you'd better get practising then,' I say, not having the first clue what an Oculus VR headset is but suspecting that it probably costs more than my monthly salary. 'Let's hear it.'

He lifts his bow and, after three false starts, he drags it over the string and my ears immediately start to weep blood. It sounds like a live cow being pulled through a mincer, and straight away I know that the boy will not be getting his Oculus headset and, worse still, that his papa will probably hold both Nikki and me responsible.

'Okay,' I say chirpily, 'how about we try it again, but this time I want you to stroke the string like you are stroking a little puppy.'

And ten seconds later, the puppy is dead.

The bell for lunch goes at 12.30 p.m. and I make my way through the landscaped grounds to the staff canteen. I can already detect the familiar metallic smell from outside the building, and when I enter, I see that I'm right: mass-produced chilli con carne and undercooked rice is still on the menu. If memory serves, it will cause explosive farting for the rest of my week, but there's nothing else on offer apart from cold artichoke salad, crumbed ham and hard-boiled eggs. So, I take a plate of it and, once sat at the table, I discreetly undo the top button of my trousers, force it down and wait for the bloating to kick in.

I sit sandwiched between Mrs Humphreys, the partially deaf piano teacher who's been working here for over thirty-five years, and the new percussion teacher, Mr Lewis. He is fresh out of music college and still in the I-can't-believe-that-I-work-here phase of total euphoria. He started just before I left to have Jack last year and is still super enthusiastic about his job, but a year from now, after ninety-odd servings of the chilli con carne, I'm confident that both he and his bowels will feel differently about his new career.

They both ask how Jack is and I tell them that everything is great, then show them a few pictures of him and soak up their compliments about how adorable he is. With that out of the way, we move on to the usual chit-chat that music teachers have over lunch – namely, which kid is doing what grade, who has been picked to perform solos at the summer concert and which parents have kicked up a stink at said decisions. Strategies are discussed regarding how to handle these difficult millionaire parents when they come to hunt us down, and Mr Lewis – who is still relatively new to all of this – listens intently and even jots down some tips in a notepad that he pulls out of his blazer pocket.

I'd already made the grave error of checking my school email during this morning's break, and at the top of my inbox (2,342 unopened emails in total) was a classic one from Louis Robertson-Wade's dad.

I demand to know why Louis hasn't been chosen to play in the summer concert and I expect a full explanation by the end of the working day.

His email wasn't just addressed to me and the head of music, but the head of the school and chair of the board of governors too. Part of me was genuinely surprised that the prime minister and the head of Scotland Yard weren't also cc'ed. The death note was signed 'best', which immediately sent shivers up my spine because, from experience, I knew this meant that he was more pissed off than usual.

Last year, this father was always on my case, and the night before my teaching days, I used to lie awake in a panic about what I was going to find when I opened my inbox the following morning. The man is an internationally renowned criminal barrister, so I never stood much of a chance.

In a perfect world, I would have replied to his email with the truth:

Dear Mr Robertson-Wade,

Many thanks for your email. I have been on maternity leave since last September so, to be frank, I have no idea why Louis has not been chosen because I've been burping babies and inhaling doughnuts around the clock.

If I had to make an educated guess, I'd say that Louis has not been chosen because, despite playing the cello for three years, he still rested the neck on the wrong side of his head when I taught him this morning. He is a lovely boy – gentle, kind and adorably sweet – but, in truth, he prefers to spend his lessons talking about Minecraft (or scraping out the contents of his nostrils and smearing them under the chair) rather than ploughing through a snail-paced rendition of 'The Drunken Sailor'.

I can only assume that Ms Nicola Feaver – my esteemed colleague and maternity cover – hasn't chosen him to play in public to spare both his and your dignity. Describing Minecraft houses in minute detail and rolling boogies for half an hour a week does not make for a fine cellist. Perhaps if you encouraged him to practise at home once in a while, he'd have a fighting chance of getting through one line of his piece without having to stop every ten seconds for a nasal cleanse.

You would do well to take some responsibility for your child's musical education and not blame everyone else for your lack of effort.

Kindest regards,
Mrs L. Wright
Bachelor of Music (First Class), LRAM, PG Dip (Distinction) KISS.MY.ARSE

In the end, I wimped out and didn't bother to reply at all. For now, he is Nikki's problem and she'll have to deal with the obnoxious jackass when she comes in next week.

Sitting in gridlocked traffic on my way home at 5 p.m., stuffed to the gills with kidney beans, exhausted and in dire need of some Gaviscon, I realise that I haven't really missed any of this. I've been so desperate to get out of the house and reclaim my old life, but now that I've dipped my toe back in the professional waters, I'm not sure that I ever want to dive back in.

Sure, my students are sweet. They're polite, articulate and often quite fun, but they only learn the cello because their parents want them to have extra-curricular activities to add to their Oxbridge applications. In all the years that

I've been teaching, I've only come across two or three boys who were genuinely talented. Even then, none of them were ever going to pursue music professionally because by the age of eight their dads had already mapped out lucrative careers for them in finance, business or politics. It's quite sad, really – for all concerned. The most fruitless of endeavours.

Right now, I'd quite happily never return to the place again, and if I could afford to quit, I'd do it in a flash, but working here is my bread and butter. Teaching and background gigs are what keep the musicians of London afloat, and until my phone starts ringing off the hook with well-paid performing opportunities, then things will stay as they are.

I still have a few more months until I have to face the 'music' so for now, my eardrums and my bowels can relax, and I can make the most of my time at home with my boys.

16

To Compare Is to Despair

Facebook has been a real thorn in my arse lately. Being wrenched from a deep sleep at 3.32 a.m. to feed Jack after a long day of teaching is hard enough, but what makes it worse is scrolling through my feed and discovering that every friend and colleague I've ever had is having a much more exciting time than I am.

I read Nikki's Facebook status at 3.45 a.m. as I wait for Jack to burp:

> **Nicola Feaver** is at the **O2 Arena.** 5 May at 22.17
> Just met Keanu Reeves backstage at my gig!
> Can't believe it! Nice guy!
>
> #LoveMyJob

There's a photo of her standing on his left, eyes beaming, looking slim and stunning in her sparkly black dress with her cello in hand. It suddenly becomes clear why she was so eager to ditch my teaching for the day. Keanu Reeves or Mr Robertson-Wade? There's *no* contest.

Adding fuel to the fire, I also discover that Charlie had been doing the same gig. Her status that I read at 3.46 a.m. (after I've been blasted over the back of the shoulder with hot vomit) is:

Charlotte Danvers is at the **O2 Arena**. 5 May at 23.49
So Keanu was watching our gig tonight. He's lucky that I'd already had dinner or I would have eaten him there and then.

#UnleashMyInnerCannibal
#Tasty
#WithFavaBeansAndANiceChianti
#FuhFuhFuhFuh

To the right of the photo is Charlie with her violin in one hand and her free arm wrapped around Keanu. One knee is up over his groin and her exposed tongue is just inches from his face, like she's about to lick him. The girl has *no* shame.

Scrolling further down my feed, I see that Nick Harrow has 'checked in' to *Hamilton* just to remind everyone that he has the percussion chair on a major West End show. Annabelle Whitson has a 'hilarious' tale to tell about her gig with the BBC Concert Orchestra, and Simon Monroe has tagged half of the London music scene at Abbey Road Studios where they've been recording the soundtrack for a 'top-secret MAJOR blockbuster.' It's a gig that he 'really shouldn't talk about', but he is talking about it. He's making sure every musician in the UK, if not the world, knows about it.

Aside from my friends and colleagues letting rip about their impressive gigs and encounters with Hollywood heartthrobs, my old school pal Sarah has posted a selfie holding her new baby boy with the caption 'SOOOOOO in love!' Her make-up is flawless, her hair shiny and sculpted to perfection and the backdrop in the photo depicts an immaculately tidy home. Her baby is smiling, of course, with his hand sprawled out on her upstanding rack.

I have two choices: either I can admit defeat and accept that I'm failing miserably as both musician and mum, or I can decide that Sarah is full of shit and her photo has been heavily edited to show just 10 per cent of the full picture. For the sake of my mental state, I choose the latter. Her life can't possibly be as picture perfect as she is making out. I have to believe that behind the scenes her sofas are stacked high with dirty washing, her baby is screaming like a banshee around the clock and her three-year-old is defiantly lobbing cold spaghetti at the walls. I convince myself that her leg hair is so long that Tarzan could swing off it and she, like me, hasn't washed her bra in over a month.

Sarah's post is a blow to the guts, but if there's a prize for being the champion gut-basher, then Marsha would definitely win it without contest.

Her most recent post:

 Marsha Dunn is with **Jane Hudson-Phillips** and 6 others at **Legoland.** 5 May at 18.32
Had a wonderful time with Hugo and his lovely friends at Legoland. We've done the mini Viking ship, the Spinning Spider and the Dragon rollercoaster today and we're going back tomorrow to cover Duplo Land!

#PremiumPasses
#FunFunFun
#ThrillSeekers

When I first met Marsha, she was a barmaid at our local pub, The Lodge. She was a good-time girl, a celebrated party animal, who loved her cocktails and *adored* her men. Popping into The Lodge with Charlie and Jen for a quiet drink on a weeknight was *never* an option if Marsha was working. A quick pint would often descend into absolute debauchery, as she would sneak us free shots of tequila when the manager's back was turned. More often than not, she'd drag us all to The Barracuda Club after finishing her shift, and there we would stay until the sun came up, drinking, dancing and listening to countless tales of her most recent escapades. Then, the moment she bagged herself a local, wealthy property developer, she quit her job, became pregnant and abandoned every facet of her former identity to play the perfect mother to Hugo. And now, she acts like she barely knows us, like our history together has been wiped clean from her memory.

We became pregnant at around the same time, and from the off, she took a very different path to me. Whereas I hid my pregnancy from every music agent in town to keep hold of my TV work, Marsha did the opposite. The woman screamed her news from the rooftops and filled her Facebook feed with pictures of scans and pregnancy updates – the sort of irritating posts that aggravated my already intense nausea.

 I can't believe **Little Bean** is the size of an apple now!

Little Bean has been to the swimming pool today. Judging by how much he kicked, I'd say he's going to be a water baby.

Put Little Bean's name on a waiting list for nursery today. This mumma is getting organised! LOL!

Alongside her active presence on social media, she also joined a pregnancy group and made friends with every knocked-up woman in West London. They spent their mornings in Starfucks and Cost-ugh together, sharing tales of swollen boobs and morning sickness, while I was playing behind contestants on the *X Factor* – puking during the loo breaks down the corridor from Simon Cowell's dressing room.

It's a no from me.

In the second trimester, I took on orchestral tours and lugged the cello and my swollen belly all over Europe. I slept in grotty hotels, ate vending-machine snacks for breakfast and managed to combat the crippling fatigue to stay awake on-stage. When I became too fat to play on TV or to board a plane, I played brides down aisles and serenaded businessmen in the lobbies of the Savoy and Claridge's instead. I took every gig possible at every stage of my pregnancy and kept going to the bitter end. As much as I would have liked to put my feet up, Ed's work was unreliable, we were skint and, with a baby on the way, taking time off was not an option.

A few weeks into motherhood, I didn't even think of heading out to meet other mums. With a colicky baby, I was so exhausted that making small talk with strangers would have pushed me over the edge and into an asylum. Instead, I took Stanley to the pub, where I spent time with Charlie and Jen. As my best friends, they knew how to support me through the chaos that life had become and, thanks to them, I got through it. When Stanley was two months old, I met a lovely local babysitter called Mandy and started accepting work again. I had no choice because in the music industry vanishing off the scene for a year's maternity leave would have amounted to career suicide, and we had bills to pay and a child to support.

Now, nearly five years down the line, I look at the photo of the wildly transformed Marsha and her gang of mummy friends and see that her decisions have really paid off. Hugo is thriving and has a social calendar to rival Kim Kardashian's. Not only does he do karate, dance classes, swimming and football, but he also has a large group of friends by his side through it all.

Stanley, by comparison, still has no friends. There are no party invitations flying through the letterbox, no playdates around other kids' houses and no trips to Legoland in the diary. I can't help but think that if I'd joined the coffee-shop clan from day one, then things might have worked out differently.

I compare and therefore I despair, but come dinner-time, I've managed to get a grip and pull myself out of the well of misery. This guilt isn't doing anyone any good and I need to tackle it head-on. My decision is made. Tomorrow: no Facebook! I'm logging out and *going* out with Jack to a baby class at the town hall for some quality time, just him and me. Then, on the way home, I'm picking up Stan from nursery and hunting down Emmanuel's mum to set up a playdate.

Fuck Keanu Reeves, Simon Monroe, hairy-legged Sarah and Marsha with her 'premium passes'.

No more comparing, no more despairing.

17

Tiny Tots Tambourine Time

A new day begins, and after a brief shut-down, I've rebooted and feel ready to face the world. Ed is out at Angel Studios recording an album all day, so Jack and I are heading down to Tiny Tots Tambourine Time for a mother–baby bonding session as promised. I admit that I'm hardly thrilled at the thought of it, but it's time to take him somewhere other than a place that sells anatomy sticker books or beer. This isn't about Stanley or me, for a change. It's about Jack.

First, I must prep Stanley for his morning session at nursery. By speaking endlessly of Emmanuel, I'm hoping that I can point him in the right direction and steer him towards making his first friend.

'Are you going to play with Emmanuel today, Stan?'

He doesn't reply, so I try again. 'What toys does Emmanuel like to play with? Do you know?'

Stan lifts a piece of banana off his plate and holds it up close to his eyes to inspect it. 'I like to play with the number puzzles and the body books,' he says before putting the correctly shaped banana slice into his mouth.

'I know you do, Stan, but what does *Emmanuel* like?'

He lifts the next bit of banana and continues his thorough inspection. 'Emmanuel likes trucks and cars.'

'Well, that's brilliant! You like cars too. You should ask him to play cars with you today, like you do with Daddy. That sounds fun, doesn't it?'

'Excuse me, but what about numbers?' He tosses the banana on the floor and reaches for another piece. 'I always play numbers when it is a Thursday.'

'Well, Mrs Kinsella told me that Emmanuel *really* wants to play with you, but he's a bit shy,' I say with the animation of a CBeebies presenter. 'If you both like cars, then you could play with them together. We might even ask him if he wants to come here to play with them in your bedroom. Sound good?'

He doesn't respond, but the seed has been planted, and one can only pray that it will grow into something wonderful.

After breakfast, we walk to nursery and, to my surprise, Stanley goes straight in without creating a fuss. It's a promising sign and I leave optimistic that by the end of the day he'll have a friend to call his own.

I wander down to Ealing Town Hall with Jack and arrive bang on time but push the pram through the door to find that it is already packed. A large circle of parents sit on the floor with their babies lying on mats in front of them. A quick scan of the room reveals that virtually every baby is fast asleep apart from one, who is howling at a decibel level so great that the old wooden window frames of the hall shake. The baby's mother, clearly frazzled, alternates between bouncing him up and down and shaking a tambourine in his face, which only makes him cry harder.

I find a space in the circle, lift Jack out of the pram and plonk down between two mums: one who is trying to get her baby to latch on to her swollen tit and another who looks like she is next in line for the lethal injection on Death Row.

'Hi,' I turn to her, 'I'm Lu—'

'Welcome, mummies! Welcome to Tiny Tots Tambourine Time!' This interruption comes in the form of a penetrating squeak and is delivered by a woman who bounces over to me, dressed in what I can only assume is Joseph's amazing technicolour dreamcoat. She thrusts a tambourine into my hand. 'Hello, Mum. I'm Tilly and we're going to have lots of fun here today!'

Tilly has pink braided hair all the way down to her waist and three silver rings through her right nostril. She's a definite quinoa enthusiast, the sort of woman who never shaves her armpits, who probably sprinkles flax seeds over all of her meals and who has a child named Earth or Tree. She bursts into a song about a dizzy elephant and skips to the other side of the circle, rattling her tambourines over her head as she goes. A quick glance up her sleeve and straight away I see that I'm spot on about her armpits.

Jack becomes hysterical. Clearly, she's scared the shit out of him, as she has me, and it's now abundantly clear why the woman next to me looks like she is facing imminent death.

'It's not your first time, is it?' I say.

She sighs, then nods and lifts her tambourine up and starts tapping resignedly.

The next forty-five minutes are a total blur. I know that there is singing – a lot of singing. Tilly, to her credit, has a range to rival Mariah Carey's, and I'm certain she could fill the O2 Arena without the need for a microphone. She moos, meows, then clucks and skips around the room, slapping her tambourine with the enthusiasm of a coked-up cheerleader on a pogo stick.

Some of the mums hunch over their babies, changing nappies as they reluctantly sing along, and the more eager ones join in by joyfully tapping their tambourines and waving them in the faces of their sleeping babies. Other members of the group have abandoned the circle altogether and sidestepped towards the plate of chocolate digestives located by the exit. I do none of the above. I just sit there, rocking a screaming Jack for the entire session, wondering why they don't sell beer or something stronger in this godforsaken hell-hole.

Eventually, the glorious words that I've been waiting to hear since I arrived come from Tilly's dry lips: 'And that's it for today, everyone. I shall see you all next week for more Tiny Tots Tambourine Time!'

No way! Never again!

'So, how was it today?' I say to Stan when he comes out of nursery plastered in paint. I frantically scan the crowd for Emmanuel, and more importantly his mother, but neither is anywhere to be seen.

'I didn't do numbers,' he replies, his tone wooden. 'Mrs Kinsella told me to paint pictures, even if it is a Thursday.'

'Oh. And were you okay about that, Stan?' I say, knowing that he would not have coped well when Mrs Kinsella changed the schedule without warning.

He doesn't answer but the red rings around his eyes indicate that he'd had a negative reaction, the extent of which I will only find out if I hang around and wait to speak with Mrs Kinsella. But there is no time – I have more important things to see to.

'Has Emmanuel gone home already, Stan?'

'I painted a green ghoul-bladder and a purple pancreas and a brain. They did not have grey, so I did it yellow.'

I bend down, put my hands on his shoulders and gently turn his body to face mine. 'Stan,' I say slowly, 'I asked if Emmanuel has gone home already?'

'Emmanuel got out of the door first, and then Anika, and then Michael, and then—'

'Okay, love,' I interrupt to spare myself from hearing a list of thirty-odd names, 'let's just go home.'

With Cheetos in hand, we cross the green and start walking down Windsor Road. I decide to subtly question him to see if the seed that I'd planted earlier had sprouted.

'Stan, did you play with Emmanuel today?'

'He painted a red car and a smiley face and a dog, but it didn't look like a real dog because he did it green.'

'But did you play *with* him?'

'I said to him that I like body parts and numbers and letters, and he said that he likes cars and *SpongeBob SquarePants* and hamsters.'

'That sounds great! Maybe we should watch *SpongeBob SquarePants* when we get home? If he likes it then it *must* be good.'

'Excuse me, but I have to watch my ghoul-bladder video first.'

It's not the Earth-shattering result that I was hoping for, but it's a start. He'd had a rough morning, but he'd still made an effort to converse with Emmanuel, which is definitely a step in the right direction. And if nothing else, there's a chance that we'll be watching something other than gall-bladder videos when we eat our dinner later.

That, surely, is something to celebrate.

18

The Welsh Girl Who 'Did Gud'

With Ed still at the studio I spend the evening alone, but instead of vegging out in front of Netflix, I decide to open a bottle of wine and call my mum. A bit of adult banter is more than needed to erase the hideousness of my tambourine-slapping day.

My tear ducts instantly swell when I hear her soft Irish voice down the other end of the phone.

'Hello, my wee darling. I saw your old maths teacher at work today. Mrs Smith, is it?'

By seeing my old teacher 'at work', my mum means that she'd given my old maths teacher a smear test, and that she'd actually seen far more of the woman than her own husband ever has.

'You mean Mrs *Smithe*, Mum.'

'Och, that's it. Mrs Smithe. She was asking after you.'

Even now, at the ripe old age of thirty-three, I'm still known locally as the Welsh girl who 'did gud', and over the years, I've grown to accept that my mum likes to brag to her patients about my 'exciting life in London' whilst she prods a speculum up their fannies. As the resident practice nurse at the local surgery, she's the only smear-test giver in Tref Y

Glaw – the small Welsh village where I grew up – and she's probably seen more vaginas than Russell Brand.

It's a common misperception that classical musicians are the spawn of the rich and privately educated. A passion for Mozart and Beethoven is typically associated with posh, pretentious or old people, and it's often assumed that I was raised spreading caviar over my toast for breakfast and attending operas from the age of three. But this couldn't be further from the truth. I was an ordinary kid from an ordinary family, and aside from my dad playing the bagpipes in his weekly sessions with the county pipe band, no one in my family has a clue about music.

I was only five or six when my family relocated from Northern Ireland to Wales, after my dad was offered a promotion at work. I don't remember much of Ireland at all and my fondest childhood memories are of Wales, playing Barbies, Cabbage Patch Kids and My Little Ponies with Rachel in her bright pink shoebox bedroom. We had farting competitions in the bathtub, watched *Stars in Their Eyes* and *Gladiators* every Saturday night without fail, and we ate Findus Crispy Pancakes, Chicago Town Pizzas and Pop Tarts by the truckload. We made perfume from flower petals and water, then sold it to our neighbours for two pence a squirt, and we wrote hilarious five-minute-long musicals which we performed in our small back garden – usually to an audience of one leg-humping springer spaniel, Harry.

Bingeing on Walt Disney movies meant that our only dream was to grow up to become princesses. We'd dress up in old bed-sheets and ride around the streets on our bikes, pretending we were clothed in elaborate gowns, galloping on our unicorns to meet our handsome princes at the ball.

A few months shy of my ninth birthday, every girl in the village became sucked into the revolutionary pop phenomenon that was the Spice Girls, and both Rachel and I followed suit. We ditched our imaginary gowns and replaced them with cheap Union Jack leotards and girly pink dresses, then re-enacted scenes from the Spice Girls' videos in our parents' bedroom. Rachel was Baby Spice out of sheer convenience because her wardrobe was already bulging with pink clothes, and I was Ginger, which was only made possible by colouring in chunks of my blonde hair with orange permanent markers. Countless hours were spent singing songs about girl power down our hairbrushes as we admired ourselves in the mirror, and before long, we recruited a few of our friends to play the roles of Posh, Scary and Sporty Spice so we could perform as a complete group at the school talent contest.

A year or so down the line, my life took a sudden and dramatic turn after watching *The Sound of Music* with my gran when on holiday in Ireland. I was so blown away by it that, upon returning to Wales, I called a family meeting and announced that I wanted to become a nun. Rachel declared me a 'weirdo', and like every pre-teen in our village, she went on to develop a gross infatuation with Ricky Martin and covered every inch of her walls with posters of his baby-oil-slathered biceps. I broke away from the pack, choosing instead to learn 'Edelweiss' and spend months relentlessly strumming duff chords on a guitar that my dad bought me from Argos.

Just after I'd started secondary school, a cheesy eighties movie changed the direction of my life forever. It was called *Electric Dreams* and it was the story of a computer that falls in love with a beautiful blonde cellist. The plot was beyond ridiculous but sometimes inspiration comes from the weirdest of places. After watching it, I was immediately hooked on the cello and begged my parents for lessons. Relieved that I no longer wanted to pack my bags, don a habit and move into a convent, they agreed, and I started having lessons at school soon after.

Music instantly took over my life and I became so obsessed that within a month I'd bashed my way through all three beginner books and was thirsty for more. I played every piece of music that I could get my hands on, always wanting to challenge myself, and my cello teacher struggled to keep up with my appetite. It didn't take long for me to discover the works of the great composers and, to the annoyance of Rachel, I ditched my Foo Fighters and Bon Jovi CDs and started blasting Beethoven and Brahms out of my bedroom speakers. Whilst she was rocking out to Aerosmith in her room, I was dancing around to Mozart symphonies in mine; and whenever the chips were down and the boy she fancied had snogged someone else, she'd play 'I Don't Want to Miss a Thing' on loop, while the soundtrack that accompanied my intensive bouts of teenage angst was the slow movement of Grieg's piano concerto. My devotion to classical music was unrelenting, and by age seventeen I was winning national music competitions performing the Elgar Cello Concerto on-stage. And overnight, I was propelled from the status of quirky, spotty teenager to local celebrity.

Tref Y Glaw was full of men called David, and the only way to distinguish one from the other was by their trade. Dai Clips was my dad's barber, Dai Chops was the respected family butcher, and Dai Hops was an old boy who'd had a nasty run-in with an industrial lawn-mower some years earlier. The photographer from the local paper was also a

David (known as Dai Flasher on account of his talents with a camera), and when I started winning prizes, he would often turn up at my school unannounced to take pictures of me.

Over the space of a year, I ended up being in the paper quite a bit, so I got to know Dai Flasher pretty well. He was a young guy in his late twenties who'd dreamt of shooting models for London's top fashion magazines, but his plans all went to shit after getting his girlfriend pregnant at age seventeen. Instead, he wound up taking pictures of ageing councillors and school sports days for the *South Wales Echo*.

The guy was creatively stifled, and I became his muse. He used to whisk me off on obscure photo shoots where his 'vision' involved making me sit with my cello on a traffic cone in the middle of a busy road. Every time a car zoomed past at 60 miles per hour, he would take the shot and I'd wipe the sweat off my forehead, relieved that I hadn't been mowed down just to satisfy his creative urges. The headmaster loved me so much that he filled the walls of the school's reception with blown-up prints of Dai's pictures, and he even invested in a large glass cabinet to show off all my trophies.

After I moved to London at nineteen, to study at one of the world's most prestigious music colleges, my mum continued to keep the locals up to date on my 'fabulous life' during her smear clinics. No one was particularly interested in hearing about my classical music achievements, but once I started getting pop gigs and my face was appearing behind major celebrities on TV, I was receiving congratulatory messages from every Welsh man and his dog (or every Welsh woman and her recently serviced vagina to be more accurate).

And now, all these years later, after everything that I've done to get to where I am today, there is little, if nothing, to report. Aside from one day of teaching millionaires' kids and a miserable trip to Ealing Town Hall with Jack, there's nothing to say. There are no wonderful concerts in the pipeline, there've been no brushes with celebrities, and there's no promise of anything vaguely interesting that would excite Dai Flasher or entertain Mrs Smithe when she comes back for her next smear.

So, in light of the tedium that has become my life, I let my mum do all of the talking. I listen to her blather on about how my dad's constant bagpipe practice is pushing her to the edge, and how the village's handyman – Bungalow Baz – had been over to lay the new laminate flooring in their conservatory.

'That brute has made a right mess of it,' she says, 'and your father is *not* happy. But will he call him to make him come and sort it out?'

'I'm guessing not,' I say, my face aching from smiling so hard.

'Of course not. He'd rather moan about it for the next thirty years than do anything about it. Your father is a pillock!'

Barry Jenkins – fondly called 'Bungalow Baz' on account of him having 'nothing upstairs' – is the master of botch jobs and has been slowly destroying every house in Tref Y Glaw since the mid-eighties. The man will do anything for fifty quid and four cans of Strongbow, so regardless of his shoddy workmanship, he's the busiest tradesman within a ten-mile radius. My dad, like every other man in the village, loves a bargain. He would rather spend his cash on malt whisky or random tat from the middle of Lidl than invest in a real professional, so it's hard to have any sympathy for him.

After finishing the call, I mop up a few tears, then finish my wine and zone out in front of another episode of *SpongeBob*. The kitchen is trashed, the bins need emptying and wet clothes are growing mouldy in the washing machine, but I can't face any of it. With the likelihood of Jack waking up screaming within the next few hours, I force myself to hit the hay. The flat will still be a shithole in the morning.

Once I've collapsed on the pillow and turned off the bedside light, I foolishly succumb to the temptation to log in to Facebook again. Marsha's most recent update is the first thing I see on my feed:

 Marsha Dunn is 'feeling excited' at **Legoland** with 8 others. 6 May at 16.23

Second day in a row with Hugo and his friends at Legoland. So much fun in the sun! Is it wrong if we all go again tomorrow?

#PremiumPasses
#ThrillSeekers

Further down, I spot that Ed has been tagged by one of our musician friends in a recent update:

 Ben Johnson is 'feeling merry' at the **Salmon and Compass**, Islington with **Ed Wright** and 3 others.
6 May at 23.35

Great recording session today working with some real legends! Cheers guys. To the bar we go!

#MusiciansLife

And, just like that, this Welsh girl is *not* doing so 'gud' any more. I've fallen back down the well, neck deep in the dirty waters of despair, and it's clear to me that the only way to pull myself out is to *go* out.

To play.

19

The Blue Shit

Most of my day has been spent emailing CVs out to as many agents as I could think of to try and generate some work. Shitty background gigs and a bit of teaching isn't enough for me: I want the *real* work, real playing to real audiences just like the good old days. I want to perform the symphonies of Mahler, Brahms and Shostakovich with major orchestras again ... my soul craves it. I want to experience the enormous prestige of recording soundtracks for blockbuster movies and to soak up the excitement of performing behind pop stars in huge arenas filled with thousands of screaming fans.

After having Stanley, I managed to claw my way back into a few orchestras, so I know that with effort it is possible. The striking difference this time is now I have *two* children, so my brain has taken *twice* the beating, and most days I feel like someone has yanked it out of my skull, chucked it in a blender and hit Blitz. Since having Jack, I don't know what day it is, how old I am or when I last washed my genitals, and that's just for starters.

Last week, I walked around the whole of Westfield shopping centre with a soiled nappy dangling off my cardigan sleeve and didn't notice until an old lady pulled it off. I then couldn't remember where I'd parked the car, and after wandering around for twenty minutes, I broke down in tears on the parking attendant and was sent to the security office for assistance. The following day, I torched three batches of fish fingers in a row and put my phone in the fridge. And the day after that, I spent twenty seconds leaving a voicemail for my sister Rachel, only to discover that I was talking into the remote control. These kinds of things have been happening more often lately, so trying to construct a grammatically correct sentence in a professional email was no easy feat.

Dear Malcolm,

Its Lucy Wright hear. I just thought that I would get in touch to let you know that I have come to the end of a busy patch and I am avalable for any last-minute work should you need me at the BBC Philharmonic Orchestra.

I hope all is well you're end,
yours sincerlay,
Lucinda Wright
Bmus PG Dip LRAM
Cello

Staring at the laptop screen for so long this morning, whilst holding a sobbing Jack, made my head explode. Was it 'your' or 'you're'? And why did the word 'here' look so weird on the page? Surely 'hear' made more sense? Why did all the words look so weird? Or was it 'wierd'? I have an A grade in A-level English, for feck's sake, but I guess that's been blitzed in the blender along with my ability to grill a fish finger.

Ed finishes his last day of recording sessions early, and instead of going for his usual pint (or three) with the producer, he comes home of his own accord and insists that I go out with my pals.

'You need a break,' he says. 'Go out and enjoy yourself.'

I'm caught totally off-guard by his suggestion. I'm not prepared! I need to shower, to shave, to scour the wardrobe to find something to wear, and all of this before even getting started on what needs to be done for the kids. 'But I haven't done bath-time yet! Stan needs his hair washed,' I say, mildly panicked. 'That's not an easy job.'

'I'll do it. Just go.'

'And remember, Jack takes eight ounce bottles now. He has been for ages. So don't just give him six like you always do.'

'Okay. Go!'

'And Stan didn't eat his dinner, so he might need a snack before bed. Maybe a bit of toast? But *don't* forget that you have to give it to him on the red plate – with your left hand, not your right – or he'll kick up a stink.'

'I know. Go!'

I'm straight on the phone to Charlie and Jen, who are delighted to hear of my sudden freedom. Miraculously, they are both around to hit the pub. I quickly throw on a long black cardigan and my maternity leggings from Asda, then slather my blotchy complexion in thick foundation.

'How do I look?' I say to Ed as I twirl around to show off my outfit.

'Yes,' he replies, having not looked up from the TV.

'Do I look really spotty? I feel *really* spotty, do I look it?' I wait impatiently for an answer, but nothing comes, so I lift a cushion off the sofa and lob it at him to get his attention. 'Ed! Hello?'

'Wait! Give me a sec,' he says grumpily. He pauses the TV and struts over to examine my face up close as if he is a microbiologist. 'There's just that big one there,' he says, pointing at a mole that has been on my chin since birth.

'Never mind.' I roll my eyes. 'I won't be late.' I plant a sloppy kiss on his bald head then stuff a few bits of make-up into my handbag. 'Do you know what, Ed?' I say as I'm zipping up my boots. 'Every once in a while, it would be nice if you told me that I'm beautiful.'

His face is a ball of confusion. 'But you *are* beautiful. You know this.'

'Actually, no. I don't. I need to be told, just every now and then, to give me a boost.'

He sinks back down into the recliner and lifts the remote. 'You're beautiful,' he says.

'So are you.' I wink seductively and blow him a kiss, but he doesn't notice as he's already pressed Play and the TV has sucked him back in.

I'm out of the door and in The Lodge by 7.05 p.m.; bullets have left guns slower. The Lodge is the hang-out pub for all the musicians who live in Ealing. You could walk into this place any time of day or night and find a bunch of musos knocking back beers whilst chatting about gigs: who is doing what (or who), who's been scrubbed off which fixer's list and why, who has got shitfaced and fallen asleep in *The Book of Mormon* theatre pit and who is about to go on tour with Rod Stewart.

Drummers, guitarists, singers and string players *all* hang out here most nights (as did I, before having kids) and there is often a lock-in. Harvey, the manager, and his boyfriend, Pete, *love* us, and a simple pint usually ends in trays of sambuca shots being passed around until the early hours of the morning. God, how I've missed it!

Charlie is already leaning on the bar holding a large glass of wine when I arrive. Clothed in skinny jeans and a tight black top, she is effortlessly beautiful and completely unaware of it. Her long dark hair is thrown up in a messy ball on top of her head, an indication that she'd left the house in a hurry, and her thick black retro glasses suggest that she'd been practising her violin when she got my call.

'So, Ed actually took my advice, I see?' she says casually.

'Uh, what advice?'

'I texted him and said in the clearest way possible that you needed a break. I think I might have said a "fucking break".'

'You did? God, I love you, man.'

'I know, I'm a genius, but how else was he going to get the hint? So, now you're here, time is *not* to be wasted if we are to *get* wasted. What's your poison?'

'A pint, please, love.'

'A pint and a couple of sambucas it is, then.' She smiles wickedly and inhales the whole glass of wine that is sitting on the bar, then calls out to Harvey to come over and serve us.

Jen arrives within minutes, clutching her new leopard-print Zara handbag, followed by Will, who straight away orders two pints – one for each hand.

'He's celebrating,' Jen tells us. 'He's literally just got the call to play on *Wicked*!'

'Wowsers!' says Charlie. 'Harvey, hun, can you double up on those shots? Will here has bagged himself a West End show, clever bastard that he is.'

'Sure thing, Charls,' yells Harvey from the other end of the bar. 'May as well just give you the bottle, eh?'

'Hell yes, Harv. Genius idea!'

With beers, shots galore and large glasses of wine crammed on to a tiny tray, we park in our usual seat in the corner, ready to indulge in a long-overdue catch-up.

Charlie gets straight to the point. 'So, great news about the show and all, Will, but we've more important things to discuss first.' She knocks down a shot and turns her whole body to face mine. 'So, Luce, had sex yet?'

Will shifts uncomfortably in his seat and starts fiddling with his phone.

'You're kidding, aren't you?' I say. 'Ed's been working like a dog, and if he's ever home, he's out cold and snoring by 8 p.m.'

Charlie tuts, clearly disappointed that I don't have any raunchy stories up my sleeve to share with the group. 'Didn't I warn you not to marry an older man?' she says. 'Ed has, what, ten years on you, right? So, while you're approaching your sexual prime, he's close to drying up.'

'Nine years. And thanks a bunch, pal. Thanks for bumming me right out.'

'Mark my words, Luce, you'd better hop on him now before he needs a suitcase full of Viagra to get going! That shit costs mega bucks.'

Will smirks, his eyes still focused on his phone.

'All I want inside me of an evening is a hot meal and a bottle of wine, Charls. Sex isn't exactly ranking high on my list of priorities,' I say defensively. What I don't say is that, even though I don't particularly want to have sex, I still want Ed to initiate it. I just want him to make a move, any kind of move, to show that he still finds me desirable because, deep down, I'm terrified that he doesn't any more.

'All I'm saying is use it or lose it.' She nods firmly.

My mind starts to wander down a depressing, sex-less road, and just before I slip into a state of full-blown internal misery, Jen steps in and steers the conversation towards someone who definitely is getting some action, and probably an abundance of it too: Charlie.

'So, what about Dr Tom? Are you ready to bring him out for a good old-fashioned scrutinising yet? We need to give him the thumbs up before you waste any more time on him.'

Charlie slides back in her seat and drops her eyes down towards the table. She lifts her drink up to her lips to hide the smile that is creeping onto her face. 'Not yet,' she says sheepishly, 'but I'm meeting his parents this weekend.'

'No way!' squeaks Jen. 'Exciting!'

'Calm yourself, Jen. No shopping for bridesmaids' dresses yet, for fuck's sake!'

'What? I wasn't thinking that at all!' she says, even though she most definitely was.

'If these parents are good people and not a bunch of psychos, then I may decide to keep him a bit longer. And then, I may just bring him out to meet you guys soon. But you've got to be nice, you bitches!'

Meeting parents is a first for Charlie. In all the years we've known her, she has only ever had one boyfriend who's lasted more than three weeks: a guy called Matt who was the sound engineer from a big tour she did. They had a wildly passionate shag-athon as they toured America for a month, but when the tour finished, he went back to California and she never saw him again (aside from the occasional dick pic that he sent her on Snapchat). This doctor must be special to hold her interest for so long.

The rhythm-section lads all pile in at around 9.30 p.m.: Fit Ben the drummer, Rob the sax player, Niall the keys player, and his girlfriend Cat (a well-respected session singer who is always clothed in leather regardless of the weather). Will is immediately relieved to have some men to chat with and is excused from the table and from participating in any more girl talk. Within the hour, almost fifteen musos have stopped by on their way home from gigs and pints are flowing from all angles like Niagara Falls. It's the first time that I've felt like myself in ages.

At around 11 p.m., I try to slip off to call Ed to check on the kids, but Charlie grabs my arm and yanks me back down into my seat.

'Leave it, Luce! The kids are fine. Ed has it under control, for fuck's sake. This is your night off!'

I playfully slap her hand away and get up again. I *have* to check. 'I just need the loo. Jeez!'

From the privacy of a toilet cubicle, I call Ed and, after several attempts, he eventually answers. The first thing I hear when he picks up is shouting.

'Stop that! *Stop!*'

'What's going on? Ed, what's happening?'

'Stan is doing my nut!'

'Why is he even awake? It's nearly midnight!'

'He wouldn't get in the bath. And he didn't eat the toast because the red plate was in the dishwasher. And Jack only took four ounces even though you said to give him six—'

'I said eight!'

'And Stan threw the iPad and cracked it and now he is – *Stan!* Stop that! Stop! I've got to go.'

The line goes dead, and I'm left in a state. I have to leave – Ed isn't coping. I pull up my jeans and dash out to the bar to explain the situation to the girls, but Charlie isn't having it.

'I don't care if the kids are kicking off. I don't even care if the place is on fire. Ed *has* to handle it, Luce. He's their dad, isn't he?'

'But he's losing his shit.'

'So what! You deal with it all of the time, so let *him* do it for once,' she says dramatically. 'You might never get this chance again!'

Charlie is acting like the apocalypse is imminent and she's right. I never go out and this might well be the end of days – for my social life at least. Ed has to learn how to handle Stanley's explosions – how to control his own, even – and tonight is as good a time as any for him to get started. So, at 11.55 p.m., I resist every natural urge to run home to my traumatised husband and, instead, I wash away my guilt by sharing another tray of sambuca shots with my friends. The shots are soon followed by a blue concoction, a new invention of Harvey's that he has aptly named the Blue Shit. It's blue and it tastes like shit, but it is Harvey's baby and it would be rude not to try it. So we drink two jugs of it to show our support.

Come 3 a.m., Jen has fallen asleep on the table using her new bag as a pillow, and Will is bashing out his party piece on the clapped-out piano in the corner: 'All You Need Is Love'. If Will is ever hammered and within a few yards of a piano, we are always treated to a blast of his best Beatles. Every *single* time.

'All ya need is love!' he yells, slamming his hands down on the piano.

'Da, dah, dada, dahhhhh!' we sing whilst merrily swigging back the Blue Shit that Harvey keeps pouring into our pint glasses.

Leathered-up Cat shows off her professional skills by singing some complex harmonies, and after minimal encouragement, Rob whips out his saxophone and explodes into an incredible ten-minute-long improvisation.

The night ends with a blue puddle of puke and a half-eaten kebab being dropped in the drain outside the flat.

Best night ever.

I am BACK!

20

The Hangover

There was puke everywhere.

Blue puke. In my hair, on my clothes, in the hallway, in the kitchen and, worst of all, on Ed's precious cream rug.

He has cleared it up, but he hasn't said a word. From what I can gather, he's done everything: the feeds, the nappies, the nursery run, the shopping – all of it. And Jack, as I've heard from a horizontal position on the bathroom floor, has screamed through *all* of it. Maybe he's testing Ed, seeing if he can break him? Or maybe he's punishing me for abandoning him to lie on the floor, screaming until my skull cracks open to teach me a lesson for my shameful ways.

Stanley came into the bathroom and said one measly sentence to me before he left for nursery this morning. 'Excuse me, but you're in the way! My numbers! Get off my numbers!' he screeched. He dived onto the floor where his perfectly placed row of foam numbers were scattered in total disarray after I'd collapsed on top of them in a drunken stupor in the early hours of the morning. He realigned them, placing them exactly one centimetre apart, and left the bathroom in total silence. And then I was alone, lying next to twenty numbers that were more deserving of my son's love and attention than I was, his own mother.

Oh God! I am a terrible mum! A selfish, horrible, disgraceful mum whose priorities are all wrong. Blue Shit? What kind of mother drinks Blue Shit? What will the kids say when they're older? 'My mum is a heavy Blue Shit drinker. She wrecked the cream rug, so my dad left her for a tap-water-drinking woman who doesn't have blue puke in her hair. She's a better mum than my real one. She bakes cupcakes and reads me stories every night about fairies and magical lands whilst my real mum lies on the floor in a puddle of her own multicoloured vomit.'

By the time Stanley returns from nursery, I've crawled out of the bathroom and climbed into bed to sleep off the remainder of the brain pain. I wake an hour or so later to the sound of hysterical, highly infectious belly-laughing.

'Okay. Are you ready, Stan? Five, four, three, two, one … Thunderbirds are … GO!' Ed yells playfully through the wall.

Another belly-laugh comes followed by a loud bang.

'Again, again, again, again!' Stan squeals in excitement.

The same happens over and over, and each time, Stan's laughter becomes more excitable and more infectious, to the point that I too find myself belly-laughing as tears soak into the pillow and my cheeks start to throb.

'I need a rest, little man. Daddy's arms are tired. Shall we play numbers instead?'

'Yes. Yes. Yes. YES!'

'Shall we ask Jack if he wants to play too?'

He screeches 'yes' again, exactly four times, and I chuckle out loud, imagining how long it will take him to answer a simple question when he is twenty-four years old – or forty-eight, even.

'Sssshhh! Stan. Indoor voice,' I hear Ed say. 'Let's go into the living room with your numbers because Mummy is sleeping next door.' And off they go, and I stay put, my heart on the verge of exploding with love for all three of them.

Come dinner-time, I'm finally vertical. Sitting on the sofa, I sip a cup of lukewarm water and nibble dried crackers as I stare at the faint stain of my blue puddle of vomit which lies in the centre of the cream rug. Stanley is lying on the floor next to his mini body parts and foam numbers, which are placed perfectly around the circular stain, as if they are enjoying a nice picnic together by the edge of a huge lake.

Ed slips in through the door with both hands behind his back, a mischievous look on his face. 'I was going to wait until you felt better before I told you, but guess what?'

'What?'

'I've just got off the phone and it's *on*!'

'What's on?'

'I'm going on tour to … wait for it … the US of A!' And he pulls a bottle of Prosecco out from behind his back. 'We're having this!'

Before I have a chance to react, he has already launched into a monologue of triumph, so I sit and wait for him to get it all out, poised ready to resuscitate him if he ends up hyperventilating.

'Yeah, yeah – so the American singer that I've been recording with all week is releasing the album next month and he's going straight on tour to promote it—' He gasps for air. 'He's already a big deal in the States so he's starting there and if that goes well, shit, who knows?' He fiddles impatiently with the wire on the top of the bottle and continues. 'It might go on to a European tour, maybe Asia … maybe,' he twists the cork, 'maybe another album that I might get to play on—' Then it shoots off the bottle, smacks the ceiling and the bubbles spray all over the floor. 'Fuck's sake! Cloth, cloth!'

'My heart!' yells Stanley. 'It is wet! Wet!'

Ed dumps the bottle on the coffee table and dashes to the kitchen. He returns, totally flustered, with a thick wad of cloths, a couple of kitchen rolls and a bath towel in his arms, then proceeds to lie them all down carefully side by side across the floor as he curses angrily. 'Shit! The rug's ruined! Fuck's sake!'

'My kidneys! My lungs! My number four … my number nine! Wet! Wet! Wet! WET!'

'Okay. Everyone calm down. And watch your language, Ed,' I say with a forced softness. 'It's just a bit of liquid, hardly hot lava.'

'My bladder!' shrieks one and, 'It's going to stink the rug out!' yells the other.

'Right, the pair of you – back up! Let *me* do it,' I say, desperate to defuse the chaos, preserve what's left of my eardrums and spare my favourite towel from getting saturated in cheap fizz. I usher them both out of the way and get on with mopping up the spillage while Ed pours what's left of the Prosecco into a couple of glasses and resumes his monologue.

'So, I go July third and it's just over three weeks around the States. Boston first, then New York, Washington …'

My heart stops dead in my chest. 'Three?'

'Atlanta, Miami, New Orleans, Dallas, Austin.'

'Did you say three weeks?'

'Then Phoenix, San Diego, LA, San Fran, Portland and we finish up in Seattle.'

'Ed! Stop listing cities. I asked, is it *three* weeks?'

'Yep … it'll be a huge chunk of cash.' He beams.

'That's so good, love,' I say out loud, battling to reverse the corners of my mouth, which are curling downwards. 'I'm so chuffed for you and so proud. Come here.'

And then I hug him, just long enough for the initial shock of the news to subside.

It's tough to digest – not being asked but being *told* that my husband is clearing off to the US and leaving me here with our kids. Three hours alone with them is challenging enough, but three weeks?

Most wives would probably flip out at such decisions being made without their consent, but in the music industry, this is just how it is. Ed and I, like every other musician we know, are at the mercy of 'the gig'. If the gig says 'jump', you jump. And if it says 'abandon your wife and kids for three weeks', then you do just that without hesitating. If you don't, your mortgage won't get paid.

I hate it, but I get it.

Playing with an American pop star in 'the land of opportunity' will give Ed's career a huge boost, and he's right, there's potential for it to lead to all kinds of other exciting things. In times like these, it's pointless wallowing in self-pity and I must force myself to look on the bright side. Maybe Ed will rocket to stardom and we'll end up moving to Hollywood? Perhaps we'll ditch our tiny flat and buy a Beverly Hills mansion with a pool? It's a long shot, but he might even make a million bucks and be invited to appear on *Oprah*. And, who knows, but a year from now, Stan could be introducing himself to his classmates in his swanky new school in LA – 'Excuse me,' he might say proudly, 'but my daddy is a rock star!'

And maybe, just maybe, he'll be the kid that *everyone* wants to be friends with for a change.

A couple of glasses of bubbles down the hatch later and my inner calm is temporarily restored. Ed suggests that we go out to celebrate his news, so with the kids and Stan's newly washed organs and numbers in tow, we head down to The Lodge for dinner. 'Order whatever you want,' he says, 'don't even look at the prices,' and so we do. Stan chooses chips and ketchup because 'ketchup is red, and red is my favourite colour' and Ed insists on splashing out on fillet steak with sides of onion rings and garlic bread: the ultimate feast for a rock star and his bum-wiping wife.

'I'm just going to pop to the loo quickly before the food comes,' I say, and once in the cubicle, I pull down the toilet seat, park up and call my mum just to hear a comforting voice.

'How are you, my wee pet? How are my boys?'

'They're great. I'm great. We're all great,' I lie.

'Well, I'll tell you what, the whole village is in an uproar here,' she says. 'Ozzy Jones is on the keto diet and he's bought up every pack of pork scratchings in a five-mile radius. The village is gearing up for a witch hunt!'

I'm in fits of laughter within seconds.

Ozzy Jones – owner of a tiny shop called 'The Sandwich Co.' – is one of Tref Y Glaw's most-celebrated residents. Not only is he the creator of the world's most unique and delicious sandwiches, but he and his wife, Claire, invented the Slutty Brownie: chocolate brownies so outrageously naughty that people from as far as Australia order them by the dozen. Radio DJs, TV personalities and half the Welsh rugby team have been photographed with one of them in hand, so Ozzy sure has put the village on the map. But now that he's been hoarding the pork scratchings, the villagers are turning on him and it's possible that his empire stands to collapse.

'Well, is his diet working at least?' I say.

'Four stone down so far!' she replies. 'And he's been going to the gym an' all. I popped in to get an Arnie Sarnie for your father yesterday and Ozzy made me feel his bum. And I tell you what, it was solid!'

'Arnie Sarnie? Ooh, is that a new one?'

The invention of a new sandwich is much bigger news than hearing that my mum has groped Ozzy's bum. Most of the village has copped a feel of his rear at one point or another, and the vast majority have seen it in the flesh after he donned a mankini and ran through the crowd at the Christmas fair last year. So, Ozzy's arse is pretty much old news.

'The Arnie is this week's special,' she continues. 'It's got chicken, a wee bit of chorizo, bacon, cheese and a few of those jolly ponies.'

'Um, and what exactly are "jolly ponies", Mum?' I tease.

'Y'know, those wee green chillies that you get on the nachos in the cinema.'

I roar with laughter down the phone.

'Stop it, you wee rascal! Don't you be laughing at me!'

'Jalapeños, Mum. They're called *jalapeños.*'

'That's what I said – jolly ponies,' she says in her thick Belfast accent. 'Enough, young lady! Anyway, you're okay? The boys are okay?'

I briefly toy with the idea of telling her about Ed's tour, but decide against it for now. She'll blow it up into a huge drama – her 'poor wee daughter' being left alone with 'two wee children' is just the sort of news that will have her calling me every ten minutes for the rest of my life. From experience, I've learnt that it's better to be selective about what I tell her because her nerves can't handle the truth.

I head back to the table, and just as our food arrives, Fit Ben and Niall stroll in through the door and Ed waves them over to join us. It seems that they've also got the call to do the same tour, so naturally Ed had invited them out to gatecrash our family dinner without consulting me first.

With pints in hand, the three of them discuss their impending trip of a lifetime, the conversation revolving exclusively around the cities that they'll be visiting and the 'insane bars and clubs' in Seattle and LA that Ben plans to take them to.

'The hotels are gonna be good too,' he says coolly, 'at least four star, but probably five, I reckon.'

I sit there and soak it all in as I try to persuade Stanley to eat a chip that isn't shaped exactly like the ones you get in McDonald's, which, eventually, he does.

Success! Not quite international, and not likely to be of interest to Oprah, but it's all I have.

21

'My Mummy Is a Pop Star!'

*F*ive days later

By 9.49 a.m. this morning, I'd:

- Lifted screaming baby from cot, fed him, changed him and binned his tie-dyed brown babygro
- Gagged a little
- Sliced banana into identical semicircles and passed it to Stanley with left hand, *not* right
- Picked banana bits off cream rug after they'd been lobbed there from other side of room – rejected for being 'wrong shape' (Note to self: next time, use ruler)
- Removed yesterday's coffee from microwave and inserted current one
- Distracted Stan with favourite video about gall-bladder and shovelled Weetabix into him
- Pondered how long it would be until he learnt how to use a spoon by himself (Weeks? Months? Decades?)
- Filled out Ed's application for American visa and left it on counter ready for him to sign

- Changed Jack's clothes for second time and made mental note to shop around for more effective bib
- Peeled and chopped organic carrots, parsnips, sweet potatoes and a large onion and diced two chicken breasts to make stew
- Blitzed stew into mush and froze in fifteen tiny tubs
- Said a little prayer to good Lord above that stew was going to be 'the one'
- Removed tubs of organic cauliflower gloop and broccoli mush that have been clogging up freezer for over two months
- Answered door to neighbour Alan who had parcel for me. Suffered long-winded update about his recovery from recent knee surgery, all the while with chest unsupported
- Put on bra
- Removed smear of baby shit off shoulder and hoped Alan hadn't seen it
- Gagged a lot
- Bleached toilet
- Binned four empty toilet-roll cylinders that were on bathroom floor and clipped new toilet roll into holder on wall
- Plucked two stubborn black hairs from chin and one from left nipple (another joyful side effect of pregnancy)
- Sighed and worried about prospect of having fully grown beard and hairy chest someday
- Googled 'Can you die from lack of sleep?'
- Realising death not imminent, heated same cup of coffee in microwave and powered on

- Sterilised six bottles and unloaded dishwasher
- Lifted Ed's pants off hallway floor, plus jeans, socks and two T-shirts and placed them *inside* laundry basket
- Sighed before nuking coffee for third time

All in all, a typical morning's work for the average mother. And what had Ed achieved by 9.49 a.m.? Well, he'd:

- Woken up
- Walked into kitchen
- Scratched his arse
- Guffed
- Flicked kettle to On position
- Then said, 'God, I'm knackered'

I won't lie, the temptation to throw my icy-cold coffee in his face was strong. But I didn't, simply because he'd been working late last night. I reasoned, as I have to most days, that he is making his contribution to the household as the financial provider, even though last night's 'work' involved playing one song behind some reality-TV-star-turned-pop-star on the *Graham Norton Show*. These three minutes of hard-core labour were followed by an after-show party where he probably downed gallons of free beer, ate delicious canapés and took a complimentary taxi home at 2 a.m.

I look down at my hands, my amazing, high-achieving hands that have played symphonies in the Albert Hall, that have backed international artists on-stage in New York, that have appeared on dozens of TV shows watched by millions.

What's happened to them?

Now, my sad mitts are dry and cracked from washing bottles and mopping floors. They're tired and disgusted from changing nappies and scraping other people's skid marks off the toilet bowl day after day. Their spirits are low from liquidising organic vegetables that have been spat out in disgust. Beethoven symphonies and hobnobbing with the rich and famous are a distant memory for these poor babies.

I'm not going to pick a fight with Ed about any of this shit today, for a change. Even when he looks up from the comfort of his recliner and says, 'Have you seen any of my black shirts? I need a clean one for my show later,' I manage to resist the urge to rip his eyelashes out because, today, I'm in an unusually good mood. Lingering in the air is the smell of hope, the sweet stench of opportunity and excitement.

My mitts and I have been asked to appear in a music video!

Charlie called yesterday to say that one of her record-company contacts wanted her to put together some string players to feature in a video for a new indie artist – Patrick something. He's signed to a major label and the video is for his first single, which will be shot in a manor house in Gloucester.

'The fee is £250, they'll put us up in the mansion and Jen is already on board. So, you're in?' she said.

I was more than tempted by her offer, but it was just too short notice. 'There's no way, Charls. I can't leave the kids overnight. Jack still isn't sleeping through and Ed won't cope.'

'He'll be fine, Luce. You cope every day, don't you? If the shoe was on the other foot, he'd accept the gig in a fucking heartbeat, and you know it!'

'But, I—'

'No. I'm *not* having it! We *are* going to Gloucester. We're going to hang out with a pop star, drink whatever we can get our hands on, sleep in a luxury manor house and laugh our tits off. Oh, and we're going to have a lie-in.'

The words 'lie-in' glided down my ear canal like a gentle harp glissando strummed by the fingertips of a heavenly angel. And, in that brief moment, I was lost. My weary body floated up to the sun-filled skies and embedded itself in the warmth of the fluffy clouds. Then I heard a voice, a sweet, quiet voice. It was Stanley, and he was chanting beautiful words to a room filled with his adoring classmates and teacher, the words, 'My mummy is a pop star.'

'Charls, I'm IN!'

In the cold light of day, I don't feel even remotely guilty about my decision. Ed accepted a long international tour without even checking with me first, so I figure that I'm next in line to squeeze the milk out of life's coconuts. I'm done with tap water. This is a proper gig, not a demoralising background function for rich, pervy businessmen who hoover up free champagne and unashamedly slap their hands across the arses of waitresses. It's a gig that has the potential to lead to much greener pastures, not just for me, but for the whole family.

One sleepless night won't kill Ed. Hell, I've survived hundreds and I'm still breathing. I've reasoned that if everything falls apart and I come home to find him in a semi-comatose state, suffocating under a pile of empty crisp packets, foam numbers and rubber organs, then at least he would've experienced what it's like to live in my shoes for a change. And that can only be a good thing.

Of course, when Judith heard I was abandoning my family for my own personal gain, she cancelled her plans and is arriving later today to rescue them from their demise.

The rest of my day will therefore be spent cleaning in preparation for her visit.

Things to Do Before Judith Arrives
HIDE vibrators from bedside drawers.
BIN pile of odd socks: must escape criticism about
    profound inability to keep track of location of
    every sock in household.
BIN all Tupperware which doesn't have matching
    lids; so, basically, bin ALL Tupperware.
PUT all of Ed's Pot Noodles and my multipack of
    crisps in black bag and HIDE in boot of car.
REMOVE wine bottles from recycling bin so she
    won't perform usual rant about recommended
    daily alcohol units as stipulated by NHS.
POLISH light switches, skirting boards and remove
    disgusting balls of hair from all plugholes.
LOB dirty washing in bin bag and put in bottom of
    my wardrobe to leave a pristine empty basket,
    thus projecting image of being admirable
    domestic goddess.
BIN several bags of soggy uneaten salad, plus
    four jars of opened pesto that have black shit
    growing on top of them.
DYE hair and shave legs (cannot risk her shoving
    hand up trouser leg, stroking calf and passing
    comment on upkeep of femininity).

All possible ammunition to be used against me needs to be removed/hidden/lobbed/shaved off. The woman won't have a cleanly shaven leg to stand on.

22

The Puddle

Judith has been much better behaved than I expected. She arrived yesterday afternoon to hold the fort while I packed for my trip to Gloucester and, surprisingly, not one toxic remark has been made about my weight, which is a first. At one point, she even mentioned that she liked my new hair colour. (What she actually said was 'Oh, that's a Nice'n Easy dye is it? Well, it does look nice and definitely *easy*', which she followed with a short, squeaky giggle.)

Although the woman has an extraordinary talent for turning an observation into a criticism, she'd at the very least made an effort to say something vaguely pleasant. Of course, it has always been impossible for her to keep up the pretence that she likes me for a sustained period of time. I knew that sooner or later she would break, and her true colours would start leaking out all over the place.

At 8.25 a.m. this morning, she starts to curdle, right on cue.

It begins when I strip Jack naked and lie him down on his playmat for some free-willy time before breakfast. I've always done this to allow his bits and bobs to get a little fresh air after being barricaded behind a thick nappy all night long. Jack – like every man I've ever met – has a *total* fascination with his bobs. Both he and Stanley fiddle with them any chance they get, and sometimes they tug on them so hard that I'm convinced one day they'll pull them clean off and ruin my chances of ever becoming a grandmother.

This morning, during an ordinary free-willy time, Jack achieves a major milestone: he can now travel! In the thirty seconds that I'm in the kitchen getting his breakfast, he has spontaneously sprouted the muscles required to drag himself all the way across the room from the playmat where I've left him tugging on his bobs. And how do I find out he is capable of such an almighty task? When I open the door, skid two metres across the floor and crash in to Ed's recliner.

After the shock subsides, I steady myself and turn around to see the cause of my sudden flight across the room: a large yellow puddle positioned directly behind the door. It may seem strange to some, but I'm not repulsed: I'm excited. It's a great sign, a sign of progress – our baby can move! I lift him in the air and swing him around in excitement, delighted at his amazing achievement.

Judith struts into the room with a bowl of strawberries in hand and, before I can warn her, she slips in the puddle and is knocked flat on her arse.

'Judith!' I screech. 'God! Are you okay?'

The woman is winded, silent, for the longest I've ever known her to be. She lies there in shock, surrounded by piss-sodden strawberries, taking an age to process the disgusting situation in which she finds herself.

Finally, she lets rip. 'No!' She gasps. 'Oh no, oh no!'

I plonk Jack back in his highchair and hurry over to help her up, but she slaps my hand away. 'I'm okay. I'm okay, Lucy. Give me a minute. Please!'

She rolls over on to all fours, grabs hold of the door handle and awkwardly pulls herself up on her feet. Glancing down her back, I see that her beige trousers are soaked – positively drenched, even.

'Was that Jack's doing?' She tuts.

'I think so,' I reply sheepishly, doing my best to keep a straight face.

'Well, for God's sake put a nappy on him, Lucy! I could have broken my back!'

The guilt kicks in thick and fast. 'I'm so sorry, Judith. Have you hurt yourself? He *never* normally does this, it's the first ti—'

'I never had *anything* like this to deal with when Edward was a baby,' she interrupts sharply. 'I had him fully potty trained by six months old.'

Really, Judith? Potty trained at six months? Well, your son has certainly regressed over the years, given that I have to mop his piss off the bathroom floor on a daily basis. And, let me guess, was he quoting Shakespeare by seven months? Enrolled in the Olympic running team by eight months?

'Do you want to borrow some clothes while I put those in the wash for you, Judith?'

'No. Your clothes will be far too big for me. I'll just have to wear my dressing-gown.' She huffs exaggeratedly, then limps off down the hall to change.

As I'm cleaning up, she returns and hovers in the doorway, tutting and groaning to alert me to the seriousness of her bruised buttocks.

'Could you get me a bag of frozen peas, Lucy? If you have any vegetables, that is?'

'I do. Just a sec.'

'I think I'm starting to swell up.'

She hobbles to the sofa and plumps up some cushions before carefully lowering herself down. 'And a cup of tea would be lovely. Peppermint, if you have it? It's the best one for stress.'

'Of course,' I say.

With a cup of peppermint tea in hand and a bag of peas positioned on her forehead, she proceeds to offer me tips on how to mop up the puddle effectively. And after the floor is inspected and considered sanitary enough for the Cambridges' to eat their dinner off, I'm free to resume my breakfast duties.

As usual, I give Jack a banana that he smashes into his hair, followed by some organic baby porridge ('Out of a packet!'). I shovel it into his mouth with one hand and feed Stanley his yoghurt with the other while the tinky-tonk arpeggios of *Peppa Pig* draw their attention towards the TV.

Judith dabs the bag of peas on her chest. 'Shouldn't Stanley be feeding himself by now?'

'Yes. But he finds it difficult. We're working on it.'

'You really mustn't do everything for him, Lucy, or he'll grow up to be lazy.'

'Oh, I know,' I say, then bite the inside of my cheeks extremely hard.

'Too much television at this age can be detrimental to a child's development,' she remarks casually as she sips her tea. 'Screen time can make children emotionally volatile. Apparently, it's as addictive as crack cocaine! It is, isn't it? Yes, it is, my little sweetie,' she coos at Jack.

My poor, coked-up Jack.

'We didn't have a television when Edward was growing up,' she says proudly.

Of all the nonsense that spews out of the woman's mouth, this is the only bit that I can believe, because the way in which Ed becomes totally transfixed by the colourful glare of our TV suggests that he was deprived of watching one as a child. The lure of our Samsung 42-inch screen is so powerful that I could be doing naked cartwheels across the living-room floor and he wouldn't notice.

To stop myself from gnawing right through my cheeks and drawing blood, I slip out to the kitchen to stick my head in the fridge. I toy briefly with thoughts of necking a few shots of neat vodka but manage to resist, and after inhaling a fun-size Mars bar, I return to my duties a few minutes later, emotionally calmed. Judith is back on her feet, attempting to feed Jack blueberries in his highchair. The TV is off, and Stanley is *not* happy about it.

'Be quiet, Stanley! Quiet, now!' she snips. 'Stop all of your drama! See, Lucy – didn't I just say? Look at your baby brother,' she continues, 'he's eating some tasty blueberries. Of course, strawberries *were* on the menu, but these are just as nice. Much nicer than that gloopy stuff out of a packet. Why don't you try one?'

'They are blue,' shouts Stanley, 'and my favourite colour is red!'

'But they're delicious. Here, try one.' She lifts a blueberry and dangles it close to his lips. Far *too* close.

'No!' he yells four times and smacks her hand away, sending the berry flying across the room, then runs under the dining table to take shelter.

'Well, if you're going to make such a fuss about it then forget it!' she says, her mouth shrivelling tighter than a duck's bum. 'I've said it before and I'll say it again, that child needs a little tough love, Lucy. His unruliness is getting beyond.'

I choose to ignore both her comment and the fact that my blood pressure is escalating to dangerous levels and lean down to pull Stanley out from under the table for a reassuring hug. 'I'm not sure that Jack is old enough for blueberries, Judith.'

'It's just fruit, Lucy. Hardly as damaging as the television. And they're rich in antioxidants. Look, he loves them.'

Jack puts one in his mouth and uses this moment to reveal the widest, gummiest smile in his repertoire (the little punk). Judith delivers the finest, smuggest one in hers and saunters into the kitchen to inspect the contents of our fridge.

Ed emerges from the bedroom, having missed all of the action as usual, and yawns so wide that I can see the dangly thing at the back of his throat.

'You're awake!' chirps his mother, who – now miraculously recovered from her crippling fall – virtually skips over to greet him. 'What can I get you? How about some lovely oats with blueberries and sunflower seeds? I bought some from Holland and Barrett.'

'Uh. Yes, please, Mum. That sounds, um, great,' he says before collapsing into the recliner and pulling the lever to launch his feet up into a horizontal position. 'Where's the remote?'

What, Ed? No toast cut into triangles with the crusts off, served with two slices of rind-less bacon on a separate plate? You're actually going to eat something different for breakfast for the first time in nine years? Do you even know what a sunflower seed is? Or a blueberry? And good luck finding the remote. Your mother's probably binned it to save what's left of our fried brain cells!

The buzzer sounds, a glorious cue that Jen and Charlie have arrived in Will's chariot to rescue me from a double murder most horrid. I yell down the speakerphone that I am on my way over the excited voices of Charlie and Jen who are whooping and cheering on the driveway. I just have to dress the kids quickly and then my work is done.

I lift Jack for a final embrace and I'm immediately splatted on the foot by a squashed blueberry that rolls off his lap. After stripping him naked, I find another two stuck in his belly button, four in his nappy, one in his ear and the remainder of several embedded under his tiny fingernails.

So, the scores are:

Baby porridge ('gloopy stuff out of a packet'): 1
Organic blueberries: 0

Or, in other words:

Me: 1
Judith: 0

And I'm willing to bet good money that a shower of hidden sunflower seeds will fall out of Ed's pyjamas when he goes for his morning shit. But I'm not going to stick around to find out.

I have a video shoot to get to.

23

The Shoot

Speeding down the M4 in an old Fiat Panda with the windows rolled down and my best friends beside me is pure bliss! I'm like an excitable dog with my head hanging out of the window, sucking in the delicious fresh air of late spring. The sun is a-shining, the birds are probably a-chirping, and I have two full hours to talk to my friends without any distractions.

The first nugget of delicious gossip: Charlie has met Tom's parents.

'Fucking fantastic people!' she declares as she chews her way through a packet of nicotine gum. Tom's mum is a 'classy, well-dressed Emma Thompson type' and a top family barrister for a major London firm. The dad she describes as 'an older, but still quite fit, highly shaggable Pierce Brosnan kind of guy', who is a banker in the City. They live in a massive house in Wimbledon with six bedrooms, five bathrooms and an indoor swimming pool and have three posh cars on the drive (two of which are 'BM-fucking-Ws').

Charlie tells us how she spent the evening drinking port and chain-smoking Vogue cigarettes with Tom's mum on the balcony of their luxury home. They cooed over Tom's baby pictures, listened to jazz and by the end of the evening had made plans to meet for lunch next week.

'I didn't even steal their soap. And it was Jo Malone as well.'

'Wow!' Jen laughs. 'This is getting serious.'

Jen is not in such a good way. She's been really busy playing with the London Philharmonic Orchestra and has been dragging herself all over the UK for the last couple of weeks. Will has been out most nights blowing his trumpet in Wicked in the West End and has headed to the pub straight afterwards, so she's barely seen him. When they've both had a day off, he has just wanted to nurse his hangover by lounging around in his pants playing on the Xbox. He's been inexplicably moody and withdrawn and poor Jen is fed up. Things between them are growing stale and she's desperate to return to the early days of their relationship when he would throw her up against the washing machine without warning. (Truth be told, I hope those days never happen for me again. I am done with sex on the washing machine. I spend enough time with the damn thing as it is.)

We pull up at Ramona House: an absolutely massive mansion in the middle of a National Trust forest. Most people would probably gasp at the sight of a house so posh, but we aren't bothered by the grandeur of it all. Between us, we've played about four thousand brides down the aisle in manor houses exactly like this over the last ten years and, quite frankly, after a while, once you've seen one forty-five-bed mansion, you've seen them all.

'A bit over the fucking top, as usual,' says Charlie. She spits out her nicotine gum and lights up a fag.

Waiting on the driveway is the estate's chauffeur, a smartly dressed man who introduces himself as Gordon. He informs us that he is there to park our car, and after unloading the instruments and suitcases (plus empty crisp packets, Starbucks coffee cups, M&S tubs of brownies, satsuma peelings and a few empty foil sheets of nicotine gum), Jen hands over the keys. We stand cringing as we watch Gordon park Will's shitty Panda next to the Bentley, the Porsche and the two Ferraris in the car park to the left of the roundabout; and by roundabout, I mean an elaborate stone fountain of water-squirting cherubs that sits directly in front of the entrance to the manor.

I'm startled when I feel a rapid tap on the back of my arm and swivel around to find a strange little woman standing behind me. On one side of her head, her thin purple hair touches her shoulder, but the other side has been shaved clean off to reveal a tattoo of several entwined black roses across her bare scalp.

'I'm Martina, assistant to Fabio,' she says in a squeaky little chipmunk voice that doesn't match her appearance in the slightest. Her bosoms are substantial and bulge over the top of a tight red PVC corset, while the bright pink tutu that sticks out at least a metre from her waist makes her resemble a life-sized ball of candy floss. She looks like she's wandered off the set of the *Rocky Horror Picture Show*, and if I bumped into her in a dark alley, I'd probably scream, whack her with my handbag and make a run for it.

'Fabio?' Charlie says casually. 'Who's he?' She exhales a thick cloud of smoke and tosses the butt of her cigarette onto the gravelled drive.

'Fabio Bianchi … *the* Fabio Bianchi!' squeaks Martina.

Charlie and Jen say nothing and just stand there gawping at her scalp tattoo, so I pipe up. 'Oh, yes! *The* Fabio Bianchi – what a treat!'

'Come,' she says, 'he's waiting for you in the drawing room.'

She ushers us into the house and scurries across the creaky floorboards, and we follow, trying to keep up as we drag our suitcases and instruments up a million steps past rows of stuffed deer heads mounted on the crimson walls.

'Darlings! Is that you?' comes a voice from the drawing room. 'Come, come! Don't be shy.'

Stepping through the door, we are stung in the eyeballs by the sight of *the* Fabio Bianchi. His fluorescent yellow fishnet vest is one thing, but his white denim hot pants are so snug that they show off far more of him than I'm comfortable seeing. People have certainly been arrested for exposing less.

'Welcome, ladies,' he purrs. 'Fabio, I am Fabio Bianchi.' With one hand resting on his hip and the other swinging rhythmically by his side, he struts across the room towards us. Towering over Charlie in a pair of patent red platform boots that add an extra foot to his height, he leans in to blow kisses on each side of her face. 'Mwah, mwah.'

With a name like Fabio, I was expecting him to be Italian, but hearing his thick cockney accent, I conclude that his real name is probably Phil or Steve – maybe even Brian.

'Jesus!' mouths Charlie once he's moved on to air-kissing Jen. 'What the fuck?'

'Right. Let's begin, ladies. I'm thinking gold, I'm thinking silver. Lace, velvet, silk … leather! I'm thinking Queen Elizabeth I meets Lady Gaga. Here, sit. Sit!' He reaches over to a clothes rail, lifts off several items and holds them up to the bay window to inspect them in the natural light.

'Right, you. Darling, yes … *you*.' He points at Charlie. 'Strip off and try this on.'

He lays a long silver and white backless gown in her arms. 'These dresses are all from my last show. Fresh off the runway. They're just *divine*, aren't they?' he gushes before striding over to Jen to give her an embroidered corset and a bronze velvet skirt. 'Martina, help. Don't just stand there. Help these ladies, please!' He clicks his fingers in the air impatiently then turns around and glares intensely at my chest for a wildly inappropriate amount of time. 'Right, right. Um … you're a bit of a tricky one. Maybe the leather – or the fur? No! Wait!' He throws his arms up in the air jubilantly. 'I've got it!' He lifts a tiny gold corset off the rail and presents it to me with an exaggerated curtsy. 'For you, darling.'

I'm horrified by the sliver of jewelled fabric that I hold in my hands. 'What, uh, what size is this?' I say.

'Six, darling. Everything is a standard six. There's a screen there if you want to strip off.'

I take the corset, slip behind the wicker screen and pull off my elasticated maternity leggings. 'Look, um, Fabio. I had a baby not long ago,' I say quietly as I attempt to squeeze my rolls into the corset. I give up almost instantly. 'Nope. It's not going to do up. No chance, none.'

'Not to worry, darling. Out you pop – come on.' He drags the screen to one side and unabashedly scans the full length of my body before clicking his fingers in the air once again. 'Gaffer, Martina, bring me the gaffer!' and Martina comes running.

Mortification levels reach dizzy heights when Martina and Fabio each take one side of the corset and pull it so tight over my gut that I fear they've cracked my ribs. Before I can object, Martina scoops my boobs up and forces them into the cone-shaped cup-holders at the front of the corset, while Fabio wrenches the back of it closed. He secures it with strips of thick black gaffer tape that he rips off the roll with his row of perfectly polished veneers.

'There, darling! It's on,' he says proudly, standing back to admire his work. He wipes the sweat from his forehead. 'And this is the skirt.' He holds up a large ball of white net fabric then barks his orders. 'Gaffer, Martina, more gaffer! And bring the scissors. We're gonna have to cut this skirt open to get it on her. Quickly now – the clock is ticking!'

And moments later, there the three of us stand, taped and pinned up to the rafters, too terrified to move in case we burst out of our outfits.

'Have you got a mirror, Fabio?' I say tentatively.

'Of course, darling. Here, here,' he says, ushering me over to the far side of the room where a full-length mirror is propped up against the wall.

Surprisingly, I look rather nice, and even though I can hardly breathe, I'm just about pulling off the 'Queen Elizabeth I meets Lady Gaga' look. But then I make the mistake of turning around to check out the view from behind. It's not pretty. Not at all. With the corset and skirt only managing to stretch across the front of my body, the entire rear is grossly exposed. We're talking polka-dotted full briefs, my off-white bra and every ounce of excess fat that I have bunched together and bound tightly with more strips of tape than you'd find at a cordoned-off crime scene.

'Okay, and now for the finishing touch. Martina, get the unicorn!'

'Unicorn?' I say.

'Yes, darling. *The* unicorn – quickly!'

Martina dashes over and hands him a large golden spraycan with a white unicorn pictured on the side of it. He pulls off the lid, struts over and blasts me in the chest with it. A spray of golden glitter shoots out and I start to cough, but he doesn't hold back. He moves on to my arms, then my hair and, without releasing his finger off the trigger, he side-steps towards Charlie, then Jen and manages to plaster us all in the stuff within seconds.

'Done! Happy, ladies?' he says, but he doesn't wait for a reply. 'Martina, tell Patrick that we're ready for him. And hand me a towel, for god's sake – I'm sweating like a pregnant nun over here!'

Six hours drag by, each one seemingly longer than the last. We sit by the bay window in direct sunlight, playing the same track on loop, with the star, Patrick, a young man whose rising fame has already swelled his ego enough for him to justify totally ignoring us. Squeezed into the tight underwired corset, I am sweating in places that I didn't know one could sweat from (inside of the elbows!) and feel like I haven't inhaled a decent amount of oxygen since I left the flat this morning. The pins on Charlie's dress have dug into her skin to the extent that she is bleeding, and every half an hour or so she declares, 'Fuck this!' She virtually throws her violin down on the chair and runs outside to cram in as many fags as a five-minute break will allow. Her patience has long gone and she doesn't give two shits what Patrick, Fabio or the cameraman think.

Jen and I put on a brave face for most of it and try to remain polite and professional to compensate for Charlie's colourful outbursts. But deep down, I know that Jen is just as close as I am to ripping one of the deer heads off the wall and beating everyone to death with it.

Two hundred and fifty quid for this torture? How could I leave my baby for this? He's probably choking on an organic blueberry right now, or being held over a potty against his will by Judith, desperate to catch a trickle of urine so that she can prove a point.

And I bet she's cleaned away the row of numbers off the bathroom floor and Stan is going crazy!

After hours of the usual 'Let's do another one, but this time, I want you two looking down and you on the big violin gazing thoughtfully out of the window' or 'Another one, but more pout from Patrick, please' and 'Another one, but let's get those unison C sharps really in tune, ladies', we are finally cleared. It is a wrap.

'Thank God for that!' Charlie sighs.

Off comes the gaffer tape, along with 80 per cent of my back hair and skin cells, and on go my trusty maternity leggings. Never has Lycra felt so amazing! Patrick is whisked off in his private car along with Fabio and his rail of minuscule corsets, and we are left to enjoy the complimentary dinner offered to us by the lord and lady of the manor.

It's late, we're starving and we need booze urgently. So, we accept.

The lady of the manor is an old woman called Margot. Dressed in a green velvet robe with her thin grey hair sculpted into a small, elegant bun, she looks as posh as you'd expect for a woman of such wealth, but when the butler sits me down next to her at the dining table, I soon discover that she doesn't smell nearly so ladylike. The woman reeks of tobacco and stale alcohol, and I find myself gagging on the sickly sweet stench that she exhales all over my prawn cocktail. The only words she is capable of articulating are 'Yars, yars, yars' as she sips her large glass of sherry and mops up the spillages with her napkin as and when they occur. More of it seems to be landing on the table than in her mouth, so it's a wonder how the old dear has managed to get herself quite so drunk.

The dining table has over twenty chairs, but we're all crammed at the top next to our hosts. While I have to tolerate Margot's sherry breath, poor Charlie is stuck next to her husband, Rupert, who very quickly reveals himself to be a Grade-A pervert.

'Tell me, do you have a husband? Or a gentleman friend, perhaps?' he says to Charlie, as he stares down her top for the entire duration of the starter, unashamedly licking his lips. 'Do you like the prawns, dear? I find it best to suck them slowly … to really *extract* the flavour.'

Jen is lucky that she's spared most of this hideousness, as she is sitting on the other side of me. Her only concern is having to hide her prawns in her handbag after her announcement that she is vegetarian has fallen on the deafest of ears.

Charlie bolts up abruptly halfway through the lamb main course. Either she has been struck by lightning or Rupert's sinewy hand has made it onto her thigh. Judging by the look on her face, I suspect the latter.

'Time for bed,' she says firmly. 'Come on, girls.' She grabs us by the elbows and pushes us out of the room just as a string of drool escapes Rupert's lips and lands on his boiled potatoes.

'Yars, yars. Of course.' Margot nods.

'You must be simply exhausted. Time to put on your nighties, I suppose?' Rupert says with a smile. He stands up to show us out and his napkin falls off his lap to reveal a sizeable boner protruding through his high-waisted beige trousers. It's either that or he's storing a baguette in his pants for a midnight snack.

The butler leads us by candlelight to our rooms – a good ten-minute walk to the back of the mansion. Passing the best part of fifteen bedrooms, he stops at a door at the end of a long deer-head-filled corridor.

'This is your room. The water closet is four doors down on the right. Goodnight.'

He leaves all three of us standing inside a small damp room with just one double bed.

ONE. FUCKING. DOUBLE. BED!

'I don't mind going in the middle. Don't worry, girls, I shaved my legs, so you won't get stubble rash,' says Charlie, who is past the point of caring.

'Awful. It's just so shit,' sighs Jen as tears start running down her glittery cheeks. She opens her handbag, pulls out her rack of lamb and a napkin filled with prawns and chucks them out of the window.

'Yep. Fuck our lives … But I wasn't going to sit there a minute longer and wait for that man to ejaculate all over his rack of lamb,' says Charlie, totally deflated. 'Let's just sleep it off and forget the day ever happened.'

On our jammies go and into the tiny damp bed we climb, desperate for the day to be over.

I wake up suddenly, hot and bothered, with a bony arm slung over my shoulder.

Jack? God! Is that you? Have I squashed you? Are you breathing? Or is it you, Stanley? Having another bad dream, my love?

Blinking, then furiously rubbing my eyes, I eventually focus on the ominous shadow of a deer head hanging over the bed and remember where I am. It all comes screaming back to me.

Ramona House. Size six corsets. Fabio. Gaffer tape. Prawns. Rupert. Rack of lamb. Boner. Double bed!

I elbow Charlie to get her off me. Suddenly, she springs upright, slams on the bedside lamp, then opens her mouth and pukes all over the duvet.

'Oh, fuck! There's more,' she cries, then clambers over Jen to get to the window, but she's too late and the puke hits the wall and runs down the William Morris wallpaper.

'Jen, towels! I'll get the window!'

Jen is quick to react and leaps out of bed in search of a cloth while I wrench open the old window and push Charlie's head out into the cold air. 'You okay? Is there more?'

'Yep. There's mo—' and she is sick again. Litres of prawn cocktail fly out of her on to the rose garden below. Then, just like a tiny child, she starts to cry.

And I, like a mum, hug her until she feels better.

Our coats are on and we are sneaking out through the front door within twenty minutes, dodging deer heads in the dark as we go. Still in our pyjamas, we creep out to the driveway, past the water fountain, dive into Will's Panda and speed down the country lanes of Gloucester as fast as our clapped-out chariot will allow.

Freedom. The sweet, sweet smell of freedom.

And prawn vomit.

24

Where the Heart Is

When I tiptoe through the front door at 4.30 a.m., Ed is sitting in the living room in the dark burping Jack.

'Honey, I'm home,' I whisper.

'Already?' He springs to his feet with Jack in his arms and flicks on the big light. Hooking his hand around the back of my neck, he pulls me towards him and attempts to kiss me but instantly backs away, his face a picture of disgust. 'God, what's that smell?'

'I was going to say the same to you,' I say, equally repulsed. 'Eww.'

'Jack just puked on me.'

'Well, same here – but Charls was the culprit and there were dodgy prawns involved.' I pull off my coat and toss it on the sofa then kick off my shoes.

'Uh, why are you wearing pyjamas?'

'Long, *grim* story, love. Where's your mum?' I say, glancing over his shoulder at the pile of clean bedding on the sofa. 'Did she go?'

'Yep. At dinner-time. Stan was kicking off because he didn't want peas and she had a migraine coming, so she went home early.'

'Well, that's *your* fault, Ed. If you'd shown him some "tough love" then maybe he wouldn't be so unruly!' I say pointedly, mimicking Judith's patronising tone perfectly. He stares at me blankly, my uncanny impression of his mother totally lost on him. 'Okay, just hand over that baby – I need a sniff of that neck right now, smelly or not.'

I pull Jack into my arms and take a long hard sniff of the top of his head. It stinks of stale cheese thanks to the lingering cradle cap that no cream or lotion on the market has been able to shift, but it's a stink that I've sorely missed.

'Wait there a sec,' Ed says. He nips into the kitchen and returns with a carrier bag then lays out two steaks, a bottle of Pinot Grigio and a multipack of KitKats in a straight line across the sofa. 'A welcome-home gift,' he beams, 'for later.'

The treats are a wonderful surprise, but what's even better is that the flat is immaculate. Within fifteen minutes of arriving home, I notice that the toilet seats are down, the nappy bin is empty and there isn't a dirty mug or a discarded pair of boxer shorts in sight! Obviously, I know that none of it is Ed's work, and the Post-it notes that I find dotted around the place soon confirm it.

The one on the fridge says:

Lucy,

You need skimmed milk, yoghurts and butter. I threw your margarine out. It was four weeks past the sell-by date. Butter is much better for you all. Unsalted.

Much love, J xx

The one stuck to the washing machine:

Lucy,

I cleaned out the soap drawer. It was full
of black gunge. It will not need doing for
another three weeks now.

Much love, J xx

And on the sink:

Lucy,

I found twenty or so dummies behind the
sofa and put them in Milton at lunchtime.
Perhaps time to wean them off the dummies.
They cause overbites.

Much love, J xx

I crumple the notes up in a ball, toss them in the bin and
then lie down on the sofa to decompress for a while, and
Ed takes Jack back to his cot.

I wake up on the sofa and find Stanley pacing around in a
circle, totally naked with his arms flailing around excitedly.

'Excuse me, but there are four things that you need to
know.'

Disoriented, I wipe off the dribble that has crusted around
the corners of my mouth, then briskly rub my eyes. 'What,
um, what time is it?'

He starts: 'Number one, I have to wear a green T-shirt
today because we are playing games and I am in the green
group. Number Two, I now want my bananas in circles and
not semicircles, because circles is my new favourite. Number

three, Jack pooed in the bath and Daddy said "Fuck", and number four, you're not allowed to touch my squashy body parts or my numbers if you don't wash your hands first. Daddy says you will make them dirty because hands have lots of germs and that's why we all got poorly at Easter.' Totally unprompted, he then paces over to me and leans down to deliver a stiff hug. 'You smell bad,' he says.

'I know,' I chuckle, 'I guess I'd better brush my teeth.'

He's missed me!

Jack is all smiles when he wakes, as am I when I undo his nappy and find a perfectly formed, golden glittery poo. It takes a few seconds to figure out why it's shimmering like a Christmas tree decoration, but then I remember Fabio's Unicorn spray. The glitter must have somehow made its way from my chest into Jack's mouth, then through his digestive system and out the other end. I have no doubt that Fabio would be impressed. It's possibly the most beautiful stool that I've ever seen and its almost a shame to throw it away, so before lobbing it, I take a quick picture first, send it to Charlie and Jen with a unicorn emoji attached and then stuff it in the nappy bin to fester with its less glamorous friends.

After I've dressed Jack, I bring him through to the living room for breakfast, but he refuses to let me put him in his highchair, making it crystal clear that he just wants to be in my arms. Normally, this level of unrelenting clinginess would drive me to the fridge to face-plant a whole cheesecake, but it doesn't. It's really special to just sit down and hold him.

'Ah, we've missed you, love,' Ed says as he brings me a coffee from the kitchen. 'It's not been the same without you.'

Jeez. Gone for half a day and he's acting like I've just returned from a highly dangerous expedition around the Antarctic. I guess I'm appreciated after all. Either that, or his emotional display is actually just an expression of the intense relief he feels now that his mother has gone and he can sink a six-pack of Becks and a Pot Noodle without judgement.

I find the final note on my way to the shower. It's a three-parter that is taped to the laundry basket:

Lucy,

I hope you enjoyed your little trip away with your friends. Just to let you know that I found some dirty laundry in the bottom of your wardrobe and I have sorted it out for you. I had to throw out some of your pants as they were discoloured (!) Remember to separate your whites and colours and this won't happen.

Much love, J xx

PS. Also managed to pair up all of the odd socks! And have left a new punnet of blueberries in the fridge for Jack x

Although I don't welcome the idea of Judith touching my dirty pants, I have to admit that it's rather nice to come home to a clean flat. And in the spirit of positivity, I'm sure that I will sleep soundly in my own bed later knowing that all of the odd socks have been reunited with their long-lost partners.

The woman, for all her faults, has her heart in the right place.

And now that I'm home, so do I.

25

IKEYYYYAAAHHHHHHH!

It's taken over a week to return to normal after the encounter with Rupert and his bulging beige trousers. Every night since the ordeal, I've woken up feeling the stifling heat of Charlie's body next to mine and I've jumped upright in bed, believing that I'm still in Ramona House, lying in the centre of a pool of prawn vomit. When I've regained full consciousness and adjusted to the darkness, I've been hugely relieved to discover that I'm actually at home in my own bed, and the stifling heat is just Stanley's little body, which is snuggled up next to mine as usual.

The child has never slept a whole night in his room and it hasn't been for my lack of trying. I've googled and experimented with all of the usual tricks: white noise, jungle animal sounds, singing 'Twinkle, Twinkle, Little [Bastard] Star' on loop. I've even offered him cash, but nothing has worked.

His bedtime rituals are incredibly specific and painfully time-consuming. For starters, he insists on having four sips of water before brushing his teeth and four directly after. Aside from demanding his red dummy, the light-switch must be flicked on and off four times when I leave his room. Each of his ten foam numbers from his jigsaw playmat need to be kissed goodnight and stacked up in order on his bedside table. And the newest addition to the schedule (thanks to Ed rabbiting on about germs) is that he must clean his hands with four squirts of sanitiser. Only after all of these things are done will he agree to be left alone. Of course, when he wakes up exactly three hours later, he always climbs into our bed, and most mornings I'll wake up to find him lining up numbers along my spinal cord.

Suffering multiple kicks to the guts, tiny hands pulling out my hair and sleepy conversations at 3 a.m. about the differences between equilateral and isosceles triangles doesn't make for a peaceful night's sleep (nor does waking up every ten minutes to check that I haven't accidentally rolled over and suffocated him to death). Enduring all of this, however, is easier than having to constantly climb in and out of bed to settle him in his own room. Exhaustion is no joke, and for the sake of my very survival, I discovered that remaining in a horizontal position for longer than an hour per night was essential. So, against the advice of every parenting website out there, he has become a frequent guest in our bed (as has Jack, for my sins).

Where having two kids in our bed night after night has made a minor improvement to both mine and Ed's sleep quota, it has been one of the major contributors to the demise of our sex life. I was already worried about it, but having listened to Charlie blather on about her recent raunchy escapades on our road trip to Gloucester, I have been propelled into a state of full-blown panic.

If Ed and I don't do it soon, I've convinced myself that we'll turn into one of those couples who wear matching raincoats from Regatta, who sleep in a room with identical single beds and whose only moments of excitement involve completing the *Sunday Times* crossword every week. Worse still, I'm now worried that the lack of action at home might drive him to have a sordid affair with one of the sexy backing vocalists on his approaching tour. He will be surrounded by young hot American women who have no stretchmarks or traumatised vaginas, whose blow-up boobs sit perpendicular to their shoulder blades. Although I've never questioned his loyalty, I know that everyone has their weaknesses. It's not unthinkable that he might allow himself to be seduced by a twenty-three-year-old, hot-pants-wearing vocalist called Cherry.

My overactive imagination has pushed me to take action. If we're going to have sex, then I need to invest – *not* in a load of red silky underwear or strawberry-flavoured lubricant, but in a new bed. Stanley needs a good reason to stay in his room and I've decided that a trip to IKEA to buy him a super-cool, profoundly enticing 'big boy' bed might just do the trick.

A trip to IKEA has always brought out the beast in Ed. Perhaps it's the strip-lighting, the preservatives in the hot dogs or the fact that he always has to lug the bulky boxes of furniture out of the car and up two flights of stairs, but his temper *always* flares up every time we set foot in the place. Based on this, I make a solemn promise to him before we leave that we're going in for one thing only.

'I won't buy tea-light holders,' I say.

'Or random boxes to store stuff in?'

'Okay, love, *no* random boxes. I promise.'

'Or massive houseplants that you'll kill by the end of the week?'

'Promise. I really do. Just the bed … and a hot dog on the way out. Because it's only natural. Deal?'

He frowns intensely. 'Deal.'

Amazingly, the trip is a success! After a brief delay caused by Stanley insisting that he spin four times on every single office chair on display, we leave the building with just the big-boy bed and a couple of hot dogs in hand ... and with Ed's rage totally under control. A first!

With Stan glued to the telly and Jack enjoying an afternoon nap, Ed and I start building the monstrosity of a bed that comes in over two hundred pieces with a forty-eight-page instruction manual to boot. I put on some light Mozart piano sonatas to create a peaceful ambience, pour him a beer, open the manual and we set to work with our Allen keys in hand.

Interpreting instructions from an IKEA manual isn't easy, and most NASA engineers would find it a challenge, let alone a bald guitarist with a dislike of anything DIY. The whole process is designed to test a man's masculinity so, naturally, there are going to be highs and lows when trying to execute a perfect performance while your wife watches from the wings.

New and highly creative phrases that escape Ed's lips throughout the arduous task include: 'Son of an arse-muncher.' 'Kiss my arse, you wanktard!' 'You shit stain! Stay in there! You SHIT!' And my personal favourite, yelled while trying to drive a screw into a hole that isn't quite wide enough: 'Allen key. You bastard!'

Four hours and thirty-eight minutes, three KitKats, six beers and one lingering bear hug later, the bed is ready and not once have I googled 'local divorce lawyers'. Like I said, I'm a woman on a mission. This new bed could potentially lead to a lifetime of sexual bliss, thus keeping Cherry and her leather hot pants at bay, so it was in my interest to control my own rage.

After the boys enjoy a brief free-willy time in the living room, we chuck them in the bath and then perform the usual bedtime rituals, making sure that we are careful not to forget any of the crucial details that might cause any delay in our mission. Surprisingly, Stan is a total angel. He's very excited about his new bed, particularly because I've bought him a new duvet cover which is plastered in brightly coloured numbers.

'There's numbers on my bed! Look, the number four! The number eight! The number ten! LOOK!' he flaps.

He's so ecstatic that he dives straight in, and after I've kissed goodnight to each of his foam numbers, he's happy to stay in his numerical haven without resistance.

Jack takes more convincing to settle down for the night (forty-two minutes of white noise, bum tapping, an extra bottle of milk and countless renditions of 'How Much Is That Doggy in the [Fecking] Window') but, after a heroic effort on my part, he finally falls asleep in his cot and I tiptoe out of the room ready for action.

Ed is in the living room watching Spiderman cartoons.

'Right, Ed. Limber up. We're having sex in two minutes. Here's the to-do list. Number one, find the condoms. Two: get the wine. Three: get the Pringles. I'll meet you in the bedroom.'

'Uh. What do you mean?'

'I *mean* get your dinger out. We're having sex!'

He pauses the TV and looks at his watch. 'Can I just finish this episode first?'

'Nope. There's *no* time. Get the supplies, get naked and get in there!'

I dash to the bathroom, shave all unsightly hairs from every part of my unsightly body and force my excess flesh into the red lacy bra and pants that I bought from H&M back in 2015. I spritz Marc Jacobs Daisy into every pore of my body, roll down the blackout blinds, draw the blackout curtains and turn all the lights off.

'Right. Get in here, baby. I'm ready to go. *Quick!* Before Jack wakes up!'

Seven minutes later: 'IKEEYYYAHHHHHH!' comes the passionate cry from Ed after he explodes and collapses back on to the pillow, panting like a pug in the summertime. As the light comes on, I look down towards the foot of the bed to see, to my horror, a very wide-eyed Stanley clutching a yellow number four in his tiny hands.

'Excuse me. But can I have some of those paraboloids in the red cylinder?'

'Stan! What are you doing up? Daddy and I were just … um. Yes, you can. Here you go, babe.'

He climbs up on to the bed, pulls the covers over his lap and delves into the tube of Pringles that is sitting on the bedside table. He munches his way happily through the remainder of them in utter silence.

I give Ed the thumbs up. 'It's okay,' I mouth, 'he didn't see.'

Ed exhales loudly and his eyes return to their usual size. He turns his back and quickly pulls on his Spiderman pyjama bottoms, then slides under the duvet and turns out the light.

Lying in pitch darkness, my heart throbs wildly and my limbs quiver as though electricity is dancing inside them. I'm elated. We've done it. We've sealed the deal! The first step towards getting our relationship back on track has finally been taken.

Then, just as I close my eyes, hoping to drift off into a peaceful sleep:

'Excuse me, but what is Ikkkkeeeyahhhh?'

26

The Vault

I've been on cloud nine thousand and ninety-nine ever since mine and Ed's quickie earlier in the week. Our brief flurry of passion has given our relationship a mega boost and I've noticed him being much more affectionate towards me.

On Monday night, he abandoned his recliner and instead chose to sit next to me on the sofa, then held my hand through an entire episode of *Game of Thrones*. On Wednesday, he devoted the entire day to making Gordon Ramsay's Malaysian chicken curry for me. Hell-bent on following the recipe to a tee, he dragged his arse around four different supermarkets on a quest to locate palm sugar and kaffir lime leaves, and when the meal was finally served at 10.15 p.m., I didn't even complain that he had to wrench me out of a deep sleep to eat it. It was so delicious and more than worth the seven-hour wait.

On Thursday, when I was hiding behind the kitchen door scoffing a huge bag of Cheetos, he pinned me up against the wall and snogged me, then a couple of days after that, totally unprompted, he told me that I looked sexy. I was wearing milk-stained mismatched pyjamas, no bra and my hair was tied back with a scrunchie that I'd won in a Christmas cracker last year, but I didn't care. The man said it.

I was significantly more patient with him when I walked into the living room yesterday and found him knee-deep in a mountain of DVDs that he'd pulled off the shelves. He was frantically opening the cases, then slamming them shut before chucking them down on the floor in a rage. Instead of chastising him for trashing the place, I just rolled with it.

'What are you doing, love?' I said sweetly.

'Looking for cash,' he replied as he tossed *Ocean's Eleven* down on the pile.

'In the DVDs?'

'Yeah. I hid some in here. It was in *The Little Mermaid,* but it's gone now. I must've moved it, but I can't remember where.'

'Okay. So, call me stupid, but why are you hiding cash in the DVDs?'

'So the burglars won't find it.'

'Well, that makes total sense. I mean, it's so well hidden that you can't even find it, so I'd say the cash is pretty damn safe. It's the ultimate vault.'

'Oh no! Where's *Titanic*? It's missing,' he snapped. 'It should be here in between *Shakespeare in Love* from '99 and *The English Patient* from '97.'

'I lent it to Jen – she wanted to have a good cry and clean her tear ducts out.'

'Well, get it back! Call her now. All the Best Picture winners are supposed to be in chronological order!'

'Says the man who's just turfed three-hundred-odd DVDs all over the floor. I'd say your order is pretty fecked, love.'

Over the years, I've grown used to the idea that if Ed was ever to walk in one day and find me straddling Hugh Jackman on the recliner, he wouldn't bat an eyelid. But if he walked in and found one of his DVDs out of place on the shelves, I know that he would totally lose his cool. Every. Single. Time.

'So how much cash are we talking about?' I say.

'A few hundred. For a rainy day ... God! Where is *Rainman*, 1989?'

'Ed! Cool it with the accusatory tone. Rach borrowed it. It's in Wales.'

'I'm ordering a new copy. I'm doing it now.'

I sighed and left him to it. He would be there for ages buying missing DVDs and getting himself in a flap, and if he ever did find the cash, I knew that the rest of the day would be spent restoring his beloved collection to its formerly perfect order.

I feel particularly enamoured with Ed this morning when he strides into the living room, opens his wallet and throws a pile of ten- and twenty-pound notes down on the coffee table.

'We got cash last night,' he beams, 'two hundred and fifty smackers.'

He stands tall and proud, with his hands on his hips and his head up high, towering over the table where the cash lies fanned out in all its glory. He is like a caveman dragging home a dead deer and throwing it on the floor for his starving wife and kids to feast on. I almost expect him to rip open his Spiderman dressing-gown and start drumming his fists on his hairy chest, but he doesn't.

'Awesome! But where are you going to hide *this* wad?' I say.

'I was thinking inside *Brewster's Millions* on the 1980's shelf. But maybe that's too obvious ... for the burglars?' he says in a deadly serious tone.

'Just leave it on the table and I'll have a think,' I reply, doing my best to stifle a laugh.

Annoying obsessiveness aside, my caveman has come through for us. I couldn't love him more.

*

The phone rings at dinner-time and I glance down to see Jen's name flashing on the screen. Ed is at work, Jack is lying happily on his baby gym and Stanley is distracted watching a video of a singing colon, so I'm totally free to indulge in a long, uninterrupted conversation with her. A rare treat.

I answer the phone and I'm greeted by a piercing squeal and can only make out two audible words: 'Will' and 'proposed'. Within ten minutes, she rolls up on the driveway, or rather she *scrapes* up on the driveway. Taking several attempts to squeeze Will's Panda into the minuscule space next to the wall, she eventually grinds to a halt by scraping the entire right-hand side of the car against it. I can hear the cold screech of grating metal from our lounge, and when I peer through the window, I can't help but laugh at the sight of her awkwardly climbing over the passenger seat to get out.

I buzz her in to the flat and she runs up the stairs, in through the door and thrusts a sparkling diamond ring in my face.

'He proposed!' She bursts into tears. 'It's a real diamond!'

'Amazing!'

'Charlie's on her way with bubbles. We're having a party right this second. And just so you know, the wedding is soon – August 20th – so the planning starts now.'

Charlie arrives within fifteen minutes and dances through the door with two carrier bags full of Prosecco and treats. 'Right. I'm here with the booze. It was buy one get 20 per cent off another, so I bought four. Now, let's get fucked up,' she shrieks before ripping the foil off one of the bottles with her teeth.

I cringe as the word 'fucked' hangs like a dirty black cloud over Stanley, who is sitting on the floor in front of the TV, then I go to find the champagne flutes.

The engagement story is like something you'd see in a Hollywood romcom, and if Steven Spielberg got wind of it, he'd probably snap up the movie rights and churn out a blockbuster.

Will had booked a table at their favourite restaurant in Chiswick to celebrate their anniversary before heading to the airport to fly to a top-secret destination for the weekend. Halfway through the starter, he handed Jen a card with a picture of an apple on it and the caption inside said 'Start spreading the news, we're leaving today'. The waiter then appeared at the table and presented her with a red apple on a silver plate. Carved into the apple was a heart-shaped hole, and in the hole sat a Tiffany diamond ring.

'Jesus!' Charlie says. 'The romantic bastard.'

'I know,' gushes Jen. 'So, he dropped to his knees and proposed. I cried, he cried and after I said yes, the whole restaurant burst into applause. And then, after dessert, a freaking pink limo pulled up and took us to the airport and we flew to New York! He said he'd been saving up for three years to pull it off!'

'Bloody hell, Jen. That's insane!' I say. 'It makes Ed's proposal look sad and pathetic.'

'Well, it wouldn't be hard to top his, Luce,' Charlie says.

The woman isn't wrong. Our shotgun wedding was all booked and paid for, but two weeks before the big day, Ed still hadn't officially proposed. I'd dragged him out to Argos, showed him the ring that I wanted and even bought it there and then using my own credit card. All that he had to do was book a restaurant, get down on one knee and pop the question, but organising it proved to be too much for him. With time against us, I ended up having to sort it out by myself and a few days later, when sitting in Tandoori Villa, stuffing down poppadoms and onion bhajis, I handed him the ring and told him exactly what he had to do and say.

'Check out my ring now,' I say. 'It's sporting a lump of tinfoil.'

I lay out my hand and show the girls my budget engagement ring which, as of last year, is missing a diamond after one fell out when I was rescuing Stanley from the ball pit at Cheeky Charlie's Fun House. Ed promised that he would take it to the jeweller's to get it repaired, but of course he never did. In the end, I had to superglue a tiny ball of tin foil into the hole to stop it catching on my clothes.

'Ah, classic. Romance is dead, eh, Luce?'

'Not sure it was ever alive in the first place, Charls.'

Jen has been super-efficient as expected and has already booked the Ealing registry office for the ceremony. The reception will be a carvery dinner at The Lodge for seventy-five guests, and in the evening, the entire music industry will be invited for a mammoth jamming session in exchange for free booze.

'Obviously, you're both my bridesmaids, but Charlie, I *don't* want a stripper for my hen do, so don't even think about it.'

Within the hour, Jen is scrolling through pictures of wedding dresses online, Charlie is secretly googling 'hot London strippers' and reading through the reviews, and I'm in the bedroom dressing Jack, having just given him a quick top and tail in the sink.

Suddenly, I hear an explosion of sound coming from the front room.

'Stan! What's that? Shit!' I hear Charlie yell. 'No! Give that to me! Shit, *Luce!* Get in here!'

I quickly dump Jack in his cot and dash down the hall to the living room where I find Stanley lying on the floor with his hands cupped over his ears. He is rocking rapidly back and forth, monotonously chanting, 'Shit.'

'I'm sorry, Luce,' Charlie cries in a panic as she hovers over Stanley, not knowing what to do. 'Oh, fuck! I'm *so* sorry.'

'Language, Charls!' I snap.

'Sorry, sorry, Luce. Oh, *fudge.*' She tries to stroke the back of Stanley's head, but he butts her away. 'I didn't mean to scare you, Stan. I'm sorry. I'm so sorry.'

I scoop him up in my arms and squeeze him as tightly as I can to calm him down, and after fifteen long minutes of thrashing around, he finally goes limp and his little body slumps down on the rug, exhausted. It's only then that I notice the cause of his explosion.

Lying on the floor in tatters is the wad of cash that Ed left on the coffee table this morning.

The damage:

£40 chewed, wet, demolished.
£10 ripped
£10 semi-digested and on its way to Stan's colon
£190 wet and soaked in dribble

'Fudging hell! I really didn't mean to freak him out, Luce. I just saw him eating the dosh and I panicked. So, so sorry. Is he okay?' says Charlie, still totally flustered.

'Calm down, love,' I say, leaning back against the sofa to catch my breath, 'everyone's fine.'

'Why don't we put them on the radiator? I'm sure they'll dry out,' suggests Jen as she kneels down and carefully lifts the soggy notes off the floor. 'We can always Sellotape the ripped ones.'

Charlie is visibly crippled with guilt. 'I should have been keeping an eye on him – it's all my fault.'

'Seriously, Charls, chill. If anything, it's kind of a good thing – the kid has finally tried something new. Maybe I'll add cash and chips to the meal planner from now on.'

Once both boys are settled in bed, I sneakily call Will to ask him to come and collect his fiancée. She and Charlie are both totally hammered and I still need to sterilise Jack's bottles, fold a pile of washing and pack Stanley's bag for nursery tomorrow. In short, I have shit to do and I'm not up for an all-nighter.

'Oh, God. His car,' Jen shrieks when I inform her that Will is on his way. 'He's going to flip!'

From the window, I watch my drunken friends colour in the thick white scratches that run down the side of Will's beloved Panda with a couple of red Sharpies. When he arrives ten minutes later, they are leaning against the car, cleverly blocking the damaged paintwork. Jen masterfully reaches over to hug him and then dives in for a passionate kiss. The man will never know about his savaged Panda ... at least not until morning.

Ed arrives home from his gig just after midnight. Inspired by Jen's impressive distraction tactics, I greet him by the front door in a different manner to usual (wearing nothing but a leopard-print thong with a metre-long reel of condoms in hand).

And, thanks to the magical powers of another eight-minute-long fudge in the dark, he fails to notice the rows of half-mangled ten- and twenty-pound notes draped over every radiator in the flat.

27

Fastest Finger First

The fixer of the BBC Philharmonic Orchestra has just sent me a text:

> URGENT
>
> Cellist needed TODAY
>
> Rehearsal 2–5 p.m.
>
> Concert 7.30 p.m.
>
> Bridgewater Hall, Manchester
>
> Programme: Beethoven 6
>
> Reply ASAP.
>
> I have other calls out.
>
> Regards, Malcolm

The Universe has read my mind and I'm beyond chuffed at the offer, but within seconds, the elation evaporates and is replaced with blind panic. Malcom has 'other calls out', which means that he's potentially texted every cellist in the country and whoever replies first will get the work. Annoyingly, this is often how fixers book players at short notice. They throw the gig out like a slab of steak amongst a pack of wild dogs and whoever dives in first wins.

Ed had a gig in Glasgow last night and won't be back until this afternoon, and there isn't time to get Judith to drive down from Aylesbury and hold the fort so I can make it to Manchester for 2 p.m. With the clock ticking and my adrenaline pumping, I grab the phone and call Mandy. She is our only tried and tested babysitter, but I haven't used her since I was heavily pregnant with Jack. There's no answer, so I leave a rambling message and start scrolling through my contact list looking for an alternative.

Charlie? No, Tom has the day off so she'll be busy bonking.

Jen? Nope, she's teaching all day.

Will? No clue about kids.

Fit Ben? He'll probably give them beer.

Annoying Alan? Too old, and just too annoying.

Marsha? Hell no!

I get all the way down to W in my contacts list when my phone pings. It's a reply from Mandy:

> Hi hun. Sorry I missed you. At work and can't talk. Me and Mike moved back to Wolverhampton two months ago. He's got new job managing a Wetherspoons! Did you not get my messages? Tell Stan I miss him ☹
> Let's catch up on phone later. M xx

Mandy is gone. Fun-loving, patient, kind, alphabet-embracing Mandy ... gone forever! The news is devastating; I've lost our only Stanley-approved babysitter in the blink of an eye. And so, with the heaviest of hearts, I lift my phone and reply to Malcom's text with a classic black lie:

> Thanks so much, Malcolm, but I'm afraid that I'm already working.

It's quite clear that, given my current situation, I'm never going to be able to accept work at short notice, and the more I say no, the higher the chances are that Malcolm and every other fixer in the UK will eventually stop calling altogether. The bottom line is that to be a successful musician in London, you have to be a 'yes' person.

Can you be in Manchester by 2 p.m. to perform a rock-hard orchestral piece that you've never seen before?

YES! (And I'll cry about the fact I couldn't play it into a pint of gin in the pub afterwards.)

Can you get to Heathrow airport in the next two hours and fly to Morocco for a seventies tribute show tonight?

HELL YES! (Hand me the sun lotion! Do I need jabs? Feck it, hepatitis A can't be that bad!)

Can you dress up in a size-ten silver spacesuit and mime behind Bjork on the *Jonathan Ross Show*?

YES! WHY NOT? (As long as I can get my hands on some suck-in pants, a roll of gaffer tape and an ultra-minimising industrial-strength bra.)

It's always been this way; the more you say 'yes', the more you get booked, and vice versa. Fixers don't have time to wait for a player to sort out babysitters or find their suck-in pants. They just want a quick 'yes' and a bum on a chair, and as it stands, I'm never going to be able to do this.

Several hours after losing the gig, I'm still moping around in my pyjamas having achieved nothing worthwhile all day (aside from cleaning the mould off the shower curtain and using a chopstick to extract a disgusting hairball that was blocking the hoover). Thankfully, Jen stops by to drop off a wedding invitation on her way home from teaching, and after seeing the sorry state that I'm in, she ends up staying for a cup of tea and listens to my monologue of pessimism.

'Why, Jen? Why didn't I get a normal job,' I whinge, 'like an office job for a reputable company where I get maternity pay for a year?'

'Because you love what you do, Lucy,' she says, 'and you're amazing at it too.'

'But I can't pay half the mortgage playing fastest finger first with every cellist in the country every time a fixer texts me. Not when I have kids to think about.'

'It's so shit when they do that.' She tuts. 'I think you need to line up a couple of new sitters, so next time you get the text, you'll be ready to pounce.'

With Mandy gone, I know that I need to get on the case, but finding someone who Stanley likes is going to be difficult and, to be frank, I'm dreading it.

'I've been putting it off, but I know I've got to crack on with it soon, or else Ed and I will have to sell our organs on the internet just to keep the roof over our heads.'

'Well, *no* one will buy your liver,' she says. 'What about Judith? She's only an hour down the road, isn't she?'

'I'd rather take a bullet to the skull, Jen, or a knife to the jugular.'

'Fair enough,' she laughs, 'I get it. So, stop your whining, get on the internet and lock someone down. I expect a full report on your progress by the end of the week.'

Once the kids are sleeping, I resist collapsing on the sofa with a glass of wine and a slab of chocolate, and instead, I take Jen's advice and devote my free time to some intensive childcare research. I stumble across a few recruitment websites and decide to put up a post to see if I can attract the attention of a worthy suitor.

What I want to write is:

> Desperately seeking a flexible, friendly, non-smoking, non-violent, non-paedophile and very responsible person to look after an extremely sensitive four-year-old anatomy expert and an adorable (but clingy) ten-month-old baby. Must have the heart of Mother Teresa, the patience of Job, the stamina of an Olympic triathlete and the fun-loving nature of Mr Tumble. Must be wholesome, pure and not have any child-trafficking/coke-sniffing tendencies. Gall-bladder/pancreas enthusiasts encouraged to apply.

But what I actually post is:

> Seeking a flexible, experienced childcare professional to look after our sensitive four-year-old and ten-month-old sons. My husband and I are musicians by trade and often work antisocial hours, so we are looking for someone who could potentially work weekends and evenings until late, and often at short notice.

Scrolling through hundreds of online profiles, I'm appalled to discover that the vast majority of babysitters charge a minimum of ten pounds per hour! It is so expensive and painful to swallow, especially when Mandy used to do it for a fiver an hour, a frozen pizza and the password to my Netflix account to use at her leisure.

Nevertheless, if I want to work, then this is what it's going to cost, so I just have to suck it up and embrace it. The post is up, and all being well, I'll bag us a non-heroin-injecting Mary Poppins soon and, finally, I'll get my career back on track.

28

'Yes' Woman!

Almost a full week later, I receive a five-page article from Judith in the post entitled 'Top 20 Nannies from Hell'. Ed had obviously told her that I've been looking into hiring a babysitter, even though I explicitly told him not to. Now that the cat is out of the bag, she is using the powers of the Royal Mail to voice her opinion about it, which I suppose is marginally better than suffering one of her lectures in person.

Annoyances aside, I've had some promising replies to my post online and I've set up some interviews for this morning. The flat is immaculate, the cookie jar is stocked up and I've typed and printed out my list of questions ready for interrogation. Ed has kept his diary clear to be around to give a third opinion (the first, obviously, will come from Stanley, who is by far the toughest member of the family to impress). I can't deny it, I am ridiculously excited about the prospect of getting some regular help. If one of these people is suitable, I'll have some support in place before Ed goes on tour, and doors that have been closed for so very long might finally be opened.

As it happens, finding someone you can trust implicitly with your children's lives is quite tricky; someone who won't abduct them, flee to Mexico and sell them to an international paedophile ring.

Thanks for that article, Judith, really insightful as always.

Our first interviewee of the day is Veronika. Her credentials online were so promising that I purposely scheduled her first, hoping I could sign her up quickly and call off the search.

Upon opening the front door to welcome her in, I'm immediately alarmed to find a frail old lady propped up with a wooden walking stick. At the very least, she looks to be in her eighties, *not* in her fifties as her profile picture on the website implied.

'Hi. Veronika?'

'Da,' comes her croaky reply.

If this was a Tinder date, I'd be subtly speed-dialling Charlie to call me back with 'a big emergency' to help me escape, but that isn't an option. Instead, I find myself taking her by the arm and helping her into the living room where I offer her a cup of tea and a chocolate Hobnob.

Aside from Veronika's age being a major disadvantage, her English is virtually non-existent. Just spending ten minutes trying to talk to her has Ed and me reaching for the Red Bull to reboot.

'Veronika, do you have any experience with young babies?' I say.

'Da.'

'So, um, what kind of experience?' I continue uncomfortably. 'Have you worked for other families with young babies?'

'Da, bebe? Famileeee? Da.' She pulls a few black and white photos out of her purse, all of which feature what appears to be a twenty-year-old version of herself holding a baby. So, yes, she does have experience with babies, albeit from sixty-odd years ago. Her 'bebe' must be a pensioner himself by now. In fact, they probably ride side by side on the bus together with their free passes.

'Any *recent* experience with babies?' I continue.

No reply comes. She shrugs her bony shoulders and smiles sweetly.

'Re-cent ex-per-i-ence, you?' says Ed, with the enunciation of a Shakespearian actor.

She shrugs again, then points at the baby in her photo.

'Excuse me, but you are very old,' comes an ear-splitting voice from behind me. Stanley is standing in the doorway holding a miniature rubber bladder. 'Are you going to die soon?' he continues matter-of-factly.

'Stanley! Sshhh! That is a *very* rude question to ask a grown up.'

I'm horrified and floundering to find the right words to excuse him, but Veronika simply shakes her head and nibbles on her biscuit like a fragile little mouse.

'Is your bladder broken yet?' Stan continues, a smidge quieter.

There's no point chastising him for his rudeness. Veronika has no idea what he's saying and, even if she did, he's only articulating what Ed and I are both thinking. Irrespective of how well her bladder is functioning, this frail old lady probably won't make it to the end of the year, and although I don't want to be prejudiced, I need a babysitter who, at the very least, will remain alive through one shift. So, we fill her up with tea and biscuits, smile continuously at her and fawn over her baby pictures. Then I hand her a tenner and instruct Ed to help her down the stairs and put her in a taxi to take her home.

Half an hour later, our next potential suitor arrives.

Sam has it all: official qualifications, new-born experience and first-aid training. She's in her early-thirties, casually dressed without a stitch of make-up on, and is sporting one of those trendy pixie haircuts.

'So, Sam, tell us a bit about yourself,' I say, squeezing Ed's knee in excitement.

'Excuse me, but do you have a penis or do you have a fah-gina?'

'Stanley! Gosh, I'm so sorry, Sam.' The blood rushes to my cheeks and I pray for the floor to swallow me whole. 'He likes talking about body parts. Please ignore him.'

'Don't, um … don't worry about it,' she says, shifting uncomfortably in her seat. 'Kids will be kids.'

'A penis or a fah-gina?' Stan repeats, determined to get an answer.

'Shhh! Stan, stop! Go and get your sticker book and let me speak to Sam in peace.'

'I think penis,' he says nonchalantly before wandering off to his room to find his book.

She slides all the way back in her seat and clamps her hands together. 'Well, um, that's one I've never heard before.'

'So sorry. Biscuit?' I dangle the plate of cookies in her face and she accepts. 'Please, Sam. Go on.'

'Okay, well, I am fully trained with a level 3 NVQ in early years care and education, plus I have plenty of new-born experience. My sister-in-law had twins last year and she's only down the road in Twickenham, so I help her and my brother out a lot.'

'Oooh, how lovely!' I say, totally thrilled, even though I have no idea what a level 3 NVQ is.

'And I'm fully trained in Makaton, plus I love music and play the guitar,' she continues.

'Fantastic!' I gush, even though I have no idea what Makaton is.

'I've just got married,' she continues, 'and my wife lives in Africa.'

'Africa?'

'Yeah. We're waiting for the paperwork so I can join her in setting up a new orphanage in Burundi. We're hoping it will come through any day now so I can get going.'

Well, why are you here, Sam? Just to brag about your qualifications? Dangle them in my face and then snatch them away from me along with the last of my Oreos? An outrageous tease you are! Just get out, and take your fancy Maka-whatever and guitar-playing skills with you.

When I woke up this morning, I was stupidly confident that a Mary Poppins or a Mrs Doubtfire was going to waltz through our front door and sweep Stanley off his tiny feet. But as time goes by, it's becoming increasingly clear that I'll be lucky to find a candidate with four functioning limbs and decent bladder control who actually plans to stay in the country for more than five minutes.

A while later, I'm ripping open the next packet of cookies to replenish the empty plate on the coffee table when the buzzer goes.

Zzzz. Zz. Zzzzz. Zzz. Zzz. Zz … Zzzzzzz … Zzzzzzzzzzz … Zzzzzzzzzzzzzzz …

'STOP!' screeches Stanley. He charges down the hallway with balled-up fists knocking on his temples. 'Stop it! Stop!'

I dash to the intercom and lift the handset to put an end to the incessant racket. 'Hello? Hello?'

'Hiiii! It's me,' comes the shrill voice on the other end of the intercom. Zzz. 'Can you hear me?' Zzzzz. 'Hello? It's Claudia. Sorry I'm late, I lost track of ti—'

'Yeah, okay. Okay! Can you stop hitting the buzzer? Just come on up – the door's open.'

'I've had a hell of a night!' I hear her say as she slams the front door closed and stomps up the stairs and around the corner to where I'm waiting.

'Claudia?'

'Claude, hi. So, yeah, I'm *sooo* sorry I'm late. It's a long story.'

With bloodshot eyes, cheeks stained with running mascara and stringy blonde hair that's crying out to be brushed, the girl looks rough.

'So, I was in Crazy Larry's last night. Have you been? It's immense! They do two for one on cocktails on weeknights, so I thought, perfect! You're only down the road, so I may as well swing by here on my way home – save me going back and forward, right?'

I blink repeatedly, my eyes instinctively trying to spare themselves from being blinded by the light bouncing off her silver sequinned dress. 'Oh-kay. So do you, um, want to come on in and meet Stanley? He's waiting for you.'

She walks through the door, stops briefly to kick off her stilettos, then follows me through to the living room where Stanley is now under the dining table, clutching his sticker book.

'Stan. Claudia is here. Do you want to come over and—'

'Oooh! Are these for me?' Claudia butts in when she clocks the plate of cookies on the coffee table.

'Sure, um, help yourself.'

'Great! I'm *starving*! I was going to pop to Greggs but they stop doing breakfast at eleven, and the Central Line was …' She pulls off her jacket and casually tosses it on the sofa while she waffles on, then grabs the bottom of her dress and tries to pull it down a bit, but it doesn't budge. It's short – like, barely covering her essentials short – and I pray that she is wearing a robust pair of knickers underneath. The thought of a stranger's scantily clad undercarriage sitting on my furniture is just too much to bear.

'Sit anywhere,' I say, but point towards Ed's old, shabby recliner.

She grabs a thick wedge of cookies off the plate and plonks herself down onto the chair. 'Are you putting the kettle on?'

I manage to squeeze out a 'Yeah. Of course. Tea or c—?'

'Coffee would be *immense*,' she says while throwing out a thumbs up in my direction. 'Black, extra strong, no sugars. Thanks, hun.'

When I return from the kitchen with the drinks, she is nattering away *at* Ed, who had made the mistake of introducing himself before I could warn him. He feigns interest by nodding and tutting, but doesn't stand a chance of getting a word in edgeways.

'Here you go, Claudia.'

'*Claude*,' she says without looking up. 'My mates call me Claude.' She takes a quick swig of her coffee and continues to witter on to Ed about the 'insane' delays on the Central Line, how the escalator at Notting Hill was broken and how she had to take the stairs 'in heels!'

I glance over at Stanley, who is chewing the collar of his T-shirt, his little body rocking ever so slightly.

'Okay. Let's get started, shall we?' I say, urgently.

I sit next to Ed on the sofa opposite and skim down my list of questions that I've saved on my phone. 'So, Claude, you said in your email that you've recently graduated, right? Remind me, what did you study?'

I instantly regret the question.

Every detail of her work experience from the last ten years spews out of her mouth in one long, breathless monologue and my head is left spinning. Is she a professional Instagrammer or a hairdresser? A make-up artist, a fitness instructor or a 'sandwich designer'? I literally couldn't say. But what I do notice is there's no mention of any work experience involving children.

'And what about working with kids?' I cut in sharply. 'You said in your email that you've done a fair bit, right?'

'Yep.' She straightens up in her seat and crosses her legs. 'I did half a year in a nursery in Paddington and three months at another one in Vauxhall.' She bites into a cookie but half of it breaks off and lands on the floor, so she uncrosses her bare legs and bends over to retrieve it. For a split second, I'm reminded of Sharon Stone in *Basic Instinct* and pray that Ed and me aren't about to get a flash of her beaver. I squeeze my eyes shut to protect them, and when I open them, I watch her shove the fallen cookie back in her mouth before she starts rattling off the name of every child that she has babysat since she was fifteen years old.

It's Stanley who finally puts a stop to the madness. 'Stop talking!' he shrieks. He crawls out from under the table and crosses the floor, stopping only when he reaches Claudia's feet. 'Stop talking, stop talking! Stop!'

Miraculously, that does the trick. The girl is stunned into silence. Sweet, blissful silence.

'Stan,' says Ed gently. 'Don't be rude to Claudia. That's not very nice, is it?'

'But she is *so* loud!'

Stan and his sensitive ears are right. Claudia is loud – foghorn loud. But there's more going on here. She is restless, she is unbearably overconfident, she is irritatingly animated. Hell, she's practically bouncing off the walls.

Seconds later, I decide that enough is enough. I can't listen to any more of her yabbering, nor do I want to sit back and wait for her to snort up the last of my cookies with a rolled-up fiver. I thank her politely for coming, tell her that I'll be in touch, then show her out and listen to her prattle on as she makes her way down the stairs and out the front door.

An hour after she leaves, I'm scrubbing the sofa with Dettol and blitzing the air with lemon Febreze when the heavens open and down floats a pure angel of God. She is a fresh-faced young woman with a wide smile full of pearly white teeth. Her name is Amy.

Amy tells us that she is a student and is planning to graduate and become a children's nurse in two years' time. She presents a folder stuffed to the brim with references and photos of the other families she's worked for, and a quick flick through the file leaves me feeling positively ecstatic. She's a girl who takes small kids to the Natural History Museum, the park and the swimming pool all by herself; one who bakes cookies, makes sculptures with PVA glue and isn't afraid to get the paints and brushes out. There are no needle marks on the inside of her arms, no offensive tattoos, and she smells of washing powder, not illegal substances. Throw her medical training into the mix and, boom, I'm in the presence of a bona fide Supernanny!

When Stanley discovers that she is a nursing student, he immediately comes out from under the dining table and bombards her with questions about organs. He slowly flicks through his picture book, telling her all of the things that he knows, then he gets out his bag of toy organs and, after she sterilises her hands, he actually lets her hold his gall-bladder. Judging by how he bounces on the spot and flaps his arms, I know that she is an immediate hit.

Jack's test is simpler. He sits on her knee and playfully slaps her chest whilst giggling. The fact that she isn't remotely fazed by being groped with a set of tiny mitts clinches the deal. She is a natural – gentle, sweet and caring – and definitely not a nanny who will shake your child to death in a fit of all-consuming rage.

Again, thanks for the article, Judith. Very reassuring.

I spend the rest of the day googling 'Amy Forrester' and click on as many of the 3,940,000 results as I can before Jack wakes up for a bottle. From the articles that I've read, there are no violent crimes or unexplained child deaths associated with her name. No warrants are out for her arrest, and there are no explicit pictures of her half-naked up a pole on Instagram.

After speaking to three of her former employers and getting a character reference from her old biology teacher, I feel perfectly satisfied. I make the call and book her to start next week.

I'm finally going to be a YES woman.

29

Independence Day

'Excuse me, but what if her hands are dirty?'

'Amy is a nurse, Stan. So she always has to make sure that her hands are very, very clean.'

'What if she makes my fish fingers wrong?'

'She won't. I heard that Amy is the best fish-finger chopper in the whole of London, so I know that she'll make them perfectly.'

'What if she doesn't like intestinines?'

'I don't think anyone likes *intestines* as much as you do, but maybe you can teach her all about them and she might love them too.'

Stan and I spoke about Amy as much as possible in the run up to her first visit. In an attempt to arouse his curiosity about her, I loaded his little brain with questions that he might like to ask, hoping to extinguish his anxiety about being left alone with her.

'I wonder what Amy eats for breakfast?' I said. 'Do you think she likes chocolate pancakes and yoghurts? Or maybe she has bananas and bagels?'

'I think bananas. But I think she likes them in circles and not semicircles.'

'Well, you must ask her when she comes, Stan. And what do you think her favourite chocolate is?'

He shrugged his shoulders.

'I have a feeling that she likes Maltesers,' I said chirpily.

'I like Maltesers because the packet is red, and red is my favourite colour.'

'I bet she likes red too,' I said. 'I wonder if she also likes gall-bladders like you do, Stan?'

'I don't know.'

'Well, you must ask her when she comes and you'll find out.'

By the time Amy arrived for her first session on Saturday afternoon, Stanley was waiting in the hallway with a long list of questions that had taken him most of the week to compile. The second I opened the front door, his words shot out of his mouth like popcorn exploding from a hot pan. 'Excuse me, but do you like intestinines? What is your favourite colour? Do you like Maltesers? What is your favourite shape?'

'Stan, Stan,' I interrupted, 'let's wait for Amy to come inside and take her coat off before you ask all of your questions, shall we?'

He nodded stiffly and waited, his clenched fists gently knocking on both sides of his forehead. Amy walked through the door, pulled her denim jacket off her shoulders and handed it to me, which gave Stanley the green light to continue his interrogation. 'Do you like your bananas in circles or semicircles? Are you actually the best fish-finger chopper in the whole of London? Do you like McFlurrys? Would you rather eat a burger with ketchup or a burger without ketchup?'

He took a short gulp of air and continued all the way to question number twenty-one, after which he paused and waited for her reply with his eyes glued to her shoes.

'I'll tell you what, Stanley,' she said softly, 'how about we go and sit together with Jack on the sofa, and I will answer all of your questions after your mummy goes to work? Okay?'

He took her outreached hand. 'That is okay.'

But it was more than okay. So very much more.

Amy's first stint was an absolute jaw-dropping triumph! In the short time that I was out playing string quartets for some diamond-smothered socialites, she sent cute photos of the boys to reassure me that they were in good hands. My favourite was of Jack sleeping with the caption 'Dreaming about my mummy', and the other was of Stanley making a model of the human body using dried pasta, red paint and PVA glue. When I arrived home, Stanley was sitting next to her on the sofa eating his yoghurt with a spoon (all by himself!), and she told me that he'd also helped her to feed Jack.

The flat was immaculate too. The dishwasher had been unloaded, the clean washing folded and the bottles sterilised. She'd even stacked up the loose change from the bottom of the fruit bowl in order of size and left it on the window sill in the kitchen. The young woman had achieved more in three hours than I had in nearly five years, which weirdly made me happy and not jealous at all.

Two weeks have since passed and Amy has been over several more times after I've said 'YES!' to every work opportunity that has come my way. I've played string quartets at an exhibition in a swanky art gallery (where I spotted Elton John eating a lobster and avocado hors d'oeuvre!), I've recorded some student compositions at the local university, coached the cello section of the Ealing Youth Orchestra and serenaded a bunch of brides down the aisle.

Although my workload has more than quadrupled due to the amount of physical and mental preparation that I've had to do before leaving the boys, it has been worth it. Thanks to Amy, I've put on proper clothes, left the flat, conversed with adults and actually made my own money doing what I've trained years to do. The scales are more balanced and I now feel that I could take on the world as a fully functioning working mum.

(And Red Bull addict.)

I want to scream it from the rooftops for all of the world to know:

I LOVE YOU, AMY!

I LOVE YOU, I LOVE YOU, I LOVE YOU!

I love her in the way that a little girl loves her new best friend. I want to brush her hair and give her a French plait, to play Barbies with her and to eat Curly Wurlys and watch *The Little Mermaid* together. She's not just fun, kind and a total hit with Stanley and Jack, but she has given me the best gift that I could have ever wished for: my independence.

30

Horror on the Dance Floor

A busy working week has flown by and I've been juggling more balls than a circus performer. My brain has been firing on all cylinders, all day, every day, making sure that everything is running like clockwork.

Pack for the gig, text Amy final details, wash Stan's favourite T-shirt, stock up on potato waffles, shave pits, PELVIC FLOOR, email Miguel about the gig, pluck brows, get Ed to take bins out, change tampon, pay nursery bill, put Stan's body parts in Milton, pluck solitary hair from left nipple, buy formula, defrost lasagne for dinner … go, go, PELVIC FLOOR, go!

Just as I'm starting to settle into this new chaotic role as a working mum, it all goes to shit when I receive a nasty message from the bank telling me to check my balance. Horrified that I've taken my eye off one of my balls, I log in to my account and discover that every penny I've earned so far has gone straight into Amy's pocket. My balance is in the reddest of reds, and given the dire situation, I've had no choice but to ask Judith to come and watch the boys tonight so Ed and I can go to Jen's engagement party.

She arrives after dinner carrying two grocery bags from Waitrose containing the absolute essentials that she needs to keep herself alive overnight: herbal tea, organic bananas, natural Greek yoghurt, a bag of mixed seeds, dried apricots and a Snickers bar.

'Snickers?' I say. 'Ooh, you're a rascal, Judith!'

'Yes, well, everyone deserves a little treat every so often, Lucy,' she says defensively. 'It's when you start treating yourself *every* day that it becomes a problem.' She smiles, rubs my shoulder and then opens the kitchen cupboard to put her groceries away. 'Glad to see there's no Pot Noodles in here, it looks like Edward has taken my advice.'

(Actually, he hasn't. If she peered into the recycling bin outside the flat then she would have been faced with the full extent of Ed's nocturnal Pot Noodle addiction.)

I leave her rummaging through the fridge looking for expired products while I straighten my hair and cake on foundation. I am ready in under five minutes and manage to escape the flat before she can pass comment on the fact that I'm still wearing my maternity jeans.

Eager to see all our friends for what is to be our first night out together in months, Ed and I practically run to The Lodge. He pushes through the door first and is immediately accosted by Fit Ben, who throws one arm around him and plonks a pre-ordered pint in his hand. He's going to be there for the rest of the night blathering on about the impending American tour and I need a drink down my gullet pronto, so I wade through the crowd to the bar, where I find Charlie holding a glass of what looks like water.

'God, what's happened to you?' I say. Her complexion is stark white and her eyeliner has run under her eyelids. 'You look rough, Charls.'

'Well, thanks a bunch, mate. I *am* rough. Think I may have a bug or something. I just puked in the toilets.'

'What, again? What is it with you puking lately?'

'I know. I can't catch a break.'

'Keep away from me, in that case. I've already exceeded my vomit-mopping quota for the day. Tonight's my night off. Away, demon, be gone!' I say as I make a cross of my fingers and hold them up to her face. 'Where's Tom? And Jen – have you seen her yet?'

'She's over there in the corner with Maz and So Jung. They're already on the shots, I think, and Tom's on his way. He finished work a bit late.'

She burps, then swallows hard. 'Ugh. Got to … go.'

She chokes and pushes through the crowd with her elbows to get to the toilets, and being the fabulous friend that I am, I leave my place in the queue and follow her to assist. With a packet of baby wipes and hand sanitiser in my bag, I'm prepared for the impending vomit, as any mother would be.

Twenty or so minutes later, after holding Charlie's hair back over the toilet bowl and dispensing a ridiculous amount of wipes, she's feeling better and is ready to return to the party.

'So, what's the deal?' I say. 'Reckon you've eaten something dodgy?'

'I guess so,' she replies casually as she reapplies her lipstick. 'Everything I put in my mouth these days is dodgy.' She winks. 'But if I had to narrow it down, I'd say it was the prawn sandwich that I bought from that place on the Broadway that did it.'

'What place?'

'Y'know, the place on the corner that sells batteries, random ornaments, plantain, hashish pipes, milk and … prawn sandwiches.'

The girl is a moron. Most intelligent human beings would avoid prawns at all costs after what happened the last time she ate them, but not her. And buying a sandwich from a questionable establishment – one that's probably been sat on the shelves for weeks past its sell-by date – is even more stupid.

'Tom is here. He's just texted!' She stuffs her make-up back in her bag, poofs up her hair and checks herself over in the mirror quickly. 'Got any gum and perfume, Luce? I stink like a Sumo-wrestler's thong here.'

'Um … yeah,' I say, mildly disgusted, and hand over my bag for her to help herself.

With the stench obliterated thanks to my minty gum and Marc Jacobs Daisy, we head back out to the bar to meet her new beau at last.

'There he is – Tom!' she shrieks animatedly.

A hunky stallion of a man with floppy sandy-blond hair turns around and smiles over in our direction. As he walks towards us, I study his handsome, chiselled face and within seconds a gush of hot blood hits my cheeks.

'Hi, Lucy, I believe we've met before, but in very different circumstances.' He smiles warmly and then leans in to kiss me on the cheek.

It is Dr Tom. My Dr Tom!

The hot doctor who sewed up my mangled vagina minutes after giving birth to Jack! The hot doctor who I'd asked to clarify whether he'd passed GCSE Textiles! The hot doctor who entered the room moments after I shat on a fecking table!

'What are you ladies having to drink? It's on me,' he says, pushing his floppy fringe off his forehead in one cool, sexy motion. 'I've had a hell of a day so shall I get a couple of bottles of wine?'

Charlie nods and strokes his arm affectionately. 'Yep. Pinot Blush. Thanks, hun.'

I shoot her a look of venom and elbow her hard in the back. 'Why didn't you tell me?' I yell furiously into her ear over a thick wall of sound being blasted out from the speakers overhead.

'I was going to, I *really* was ... I—' and just like that, her mouth drops open in shock. Cupping her hands over it, she bolts back to the toilets to offload the rest of her stomach lining and leaves me to face the fanny doctor alone.

Tom returns from the bar with a tray full of wine and crisps and lays it down on the edge of the nearest table. 'Where's Charlie?'

I grab a glass off the tray and neck the whole lot in one go. 'Toilet.'

He smiles, flicks his fringe off his face once again and lifts his glass up to toast my empty one. 'Cheers!' he says. 'Nice to see you again, Lucy. So, how's the little one?'

By 'little one' I can only assume that he's talking about Jack, and not my vagina. He of all people knows that my 'little one' is now a massive one (although probably not as massive as it could have been if it wasn't for his expertise with a needle and thread).

'Oh, you mean Jack?' I eventually reply, distracted by thoughts of my Grand Canyon vagina. 'Yes, he's great, thanks. Super cute by day, but the Antichrist by night.'

He laughs briefly, then sips his wine and refills my glass.

Silence follows: the *most* awkward of silences. In a room filled with drunken people singing, chatting and dancing, I simply don't know how to converse with this gorgeous man. All I can think is YOU'VE SEEN MY FANNY!

211

As I struggle to string together a sentence that doesn't involve using the words 'fanny', 'roadkill' or 'Predator', Jen pushes through the crowd gripping a tray of shots in her hands.

'You're here!' she screeches excitedly. 'Lucy, get one of these down you, love. Where's Ed? And who's this?'

I knock down two of the shots in one go before introducing her to Tom.

'So, *you're* Tom.' She shakes his hand and scans his whole body from top to toe, unashamedly soaking in every ounce of his ridiculous beauty. '*So* nice to meet you. Gosh, so you're a doctor, right? What kind of doctor? Charlie hasn't told us.'

He looks over at me and with a slight smile says, 'Obstetrician.'

'That's *so* amazing – to spend your days delivering babies.' Jen is positively swooning and bombards the man with questions about his job and he reciprocates by asking about ours, but I struggle to make a decent contribution.

Out loud, my mouth is saying, 'Oh yes, we must, um, see if we can get you tickets to one of our concerts,' and, 'Yeah, that's right, Ed is, uh, off on tour in a couple of days' – but inside my head, I'm composing a new West End musical entitled *You've Seen My Fanny*, the set design of which is a giant pair of spread legs and, dancing in between them, a row of sexy needle-wielding doctors.

Not even two more shots and the rest of the bottle of wine can stop the lyrics from forming in my overactive brain.

You have seen my fanny. Oh no! What shall I do?
You have seen my fanny, but did you see me poo?
You sewed up my fanny, with your needle and your thread,
And 'cos you've seen my fanny, I now wish I was DEAD!
La, la, laaa, la, la laaaah!

31

The Visitor

Needless to say, the engagement party doesn't go quite as planned. Charlie eventually emerges from the toilets greener than Kermit, and she's right, she does reek how I imagine a Sumo-wrestler's thong would. Tom, having fulfilled his boyfriend duties by chatting away in a blissfully charming manner with us, insists that he take her home. She leaves early with her hot man on her arm and the rest of my chewing gum in her pocket.

I don't see much of Ed at all. As usual, he's transformed himself into his mega-social mode and spends the whole night downing pints and gearing up for his tour with his buddies. His banter is so animated that, despite the pumping music, I can hear every word he says from the other side of the room. He, like Stanley, hasn't quite grasped the concept of the indoor voice, but in a busy bar, he can get away with it.

Still shuddering from my embarrassing encounter with Tom, I sedate myself with as many large glasses of Pinot Blush as I can tolerate and cringe into Jen's earlobe for hours.

'I wouldn't worry,' are her words of reassurance, 'he probably sees a million fannies a day in his job. I mean, fannies to him are like wanker bankers to us, right? Eventually, they all start to look the same.'

After last orders, Ed and I resist following the rest of the party to Crispin's Wine Bar for more drinks and head home at a reasonable hour to limit the grief that we'll undoubtedly get from Judith.

It takes several attempts to get the key in the lock, and when we finally do, we stumble through the front door and into the lounge where we are greeted by the most incongruous sight: Judith and our neighbour Alan, sitting on the sofa sipping tea!

'Oh, you're home!' Judith says in a weirdly chirpy tone. 'Did you have a lovely time?'

'Hi, guys. Har yooouu both?' Ed slurs, completely unfazed by the fact that Alan is cosied up to his mother on the sofa.

'Hello, Ed,' Alan replies politely. He subtly shifts away from Judith. 'I just stopped by with a parcel for you, Lucy. I signed for it yesterday when you were out and noticed that your light was on, so I popped over to drop it off.'

'Lucy, did you know that you'll be getting speed bumps on the street soon?' Judith interrupts. 'Alan here has sorted it out with the council. It's such a wonderful idea, don't you think?' She smiles across at him with her head tilted to one side, tensing her lips to form a self-conscious pout.

'Yes, Judith. I know. Alan *has* said. Anyway, how were the boys tonight? Did they go to bed okay?'

'And did you know that he's recovering from knee surgery?' she says, gazing directly into his eyes. 'I'm on the waiting list myself. And I don't feel nearly so frightened about it, now that I see how well you're doing, Alan.'

I try again. 'Judith, the boys – how were they?'

'It's not nearly as terrifying as I imagined it would be,' says Alan. 'I really do think it will give you a whole new lease of life. You'll be back doing cartwheels before you know it.'

Judith throws back her head and releases an irritatingly high-pitched giggle.

'How were the kids tonight?' I finally snap.

'Goodness me! I heard you the first time, Lucy. They were perfectly fine. No problems at all.'

'So Stan didn't get upset about the light switches and make you kiss all of his numbers goodnight?'

'Not at all. He had a moment of silliness about washing his hands, but I dealt with it. I really do think you pander too much to that boy, Lucy. But I'm not his mother so it's not for me to say.'

'You're right,' I say through gritted teeth, 'on both counts.'

'Anyway, I'll leave you all to have a catch-up. I still have to sort out my recycling, so I'd best be off.' Alan stands up, pulls his lilac V-neck jumper back down over his slight belly and reaches out his hand to Judith. 'Delighted to meet you, Judith, and thanks for the tea and the wonderful company. Perhaps see you again next time you visit?'

'Absolutely. Let me show you out,' and she follows him to the door, poofing up her hair as she goes.

An obligatory cup of herbal tea later, I grab my parcel and slip off to bed leaving Ed to deal with his mother. Ripping it open, I find the new bottle of Marc Jacobs Daisy that I'd ordered online and fall asleep wondering if Dr Tom had noticed this sweet smell that day. Was it strong enough to block out the stench of my bowels exploding on the table in front of him and his colleagues? Was he even in the room for that part? I can't remember, which is probably a blessing.

Nightmares of the most graphic kind follow and will probably continue to do so for the rest of my natural life.

*

Charlie finally picks up her phone at lunchtime the next day, which gives me the chance to let rip after having had an awful night's sleep. (Let's just say that the horrendously vivid dream I had in which a team of Chippendale-esque doctors were eaten by a giant fanny with razor-sharp teeth wasn't exactly pleasant.)

'How could you not tell me, Charls?'

'Well, I'm much better today, thanks for asking. I've not puked since 3 a.m.'

'*Don't* change the subject. I want to know how? How did this come about? When? *How?*'

'*Okay!*' she puffs. 'Well, after you gave birth and were off having a shower and stuff, I popped out around the back of the hospital for a fag to calm myself down. And he was there.'

'What? Smoking?'

'Hell yeah, loads of doctors smoke, y'know. Anyway, we got talking. Had a laugh. Had another fag, and before I knew it, I was offering him a comp ticket to see my *Star Wars* gig at the Albert Hall.'

'And ...? Then what?'

'Well, he actually came to the gig and we went for drinks afterwards. He was funny, interesting – had great stories and stuff.'

'Spit it out, woman!'

'Chill, Luce! Basically, one thing led to another, and the next thing I know, I'm pressed up against the wall in the gents' toilets of The Gloucester Arms. And it's sort of grown from there.'

'Gawd! So, how come you haven't mentioned it after all these months?'

'I couldn't make my mind up about him for ages, so I didn't see the point. And, to be fair, I've hardly seen you. You've been so busy with the kids and everything, but look, you know now and it's all cool, right? The pussy cat is out of the bag!'

'Don't even talk to me about pussies!' I cringe. 'Ugh. I hate you!'

'Don't be a dick, Luce. If it makes you feel any better, he's seen my pink taco too, y'know.'

'Pink taco? You're *sick*, woman!'

'It's just a vagina,' she continues as I make a mental note to bin the Old El Paso taco kit that I bought on special offer in Tesco the other day. 'He's seen thousands, Luce. Damn, I bet he couldn't even pick yours out of a line-up.'

And now my revulsion at tacos has been rapidly replaced by the image of a row of gruesome-looking fannies standing in a line-up at the police station.

'Ask your mum, she'll tell you the same. She's seen the taco of every woman in your village, hasn't she?'

The girl is right. My mum can't walk into the local Co-op to buy a loaf of bread without bumping into a woman whose smear she's done.

'If you want, I'll flash mine to Ed and then we can call it even.'

'No way! He doesn't need reminding of what a fanny is supposed to look like. He's married to *me* so he has to accept that he's stuck shagging roadkill for the rest of his life.'

'Poor Ed. Roadkill!' She howls with laughter. 'Well, let's just all go out for dinner together soon and you can get to know Tom. He's a really good laugh … and *smoking* hot, you have to admit.'

'Too hot. Far too hot.'

*

Judith leaves after lunch, but only once she's emptied the washing basket and finished up the last of my washing powder, which was nearly full when she arrived yesterday. In just twelve hours, she's used more electricity washing and tumble-drying our clothes than it would take to light up Oxford Street at Christmas. A terrifying bill will undoubtedly arrive next month as a result.

'The basket is now empty, so Edward has everything he needs for his tour,' she says proudly just as she's walking out the door. 'And don't forget to make him a nice lunch to take on the plane. Plane food is full of additives.'

'Yes, thanks, Judith. Rest assured, I'll remind him to make *himself* some lunch.'

I spend the rest of the afternoon helping Ed pack for his tour after he's wound himself up into an anxious mess. He slams drawers closed, pulls clothes out of the wardrobe and throws them in a pile on the floor, then stomps up and down the hall, angrily muttering, 'Where's my black shirts? And my tie – the thin grey one? Plugs? I can only find the European ones – that's just *great*!'

'Where's Mr Happy gone?' I snap back. 'Where's last night's life and soul of the party, eh? Please, Ed, let's have him back.'

'And my passport?' He totally ignores me and continues tossing things around the room like a mad man. 'It's not where I normally keep it.'

It never fails to amaze me how performing on-stage to an arena filled with fifteen thousand people doesn't faze him in the slightest, but the simple task of putting a few items into a suitcase is what it takes to break him. Sometimes, the man is a mystery to me.

'Ed, enough! You're just packing a suitcase – hardly defusing a live bomb. You *must* calm down.'

'I am calm!'

'Indoor voice,' I say on autopilot.

'I *am* calm,' he then whispers, his fingers drumming repeatedly on his chest.

'Look, I'll pack – you watch the kids.'

He exhales and his shoulders drop. 'You sure?'

'Yes. Please, just relax before you drop dead of a heart attack, for God's sake.'

I fill his case, pack his hand luggage and write him a list of last-minute essentials that he mustn't forget while he lies on the floor with Stan in the hallway, helping him to categorise his cars in order of colour. I make him a packed lunch for the plane, then once everything is ready I head out to work – this evening's gig being another corporate event playing quartets at the Savoy.

Looking across the ballroom at the dance floor rammed with bankers gyrating under a giant crystal chandelier, I realise that Jen is right. Once you've seen one wanker banker, you've seen them all.

The same *must* be true of vaginas.

32

Bon Voyage

The floodgates open this morning when Ed's Uber rolls up on the driveway to take him to the airport. I've known that this day has been coming for ages, but that doesn't stop me from crumbling into a pathetic heap of snot and tears. It's stupid really, he's been away plenty of times before, but this time it feels different. Now, he isn't just leaving me, but he's leaving *us* – his wife *and* two kids.

I stand in the hallway holding Jack and have one last lingering kiss with Ed before he nips into the lounge to say goodbye to Stanley.

'Bye, little man. See you soon. Daddy will try and bring you back some new body parts from America, okay?'

Engrossed in a YouTube video as usual, Stanley doesn't look up or say a word. Ed smiles and blinks away a light film of tears, then wanders back into the hallway, kisses Jack on the forehead and lugs his guitar and suitcase down the stairs to the cab.

'Don't get too drunk,' I call out to him, a standard warning that every muso wife gives to their spouse before they head off on tour.

'I won't.'

'And don't forget to call.'

'I won't.'

'And don't forget to WhatsApp me a dick pic in case I start to lose interest.'

'Maybe, if you're lucky,' he yells out before I hear the front door close.

And just like that, he's gone.

After gnawing my way through an entire family-sized bag of Chilli Heatwave Doritos in front of the telly, I decide to get a grip. No more self-pity. No more staring in misery at the Ed-shaped dent in the recliner. No more scrolling through Facebook aimlessly filling out quizzes and uploading photos to determine what I'd look like if I was a cat.

Life must go on.

I open the curtains and I'm immediately blasted in the face by the scorching heat of the summer sun. Back in the day, this glorious ball of fire in the sky meant only one thing: Ed, Charlie, Jen, Will, Niall, Fit Ben and *pub*! But now, it means something entirely different. It means that for the sake of the healthy development of my small children, I'm obligated to drag my sorry arse out to the park. I wipe the salty-red residue off my lips, throw on some clothes and, an hour of preparation later, head out down the street with my tiny companions, a bag of body parts and a bottle of hand sanitiser. En route to the park, we pass Starfucks.

I peer through the window and spot Marsha with her gang of mum friends, gassing away to each other as their kids sit quietly drawing pictures and nibbling on muffins. I hover outside and toy briefly with the idea of going in and introducing myself to Marsha's chums, but stop and reverse my pram away from the door. I just can't bring myself to do it. Not today.

Upon arriving at the swings, I'm met with the usual tedious scene: a long queue of red-faced parents being headbutted in the crotch by their toddlers as they wait their turn. Stanley immediately sets up camp on the picnic bench with his bag of body parts while the other kids his age throw themselves off the wooden climbing frame like a pack of wild animals. Seeing that he is perfectly content, I lift Jack out of his pram and join the queue, but ten minutes later we're still standing there, my back on the verge of splitting in half as we wait for a distressed woman to pull her feisty toddler out of the swing. The child just *doesn't* want to leave and, despite his mother's best efforts, all the rice crackers in the world aren't going to trick him into letting go of the chains.

'I have some Cheetos here – would he like one?' I offer in an attempt to be helpful.

His mum shoots me a look of disgust, like I'm offering him a line of cocaine. 'No, thank you. *We* are just fine.'

Just as I'm about to abandon ship and run home with my tail between my legs, I glance over and see Stan sitting on the bench talking to a little boy. It's Emmanuel, the boy from his nursery. I leave the queue with Jack and discreetly make my way over to stand behind the climbing frame, where I can eavesdrop on their conversation.

'Do you want to see my body parts?' Stan says.

'Okay!' Emmanuel replies sweetly.

'This is the heart. It is very good because it is red and it beats like a drum.'

'Can I hold it?'

'Have you washed your hands?'

Emmanuel nods his head and, just like that, Stanley gives him his heart.

'Excuse me, but do you want to hold my kidneys too? They look like baked beans and they help you do wees.'

Emmanuel nods again and gently takes the kidneys from Stanley's hand. He examines them up close through his thick blue-rimmed glasses and gently prods them with his finger. 'They are so squashy.'

'And they are a bit slimy too.'

'Do you want to go on the slide with me, Stanley?'

And his reply floors me. 'Yes. Yes, Emmanuel. Yes. Yes.'

He carefully bags up his body parts and then runs over and shoves them into my hand. Without saying a word, he hurries back to the slide and climbs on, his little companion following up the ladder behind him. A juicy tear runs down my cheek and hits the floor before I have a chance to catch it. I mop up the next one with my sleeve, take a deep breath to compose myself, then scan the grounds looking for Emmanuel's mother.

A pretty young woman, no older than twenty, is sitting on a bench on the far side of the park glued to her phone. Every other woman is either holding a baby, pulling a kid off the climbing frame or loading shopping bags onto prams so, by a process of elimination, I decide that she must be Emmanuel's mother. I approach with caution, just in case I'm wrong.

'Hi, are you Emmanuel's mum by any chance?'

'Oh, no.' She laughs. 'I better change my moisturiser. Sister – I'm his sister.'

'God, I'm so sorry. I took a gamble – a pretty bad one, I guess.'

'Don't worry about it. Really. I'm Ayesha,' she says, holding her hand out to shake mine

We chat briefly and I learn that she's in her first year studying accountancy at the University of West London around the corner and often brings Emmanuel to the park when she has free periods. We sit together and watch the boys climb the slide over and over again and soak up the abundance of joyful energy in the atmosphere. By the time she has to leave, I've managed to give her my number to pass on to her mother so that we can arrange an official playdate.

She calls her little brother over and hands him a banana to keep him entertained while she re-ties his shoelaces.

'Bye, Stanley,' he says, 'I'll see you tomor—'

'I want the iPad,' Stan cuts in breathlessly. His fringe is soaked in sweat and his cheeks are glistening pink.

'Stan. Say goodbye to Emmanuel first.'

'Goodbye to Emmanuel first,' he pants with his back turned away from him. 'Excuse me but I want to play Chinese numbers now.'

'Yes, I know. You can play it on Daddy's iPad when we get home. Say "Nice to play with you" to Emmanuel before we go.'

'Nice to play with you to Emmanuel before we go,' he says, mimicking my voice exactly, and we leave.

Approaching the exit to the park, my heart bursting with joy, I spy Marsha and her entourage strolling in, holding their Frappuccinos. She waves and gestures for me to go over and there's no way to avoid it.

'Hi, Marsha. Look, we're in a bit of a hurry, we need to get back to—'

'Lucy! This is Jane and her son Matthew, and this is Amelia and her son Fre—'

'SHITTY!' screeches Stanley, his voice so startling that she leaps back like she's been electrocuted and drops her Frappuccino on the ground. He yanks his hand out of mine and scampers through the gates towards the bus stop where the number 17 bus is pulling in. Without thinking, I lunge into a sprint, leaving Jack's pram behind on the path, and fuelled by an intense rush of adrenaline, I manage to grab him by his collar just before he reaches the bus stop. I lift him up and he punches my chest and yells, 'It's shitty! Shitty!' in my face as I lug him all the way back across the green to get his baby brother.

Marsha and her party are standing on the gravel, gawping at us in total disbelief, but I choose to ignore it.

'Sorry about that, ladies,' I say.

'Not to worry.' Marsha smiles uncomfortably, dabbing the spilt coffee off her floral skirt with a wet wipe.

'He just really wants to get home to his Chinese number— um, his game.'

'Lucy, a word of advice,' she says sweetly. 'I hope you don't mind me saying but you might want to nip that language in the bud before he starts school. Ealing Primary has a strict policy about the use of bad language, and I wouldn't want him to get in trouble.'

One of the other mums nods and the other two look away.

'Don't worry, it's under control.' I force a smile and leave with my heart throbbing so furiously that I can't tell if I'm going to drop dead or suddenly go on a mindless killing spree using my nappy bag as a weapon.

My bra is off, pyjamas are on and five Jaffa Cakes are down my gullet within minutes of arriving home. Stanley slathers his hands in sanitiser then disappears to his room to watch his Chinese number videos. As he happily yells

'Shi-ty and shi-tio' (known to mere mortals like Marsha and her friends as numbers seventeen and nineteen) from the other end of the flat, Jack and I lie snuggling on the sofa nibbling our treats.

Minutes later, on this day where my heart has been subjected to the highest of highs and the lowest of lows, three glorious little syllables fall out of Jack's chocolate-stained lips: 'Mu, Mu, Muh.'

In this special, glorious moment, I realise that I am his world.

And both he and Stan – my Chinese-chanting darling – are mine.

33

The Tour Bubble

Six days after Ed left, I was still waiting for him to call. Cursed with my mother's colourful imagination, I'd alternated between all of the worst-case scenarios which might have explained his silence.

He'd been mugged and beaten to a pulp on the streets of Seattle and was now lying in a hospital bed in an induced coma (his iPhone having been sold down a back alley somewhere by a meth-head wearing knuckle-dusters).

He'd fallen in love with a backing singer – a busty blonde with a penchant for small bald men, who doesn't nag him about leaving his dirty pants on the floor. Perhaps he hasn't left his five-star hotel room in six days after discovering that she too is an Action Man collector, and they are now ensconced in a mammoth play session where they're lining up their dolls across a four-poster bed.

Or, and this is the one that troubled me the most: he'd forgotten about us.

It's now day seven and I'm fully immersed in the pool of negativity. My conclusion is that he must be having the time of his life and we, his family, are long forgotten. Thankfully, my sister Rachel is on her way for a 'surprise visit', which essentially means that my mum has sent her to London to check that I'm not falling apart without Ed (which, evidently,

I am). She's travelling up from Wales with my nephew George and is due after lunch, so while I wait for her to come and rescue me from my own imagination, I spend the morning mindlessly filling out 'Should I get divorced?' questionnaires online.

Of course, I don't want to get divorced, but until Rachel arrives, I have only Google to guide me, and it turns out that it is quite the pessimist.

Google's response to my plight:

94%: You SHOULD get divorced!

The right man is out there for you, so don't waste any more time staying in a bad marriage. Get some girl power and get out of there, girl!

Trade in your slime for someone sublime!

The result devastates me. The thought of splitting up with Ed and having to move back to Tref Y Glaw to raise our kids in a grotty bedsit is beyond unbearable.

And Ed? What if, heartbroken by our split, he ends up out-of-his-mind pissed, then has a meaningless orgy with a group of twenty-year-old backing dancers, contracts syphilis and dies a slow, painful death where we have to bury him in a closed casket to protect his young sons from the trauma of seeing his lifeless, sore-ridden corpse?

I'm sure that he'll call eventually. It *has* only been a week, and I must remind myself that by now he'll be firmly embedded in the 'tour bubble'. In my rational mind, I know this and I have to accept it, having been in that same bubble *many* times myself over the years.

Only musicians can truly understand the intensity of the tour bubble. Take a group of musicians, be it a rock band or a symphony orchestra, and then subject them to the following: airport calls at 4 a.m., pints for breakfast in the Wetherspoons at Heathrow and long-haul flights where they suffocate on the farts and smelly socks of two hundred strangers.

On arriving in a random country where they may not speak the language, they have to try and order edible food in a restaurant where none of them understand the menu or the currency with which they are paying. Everyone then boards the tour bus where they have to sit/sleep/shit in front of each other for periods often in excess of twelve hours, until arriving at the next city.

By far the hardest part is having to put their jet lag to one side and walk on-stage to perform like superstars in front of thousands of people who have paid hundreds of pounds to see them. Nothing but their best effort is expected so they focus what's left of their energy on delivering the goods. After the show comes the let-down: the beers, the shots, the obligatory hob-nobbing with the artist and record label representatives before they have to somehow find their way back to their hotel, remember their room number and fall asleep in a strange bed. The next morning usually involves throwing everything they own in a suitcase before jumping back on the bus to repeat it all over again (but only after they've sourced the equivalent of Alka-Seltzer and Imodium from the nearest chemist – not so easy to do if you are in the likes of Wuhan or Senegal).

It's fair to say that if you do these things day in and day out with the same group of people, you all become close. You become totally immersed in this bubble together, where all that matters is the quality of your hotel, the price of a local beer and what time your lobby call is the following morning.

The adrenaline of the previous night's gig keeps you going, even though you haven't slept properly in days. You have more beer in your body than blood, you've run out of clean pants, you've forgotten which city you are in – sometimes which country – and you haven't eaten a meal that your digestive system can tolerate since you left home.

With all of this going on, your real life fades away. You forget about the life you left behind. You forget the people you love. You forget about your gas bill that needs paying, the due date of your car's MOT and your emails that are awaiting replies. All you can focus on is the gig and the people around you who share in the madness of it all.

That is why Ed hasn't called.

I know it, I understand it but I'm struggling to embrace it, because I'm not just a tour wife any more: I am a tour *mother* too.

I guess I thought this would change things, but clearly it hasn't.

34

View from a Bench

'Whoa! What's with your hair? You're one split end away from looking like you've been electrocuted!'

Rachel's first words when she arrives with George are exactly what I'd expect from her.

I totally blank her. 'Hi, Georgie,' I gush. Making a big fuss of him, I ruffle his hair and lean down to blow a raspberry on his neck. 'I've got a cupboard full of goodies for you. But go and say hi to Stan first – he's waiting for you in his room.'

He scampers straight down the hallway, leaving me to retaliate as best I know how. 'Yeah, Rach, so Grandad just called – he wants his shoes back,' I scoff as I eyeball her sensible brown-leather sandals.

She punches me in the arm, calls me a twat, then hugs me. 'Get me some scissors and I'll sort you out,' she says.

Rachel did a night-school course in dog grooming back in her twenties, so she's just about capable of giving my straggled mane a trim. My hair hasn't been cut since before Jack was born, so I figure that a hairdresser for dogs is better than no hairdresser at all.

Stanley is terrified of haircuts, so I grab us a couple of Diet Cokes and a pair of rusty, blunt scissors from the kitchen drawer, then we lock ourselves in the bathroom out of sight. I sit on the toilet and she hacks off nearly a year's worth of dead hair while filling me in on the latest gossip from Tref Y Glaw.

Hot off the press is the news that Ozzy the sandwich man has been caught cheating!

'Dai Chops saw him through the window of the Dragon House and took a photo of him in the act,' Rachel tells me. 'Then he posted it on the Facebook community page so now everyone knows.'

'God! And what did his wife say when she saw it?'

'Claire was well miffed, of course. I mean, getting busted scoffing down a whole tub of chow mein with his bare hands? Not good. Especially when he'd spent a mint buying up every bit of meat and avocado in the village for his keto diet.'

'Not to mention the pork scratchings!'

'I know! Literally everyone is ripping the piss out of him now. Poor fella.'

In other news, she tells me that Bungalow Baz has apparently been back to fix our parents' conservatory floor, but he ended up talking our gullible dad into hiring him to paint their spare room as well. Mum is beyond livid. And, most shocking of all, Kelly Ann Evans – a girl from the year below me at school – is about to become a grandmother for the second time.

'No *way!*'

'Way!' she says. 'A grandmother, *twice*, at thirty-two. You couldn't make it up!'

Ten minutes of haphazard trimming later and my hair is finished. 'Done,' says Rachel, 'have a look and see what you think.'

I stand in the bathroom mirror flicking around what's left of my mane, trying to get it to sit right. 'It's not quite "show poodle", is it?'

'More like "rescued terrier", but it's still better than it was.'

Once Jack wakes up from his nap, Rachel suggests that, in light of the baking weather, we should all head out to the park. George has been sitting in a car for three hours and is desperate to burn off some steam, like any ordinary seven-year-old, so I've little choice but to agree.

Stanley is less enthused. 'I want to play body parts!' he screeches, then scrunches his face up in a tight ball. I've noticed that he has been doing this repeatedly over the last week – since Ed left, in fact – and after doing some googling, I've convinced myself that he either has extreme anxiety or he has a tic and is developing Tourette's syndrome. Either diagnosis is not good.

'Stanley, stop pulling that funny face. Why do you keep doing that?'

He doesn't reply and continues to scrunch his face involuntarily whilst drumming his fists on his chest.

'Leave him alone, Luce. He's fine.' Rachel throws her arms around him and gives him a gorilla hug, which makes him laugh and calms him instantly. 'Come on, kid, let's go to the park and I'll buy you a toy on the way home.'

Her offer swings the deal and we leave the flat without a huge drama, for a welcome change.

Sand is one of Stan's major repulsions, so when George makes a beeline for the sandpit, I brace myself for a potential ordeal. The ghastly stuff is right up there on Stanley's list of 'YUCK!', sharing the number one spot with Johnson's baby shampoo, wrongly shaped bananas, broccoli and haircuts. I'm just about to suggest an alternative place to go when, to my absolute delight, I watch him casually follow George into the pit without any objections.

'I can't believe it!' I gasp.

'Can't believe what?'

'He hates sand, Rach – like, *hates* it with an absolute passion. Normally, he freaks if he goes anywhere near it.'

'Well, he *loves* it now.' Rachel smiles. 'Tick that one off the worry list and chill out. He's fine … he's happy.'

Ability to touch sand: TICK. Now I just have to get him to look at me when I speak to him, to hold a conversation about something other than anatomy, to stop washing his hands every fifteen minutes, oh, and the newest worry: to stop his face twitching.

'Maybe I do worry too much.'

'No shit! You're borderline hysterical … as usual. But, to take the edge off, I gift unto you this bad boy.' She opens her bag, pulls out two cans of gin and tonic and dangles one right up close to my face.

'Rach!' I snatch it out of her hand and swiftly tuck it in between my legs. 'We're in the bloody park, woman. With three kids! What will people think?'

'People?' She shrugs. 'What people? It's just a little treat that I picked up at Reading services. I'm on my holidays, aren't I?' A wicked glint sparkles in her eye. 'Just hold your hand over it and it'll look like a can of pop.'

I scan the park quickly: there's no policeman, no priests, no social workers and not a single Yummy Mummy in sight, so I discreetly open the can and take a sneaky sip. The shame of it!

Dressed in cheap leggings and cami vest tops, we sit like rebellious teenagers on the bench swigging our cans of gin and tonic, witnessing the sheer miracle of George swinging Stanley around by his arms in a pit filled with billions of grains of sand.

I moan about Ed and how his life is all Hollywood-glamour and mine is more Shitsville-broccoli-vomit. I obsess about

Stanley's obsessions, whine about how I miss *drinking* wine with my friends and blather on about my failing career, my lack of sleep and my protruding pot belly.

Performing her assigned role on this planet as my older sister, Rachel delivers her best nuggets of wisdom to help me pull myself together. 'Forget about the size-ten waist,' she says firmly. 'Only Victoria Beckham has strolled out of a maternity ward with one of those, and that's because she was a size minus-fifty to start with.'

She lifts a tube of BBQ Pringles out of her bag, tears off the lid and swings the tube over in my direction. 'For now, focus on keeping alive so you can raise these kids, and if that means eating crap all day, then do it. Lettuce isn't going to get you through it.'

I look down at my gut that I've tucked into my maternity leggings, release a sigh then pull a thick wedge of crisps out of the tube and stuff them all in my mouth in one go.

'And cut Ed some slack. The man is out *working*,' she continues. 'Yeah, he's probably getting hammered most nights and lying around most of the day, but that's what musicians do, isn't it? And what if he had no gigs and was sat around the flat stinking up the place, eh?'

'I'd be freaking out even more about money, I know.'

'Yep, of course you would. And, Luce, I'm not being funny, but if your friends are all too busy to see you, go out and make some new ones. There's got to be other weirdo-creative types around these parts.'

'"Weirdo-creative"? Thanks for that, dickhead.'

'And quit moaning about work, for God's sake. You'll be back working stupid hours soon enough and you'll wish that you'd enjoyed this time to hang out with your kids. You'll never get this chance again – believe me, I know.'

When George was only eight months old, Rachel was offered a promotion to office manager. By accepting the job, she was forced to cut her maternity leave short and put him in a nursery for ten hours a day to be looked after by strangers. It's only since becoming a mother that I fully understand just how hard it must have been for her.

'Thank God I took that promotion now that I'm single. I'd be screwed without it.'

My guilt is immediate. 'God, I'm such a moany, selfish bitch.'

'Yep. You're a major twat.' She smiles and swigs her gin. 'As usual.'

'So, um, how's it all been ... flying solo?'

'Well, if you ask Mum, I'm "lonely, sad and miserable and in need of a nice wee man to keep me company", but the truth is I'm great,' she says. 'It's just me and my little boy and that's the way I like it.'

I squeeze her thigh and force a smile to mask the sadness that has suddenly consumed me. 'You're amazing, Rach.'

'And do you know what? So is Stan,' she says. 'I don't know any adult, let alone any *kid*, who can say the alphabet backwards and talk about colons in such detail. And, before you start, *no*, he doesn't have Tourette's, you total nutter.'

'He might have it!'

'I have one word for you, Luce.' She pauses dramatically and looks me straight in the eye. 'Syphilis.'

And we both start roaring with laughter.

As teenagers, we used to spend rainy afternoons flicking through my mum's old nursing manuals, entertaining ourselves with gross pictures of infected testicles and warty bum holes. Then one day, I found a weird sore on my bikini line and was driven in a panic to the manuals for answers.

I diagnosed myself with syphilis within five minutes and howled with tears all over Rachel's shoulder.

But in the end, it turned out to be an ingrown hair.

'I mean, syphilis!' She squeals and spits her gin out from laughing so hard. 'You haven't changed at all!'

I slap her on the arm and yank the tube of Pringles out of her hand. 'Shut it.'

A shrill interjection slices through the joyous atmosphere like a machete. 'Hiiii! I thought that was you – Lucy!'

Startled, I turn around to find Marsha standing over my shoulder with Hugo by her side, nibbling a stick of celery.

'What is that? Gin and tonic?' Her lips instantly shrivel up as she glares at the tin of shame in my hand. 'Having a rough day, are you, ladies?'

'Not at all,' I reply casually, trying my best to appear innocent, 'quite a good day, actually. Marsha, this is my sister, Rachel. We're just sat here chewing the fat.'

'Hello.' She smiles wryly, quickly eyeing Rachel up and down. 'Look, Lucy, I can't stop as I have to get Hugo to yoga by 4.30. I just spied you and quickly came to drop off an invitation for Stanley. It's Hugo's birthday next week.'

'Great, thanks,' I say as I take the silver envelope.

'Yes, it's definitely not one to miss. All of their new classmates for next term are going to be there. So far, twenty-seven have RSVPed.'

'Really? Twenty-seven? Wow. How do you know what class they'll be in already?'

'Oh, I have my ways, Lucy,' she says as she taps her temple with her index finger. 'Let's just say that I have a "friend" who has access to the right files. I can't say any more, or I shall have to kill you.'

'No! No! No! NO!' bellows Stanley from over six metres away. He runs over and catapults himself on to my lap. 'You are *not* killing! You are not killing!' His face is twitching uncontrollably.

Startled, Marsha leaps back and instinctively pulls Hugo behind her.

'It's just pretend, Stanley, just *pretend*,' I say, but he won't listen. The boy is seemingly blessed with the gift of bionic hearing, but fails to *listen* to anything that is being said. He becomes hysterical and squeezes his arms around my neck so tightly that strangulation is imminent.

'I'd better go. Sorry to cause upset, Lucy. Hope to see you at the party.'

'Looking forward to it,' I lie.

Marsha leaves behind a scene of devastation that takes over fifteen minutes to dissipate, but once we've convinced Stanley that no one is going to kill me, he skips back to the sandpit to play as if nothing has happened.

With order restored, Rachel reaches into her bag and pulls out two more cans of gin.

'Ding, ding!' she says. 'Round two.'

35

Let's Pretend

The kids scoff down a typical beige dinner of chicken dippers and Smiley Faces, and with full bellies, they're perfectly content to lie on the floor and play with the new toys that Rachel bought them. George chose a crappy plastic truck, and after digging out Stanley's Marvel superhero figures from the bottom of the toy box, he's now engrossed in a game in which Spiderman is fighting the Green Goblin.

'You can run but you can't hide. Take *that*, Goblin!' says Spiderman, unleashing his web and throwing the Goblin onto the bonnet of the truck. 'You are one ugly dude, Goblin!'

Stan lies quietly next to him on the rug lining up the numbers from the puzzle that he chose, his face now twitching constantly. We already own several copies of the same puzzle, but he refused to leave the shop without another one, and for once, I didn't try and persuade him to choose a shitty truck like George had. He wants what he wants and I've accepted that buying anything else is pointless. We have boxes full of trucks and expensive action figures which only see the light of day when George comes to visit, after all.

George lifts Stanley's numbers two and three off the rug and plonks them in the middle of the large stain that's still there after my unfortunate Blue Shit incident a couple of months ago.

'Help us, Spiderman! Help!' cries George dramatically. 'The Goblin is going to drown us in the pond!'

Stanley freezes and glares in horror at the sight of George touching his numbers and I can see his brain ticking over, deciding if he is going to flip out. But then his frown relaxes and a big smile follows when Spiderman dives into the pond to save his numbers from drowning.

'Here comes eight and nine walking to the pond, when BANG! The Goblin throws the monster truck on them, and it squashes them so bad that their brains and guts fall out. Nooooo!'

'No!' yells Stan, genuinely appalled.

'Pretend,' I interrupt, 'it's just *pretend*, Stan.'

He allows my words to sink in and forces a slight smile.

'Get me the four, Stan,' says George excitedly. 'He's going to fall off a tower, and you can be Spiderman and you've got to save him with your webs.' And, to my delight, Stanley hands over his favourite number, then lifts Spiderman off the rug and joins in.

I don't realise that I'm weeping until Rachel climbs out of the recliner and comes over to hug me. 'See, Luce, I told you. He'll be just fine.'

The boys play for ages in the bath then head to bed holding their favourite toys: the truck and Green Goblin in George's hands, and numbers four and eight *and* Spiderman in Stanley's. Distracted by the exciting presence of his cousin, he doesn't ask for his stack of foam numbers to be kissed goodnight, nor does he request his red dummy. I leave the room with the biggest of grins on my face, and a few more tears gathering on the rims of my eyelids.

'Lights!' he calls out just as I'm closing the door.

'Yes, love.'

'Lights! Lights!'

'Okay. Here they come.' I flick the switch. 'One, two, three, four. Now, goodnight to you both. Love you.'

Rachel and I spend the rest of the evening doing what we love most: eating Chinese takeaway, drinking cheap Prosecco and watching *Legally Blonde* for possibly the four hundredth time together. It's been a great day and we have much to celebrate. Stanley has played perfectly with his cousin, he's miraculously overcome his fear of sand and he's been invited to a birthday party – his first-ever invitation to date. Things are looking up for him at last and I feel my shoulders drop down to their natural position for the first time in months.

A bottle and a half of Prosecco down, Rachel pauses the TV. 'Is it time?' she says. ''Cos I'm feeling tipsy and if you want it doing, then it needs to be now.'

I tiptoe down the hall and pop my head into the boys' bedroom to confirm that they are both out for the count. 'The time, dear sister, is now.'

Armed with a pair of scissors and a comb, Rachel crouches over Stanley's bed and trims his locks as he snoozes away, totally oblivious to the fact that a terrifying set of deadly shears are just inches away from his face.

'A little more off the fringe,' I whisper.

'Shine the torch here, I can't see.'

'That's it. Just whip it off, quick, before he wakes up,' I hiss.

'Shhh! Don't stress me out! Just let me do my thing.'

Rachel trims away six months' worth of Stanley's hair and, seeing as she's there, I make her cut his finger- and toenails too. I brush up as much dead hair and nail clippings as I can see in the dark and dispose of it so he won't learn of our illicit behaviour come morning. When she's satisfied that she's done her best, we creep out of the room and crack open the gin to celebrate our cunning victory.

'Cheers Rach, you legend!'

'Cheers! And yes, I *am* a legend.'

It is the best of days.

36

The Funky Raccoon

'Lucy. *Luce!* Have you checked Facebook?' Rachel bursts through the bathroom door and whips back the shower curtain with such vigour that half of it tears free from the hooks.

'Jesus, give me a minute. I'm naked here!'

'Get out,' she squeals. 'You're going to want to see this, trust me. Come on!'

I turn off the shower, quickly wrap a towel around myself and take the phone which she dangles in front of my face impatiently.

On the screen is the latest status update from Fit Ben:

> **Ben Johnson** is with **Ed Wright** and 4 others at **Montage Beverly Hills.** 10 July at 02.35 a.m.
> Excellent gig in LA tonight. Here's my best mate Ed, renamed the 'funky raccoon' by THIS legend!

My jaw drops when I see the photo that Ben has attached. 'Holy *shit!*'

It's Ed, my 'funky raccoon', and he is hugging legendary American rocker Steve Tyler!

'See! See what I mean?' Rachel shrieks, clearly on the verge of having an orgasm. 'Can you believe it? Ed with

Steve Tyler! Do you remember that massive poster I had of him on my bedroom wall?'

'Of course I do, and do you remember the day I caught you snogging it? You freak! Your mouth was stained black with the ink from that poster for weeks.'

'Like *you* can talk!' she scoffs. 'I believe that it was Dave Grohl who you abused back in the day. Poor bastard.'

I haven't a leg to stand on here because she's right. Like every other girl in my class, I fine-tuned my snogging skills on a Foo Fighters poster when I was a teenager, and my own mouth was stained blue for a good few months.

'You've got to call Ed *now*. Do it, do it! Find out *everything*.'

Still soaking wet and half-naked, I wander through to the bedroom and she follows, hot on my tail, thirsty for details. I lift my phone and call him on loudspeaker, knowing that she won't be satisfied unless she can hear every word first-hand. To my surprise, he actually answers.

'Steve Tyler! I just saw you with Steve Tyler,' I yelp before he has a chance to say a word.

'Hi, love,' he croaks, then coughs to clear his throat.

Rachel is practically standing on my feet, rapidly fanning herself with an old copy of *Heat* magazine. 'Ask him what he's like. Ask him. Ask him!'

'*Okay!*' I hiss and lift a pillow off the bed and whack her with it. 'Ed, Rach is here with me and she wants to know what Steve Tyler is like before her head explodes.'

'He's nice,' is all he says.

Rachel tuts, clearly dissatisfied, and tries to snatch the phone from me, but I slap her away with my free hand and lose my towel in the process. I awkwardly twist down to retrieve it and cover myself up. 'We're going to need *way* more details here, love. Like, how did you meet him?'

'What do you mean?'

'How. Did. You. Meet. Him?' I repeat a little louder.

He pauses briefly then, in a blasé manner, says, 'Yeah, he watched our gig and I met him at the party afterwards.'

'Ask him what he said – ask him!' Rachel says.

'Okay, Rach. *Shhh!*' I hiss again. 'Ed, Rach wants to know what he said.'

'He, um, shook my hand and said that I played like a funky raccoon and then bought me a beer ... a Budweiser.'

'Oh my GOD!' yells Rachel. 'You're a rock star, Ed!'

The fact that he hasn't called in days has completely vanished from my mind. I'm just so elated to hear his voice at last. Bollocking him will only crush the excitement, and an encounter with one of the most famous rock stars in the world isn't something to be brushed over.

'I've got to be quick,' he continues. 'How's Stan, is he okay?'

'He's great. Like, really *really* great. He's been playing with an actual Spiderman toy, thanks to George.'

Ed suddenly springs to life. 'Has he? Brilliant! Tell him that I've got all of the vintage Marvel stuff in my wardrobe. Go and get it out now, but just make sure that he washes his hands before he touches anything though, okay?'

'Of course, love. I know the drill,' I say dismissively, 'and just to let you know, I've paid the water bill. It was over three hundred quid so the joint account is looking grim, and the electric and gas are coming up next week. Any idea as to when you're getting paid?'

'There's a Spiderman in there, and a Sandman, Dr Octopus and Scorpion, and you can try him with my Batman figures too,' he continues, having not heard a word of what I've just said, 'and if you go to the top of my wardrobe, there's an orange box with ...'

Now that we've moved on from Steve Tyler, Rachel has totally lost interest. She mouths the words 'Want a coffee?' and, with the *Heat* magazine tucked under her arm, she slips out to put the kettle on. Once she's gone, I turn off the loudspeaker and interrupt Ed who is still rattling off a list of all the superhero toys he has stashed in his wardrobe.

'That's all great. I'll dig them out, love. Anyway, tell me how the gigs are going.'

He exhales sharply. 'Until last night, good. But then I fucked it and played an F sharp instead of an F natural.'

'Crisis!' I tease, knowing that he's probably been in a total rage for the last twelve hours since this horrendous mistake. 'Even funky raccoons make mistakes, Ed.'

'I'm still fucking *furious*.'

'You'll get over it,' I say warmly, then quickly steer the conversation in a different direction to cheer him up. 'So, I *have* to know, have you fallen in love with a smoking-hot backing dancer called Cherry by any chance?'

'Cherry? I don't think she's on this gig,' he says in total seriousness. 'Maybe Ben knows her?'

I tut, my eyes rolling back a full 180 degrees in their sockets. 'Never mind.'

He doesn't say it in so many words, but I can tell from his voice that he's homesick. If he was standing in the room with me right now, I know that I would get much more out of him because he's a much better conversationalist in person and often it's impossible to shut him up. If a stranger stops him in the street and asks for directions, they'll be there for ages listening to him list the best local pubs to visit and usually I'll have to intervene to help the poor bastard escape. If I was to ask him the quickest way to get to central Edinburgh from the arse-end of England, he'd perform a long-winded monologue detailing every single A-road and motorway that I should take, without needing to look at a map.

Ask him anything about music, Oscar-winning films or *Star Wars* and you'll be stuck for hours listening to a stream of detailed facts about each of them. But pick up a phone and ask him how he is and you'll get very little, even nothing, out of him.

'Before I go, is there anything you need from the airport?' he continues.

'Do they sell new vaginas? Or bottles of sleep? Or maybe a fat-shrinking cream? I've about forty-five stones' worth of cakes and pies hanging off me right now.'

'Shall I just bring some gin?'

'Good enough.' I smile, knowing that no matter what I ask for, it's guaranteed that he'll return with a Toblerone. Nine years ago, I made the mistake of casually mentioning that I liked them and ever since he brings one home any time he's passing through an airport. Every. Single. Time.

'Oh yeah, coming. Coming now …' he calls out to a muffled voice in the distance. 'Love, I've got to go to sound check.'

'Okay. I love yoooou.'

But my rock-star husband, the funky raccoon, is already gone.

37

Nutter!

Rachel and George leave just after lunch. Over the weekend, I've seen tremendous progress in Stanley's behaviour and I know it's down to George's influence. He is Stan's hero and by copying his every move, Stan's actually played with 'normal' toys, made up imaginary games and conversed about topics other than gall-bladders. On top of all of this wonderfulness, he's somehow been cured of his involuntary twitch.

'Look!' I say to Rachel as we sit watching the kids have one last play over a can of Diet Coke. 'Have you noticed that Stan's twitch has stopped? Like, *totally* stopped.'

'Yep.' She nods, a big grin sneaking on to her face.

'It must be because he's so relaxed around you two. It's … a *miracle*!'

She bursts out laughing and takes an age to stop. 'No, it's *not*, you total dick. It's because I trimmed his fringe.'

'What are you saying?'

'I'm saying that his hair isn't in his eyes any more, you dumb ass!'

'So he's not got Tourette's?'

'The poor kid just needed a haircut. Please, for the love of God, stay away from Dr Google.'

And oh, how we laugh.

After they leave, I distract myself from my new-found solitude by preparing for Hugo's party next weekend. I'm weirdly motivated by the whole thing, and more than determined to make sure that Stan has the time of his tiny life.

Sprawled out on the sofa in my pyjamas, with greasy hair piled up on top of my head and my big toes sticking out of holes in my mismatched socks, I log on to Amazon Prime and start searching for the most impressive gift for Hugo that I can afford. I order a remote-control dinosaur and team it up with T-Rex wrapping paper and a card that roars 'Happy Birthday' when you open it. It's pricey but I'm going *all* out to make sure that Stan and I are accepted by Marsha, her gang and, more importantly, their kids.

With the basics covered, I just need to start work on preparing Stanley for what's coming: a room full of strangers, popping balloons, mixtures of smells, unfamiliar foods and games that he may or may not win. In short, I have six days to train him how to cope in a room packed with all of his biggest triggers.

I fashion the ultimate plan: every day for the next six days, we'll practise playing pass the parcel together. It will, of course, be rigged so that Jack wins one day, Stanley the next and myself the next and, hopefully, by the time we get to the party, he will be more accustomed to the concept of losing. I'll also show him some YouTube videos of parties so he'll have a better idea of what to expect, plus we'll do role-plays where I can give him ideas of things he can say to the other children when he meets them for the first time. My entire strategy might sound ridiculous, but this party will be full of his future classmates, so I'm not leaving anything to chance.

As I scroll through the Amazon website buying up small toys to wrap for our party-game practice, I receive a text from my pregnant friend Emily – a fellow cellist who I haven't seen in months on account of my being housebound with young kids.

> Lucy! Have gone into labour early! 😲😦 Have a gig tomorrow that I need covering. Solo cello in Guildford (will send postcode). Radio broadcast playing a few seconds of Bach Suite 1 Prelude. Arrive 7.15 a.m. Goes out LIVE at 8 a.m. I have no info about what to wear so just go with standard concert black in case there's a camera there. Fee £225. Are you free? Pretty please. Em xx

From pyjamas and holey socks to black gowns and heels, oh, how everything can change in the blink of an eye!

A live radio broadcast for national radio!

£225 for a few seconds' work!

Some national exposure to give my dwindling career a boost!

My gut tells me to say no. It's too short notice, I'm too rusty and the thought of playing a solo on the radio makes me want to soil myself. But once I've inhaled two KitKats and given myself the chance to calm down, I'm able to get a grip and accept that Rachel is right: I *am* becoming a nutter. I've had far too much time on my hands to obsess over Stanley. I need to get out and do something with my life before I end up diagnosing him with rabies or some other ridiculous disease. This is a proper opportunity to perform classical music, not a background gig or a hideous video shoot. So, against every natural instinct that I have to hide under a duvet, I call Amy to check that she is free to watch the kids then grab the bull by the bollocks and text Emily back to accept the gig.

With the plans changed, I devote the rest of the afternoon to blowing the thick cobwebs off my cello playing and frantically practise Bach as Jack rugby-tackles my ankles and screams for attention every ten seconds. I doubt it's how Yo-Yo Ma prepares for a solo radio broadcast, but it is what it is. Until I can afford a full-time nanny and a purpose-built practice studio in the garden that I don't have, I'm just going to have to wing it and hope that I don't play an F sharp instead of an F natural.

Because that, according to Ed, would be a *tragedy*!

38

F**k My Life!

So, in short, I *earned* my £225.

I played the solo. Live. On national radio ... for chickens.

Hundreds, if not thousands, of beady-eyed, wattle-flapping, clucking *fucking* chickens!

The 'exclusive' ground-breaking live broadcast turned out to be a seventeen-second feature about an unexplained phenomenon that has baffled the world's greatest scientists for decades: do chickens lay more eggs when exposed to classical music?

I didn't stick around long enough to find out the answer, but what I can say, with full confidence, is their arseholes *definitely* become far more relaxed when exposed to a few arpeggios. I've got a pair of chicken-shit-encrusted diamanté heels in the boot of my car to prove it.

At midnight, after a truly disgusting day which has put me off McChicken sandwiches for life, I discover via a Facebook post from Emily's husband that their baby has been born.

 Welcome to the world, **Archie Benjamin Adams**. Born at 10.15 p.m. weighing 9 pounds and 4 ounces. Mother and baby doing well!

A gorgeous picture of a wrinkly new-born boy wearing a pure white babygro is alongside the caption, which has already generated over 457 likes since being posted two hours ago.

As I lie in the dark with the stench of chicken dung still embedded in my nostrils, I find myself having a little chuckle at the classic line that all new dads write on Facebook: 'Mother and baby doing well'.

Doing well, my ass!

I know for a fact that the current scene in Emily's maternity ward will be that of chaos. I can just picture her propped up on some pillows with a set of rock-hard watermelon boobs, desperately trying to get her baby to latch on to nipples that are bigger than his entire face. Her colostrum will probably be extracted manually to start with, and if her experience is anything like mine was, the poor girl will end up with a team of midwives queueing around her bed most of the night as they take it in turns to have a tug on her udders.

It's a good job that I'm highly experienced in the aftermath of childbirth. Because of this, I'm sympathetic to Emily's plight and choose not to unleash the rage that I feel towards her after tricking me into doing her horrendous chicken gig. The girl owes me one. In fact, she owes me a new pair of diamanté heels and a tenner towards my dry-cleaning bill.

But screw it, I'll cut her some slack.

It's what us mums do.

Come Friday, solo chicken gigs and Emily's watermelon boobs have long vanished from my mind. It is Hugo's party tomorrow and I've been so busy training Stanley for *the* social occasion of his life that I've had no free brain space to think about anything else.

The party-game practice has, of course, been an absolute disaster. We had a go at musical statues on Tuesday, but he couldn't seem to grasp the idea that the prize is given to the competitor who can stand still the longest. Every time I paused the music, he froze briefly but became so excited that his limbs took on a mind of their own and flailed about until he lost his balance and fell over. Pass the parcel has been even more disastrous. The boy is the ultimate sore loser, and even though one of the prizes was *his* chocolate pumpkin lolly that had been gathering dust in the cupboard since Halloween, he still collapsed on the floor in a howling rage when he didn't win.

'I want to be number one. Number one!' he squealed.

I tried to reason with him. I said all of the things that you're supposed to say in such situations, but repeating 'it's the taking part that counts' on loop just didn't fly, and by the time we started round two, he was in such a state that I had to bear hug him for an hour to calm him down. At this late stage, I've accepted that these games aren't designed with kids like Stanley in mind. Short of calling Marsha to ask her to hire a bouncy castle in the shape of a gall-bladder, there's nothing more I can do to ensure things go smoothly tomorrow.

After picking up Stanley from nursery, we pop down to Asda to choose a new party outfit. The games might be out of my control, but I'm still hopeful that I can persuade him to wear something other than the same grotty T-shirt that Marsha has seen him in time and time again. Thankfully, after a bit of a fuss, he chooses a red top, a pair of jeans with a red belt and a red hoodie, and once they've all made it in to the trolley, I take him down the junk-food aisle hoping to stir up some excitement.

'Look, Stan. Party rings! I wonder if Hugo will have party rings to eat tomorrow. Or maybe there'll be Jammie Dodgers. What do you think you'll get to eat?'

'Jammie Dodgers because they are red. And red is my favouri—'

'Of course,' I interrupt, 'silly question, *Mummy*. Shall we go and look at the birthday cakes and guess which one Hugo is going to have?'

'Yes,' comes his flat reply.

'And how many birthday candles will he have on his cake?'

'Four.'

'And who will blow them out?'

'Hugo. Because he is going to be four years old. But my calculator said that four years is one thousands, four hundreds and sixty days, so he might have that many candles on his cake.'

'Well, it would have to be a pretty big cake!' I laugh.

'Excuse me, but I am having a red cake in November in my party, a small intestinines one. With one thousands, eight hundreds and twenty-five candles.'

'*Intestines*,' I sigh, 'of course you are.'

And this is how I discover that I have less than four months to source a cake mould in the shape of the small intestine, one large enough to hold nearly two thousand candles.

'Let's just get Hugo's party out of the way first, shall we, Stan?' I say. 'And then we can start planning yours.'

Fuck my life.

39

Chocolate Fingers

Amy arrives at 12.30 p.m. to watch Jack for a couple of hours while I take Stanley to the party. Ed still hasn't put any money in the joint account and hasn't answered my calls since Rachel left, so I've had to delve into the emergency cash from his DVD vault to pay her. I figure that it'll be worth it to be hands-free, sharp and ready to leap into action should Stanley need me.

Both of us are exhausted and not in much of a partying mood because he's been up most of the night washing his hands.

'Excuse me, but I just touched my bum. I need to wash my hands,' he said (and did) at 4.35 a.m.

'Excuse me, but I just touched my bobs by mistake. I need to wash my hands' was at 5.05 a.m.

'Excuse me, but I just touched my bum and then touched my number four. I need to wash my hands. And my number four' came at 5.31 a.m., after which he refused to go back to bed.

His hands have been washed so many times since Ed left that they're now badly cracked and bleeding. I've tried all sorts of lotions but he hates the sensation of cream being rubbed into his skin, so the only way to cure the obsession has been to give him The Rules.

'Stan,' I've said repeatedly, 'there are *three* times when you need to wash your hands. Number one: after going to the toilet; number two, before and after you eat a meal; and number three, if you have been doing messy play.'

I'm hoping that if I continue to repeat these rules several times a day for the foreseeable future, then eventually they might stick and his hands will have a chance to heal.

He's been dressed in his new party outfit since 6 a.m., but it's only several hours later, when we are walking out the door, that I notice the hole he has chewed through the sleeve of his new red hoodie.

'Are you okay, Stan?' I say as I open the front door. He doesn't answer, but just fidgets with the collar on his T-shirt. 'Do you want to change your top and put your favourite one back on?' No reply comes, so I close the door and rush to his room and lift his freshly washed favourite T-shirt out of his drawer and help him put it on. 'Better?'

He nods and picks his plastic bag of body parts off the floor and puts them in his pocket.

'Stanley. Maybe you should leave those at home,' says Amy sweetly. 'They might get lost at the party and they'll be safer here. Jack and I will look after them for you, okay?' She holds her hand out and he lays them in her palm without resistance.

I mouth the words 'Thank you' and blow her a kiss, then, with a beautifully wrapped dinosaur under his arm, we leave to meet his future schoolmates.

*

1.00 p.m., Hugo's Fourth Birthday Party, St John's Church, West Ealing

It comes as no surprise to find that Marsha has pulled out all the stops for her son's party. It isn't a typical kiddie's birthday bash with a fat guy in a clown suit, a load of crisps and chocolate cookies slung in paper bowls and a cake bought from aisle twelve of Tesco. This do is nothing short of an extravaganza, designed to wow both young and old alike.

Multicoloured helium-filled balloons decorate the edges of the dance floor and a long table runs down the side of the hall crammed with home-made cakes labelled 'gluten free', 'dairy free' and 'sugar free'. Platters of T-Rex-shaped sandwiches are laid across the table which, at its centre, has a towering chocolate fountain with bowls of marshmallows and fresh fruit waiting to be dunked. The cake is a three-tiered volcano of buttercream icing and features a pair of fondant diplodocuses holding a little banner that says 'Happy Birthday Hugo'. It's a work of art, definitely one made by the hands of a professional.

Several eight-foot-tall dinosaurs stand in the centre of the dance floor where a swarm of sugared-up kids tug on their arms, then run away in hysterics when they retaliate with a snap. A face-painting lady sits in one corner of the hall, and a balloon modeller is in another, and at the far side is a small Dino World bouncy castle packed with rowdy children. It's a no-expense-spared production that probably cost more than the Notting Hill Carnival to execute.

Marsha is virtually on top of me the moment we arrive. She strides over in an off-the-shoulder floral maxi dress, with her hair sculpted in an elaborate messy bun, which, again, is blatantly the work of a professional.

'Lucy! You came – helllloooo! Come, you *must* say hello to Jane, Amelia, Paula, Jasmine and Francesca. We're all over here. Come,' she says, grabbing me by the elbow and pulling me in the direction of the tea station.

'Give me a sec will you, Marsha?' I say, gently shaking her off my arm.

'Okay, darling. Pop over and meet them when you're settled. I'll get you a tea, or would you prefer a can of gin?' She winks, then saunters off towards her next victim. 'Hetty, you came!'

Stanley has dumped Hugo's gift on the floor and is now hiding under my jacket with his arms wrapped around my waist.

'Shall we go and check out the table of food and see what they have?' I say gently, and when he doesn't answer, I take him by the hand and lead him past the hordes of noisy kids to the buffet.

'Look! There's party rings, chocolate fingers, Oreos *and* Cheetos – all of your favourites, Stan. How exciting! What are you going to choose?'

'I want chocolate fingers because fingers are body parts,' he says quietly, his face totally expressionless.

'Okay, we'll get some later. And look at those dinosaurs. Wow! They're amazing. I think that is a T-Rex there, and that one with the spikey back is a Stegosaurus, but I'm not sure what that greenish one is ...'

'Velociraptor,' he says a little louder, 'but not a real one because dinosaurs are all egg-stink. There's people inside those dinosaurs.'

'*Extinct*. You're right. They're just pretend, but they look so real, don't they?'

I lead him over towards the heart of the action to get a better look, and once he's spent a few minutes silently absorbing his surroundings, a genuine smile creeps across his cheeks. He drops my hand and wanders on to the dance floor to join in and I discreetly back away and watch him from the wings.

He mimics the other kids and follows from the back of the crowd as they cautiously approach the T-Rex. One boy tugs on its arm, then another daring little girl pokes its belly, and when the T-Rex finally snaps, Stan, along with his peers, dashes to safety at the far end of the hall. I can see him studying the faces around him. The more they laugh, the more he laughs, and the louder they scream, the louder he does, albeit a split second later.

With my face aching from grinning so much, I take a deep breath, straighten out my clothes and prepare to hit the tea station. It's time to meet the mums who I'll soon be standing next to in the school yard for the next seven years of my life. I can't put it off any longer.

'Lucy! Everyone, this is Lucy,' says Marsha, her voice so piercing that it draws the eye of every woman in the group. They reshuffle and form a circle around me, and I feel them eyeing me up and down with their cupcakes in hand, waiting for me to say something profound.

I wave and manage a 'Hi' then stuff both hands in my pockets.

'Take that jacket off, darling!' Marsha laughs. 'Or is that you off already, before you've even had a chance to sample my lemon meringue cupcakes?'

She comes up behind me and pulls my jacket down from my shoulders as she continues her introduction. 'So, everyone, Lucy is *Stanley's* mum and he is going to be one of the *older* boys in the year. His birthday is in November, isn't that right?'

'That's right,' I say and briefly consider telling them that he has asked for a small-intestine cake for his birthday, but quickly decide against it.

'So, essentially, Hugo is nearly a full *year* younger than Stanley! Isn't that crazy?'

'It sure is,' says one of the mums and a couple of the others nod.

'And he loves the alphabet, doesn't he, Lucy? But I'm sure you said that he's not a fan of sports, so perhaps him and Matthew won't end up being friends,' she says, turning to a blonde woman who has the figure of an Olympic triathlete.

'He's not a football kid, really. He's quiet … more of a reader, I'd say.'

'He can read? Already?' gasps Matthew's mum.

'Well, I'm sure the staff at Ealing Primary will be *very* impressed with him,' Marsha interrupts, 'but don't worry, Jane. The children aren't expected to be able to read at this age. Their first year of school is all about imaginary play, and Lord knows our kids are experts at that.'

The conversation continues in a similar fashion for a good half an hour and I play along whilst keeping one eye on Stanley. I nod and say 'wow' as they gush about the wonderful things their kids have achieved in their tiny lives so far.

'Well, Matthew supports Liverpool. He's doing so well with his football that Adrian is treating him to season tickets for Christmas,' says Jane.

'Harry swam 25 metres last Sunday,' says another woman whose sculpted eyebrows have been coloured in at least five shades darker than the hair on her head.

I say very little about Stanley, partly because no one asks, but also because I sense that this crowd won't appreciate knowing he can spell 'parallelogram', say the alphabet backwards and give a detailed account of the intricate workings of the human digestive system. There's a time and place to reveal such things about your child, and this isn't it.

To my relief, there are no party games. The entertainment is just a short interactive show given by the dinosaurs and a bearded man dressed as a ranger. All of the children, including my boy, sit on the dance floor totally transfixed by the sight of dinosaurs dancing to 'Gangnam Style', and at the end, the balloon modeller gives every child an inflatable sword that they use to attack the T-Rex. Stanley loves it, but nowhere near as much as I do.

'Time for food, everyone! Take a seat and let's get started,' shouts Marsha when the show has come to an end. 'Mums, dads, can you help with the juices, please?'

Everyone ignores her request and, instead, they scramble to the dance floor, grab their children, plonk them in a chair and start snatching handfuls of food off the table like a pack of ruthless scavengers.

'Ham or egg? Want a fruit skewer?' says one mum urgently, not waiting to hear her child's answer as she loads a thick wedge of sandwiches onto his plate. 'Blackcurrant or orange, Rishi? Answer me, please!' barks another. 'Enough crisps! Put some grapes and cucumber on your plate!'

The kids couldn't give a shit about the fruit skewers and vegetable sticks. For them, the chocolate fountain is *all* that matters and they throw themselves on top of it like a bunch of rugby players diving for the ball. Fistfuls of crisps and crackers are dunked in the waterfall of melted chocolate, even ham sandwiches, sausage rolls and bread sticks, and those who can't get anywhere near it pounce on the platters of chocolate fingers and party rings instead. It's very much a dog-eat-dog situation, so I have no choice but to grab a paper plate, push my hand through a gap in the crowd and load it up with whatever I can get before it all vanishes.

I place a plate in front of Stanley, who is sitting at the end of the table by himself looking hopelessly lost. My effort is pathetic: two egg sandwiches, one cocktail sausage, a feeble portion of broken Mini Cheddars, four carrot sticks and a gluten-free cupcake. He looks down at the plate of sadness and his face instantly crumples.

'Fingers! Fingers! Fingers!' he chants over and over again, the hysteria escalating in his voice.

I crouch down to his level and put both hands on his shoulders to draw his attention. 'It's okay, Stan. It's okay. Please calm down,' I say gently in his ear. 'Just wait there and I'll go and get some.'

In a total fluster, I hurry down the full length of the table, scanning the wreckage in search of a plate of fingers. But they're long gone.

'Marsha, Marsha. You got any more chocolate fingers?' I ask desperately.

'No, darling. I only have what's out on the table. There's a few extra party rings in the kitchen, though, and my gluten-free cupcakes have barely been touched.'

'Oh ... um, not to worry,' and with my heart thumping through my chest, I return to the table to break the news to my boy.

'Stan, my love, there are no fingers left, but there *are* party rings. Do you want party rings?'

'Fingers! Fingers! Fingers! Fingers!'

'I know, I promise I'll get you some on the way ho—'

But it's too late. He's already on the floor, thrashing around manically as the room falls silent and everyone glares down at him in shock. His screams are ear-splitting and the sound of his head cracking repeatedly against the hard wooden floor makes the sick shoot up my gullet and burn my throat.

I struggle to lift him up. His convulsions are so violent that reaching him without being kicked or punched is impossible, but I resist cowering and keep trying. One of the dads eventually steps in to help, and between us we manage to lift him off the floor and carry him through the crowd of gobsmacked parents and out into the car park. I steer us over towards a patch of grass in the churchyard and we lie him down where he can thrash around safely.

'Thank you. Thank you,' I pant. 'I've got it from here.'

'Are you sure?' he mouths, pulling his T-shirt back down over his belly then wiping the sweat from his forehead. 'Want me to stay?'

I can't hear a word over the screaming, but answer him anyway. 'It's okay. It's better if it's just me. Thanks so much.'

He smiles and I see that look in his eyes, one that I've seen many times before. The look of heartfelt pity.

I'm left lying on the grass, still struggling to comfort my child. He is totally out of control, worse than I have ever seen him. He kicks and slaps, pulls on my hair and screams so wildly that if I closed my eyes I wouldn't recognise the sound as being human. I take the punches, persist with the sharp kicks to the shins and, finally, manage to restrain him. I pull him in close to my chest, wrap my legs around his and squeeze him as tightly as I can.

We are still lying on the grass when the party is over. One by one, Stanley's future classmates leave the hall with their party bags and coloured balloons in hand, each one slowing down next to their parents to gawp at the scene before them.

Marsha and Hugo are the last to come out, carrying just my handbag and our jackets. There's no balloon for Stanley, and no party bag. She stands over me, awkwardly clutching our things, saying and doing nothing. Her presence only aggravates Stanley more, so I ask her and Hugo to leave, which they do without hesitating.

When everyone has long gone and Stanley has finally come out of it, I lift him off the floor and carry him all the way home in my arms.

It starts to rain, and by the time we reach the front door, I'm crying heavier than the clouds overhead.

40

The A Word

Stanley has been very subdued since the party. He's slept solidly two nights in a row, which is unusual, and instead of hiding away in his room with his organs, he's spent both mornings hanging out with Jack and me watching cartoons. His body parts have been gathering dust.

As I try and feed him breakfast, he pushes my hand away.

'My tummy hurts,' he says over and over again. 'It hurts.'

It's not a stomach bug. He always has the same complaint after a traumatic event and, over time, I've learnt that a hurt tummy means that he's feeling anxious and sad. His explosion at the party was particularly harrowing, so his tummy probably hurts more than usual.

'It's okay if you feel sad,' I say. 'You can have a good cry and it might make your tummy feel better?'

He pulls his legs up onto the sofa and curls up in a little ball. 'Is that why you were crying?' he says. 'When your tummy was hurting?'

'When are you talking about, Stan?'

'Auntie Charlie was wearing a blue top and she said "fuck" a lot. And you cried. And you were wearing a black top and your tummy was really big. And then you went away and came back with Daddy and Jack. After three sleeps. And your tummy was a bit smaller, but not *that* much smaller.'

The penny drops. 'Oh, you mean the day that Jack was born?'

'And I still liked letters then. But now they are only my third favourite thing because my favourite thing is body parts. And my second is numbers.'

A tear slips out of my eye and I quickly wipe it away before he can see it.

I think back to the day that I was in labour with Jack, when Stan kept nagging me to find his letters and tormented me with questions about dodecahedrons whilst I was writhing in agony on the floor. He was oblivious to the pain that I was in and, at the time, I assumed that he didn't care, that he was too wrapped up in himself to notice anything or anyone around him. But now, all these months later, he's just told me that he was fully aware of how much I was suffering that day. The way in which he can relay the smallest of details about it proves that he is sensitive and thoughtful, perhaps even more so than the average kid, but he just doesn't know how to show it.

The phone rings. Glancing down, I see a number flashing on the screen that I don't recognise and instinctively go to cancel the call. But then it occurs to me that it might be Ed, so I hit the green button, jump off the sofa and head into the hall to speak to him.

'Ed? Ed?'

'Lucy? Is that you?'

Straight away, my heart sinks. I want to slam the phone down, but it's too late. I'm committed.

'Oh, hi, Marsha,' I say, trying not to sound too disappointed.

'Lucy, my darling. How are you?' she says, her voice low and loaded with pity. 'I haven't been able to stop thinking about you, so I popped in to The Lodge and got your number from Harvey. I just wanted to check up and see if you're okay after what happened at the party?'

'Hold on a sec, Marsha.'

I hurry to the kitchen and grab a pack of Cheetos for Stan and leave him contented watching one of his videos in the living room, then go to my room at the back of the flat and close the door behind me.

'Marsha? I'm here.'

'Oh, Lucy, yes … I just wanted to say on behalf of all of us, *please* don't worry. *All* children have tantrums.'

I say nothing but start rearranging the cushion display on the bed while I wait for her to finish her commiserative speech.

'Hugo can be quite the little sod sometimes too. And I just wanted to say that I hope that you don't feel too bad about it, you know, especially because *all* of the other school mums were there.'

My knuckles turn bright white from squeezing a cushion so firmly in my hand. 'I don't feel bad at all,' I say calmly, 'just guilty.'

'Oh no, you mustn't!' she gushes dramatically. 'Please *don't* feel guilty. It wasn't your fault. We can't control when our kids have tantrums.'

'Marsha, I'm sorry, but let me stop you right there,' I say curtly. 'That wasn't a tantrum but a meltdown. Stan is autistic.'

The line goes quiet. I check the phone screen but see that the clock is still ticking, the call still active.

'Oh! Oh, gosh, I'm sorry!' she stutters. 'I'm *so* sorry, Lucy. We had no idea. I, we, I, um—'

'Don't be sorry,' I interrupt.

'No, of co— of course.'

'Parties aren't something he's used to, and I shouldn't have pushed him into a situation where I knew he wouldn't feel comfortable. It was all my fault.'

'Oh, no. Don't be so hard on yourself!' she interjects, then pauses uncomfortably, clearly struggling to find the right words. But none come.

'Anyway,' I continue, 'I hope that you and the other mums will look past what happened at the party and not judge him for the way he behaved. He couldn't help it.'

Another excruciatingly long bout of silence follows.

'Okay. Okay. Rest assured, Lucy, all will be forgotten. Stanley is lovely and I will make sure the other mums know.'

'That he's lovely?'

'No, no ... that he has autism, is autistic or ... look, don't worry. We are a *very* understanding bunch.'

'Thanks, Marsha. And thanks again for the invite. See you soon.' I cancel the call before she has a chance to say goodbye, then immediately burst into tears.

I've said it. Out loud. To Marsha. The 'A' word.

This word has been lurking in my thoughts for so long, a word that I've never had the courage to say out loud, not even to myself or Ed. And now, just like that, I've released it up into the atmosphere where the whole world can clearly see it.

My son is autistic.

41

'For Some of Us, There Is No Box'

I can't stop obsessing about my conversation with Marsha. Having broken down each word and analysed it to death, I've reached the conclusion that I've made a terrible mistake. The second I ended the call, I know she would have run straight down to Starbucks to gossip with every mum in Ealing about what I'd said over a blueberry muffin and a skinny latte. The gasping, the pity and the bitchiness would have followed, and all of it at Stanley's expense.

'Well, that must be why he's so good at the alphabet, then.'

'Poor Lucy, she has her hands full with that one.'

'I hope the school know about it. How will the teacher possibly cope with a child like him? Wouldn't he be better off in one of those special schools?'

After saying the A word, I've plummeted rapidly from blissful liberation all the way down to the dirty gutters of extreme, crippling guilt. No professional has actually confirmed a diagnosis, so have I failed Stanley by saying it prematurely? Will other kids now treat him differently and avoid him because of the label that I, his own mother, have tattooed on his forehead?

I need a distraction from my torment, so my friends are

on their way over to spend the evening finalising bits and bobs for Jen's wedding. Decent adult company is exactly what I need, and I'm hoping to fill my brain with thoughts of anything other than Marsha or autism.

'Right, most important thing first. The hen!' says Charlie the moment she steps through the door. 'Jen, brace yourself. We're off to Edinburgh! One glorious night of lifting up the kilts of hot Scottish men!'

'Brilliant!' says Jen excitedly, but I'm not nearly as convinced.

'And before you start freaking out, Luce, I've already cleared it with Ed and he's around to look after the kids.'

'What? You actually spoke to him?'

'Yep.'

'I've only heard from the man once in two weeks, and I pushed his fecking babies out!'

'Well, I *did* stalk him for eight straight days until he picked up the phone. Where hot Scots and booze are involved, I'm nothing if not committed.' She beams. 'Anyway, Jen, it'll only be us three, Jungers and Maz. Hazel's got a show and Emily is out. Apparently, she "can't leave the baby".'

'Well, Archie is only a couple of weeks old, Charls,' I say.

'So what? Life goes on. Stick a bottle in its mouth and get your ass out to Edinburgh, I say. Those kilts aren't going to lift themselves!'

'Oh gawd. What have you planned, Charlie?' says Jen, her face filled with dread. 'Am I going to end up tied to a lamp post in my pants? Or, worse, in jail?'

'The rest of the details are a secret. Just bring some party

271

clothes, a shitload of Alka-Seltzer and a stack of five-pound notes and I'll take care of the rest.'

As we drink down a fridge full of beers, we move on to finalising details for the actual wedding. I'm put in charge of kicking Ed's ass to get a band together for the reception, and Charlie agrees to round up some of our pals to play string quartets in the ceremony. The table plan is the next issue. From experience, I've learnt that sitting all the single folks together is a big no-no, especially if you want to avoid making them feel unloved and borderline diseased. Shoving all the pensioners on the same table is also bad practice; you may as well hang a banner over their heads saying 'AVOID! BORING, OLD AND SOON-TO-BE-DEAD FARTS HERE!'

'Just don't overthink it, Jen,' I say. 'You and Will both have vaguely normal families so there's not a lot you could do to mess it up. It was an entirely different ball game for us, given the Judith situation.'

Charlie starts laughing. 'You really did fuck that one up, Luce. Sitting Ed's dad between his busty twenty-nine-year-old girlfriend and his ex-wife wasn't perhaps your smartest idea to date.'

'I know. Damn,' I cringe, 'I'll never forget Judith getting obliterated on white wine and lobbing her peas at the girlfriend's 36FFs.'

'That was hilarious! The woman should drink more often. She's way more fun when she's steaming.' Charlie laughs. She reaches over to the coffee table to get another beer but stops midway. 'God, look at this!' Suddenly standing, she pulls up her vest and squeezes her belly in both hands. 'I'm, like, *so*, like, so *totally* big right now,' she says in a comedy American accent as she moves her flesh back and forth to mimic a mouth talking. 'Like, so totally, like, so not gonna fit in my bridesmaid's dress.'

I whip up my pyjama top and join in, only the voice of a cockney gangster somehow slips out. 'Oim waaaay more big than you, roight!'

We fall about the place laughing.

'Seriously, though,' she says after pulling her vest back down and cracking open another beer, 'how did I get so porky?'

'Tom's fault,' I say. 'It's the curse of a new relationship. It's all wine, sex and romantic dinners at first – a total bitch for the waistline. Then fast forward ten years and, like me, you'll not be able to see your own fanny.'

'As long as I can still *feel* it, I reckon I can live with that.'

'You should both come with me to Slimmers' Weekly if you're that worried,' says Jen. 'I've lost about 6 pounds for the wedding so far and I'm still eating pasta and drinking.'

'What? You mean "Fat Club"?'

'If that's what you want to call it, Charlie, then yes. But I'm telling you, it's easy. There's one on Wednesday at eleven thirty. Let's all go and make it a fun girly trip out.'

Charlie looks down at her belly, strokes it fondly then pulls her top back up and her fleshy American friend reappears. 'Okay, like, *totally* okay! But only if we can, like, go for, like, a beer and some buffalo wings when we're done.'

And I join in once again with my cockney guts. 'Awright, geezer!'

'So that's that sorted. Bellies away – we need to crack on,' says Jen impatiently. 'Lucy, now, there's no pressure, and you can absolutely say no, but I was wondering how you'd feel about Stanley being my page boy?'

I try to hold back, but the tears are immediate. They've been perched at the front of my eyeballs all day and the mere mention of Stan's name is all it takes for them to come rolling down my cheeks.

'God! What's wrong?' Shocked by the sudden shift in the atmosphere, Jen drops the table plan and throws her arms around me. 'What's happened, love?'

Through snotty, broken sobs, I relay a disjointed account of Stanley's horrendous meltdown at the party and tell them what I'd said to Marsha on the phone this morning. 'And I think I've done the wrong thing,' I gasp, trying to catch a breath, 'telling her that he's autistic.'

'No. You didn't,' Charlie says firmly. 'You are his mother, and *you* know best. I mean, you do think he's autistic, right?'

'Yes,' I say, suddenly calm. 'I know he is. In my bones, I'm sure of it.'

'Well, you said the right thing, then. You're just trying to help others understand him, to protect him, which in my book makes you an amazing mum.'

'She's right, love. Stan might be a little different, but he's incredible and we all adore him.' Jen smiles warmly as she gently rubs my shoulder.

'Why do you care what Marsha thinks anyway?' says Charlie. 'The woman is a dick!'

'She might be a dick, but she's a *connected* dick. Every mum in the hood loves her and, whether I like it or not, Stan will be in school with all their kids in September. I just don't want them to oust him for being different.'

'Thank God he *is* different, Luce! I don't know about you two, but I can think of nothing worse than being branded as "normal". I've made it my life's mission to avoid falling into that category.'

'Me too,' says Jen. 'If you think about it, none of us would have been considered "normal" growing up. And I bet our parents were worried sick when we spent hours alone in our rooms practising as kids, but look at us now. We've all found our way in life, haven't we?'

Jen is spot on. As a teenager, I never quite fitted in. Where all my friends plastered themselves in lip gloss, stuffed their bras and rolled up their school skirts as high as they could get away with, I wore trousers so that I could practise my cello every lunchtime without having to worry about laddering tights. My friends were all 'boys, boys, boys' but my heart was always set on other things than attracting the attention of spotty boys who couldn't keep their hands off their scrotums. All my free time was devoted to perfecting my craft, and most Friday and Saturday nights, when my friends were all out snogging the scrotum-grabbers, my parents were having to lure me away from my cello to watch TV with them, concerned that I was spending far too much time alone. My dad used to force-feed me tumblers of neat whisky to try and loosen me up, as I was permanently in a state of intense frustration – a truly tortured artist if ever there was one. Jen and Charlie were much the same, as was Ed. He told me that he was very much a loner and spent his teenage years locked away in his room with his guitar. Judith once said that he used to eat every meal with it on his lap, even Christmas dinner, and straight after his brandy pudding, he would rush back to his room to resume practising.

Jen takes my hand in hers. 'Not all of us fit in boxes, love,' she says.

'Yep ... for some of us, there is no box,' Charlie adds. 'In fact, ladies, I think it might be time for a toast!' She hands over my beer then hoists hers up in the air. 'Here's to not fitting in fucking boxes, to being unashamedly and unequivocally different! Cheers!'

275

'Cheers!' we all sing in unison.

I swig my beer and dump the bottle on the floor, then pull them both up off the sofa and squeeze them in my arms. 'God, I love you girls so so much.'

'With you as his mum, Stan will be just fine. You've got this,' Jen whispers in my ear then gently pecks my cheek.

'Okay, okay. Enough! Release me! We've got a wedding to plan and I need a piss.' Charlie hurries out of the room with her forearm covering her face, leaving me and Jen chuckling at the sound of her yanking tissues out of a box in the kitchen, blowing her nose so vigorously that a cheeky fart pops out.

Our laughter is interrupted by the beeping of my phone. I reach over to grab it, hoping to find a message from Ed, but it's just an email notification. I sigh, open it and instantly feel the blood drain from my cheeks.

Dear Lucinda,

We are so looking forward to seeing you at the weekend for your performance of John Tavener's Svyati.

Rehearsal will be at 2.30 p.m. with the choir on the day. Concert is 7.30 p.m., St Christopher's Church, Southampton. Free parking is on site and your fee will be £250 as previously agreed.

I have your biography here, which I copied from the internet, but should you want to send me an updated one, it'll need to be with me by end of business tomorrow, as the programmes are being printed on Thursday.

Looking forward to it.

Very best wishes,
Theodore Robson-Jones
Musical Director, St Christopher's Choral Society

'No! No! No! NOOOOOOOO!'

'What? What? What? WHAAAATTTT?' Charlie darts back into the room, her eyes bloodshot and her cheeks stained black from running mascara. 'Who's dead? Who's dead?'

'What day is it?' I screech. 'Day?'

'Monday, why?'

'I *forgot*! Fuck, how could I forget?'

'Forget what, woman? What?'

In a total flap, I blurt out that I've been booked to perform John Tavener's *Svyati*, a deceptively difficult piece for solo cello and choir that I last played in Portsmouth over a year ago. Even though it was insanely stressful at the time, the performance was a roaring success; such a success, in fact, that I'd been booked to do it again with a different choir this year. And now, the concert is on Saturday and I'd forgotten all about it.

'It's in five days. It's impossible! I have too much on. I've got the kids. I can't do it. I can't. Help me, girls. How can I get out of it?'

'You could always fake your own death?' says Jen.

'Or tell them that you lost an arm in a freak escalator accident?' Charlie adds.

'I've got one!' says Jen. 'Tell them you've emigrated to Vegas to become an exotic dancer!'

'Or, and I know this may sound radical,' Charlie pauses dramatically, 'but you could actually get some balls, have some faith in yourself and do the fucking concert. It's not like you're an amazing professional cellist, now, is it?'

'Definitely do it,' Jen says triumphantly. 'You need to focus on yourself for once. Maybe this is the chance you've been waiting for to properly get back into things?'

I'm rather winded by my friends' outpouring of positivity. Clearly, they've forgotten the major drawback: I have two kids to raise, and I'm doing it alone because Ed is in Hollywood schmoozing with international rock stars.

'We'll watch the boys while you practise,' says Jen without hesitating. 'You've played it before, so it'll just need some brushing up, surely?'

'And isn't Ed back at the weekend?' says Charlie.

'Yep. He lands at 5 a.m. on Saturday.'

'Well, you're sorted then. Let the jackass look after the kids and you go and steal back some of the limelight for a change, Luce.' Charlie grabs my phone off the floor and starts typing. 'Right, I've just said "Great, thanks, Theodore. I'm sure the biog you have is fine. Looking forward to it, blah, blah, best wishes, blah!" And, wait, and … Send. That's it, pal. You're *doing* it.'

'Fabulous. And there'll be no chickens at this one, I bet.' Jen winks.

Charlie pats me on the back and holds her beer up in the air for another impromptu toast. 'Sometimes, we all need a little push, Luce. Now, get this beer down you and get your arse to bed. You're up early to practise tomorrow.'

'Yes, sir!'

'Here's to having balls of steel!' she says and, just before she takes a swig, she stops. 'No, wait, *not* balls … *vagina*! Here's to having a steel vagina. Cheers!'

42

Operation: Steel Vagina

There's no time to wallow in self-pity and chastise myself for being a shit mother. My life for the next few days is going to be exclusively about executing Operation: Steel Vagina.

My friends are right. I *am* a great musician and I *do* have what it takes to brush up a big solo at short notice. I have to trust my talent and prove to women across the world that just because you have kids, your life isn't over.

(Obviously, before embracing this new and profoundly positive attitude, I called every cellist in the UK to ask if they could cover me, but the answer was a resounding 'HELL NO!' Only a nutter would agree to take on such a hard piece at short notice. So, the truth is, I have no choice *but* to grow a steel vagina.)

Jen typed up a structured plan for success and stuck it to my fridge before she and Charlie left last night.

It reads as follows:

7.30 Get up. Two bananas. Pint of water. Light
      upper body stretches.
8.30 Warm up – slow scales for 45 minutes.
9.15 Quick break. Snack (not junk!)

9.30 Play first two pages. Identify problem passages and work on them <u>slowly</u>.

10.30 Break. Water. Do a few stretches.

11.00 Tackle pages three and four as before.

12.00 Lunch. Nothing stodgy. Listen to piece on Spotify as you eat.

13.00 An hour of slow practice then take kids out somewhere.

14.30 Quick break then run through piece at speed.

17.00 Dinner (include a protein).

18.00 One more hour going over tricky passages.

19.00 You're done! Rest!*

*<u>NO</u> alcohol, <u>ONLY</u> caffeine-free coffee and early night!

Repeat every day for <u>FOUR </u>days and you'll have the steeliest vagina in the land!

Love you, J xx

Jen is clueless. Love her as I do, she has totally forgotten I'm not a twenty-two-year-old student at music college any more, but a thirty-three-year-old mum who exists only to cater to every possible need of her two young children.

With this in mind, day one of Operation: Steel Vagina actually goes as follows:

4.45 a.m. Wake up to Jack screaming. Feed him and watch reruns of *Sex and the City* to keep awake.

5.50 a.m. Back to bed with Jack. Spend an hour putting dummy in his mouth after he sobs every twenty seconds when it falls out.

7.00 a.m. Breakfast: two pints of cold extra-strong coffee, three croissants with butter and a Twix (for energy).

9.15 a.m. Multiple nappy changes later, finally get both kids dressed and make it to nursery with four minutes to spare.

10.15 a.m. Back home, cello out. Manage ten minutes of warm-ups before strapping Jack to my back in the harness because he won't stop howling. He falls asleep, which gives me a full hour of peace to learn page one and watch *Hell's Kitchen* (plus inhale two KitKats and half a tub of cookie-dough ice cream)

11.45 p.m. Lunch. Two more coffees, another Twix, half a ham sandwich and an entire family-sized bag of Doritos while feeding Jack a jar of spaghetti bolognese.

12.15 p.m. Change Jack's orange-stained clothes and clean up after lunch, then we both fall asleep and I dream of Hugh Jackman wearing a studded leather thong.

1.15 p.m. Mad dash to nursery to pick up Stanley. I'm six minutes late so he throws himself on the floor. Calm him down then drag both kids to the shops to buy a tub of formula. Jack screams all the way there and all the way back.

2.45 p.m. Call Rachel and cry down the phone for half an hour. Eat nine Oreos and endure eleven sittings of 'Let's Explore: The Large Intestines' on YouTube, still crying.

5.00 p.m. Home-made stew rejected by Jack. Offer him toast instead, which is thrown on floor. Give him a jar of shepherd's pie. Eat the discarded toast.

6.30 p.m. 'Bed, Bath and Beyond', which takes ages. Jack shits in the bath and pokes it with his fingers. I fish it out with an empty Pot Noodle container. Horrified, Stan washes his hands for an hour, vowing *never* to share a bath with his brother again.

7.30 p.m. Rock, sing, play white noise, rock, shush, dance, cry, sing some more and eventually pass out in bed with Jack in my arms and Stanley on my legs (with a load of rubber organs lined up down my left thigh.)

11.45 p.m. Feed Jack a bottle and try calling Ed for tenth time. His phone is off.

The rest is a blur and I know that if I repeat this every day for the next four days, then it's safe to say that I'll *never* achieve a steel vagina. I'll just be left with the mangled one that I already have.

43

'Fat Club'

Things are getting pretty desperate. Yesterday's efforts were pathetic and Operation: Steel Vagina is failing fast.

Where Jen and Charlie had the best of intentions by pushing me to do the concert, they've been useless at stepping in to help with the kids and I haven't seen or heard from either of them. Ed is not due back until the morning of the concert, Amy is cramming for her end of year exams, and even Judith has turned me down, saying that she has 'important plans' that she '*cannot* possibly change'.

I drop Stanley at nursery, then dash home and manage one measly hour of half-arsed practice before I'm disturbed, not just by the buzzing of my phone, but more specifically by the five words flashing on the screen: Ealing Green Children's Centre Calling.

'Can I please speak with the parent or guardian of Stanley Wright?' says the serious voice down the other end of the phone.

I imagine the worst.

Stan has had an accident. Maybe he's impaled on a fence? Or choking to death on a magnetic number four? In hospital! Hurt! Alone! Dying!

'This is his mother,' I say urgently. 'Is everything okay?'

'Yes,' comes the reply. 'This is Dr Collins's receptionist at Ealing Green. I've been asked to call you because there has been a last-minute cancellation and he would like to offer you an earlier appointment with him on Friday at 10.30 a.m.'

'What, you mean this Friday? But our appointment isn't for another two months.'

'Yes, I know, and you can keep it if you prefer, but Dr Collins wanted to give you the option of coming sooner. Are you and your husband available to attend this Friday?'

My head is reeling with thoughts that are impossible to process. There's the concert, and I have no time to prepare as it is without adding more stress to the pile. Plus the fridge is empty, Jack is constipated, I've run out of binbags, Slimmers' Weekly starts in twenty-five minutes and, what's most vital, Ed isn't here. The mental load is so overwhelming that I fail to articulate a response.

'Mrs Wright, I should mention that this appointment is solely for parents and your son will not be required to attend.'

'I'll take it,' I say instantly.

If Stanley is to be left at home, then it can only mean one thing: this is it. The powers that be have made their decision, and come Friday, we will finally know for sure if our son is autistic.

I say 'we', but there is no 'we'.

It's just me.

Slimmers' Weekly is held at St Peter's Church, which is sandwiched between Greggs and KFC and directly opposite McDonald's on the Broadway. As I approach Charlie and Jen, who are waiting on the street outside,

I'm already salivating at the thought of a Big Mac and an iced doughnut for dessert.

'Nice tactic,' Charlie says when she glances down at Jack who is strapped to my torso, 'using a baby to hide your gut. Damn, I so wish I had a baby right now.'

'Wanna borrow him, love? He's due to let rip at any time, so be my guest.'

She shudders and backs away dramatically. 'Hell no! Let's just pile in and get this over with.' And in we go to mount the dreaded scales and face the truth.

I last came to this branch of Slimmers' Weekly the year after I had Stanley, and apart from the front door being a different colour, nothing has changed. Straight away, I clap eyes on Pat, who is still the session leader and still as rotund as she was all those years ago. Dressed in a lilac velour tracksuit, she waddles straight over to greet us from the other side of the room, knocking the circle of plastic chairs to the side with her magnificent thighs as she comes.

'All right, honeys. You're new?' Her voice is low and gruff, like she's smoked forty fags for breakfast.

'I've been before,' I reply, 'but years ago.'

'Oh yeah, I recognise your face,' she says. 'Well, if you've been before, you'll know the drill. Shoes off first, then get in line for the scales. Then when you're done, come and sit with the girls and we'll have a good old chat, all right?'

'Sure.'

She waddles back over to sit by the table at the far side of the hall, which is stacked high with low-calorie cereal bars and crisps for sale. I watch her rip open a box, pull out a couple of chocolate bars and munch them down one after the other.

'Jesus,' says Charlie under her breath, 'shouldn't they have someone like Naomi Campbell running the show? Someone, like, a bit more inspirational?'

I ram her with my elbow to shut her up, then we pull off our shoes and get in line.

There's a mixed bunch of people in the queue. Most are women, most are over fifty and, like myself, most have the usual lumps and bumps hanging out of the usual places. Then, of course, there's the standard gang of young mummies who, despite having pushed babies out in the last year or two, are sporting flat stomachs and svelte limbs and are clearly just here for an ego boost.

They stand directly in front of us, gassing away to each other as their toddlers sit in pushchairs, stuffing Greggs sausage rolls and maxi bags of crisps into their tiny mouths.

'I'm so miffed,' I hear one say. She is no more than twenty-five and probably eight stone in weight. 'I did so well all week, but then I had a row with Mark and ended up eating, like, a whole bag of fun-size M&Ms. I reckon I've gained.'

'Don't worry, Sadie,' replies her equally stick-thin friend. 'I ate two Snickers bars and a Scotch egg on the weekend, and then I had four double Archers and lemonade at my cousin's Ann Summers party. I'm not happy either, but we can be good from tomorrow.'

'We're still up for lunch after, right, girls?' another one says.

Sadie jumps in. 'Hell, yeah. Kel, I'm starving. I haven't even had a cup of tea yet. I've been holding off till after the weigh-in.'

I'm wonderfully entertained by all of it: the ridiculous banter of the skinnies, and the sight of the rest of us, visibly irritated as we eavesdrop on their conversation and wait like a row of lambs heading to the slaughter. And although paying to queue up and be told that I'm fat isn't the best use of my time, it's far better than sitting at home on my own, flipping out about solo concerts and life-changing paediatric appointments.

One by one, I watch each woman remove their shoes, jackets, cardigans, belts and socks before climbing with trepidation on to the scales. Pat's assistant stands at the front of the line, where she hovers over the screen waiting for the results to register. Squinting through her bifocals, she then scribbles down some digits on a slip of paper, and once she hands it over, the rest of us in the queue go silent, waiting with bated breath to see how the woman on the hot spot will react.

Some are elated, others less so, but Sadie is totally destroyed when she glances down at her results. 'I knew it!' she snaps. She crumples her bit of paper into a ball and tosses it on the floor in a huff. 'It was those M&Ms that did it.'

Her Scotch-egg-loving friend tries to hug her, but she pushes her away then yanks the sausage roll out of her toddler's hands and takes a hearty bite. Her child is still screaming for his sausage roll by the time my turn comes, and with every member of the queue now distracted by his hissy fit, I discreetly climb on the scales and wait for Pat's assistant to squint.

The results are devastating: 12 stone 3 pounds – two and a half stone away from my pre-baby weight.

I consider wrestling Sadie to the ground and prising the sausage roll out of her bony mitts, but I manage to restrain myself. Instead, I pull Jack out of Charlie's arms, strap him back on my torso and sulk over to the circle of shame, ready to confess my sins to a room full of strangers.

'Right, and how have we all done this week, ladies?' says Pat, who has now positioned herself in the centre of the circle on a plastic chair that's struggling to accommodate her rear end. 'Who has lost weight?'

A few hands go up and the rest of the group offer a limp applause.

'Okay, Maggie, what's your loss this week, honey?' says Pat, singling out a middle-aged lady from the left-hand side of the circle.

'Three pounds off,' Maggie replies proudly.

'Great! And tell the group, how have you done it?'

'No wine, no bread and I baked a sugar-free strawberry flan and brought it around to my daughter-in-law's baby shower, so I didn't have to eat her brownies.'

'Well done!' gushes Pat. 'Let's all give her a well-deserved clap, ladies!'

Maggie doesn't realise it, but she has just made twenty enemies on the spot. Sadie is particularly disgruntled at her good news and, after flashing Maggie a look of pure venom, she delves into her toddler's bag of crisps.

'And how about you, Sheila?' continues Pat, oblivious to the palpable resentment of the group.

Sheila is in her mid-seventies and sits with her shoulders slumped, clutching a Sainsbury's Bag for Life over her stomach.

'I gained three,' she says quietly.

'What? Speak up, honey. Don't be shy.'

'I've gained three pounds,' she says marginally louder, her fingers fiddling with the handle on her carrier bag.

'Ah! Never mind, honey-bun,' says Pat warmly. 'Tell us, do you have any idea how it might have happened? Where you might've gone wrong?'

'Not really,' says Sheila sadly. 'I've not eaten much but veggie soup. And I've only had those skinny hot chocolates on my daily trips to Starbucks. I don't under—'

'Thirteen units!' cries Pat. 'They're thirteen units, my honey-bunny!'

'Thirteen!' Sheila gasps, appalled. 'But they're skinny! I was told they was skinny.'

'No, my darling. *That's* how they get you! Sneaky bastards they are. You could've had nearly three KitKats for that amount of points.'

The poor old woman is beyond devastated.

'Don't panic, though, 'cos it's fixable,' Paula says softly, sensing her distress. 'Next week, you can still go to Starbucks, but drink black tea or boiling water instead, okay?'

Sheila nods and drops her head, clearly bereft that the one sliver of chocolatey joy in her life has been ripped away from her and replaced with shitty black tea.

Forty-five minutes drag on, and after listening to countless tales of gross overindulgence, the Newbie Loser of the Week is announced. We watch Maggie stride proudly to the centre of the circle to collect her prize for being the champion abstainer from wine, bread and chocolate brownies. Her prize: a box of carrots, a muddy butternut squash, a stalk of yellowing broccoli, a pineapple and a bag of new potatoes. We all applaud with forced smiles then drag our frumpy bodies out of the hall, ready to start a week of forced starvation.

'How did you do?' I say to Jen and Charlie in the car park.

'Only half a pound down,' Jen replies, a bit disheartened.

'Well, I'm a stone up from the last time I weighed myself,' says Charlie, 'but in my defence, that was three years ago when I was naked in Dan Husting's bathroom and full of champers, so it's possible I got it wrong.'

'Lunch?' I say. 'I've got loads to tell you guys.'

'Hell yes. I'm thinking pie, chips and a couple of ice-cold pints,' Charlie replies enthusiastically.

We cross the road and head swiftly towards The Grove, passing prize-winning Maggie in the window of McDonald's, a Big Mac clamped tightly in her slender fingers.

44

Odd Socks and Bones

Something jaw-droppingly shocking happened on my way back from our boozy lunch at The Grove yesterday. I'd just left the supermarket after stopping by to stock up on lean turkey mince and lettuce for my impending diet, and, while waiting to cross the road, I glanced in through the window of Starbucks and spied a truly unbelievable scene.

It was Judith, drinking coffee … with Alan!

Her 'important plans' which couldn't possibly be changed to help me out were actually plans to sit flirting with Alan, just a five-minute walk from where her grandchildren live. Oh, the deceit!

Obviously, I toyed with the idea of going in, striding right up to her table and saying something passive-aggressive like she would *definitely* do if the shoe was on the other foot. But I didn't. Instead, I promptly turned around, slipped back inside the shopping centre and left via the rear exit. As much fun as it would have been to bust her, I was genuinely pleased to see her out socialising, albeit with Alan and his dodgy kneecaps. It seems there's more to the woman than meets the eye: a spark, a naughty streak, a bit of grit to her character. Perhaps she isn't just a judgemental, seed-eating do-gooder with an abject disgust for processed foods and overweight daughters-in-law?

Perhaps, just perhaps, the woman is human after all.

Naturally, I didn't fully let her off the hook. A little deception amongst family is to be expected every once in a while, and although I'm not totally devoid of reason or compassion, I'm also not one to scoff at an opportunity when it's handed to me on a golden platter. Times are desperate, and with two kids crawling over me 24/7, a solo concert and an important paediatric appointment looming, I decided to take subtle but effective action.

Just before hitting the hay, I sent her a sneaky text with an adorable picture of Stanley and Jack attached.

> Miss you so much, Nanna. Hope to see you
> very soon for a snuggle. Love and hugs,
> Stanley and Jack xxx

At 9 a.m. this morning, the buzzer goes and I pick up the intercom to discover that we have a totally unexpected visitor.

'Lucy, it's Judith. Buzz me up, will you?'

She pushes through the door with a small suitcase and a carrier bag full of Waitrose supplies, as always. 'You look exhausted!' she gasps, then quickly scans the utter shithole that is our flat. 'Right, hand me that child and go. Get on with what you need to be doing. I'll sort all of this out. Where's Stanley?'

'What are you doing here?' I say, feigning total shock at her unexpected appearance.

'Well, I decided to cancel my plans. You need some help if you're going to prepare for your show, so here I am.'

'You're my saviour, Judith!' I say, and I really do mean it, even though she used the word 'show'.

'Gosh, well, I don't know about that,' she smiles uncomfortably, 'but um, you know me. I'm happy to help, if I can.'

I suppress the guilt of my deception and disappear to my room. With my cello out of its case and in my arms, it's time to try and perform a miracle.

But, at 9.15 a.m. – 'Lucy, do you realise that you have four opened jars of pesto in your fridge? One of them expired two months ago!' she yells from the kitchen.

At 9.27 a.m. – 'Lucy, where do you keep your fabric softener? I can only find an empty one in here.'

At 10.05 a.m. – 'Lucy, Jack has opened his bowels. Do you want to come and deal with it? I'm just taking the rubbish out.'

By 10.37 a.m. – 'Lucy, I just bumped into Alan outside. He had some knee surgery pamphlets for me. And the postman has been. There's a letter here for Edward … a brown one. It's marked "URGENT".'

Then at 11.38 a.m. – 'It's a bill from the taxman, Lucy. Quite a big one too!'

At 11.05 a.m. – 'Lucy, I've found eleven odd socks here. Eleven! And there's holes in your pants. Where's your sewing kit?'

Just as I'm about to tear down the hallway and stuff odd socks down the woman's throat, the door buzzer sounds.

'Lucy! I'm just popping out to post an urgent parcel. Stanley doesn't want to come but I'll take Jack with me. Where's his jacket? And his nappy bag? And does he need snacks?'

I carefully put the cello down, then calmly make my way to the kitchen to get the things that she needs. 'Thanks,

Judith. Thanks.' I smile, biting my bottom lip as hard as I can. 'Have a nice time with Alan. I think he's sweet on you.'

'Oh, goodness! Don't be ridiculous, Lucy. I'm only popping out to post a parcel.' She poofs up her hair in the hallway mirror, applies a light smear of nude lipstick and leaves the flat with Jack and no parcel in sight.

Hurrying back to my room, I lift my cello off the floor, and just as I'm about to stroke the A string, the door opens and Stanley appears.

'Yes, Stan. What is it? WHAT?'

'Don't shout!' he yells, clapping his hands over his ears.

'I didn't!' I snap. 'I *didn't*,' I then whisper.

'Excuse me, but did you know that the smallest bone in a body is in the ears?'

'No, I didn't,' I reply curtly, taking my bow off the string.

'And, excuse me, but I have four more things to tell you. Number one: there is thirty-three bones in a spine. Number two: there is twenty-six bones in a foot. Number three: there is twenty-seven bones in a hand. And number four: the biggest bone is a femur and it's in a leg.'

'Oh, very interesting,' I say, laying my cello down on the floor once again.

'Do you want to know which one gets broken the most times?'

'Not right now, Sta—'

'Collarbone.'

I stand up and walk to the kitchen and he follows. I tear open a packet of cookies, shove two straight into my mouth and spend the next hour enduring a detailed lesson about the fascinating qualities of the human skeletal system.

Frustrating as it is, I'm wildly relieved to see that he is back to his old self again.

45

The Verdict

The last twenty-four hours have flown by and Judith has been about as much use as a punctured condom. The woman spent most of yesterday 'popping out' for one questionable reason or another, and she has been of no help with the kids at all.

First, there was the posting of the invisible parcel, and when she returned, she stayed in the flat for less than an hour before dashing back out to the supermarket to pick up some 'urgent' asparagus, a trip which took four hours. Either she'd boarded a plane and flown halfway to Peru to handpick her own or, like a mischievous teenager, she'd snuck back out to schmooze with Alan and his alluring stack of pamphlets. The concert is tomorrow but I can obsess over it no more. I've done as much practice as physically possible, and short of running down to the park with raw steaks gaffer-taped to my arms and being dismembered by a Rottweiler, there's nothing I can do to get out of it now.

Today, I have more important things to think about. I can't waste time panicking about semi-quaver runs or entertaining repulsive thoughts of Judith snogging Alan around the back of the shopping centre. My appointment with Stan's paediatrician is an hour away, so everything else pales into insignificance.

I haven't slept a wink, nor have I mentioned anything to Judith about it. Even though she has a spring in her step on account of her blossoming romance, I know that her wicked ways will soon bubble to the surface if she gets wind of it. As always, she'll preach to me and tell me that Stanley just needs some 'tough love' and that I should 'stop pandering to him'. The woman is predisposed to criticise me, so when it comes to Stanley's potential diagnosis, I've mentally superglued my lips shut.

After she returned from her trip to Peru last night, I purposely avoided her and took myself off to bed early. Like a student studying for the most important exam of their lives, I spent the evening preparing for today's appointment. Dr Collins fobbed me off at our last meeting, and I've realised that if I'm to be taken seriously, I need to go in with solid evidence of Stanley's struggles.

I started by searching through my phone for videos of Stan chanting gall-bladder facts and reciting the alphabet backwards, then stored the best ones in one file so I could access them quickly. Next, I jotted down on paper everything that had happened over the last few months. I catalogued his meltdowns, made notes about his fixations and wrote down details of his daily routine, from his erratic sleep patterns to the specific shape in which he has to have his food served.

The deeper I delved into the past, the more obvious it became that signs of his autism had been there since he was a baby. When he should have been crawling, waving, lifting things and putting them in his mouth, he wasn't even close. And when he should have been babbling and throwing tantrums, he rarely did. For a long time, I thought that I was lucky. I had a quiet baby – placid, gentle, easy. He was my first child, so I didn't know any different, but as time went on, I started to notice how other babies interacted with their mothers, how they were able to communicate what they needed long before they'd learnt to talk. And that's when the doubts started creeping in.

As Stan got older, simple things caught my eye: toddlers holding their own cups and sucking up juice through straws, or kids – still in nappies – using cutlery and dipping their chips in ketchup. I'd watch other children in the park climbing, running, screaming, playing, whizzing around on balance bikes and interacting with each other – all things that my boy wasn't doing because, aside from the occasional emotional explosion, he was quiet and still almost all of the time.

Eventually, I opened up to Ed and told him my concerns, but he brushed them off. 'He's fine,' he said. 'He's only a kid, give him a chance.' Let's not forget that I was the girl who'd once misdiagnosed an ingrowing hair as syphilis, so I decided that he must be right. I was overreacting – obsessing about problems that would most likely iron themselves out in time.

But they never did.

In the end, I stopped talking to Ed about it. He wasn't really exposed to other kids, so how could he know what was 'normal'? He wasn't the one standing in the park day after day, nor did he sit in waiting rooms at baby clinics or drag his arse to the soft-play centres to suffer the screams of a thousand other kids. I did. And when I studied the behaviour of other kids around me, my gut told me that something wasn't right.

Dr Collins was the first one to throw the term 'ASD' at me, but with no follow-up appointment any time soon, I'd reached out to the internet for more advice. It took seconds to find links to Mensa tests and just a few more to find the term 'Autism Spectrum Disorder', and ever since, I've been pulled between the two extremes of 'gifted' and 'developmental disorder'.

On days where I thought Stanley couldn't, he would. And when I thought he'd nailed something at last, he'd suddenly regress. In a world obsessed with labels, I needed something to cling to – a word to help me understand my son. But now, after all of this inner debate that has slowly driven me crazy, I realise there's only one word that sums him up perfectly. It's not autistic, it's not genius: it's Stanley.

Whatever happens today, whether or not a diagnosis is given, it won't change who he is or how I feel about him. He will always be Stanley. Nothing more, and nothing less.

'Mine! Mine!' shouts a small girl from the other side of the waiting room. I keep my head down and try to focus on the old copy of *Yachting Monthly* that I'd lifted off the stack of magazines, but when she scurries over and throws herself down at my feet, I can't pretend I haven't noticed her.

'Mine! Mine!' she screams. 'Mine!'

I drop my magazine and lean down to help her, but her mother quickly rushes over. 'No, please. Stay there. It's okay,' she says then bends down to lift her up. 'Evie, the lady is sitting there. Let's find another seat.'

I hesitantly sit back down, return to my magazine and watch the drama unfold from the corner of my eye. Using all of the same tactics that I would with Stanley, the woman calmly tries to coerce her to sit elsewhere but she resists, goes limp and flops back down on the floor in protest.

'Evie, I think I might be sitting in *your* seat,' I say. I promptly slide across a few seats to make room. 'Ah, this is better. This is *my* seat, and that one is *yours*.'

She plants herself in the vacated chair without saying a word, and her mum, visibly relieved, mouths 'Thanks'.

We start chatting about the weather and the traffic, but soon, we cut to the chase and move on to why we are both here. She tells me that her name is Hannah. Her daughter, Evie, is nine years old and has long brown curly hair, large blue eyes and a cute freckle in the centre of her left cheek. She also has a diagnosis of autism and she is here for occupational therapy.

Hannah tells me that Evie's anxiety is crippling and that she has never slept more than two or three hours a night. Aside from frozen chips, she doesn't eat any solid foods and survives on meal replacement drinks prescribed for her by the doctor. Hannah says that Evie can be aggressive towards her and her younger brother, then shows me bite marks on her arms and a dark purple bruise hidden under her fringe from where Evie had hit her in the throes of a particularly bad meltdown a few days earlier.

'Enough about me!' she says. 'I can't stop talking. Tell me about your son. Is he autistic too?'

I don't know how to answer. She might think that I'm a fraud, a drama queen, like some fool who sits in a doctor's waiting room complaining about a runny nose when the person next to her has pneumonia. Anything I say about Stan's challenges can't remotely compare to Evie's, but autism is a spectrum – a huge spectrum at that. I've spent countless hours educating myself about it and I've learnt that no two autistic children are the same. Whether or not your child can speak, is incontinent or aggressive, sensory-seeking, obsessive or anxious, *all* of these traits fall under one blanket diagnosis: autism. My and Hannah's situations may be strikingly different, but what we share is that we're both on journeys we didn't expect to be taking when we became mothers.

I decide to answer her question honestly. 'Yes. He is, but we have no diagnosis and I've been waiting for this appointment for ages. I'm hoping I'll get a solid answer today.'

'It's *so* frustrating, isn't it? It took us four and a half years to get one.'

'Seriously?'

'Yep. I knew from when she was two, but no one would listen to me. Apparently girls are much harder to diagnose. Just go in there guns blazing. Kick up a stink if you have to.' She rubs my arm and then offers me a mint, which I accept.

A teenage boy stands in the corner next to his dad, flapping his hands as he stomps back and forth in a straight line. Every now and again he yells 'E–Or! E–Or!' which is so piercing that it makes me and Hannah jump every time he does it. His dad sits skimming through *Woman's Own* and doesn't acknowledge the racket, presumably because he's used to it. It's only when the boy starts punching his head with balled-up hands that his father puts down the magazine and calmly steps in to intervene.

'Mrs Wright,' says the receptionist, 'you can go through to room two. Dr Collins is waiting for you.'

'Oh God. This is it.'

'Good luck,' says Hannah. 'Be firm. Fight for him, because no one else is going to.'

I smile, say 'I'll do my best' and make my way down the corridor, ready to get some answers at last.

'Come on in,' calls out Dr Collins when I gently knock on the door. He is glued to his computer screen when I enter, speedily typing away as I stand there not knowing what to do with myself. Eventually, he stops. 'Please, take a seat,' he says warmly. He rolls up his sleeves, lifts a mug labelled 'Keep Calm I'm the Doctor' off the table and takes a long gulp before swivelling around to face me. 'Is your husband joining us today, Mrs Wright?'

I shift uncomfortably in my chair. 'No. It's just me.'

He nods then returns to the keyboard to log Ed's absence in his files. 'And tell me,' he continues as he types, 'how has Stanley been since our last meeting?'

It's my chance to let rip. Motivated by Hannah's 'just fight for him' comment, my brain floods with information, but I struggle to get my words out. 'He's still very anxious and obsessive and he spends hours alone with his puzzles. I've got videos to show you.' I start fumbling around in my handbag looking for my phone as I continue to ramble. 'He still gets very upset if his structure changes and he's still, um, *very* anxious. Yes! *Anxious*. And obsessive.' Finally, I find my phone and impatiently swipe my finger across it to get it to jolt to life. 'And … sleep! Sleep has been a big issue. He won't stay in his own bed. Here, I have videos. See for yourself, there's this one where he—'

'Let me stop you, Mrs Wright,' he says. He removes his glasses and lays them on the table, then looks me directly in the eyes. 'The reason you have been called in today is that the panel have come together to discuss Stanley's case.'

Perched on the edge of the chair, my back stiff, my hands clasped together in a tight, sticky ball, I glare at him, afraid to take a breath in case I miss what he has to say.

'We've collected assessments from Stanley's nursery, the speech and language team, the occupational health team, along with my own observations. We met last week and discussed his case at length and we have made the decision ...'

My heart is thumping so erratically that I can feel it in my cheeks.

'... that Stanley does meet the criteria required to be given a diagnosis of Autism Spectrum Disorder.'

'Sorry, sorry.' My heart stops dead in my chest. 'Can you repeat that? You said yes, that he *is*?'

He tilts his head to one side and reiterates his statement more concisely. 'Yes, Mrs Wright, Stanley is autistic.'

Without realising it, I'm already on my feet and halfway across the room towards the door. 'Thank you, Dr Collins, for your time.'

'Wait. Please sit, Mrs Wright. I have some information here that I'm obliged to give you.'

The door handle is now clamped in my hand and, for some reason, I can't seem to let go of it. He comes over and hands me a heavy manual and a thick wad of photocopied sheets bound together with a green paperclip, then retreats to his chair. But I don't follow him.

'There is a letter confirming Stanley's diagnosis for your records, and also some information on how to apply for Disability Living Allowance.'

The word 'disability' pierces my skin like a wasp sting.

'There's also a book which we distribute to all parents and carers after a diagnosis, and I've enclosed details of local support groups and courses that you can do. I must warn you, however, that the waiting list for the early bird course is long, so you and your husband might want to register as soon as possible.'

I glance down at the heavy textbook in my hands – *Autism: A Guide for Parents and Carers Following Diagnosis*. It's practically the same size as Tolstoy's *War and Peace*, and if I was to drop it, every one of the twenty-six bones in my foot would shatter in an instant. I tuck it under my arm and glimpse the accompanying side dish of photocopied sheets, only to be bombarded with the usual list of acronyms: NAS, CAMHS, CFT, ERT, HMIC, NCCWCH, NICE. And, without saying a word, I pull the door open and step out into the corridor.

'Do you have any questions that you'd like to ask?' he calls out.

'No. It's okay. I have the only answer I need.'

I thank him for his time and he slips his glasses back on, wishes me well, then swivels back to face his computer and resumes typing.

46

I Am a Femur

I turn left out of the children's centre and walk in the opposite direction to home. With my phone pressed firmly against my ear, I cross the road and dodge the hot fumes billowing out of the double decker buses that sit bumper to bumper on the scorching tarmac. I power down the main road, wading through the bustling crowd of shoppers without any clear thought as to where I'm going.

By the time I've made three full laps of Ealing Common, Ed still hasn't answered, so I find a vacant bench and collapse on it – boiling hot and exhausted – and send him a text.

Call me. We need you xx

I can't say how long I sit staring at my phone willing it to ring, but when I look up and see the suits from the offices on Uxbridge Road starting to arrive with their lunch, I realise that it's been a fair while. I watch the young men in the distance as they pull off their ties and untuck their shirts before planting themselves down to eat their boxed sandwiches. Smartly dressed women kick off their heels and camp next to them, resting their bare feet on the ground. Little kids chase each other across the wide expanse of dry, yellowing grass, old men walk their older dogs, couples lie on blankets having cuddles, and young friends sit with iced coffees, soaking up the sunshine as they chat.

All around me, life is going on as usual. Ordinary people are going about their business as they ordinarily would, but not me. My mind is plagued by thoughts of Stanley. Our child – so special and so unique – will grow up here, but will he ever truly find his place in this world? A world that ultimately isn't designed for the extraordinary?

Because that is what he is.

Extraordinary.

Judith is peering out of the window as I approach the flat a while later. She greets me at the door, her reception hostile. 'Lucy! I told you that I have to be home this afternoon for a very important meeting,' she says. 'Where on earth have you been all this time?'

'Posting a parcel.' I smile wryly. 'I'm so sorry, Judith.'

'What's that you've got there?'

'Just a book,' I say as I gently push past her and head straight to my room.

'Stanley refused to get dressed,' she calls out as I close the door behind me. 'And Jack is in his highchair. He still needs his lunch and I'm leaving in five minutes.'

I open the bottom drawer of my bedside table, turn around and quickly check that the coast is still clear, then lift a thick wedge of old bank statements and stuff the book and the pile of papers underneath them. I force the drawer closed and go to find Stanley.

'I'm home!' I say. I knock on his bedroom door and enter. 'Stan, are you in there? Can I come in?'

He's lying on the floor wearing nothing but Ed's Spiderman baseball cap – a sight that cheers me up instantly.

'What are you playing in here, little man?'

No response comes, so I lie down next to him and try again.

'Collarbones, femurs, spines and Spiderman,' he says after I repeat my question twice.

'And what are those numbers that you're playing with?'

'A number one, number two, number three and number four,' he says without looking up. 'Some of them are the baddies, some of them are the goodies.'

'Oooh! That sounds like fun. Can I play too?'

He pulls himself up on his knees and organises his unusual combination of toys in a row across the carpet from largest to smallest. And after careful consideration, he selects the biggest bone from the row and passes it over to me without turning around. 'You should be the femur,' he says.

'But can't I be the collarbone? Because I like the shape of it so much more.'

'No!' he snaps, and for a split second, I panic that he is about to kick off. But he doesn't. 'Collarbones break the most,' he says. 'You can be the femur because the femur is a goodie, and it is the strongest.'

'Okay, Stan,' I say, my heart melting into a pool of mushy goo. 'I *am* the femur.'

47

Death, Taxes and Toblerones

Just before sunrise, the front door opens and in staggers a figure dragging a guitar and a huge suitcase. Buried underneath the Ray-Ban shades, the wiry beard and the thick stench of farts and beer is Ed. My rock-star husband has arrived home from tour at last and, thankfully, not in a body bag as I'd feared.

'Hi, love. I'm back,' he croaks.

'Well, don't just stand there, man, ditch that guitar and give me a hug!' I hug him so firmly that it's a wonder I don't suffocate him. 'Thank God you're back. *Loads* has happened.'

'Did you get my copy of *Titanic* back from Jen?'

'Um ... *no*, Ed. Have you even checked your messages?'

He looks at me blankly. 'My charger's on the tour bus.'

'Of course it is.' I sigh. The man knows about none of it – the meltdown, the last-minute paediatric appointment, the diagnosis – and I'm no betting woman, but a tenner says he didn't get the message about my solo concert today either. 'Look, I'll tell you in a minute, just take Jack first. He's desperate for some Daddy love.'

He lifts Jack out of his highchair, and the moment his big blue eyes look up at Ed's face, Jack's bottom lip starts to quiver and tears soon follow.

'It's the beard, love,' I say. 'He doesn't recognise you with all that fur. Have a shave and maybe lose the shades. You're not in Hollywood any more.'

One long shower later, he returns looking and smelling much more like the man I married. The beard is gone and the stench of aeroplane has been scrubbed off his skin.

Stanley has woken up and is waiting for him in the living room, pacing around the rug totally naked. 'Daddy, I have seventeen things that I need to tell you,' he says without meeting Ed's eyes.

I freeze in total disbelief. 'Stan, did you just say *Daddy?*'

'Yes,' he replies, 'because that is his name.'

'Well done, Stan!' I cheer. I pick him up in the air and swing him around like a mad woman. 'Woohoo! No more excuse mes! No more excuse mes!'

'Stop! Stop laughing!' Stan yells. 'I have *seventeen* things that I need to tell you, Daddy!'

I put him down and, before I catch my breath, he begins. 'Number one: did you know that there is thirty-three bones in a spine?'

'I didn't,' says Ed as he shuffles back towards the recliner.

'Number two: did you know that there is twenty-six bones in a foot, Daddy? Number three: there is twenty-seven—'

'Stan,' I interrupt, 'you haven't given Daddy a welcome-home hug yet. He's flown all the way back from America to see you.'

'Daddy *cannot* fly! Nobody can fly, not even Superman, because he is just pretend.'

'On an aeroplane, I mean.' I suppress a smile. 'Go on, give him a big hug.'

He stops in his tracks, opens his skinny arms and loosely wraps them around Ed's torso as he continues to recite his list. I look over at Ed, give him a double thumbs up and mouth the words 'Welcome home' but he doesn't notice because he's already engrossed in Stan's anatomy lesson. By the time he has reached point twelve, however, Ed has lost interest.

'Little Man, why don't you tell me the rest in a minute? Go and open that yellow bag and you'll find a surprise that I brought for you from America.'

Thankfully, the promise of a gift outweighs his need to reach point seventeen and he opens the carrier bag and pulls out a copy of the game *Operation*.

'It's a body-parts game,' Ed says, 'all the way from America!'

Stanley glances at it briefly then drops it on the floor. To my utter dismay, he then pulls out a sodding alphabet puzzle. I huff heavily and briefly contemplate snatching it out of his hands and hiding it before he gets too attached, but weirdly, it sparks no reaction and he throws it on the rug along with the accompanying large bag of Haribo.

'So, what do you say to Daddy, Stan?'

'Thank you. I say thank you,' he replies on cue and sits down on the floor to study his gifts in silence.

Ed lifts another carrier bag out of his suitcase. 'And these are for Jack,' he says. 'I couldn't decide which one to buy, so I bought the whole collection.' He lays a selection of small cuddly animals across the highchair tray, and when he runs out of space, he stuffs a tiger and a bunny under each of Jack's arms, wedging him into his seat.

'Ed, you've gone a bit overboard, haven't y—'

'Daddy,' interrupts Stan. 'Excuse me, but, Daddy, can you open this?' he says as he lifts the alphabet puzzle off the floor.

Ed smiles, delighted that one of his gifts has passed inspection. 'Of course, little man, but put on some pants first because you don't want bum germs getting on your new letters … or the rug.'

'Ed!' I snap. 'Do not mention germs, for crying out loud.'

'What?'

'Oh, forget it!'

Stan washes his hands as instructed and skips back excitedly, ready to play with his new letters. 'I need my other letters, Daddy. I need my other letters, Daddy,' he chants.

'I'll get them now, little man.' He dashes off to the kids' bedroom to dig out the bulk of the alphabet puzzles I'd stored away on the top shelf of the wardrobe months ago.

In less than half an hour, we've plummeted down the scale from hooray to dismay. Ed has carelessly bulldozed his way through all of the progress that I've made with Stanley since he left. Now the handwashing and the fecking alphabet have been invited back into our lives. I could strangle the man!

'Right, that's the kids sorted.' He smiles, totally oblivious to the damage he has just done. 'Now, I have a little something here for you.' He reaches over and hands me a bag marked DUTY FREE.

Inside, a Toblerone – because nothing is more certain in this life than death, taxes and Ed gifting me a bar of Toblerone.

The rest of the day is not spent with my arms wrapped around my rock-star husband; nor do we crack open the champagne to celebrate his return, or take the time to sit down and discuss the huge news that has just hit our family. I have less than two hours before I have to leave for Southampton, and with the pressure knob cranked up to maximum levels, I dump Jack on Ed's lap and head to the bedroom to run through my solo one last time. Our reunion will have to wait.

As I'm sipping lemon and ginger tea and doing some deep-breathing exercises, the buzzer goes. Ed appears at the door a few minutes later holding a massive bouquet of roses with a purple GOOD LUCK balloon tied to them.

'Oh. You didn't!'

'No, I didn't,' he says matter-of-factly.

I sigh inwardly and open the card:

Good luck for today, our fabulous friend!

Face your fears! Go for it! Ride the camel! Slap the dolphin! Wrestle the mighty bull down to the ground! Take no prisoners, you hear? Stand on the edge of the mountain with your breasts held high and scream 'I CAN do it!' into the abyss! Use that STEEL VAGINA!

Call you later.

Love Charls and Jen xx

A little tear pops out of the corner of my eye and I brush it away quickly before it hits the cello.

'Can you put these in a vase, Ed?' I say. 'I've really got to crack on.'

He leaves the room, and seconds after I've started sliding my hand up and down the cello, the first interruption comes.

'Love, where is the vase?' he bellows from the other end of the flat. 'Is it the one with the …? Oh … wait. No, it's okay … I've sorted it.'

Twenty seconds later: 'Love, where's Stan's oesophagus? He says it's missing.'

One minute after that: 'Love, how many ounces of milk does Jack take? Okay, Stan. I'll look! Just wait a minute!'

Then: 'Love, where are the wet wipes? They're not in the usual place? *Okay*, Stan! Where did you last have it? It's probably under that cushion. Look for it, will you? NO! I am *not* shouting!'

And finally: 'Love, we're out of toilet roll and I need to offload. Got any more?'

I manage ten more minutes before giving up and heading to assist in the search for the oesophagus. Chances are it's sitting directly in front of Ed and Stan's eyeballs, but without my help, they will never find it (at least not without trashing the flat and getting themselves in a total state).

By the time I've found it, fed Jack a bottle, dressed both him and Stan, added 'buy toilet roll' to the shopping list, showered and removed my flowers from a pint glass of water and placed them in a proper vase, it's time to leave. I go in search of Ed, who has long disappeared to the bathroom, and find him fast asleep on the toilet, pants around ankles, legs splayed wide open, clutching a kitchen roll in both hands.

I gently shake his arm to wake him.

'What? What?' He jumps up.

'Kitchen roll? Why didn't you just use a baby wipe?'

'I couldn't find them. I told you – they weren't in the usual place.'

'Doesn't matter.' I roll my eyes. 'Look, I've got to leave soon. Put your dinger away and get in there. It's your shift.'

'Yeah. God. Sorry!'

'And lose the bunnies, love. Buy your own – maybe something a bit more rock star, eh?'

He smiles and looks down fondly at my bunny slippers on his feet. I know then that I'll have to wrestle him at some point to win them back.

With my concert dress packed, my cello polished and my stomach jam-packed with somersaulting butterflies, I kiss goodbye to my boys, twenty-six new American letters and a rubber oesophagus before heading out the door to face my destiny.

'Wish me luck, guys.'

'Wish *me* luck,' Ed replies.

'Suck it up, buddy. It's only jet lag. You won't die.'

'It feels like I might,' he moans just before knocking back the rest of his coffee in one gulp.

'Daddy! Are you going to die? I don't want you to die! I don't want you to die!' shrieks Stanley.

'Pretend, Stan. It's just *pretend*,' are the last words I say as I close the door behind me.

48

The Lord Works in Mysterious Ways

Two solid hours on the M23 enable me to collect myself and get a grip on the ridiculous situation. In light of everything that has happened over the last twenty-four hours, this concert really is no big deal. It's just a short solo with an amateur choir in Southampton, for God's sake – hardly a concerto with the London Symphony Orchestra at the Barbican. My audience will be full of incontinent old ladies with hearing aids, *not* vicious music critics from the *BBC Music* magazine. If it goes horribly wrong, no one who matters will ever know. I need to get some guts: just get in there, bash it out, grab my cash and drive back home to my husband and beautiful babies.

When I pull up on the road outside St Christopher's, the somersaulting butterflies in my stomach instantly start to turn on each other. It's not your typical church with a crucifix over the door, a few stained-glass windows and a bell tower, but an intimidating structure of architectural splendour. It's *massive* – more like a fucking cathedral and more like a venue used to host a royal wedding, *not* the solo concert of a knackered, rusty cello-playing mum of two.

Tall golden gates surround the perimeter of the extensive grounds, leading to a narrow archway with a sculpture of Jesus embedded in the keystone. I try to steady my hands then hold my breath and cautiously drive under it at 2 miles per hour, praying that I don't knock it down and send Jesus flying on to the bonnet of Ed's car. Miraculously, I make it through unscathed but continue driving at a snail's pace, taking extra care not to flatten the bountiful flower-beds that line both sides of the narrow path.

The car park is already full. Not of shit heaps like Ed's Nissan Micra, but of brand new Jaguars, Audis and Range Rovers which tells me everything I need to know about the sort of people waiting for me inside. This will *not* be a concert for incontinent old ladies who enjoy a custard slice and a cup of tea in the Morrisons café once a week. No. My audience will be ladies clothed in cashmere and pearls, ones who lunch at the golf club every Sunday, who play croquet and squash three times a week with their lord and lady friends.

Oh God!

Ignoring the instinct to bolt to the airport and buy a one-way ticket to Mexico, I squeeze Ed's car into a tiny space under a cherry blossom tree. I unload my cello and wheelie suitcase, then take several deep breaths before navigating my way back through the graveyard towards the entrance of the church.

Upon turning the corner, my eyes are instantly drawn to the large banner that hangs over the solid oak door and I puke in my mouth – the sharp burn of lemon and ginger tea in reverse.

'Well-come, oh, welcome! You must be Lucinda.' Standing just inside the doorway is an elderly man dressed in a pristine royal-blue suit with a handkerchief folded neatly in the top pocket. His white hair is slicked back with gel, and his thick eyebrows have been combed upwards to the degree that they've set up home in the centre of his wrinkled forehead. 'Here, let me take that off your back. Theodore Robson-Jones,' he says, pulling the cello off my shoulders, 'but call me Teddy.' He thrusts his hand into mine and shakes it so vigorously that he nearly pulls my arm clean out of its socket. 'We are so delighted that you have agreed to come and perform with us, Lucinda.'

'Please, call me Lucy. I'm only Lucinda when I'm in trouble.'

He snorts, then briskly rubs my arm like he's trying to spark a fire. 'The choir are positively *desperate* to meet our star of the evening. Come, *Lucy*,' he winks, 'let's go and meet your fans.'

Within five minutes, I've been hugged, mwah-mwahed and applauded by over a hundred wealthy pensioners. Princess Diana would have had less of a reception.

The rehearsal comes and goes. Although it isn't anywhere near an 'international' soloist's standard, I'm at least able to play from start to finish without bursting into tears or getting lost. I would be far more comfortable if the banner outside read 'Knackered mum of two who only realised that she was doing this concert on Monday', but it's out of my control. Hopefully, the audience will be a civilised bunch – *not* the sort of crowd that lobs eggs in protest on discovering they've fallen victim to the powers of false advertising.

After the rehearsal, I'm invited for dinner with Teddy and the entire tenor section from the choir. 'We like to treat our soloists to nothing but the best here in Southampton,' were his exact words, so when I end up with a bowl of gluten-free mac 'n' cheese being dumped in front of me at the local Pizza Hut, I realise that these people aren't as fancy as I first thought.

My dinner looks like something you'd find in the toilet the morning after a booze-filled night out, but a salad wasn't going to tame the riled-up butterflies in my stomach, nor did I want to order a pizza and risk being fat-shamed at Slimmers' Weekly next week. As I sit listening to old men argue about which Beethoven symphony is the most superior, I force down a few mouthfuls of the cheesy gloop, then politely excuse myself and escape to the church to get ready.

The churchyard is packed with well-dressed pensioners queueing out of the door, waiting to collect their tickets from the box office. It's like a scene from Last Night of the Proms, where hundreds of culture-hungry people camp outside the Albert Hall for days to get the best seats. The sight makes me retch. The butterflies have launched into a violent fist-fight (or more like a wing-slap) and my head is spinning. I fear that I'm going to regurgitate mac 'n' cheese gloop all over the cold, stony floor – or, worse, shit it out everywhere. There is no way of knowing which of the two is going to happen, but my body tells me that I need to find a toilet, and I need to do it fast.

Unfortunately, the only toilet in the building sits directly opposite the box office by the entrance to the church. In a total panic, I push through the crowd, dash inside, bolt the door, then pull down my maternity jeans and throw myself down on the toilet seat.

And, in this ghastly moment, all of the stress and anxiety that has built up in the last week, the last year, perhaps over the last thirty-three years, comes flooding out of my body in one swift, fluid motion.

In a place of God, it is truly unholy!

Terrified, I slowly turn around to face what I've just birthed, and sitting in the toilet bowl is the most gargantuan turd that I've ever seen. It is a thing of wonder – *huge!* Like something pictured in one of Stan's anatomy books under the title 'The Magnificent Capabilities of the Human Colon'. Hell, it might even be one for the *Guinness World Records* book. I chuckle to myself and immediately pull out my phone and take a picture to send to Charlie. She won't believe it.

After this rapid offloading of my tremendous load, I'm calmer. I remove my clothes, zip up my long black dress and casually press the lever to flush away a lifetime of anxiety, then head to the mirror to powder my nose. With my make-up done, heels on and my sparkly necklace in place, I lift my bag and glance back to see that the almighty stool is still there, bobbing in the water like a morbidly obese otter.

Chill! It's no big deal.

I pull the flush once again, but then I'm struck in the chest with a sharp dagger of fear as I watch the otter leap up towards the edge of the bowl.

Fuck! No!

I throw myself down on the floor, my hands looming under the bowl preparing to catch the beast.

NO! Stay in! Stay!

And it stays in!

Thank you, sweet Lord!

I curse and try again. The same. And again. I wipe the sweat from my brow, say a little prayer and try again, but the otter rises to the rim of the bowl, taunting me like a wicked minion of the devil. Consumed with panic, I then throw my full weight onto the flush handle and it comes clean off in my hand.

This, of course, is when I notice the sign:

> Please take extra care and do NOT jerk the flush handle. The flush is sensitive. This toilet is a newly restored facility funded by patrons of the church.
>
> *Thank you*

NO!

The only toilet in the building is destroyed and the stubborn otter is still in there, smiling up at me from the filthy bog waters, delighted in his victory. In a place so holy, how can this act of pure evil happen?

My first instinct is to call Ed – a total waste of precious time because his phone, as always, is off. Next, I try Charlie.

'I've blocked the fucking toilet!' I whisper. 'What do I do? What do I do? I'm on-stage in fifteen minutes.'

Her reply is short. 'Anxiety shit? Fuck! There's nothing for it, love. *Run away!*'

And so, just minutes before my 'international' solo, I cover up my heinous crime with an entire toilet roll. I hide the broken flush handle behind a can of lemon air freshener, open the door and calmly stroll away from the huge queue of well-dressed pensioners that has formed outside.

I even manage a smile.

'How did it go?' my friends will ask.

And I will reply 'I have no idea', because all that lingered in my mind throughout the entire performance were Teddy's introductory words.

'Due to unforeseen circumstances, the toilet facilities are currently out of action. Please could members of the audience use the Portaloos outside in the churchyard.' Followed seconds later by, 'And now, please welcome our soloist for the evening, internationally renowned cellist Lucinda Wright.'

'Were you nervous?' Jen will ask.

'Not in the slightest,' I will say, because there was no room in my brain for nerves. As my hands glided up and down the cello, my only thoughts were of the otter that I'd left lurking in the toilet and, more specifically, whether my audience knew that it was me, the 'international' soloist, who had released it.

'Ah, the Lord works in mysterious ways,' Charlie will say.

'Yes, he sure does,' I'll reply.

Because that's the God's honest truth.

49

Reality Bites

'How did it go? I bet you were amazing!' Ed calls out as I walk through the front door.

He is waiting for me at the dining table where a magnum of champagne is chilling in an ice bucket and a beautiful bouquet of yellow roses is spilling out of a vase that he has placed in the centre. 'I'm so proud of you! Come and sit down, tell me everything.'

But, no. This is not my reality.

The truth is that I return from my 'international solo' and *fall* into the flat, tripping over Ed's suitcase that he's left lying wide open behind the front door. In pitch darkness, I clamber up, slam on the light and, in a rage, kick a mountain of his dirty washing out of the way and make room to put my cello down. The air is thick with the stink of curry, wet nappies and farty drainpipes.

As I pass the kitchen, I glance inside and see bottles of festering formula and dirty plates dumped in the sink where they float in stale, browny-green water. My not-so-charming prince is in the lounge, sprawled out on the sofa, snoring soundly with his arms tucked behind his head. I scan the scene of devastation, not wanting it to be true. Empty bottles of Becks are dotted about and yellow-stained plates and foil boxes from Tandoori Villa are stacked in a pile on the coffee table. More crushing than an unconscious husband and a trashed flat is the sight of his phone lying on the recliner, still turned off.

This is my reality.

My husband is a rock star now, and rock stars don't wait up for their wives. They don't check their messages, or ask themselves why they have five thousand missed calls, because as long as there's backstage parties and four-poster beds to sleep in, nothing else is worthy of their attention.

With the heaviest of hearts, I slip off my concert dress and heels, scrape off my make-up and pull on my jammies, then pour myself a strong gin. I down it in one go, then pour another and set about doing the chores – chores that are apparently better suited for the international toilet-clogging soloists of this world.

And when I'm hunched over the sink rinsing out the dirty bottles, it strikes me.

The man might be home, but I'm still totally alone.

By 6.30 a.m., Ed is in no better state. Slumped in the recliner surrounded by crisp packets and chocolate bar wrappers, he sits watching Spiderman cartoons.

'Hey, love, I've got the lag,' he whines the moment I walk into the room. 'I've been sat here since four.'

'Well, you were snoring last night when I got home, so at least you've had *some* sleep.'

'Not enough,' he says, 'not nearly enough. Can you put the kettle on while you're up?'

Just as I'm about to exhale fire, Stan stomps down the hallway and unknowingly saves his father's life. He taps me on the elbow to get my attention. 'Excuse me, but I would like my apricot yoghurt, my chocolate pancake and my banana *now*. In circles.'

'Stan, I thought you were going to call me *Mummy* now.'

'Mummy, can I have circles?'

'Circles, *please*,' I reply emphatically, wondering how many years I will have to direct his speech in this laborious way.

'Daddy, you are on my chair. I need that chair. Can you move now?'

Ed leaps out of his seat without hesitating.

'He didn't say *please*, Ed. Come on!'

'It's okay. I'm going back to bed for a bit anyway.' He stretches out his arms and releases a deliberately dramatic yawn.

'Okay, whatever, but before you go, aren't you at least going to ask me how it went?'

'What do you mean?' he says, his attention elsewhere as usual.

'I *mean* my massive solo concert that I had last night?'

My words take an age to register. 'How did it go?'

'Well, I blocked the toilet with a giant shit and then spent the whole performance panicking that everyone knew what I'd done. So, pretty tragic, really.'

'Yeah,' he says vacantly. He lifts the cushions off the sofa and tosses them carelessly on the floor.

'Ed, my cushions! What are you *doing*?'

'Looking for my Hulk pyjamas … I thought I left them here.'

'Second drawer down. Clean.'

'Okay, thanks, love.' He slips out and takes himself off to bed, my cushion display demolished and our marriage on the brink of collapse.

In the hours that he is unconscious, my anger and disappointment naturally dilute. There's no time to sit around moping about autism diagnoses, blocked church toilets and jet-lagged husbands because, once again, I'm alone with two small kids who demand my attention every minute. Nappy changes, meal preparation, gall-bladder games and alphabet challenges leave little room for much else, and with Ed's dirty washing clogging up the hallway, I've been kept more than busy.

It's just after dinner-time when he emerges from the bedroom and wanders into the kitchen, where I am loading the dishwasher. He pulls a beer out of the fridge, opens it and takes a swig. 'So, I've got news,' he says animatedly.

'What?'

'I've just got off the phone to the tour manager. I've been booked to do the next tour! Four weeks around Europe in September. And, if that goes well, there's the possibility of an Australian tour over Christmas.'

And this is when I start to cry.

50

Waterworks

The floodgates have opened. First it was my bowels and now it's my tear ducts. I sob and sob, my chest convulsing as I struggle to catch a breath.

'What?' says Ed, totally dumfounded. 'I thought you'd be happy.'

I can't string a sentence together to reply.

'It'll be loads of money,' he continues.

My guttural wailing immediately becomes an annoyance to Stanley, who has appeared in the doorway holding a letter B and a rubber bladder.

'You are too loud. Loud, loud, loud! You are banging my eardrums.'

'Just leave then, Stan! Go to your room! *Get out!* Now, now, now, NOW!' I screech, my voice piercing the atmosphere like a long shard of glass. I instantly regret my outburst, but it's too late; the hardness of my voice has already hit him. With his hands held defensively over his ears, he starts to scream.

'I'm sorry, Stan. I'm sorry.' I try to hug him, but he lashes out and starts thumping my chest with his fists. 'Help me, Ed! Just hold him. Hold him as tight as you can.'

Totally flustered, Ed intervenes and manages to lift Stanley up into his arms. He carries him through to the living room, lies down with him on the sofa and hugs him until, eventually, he calms down. I'm left in the kitchen sobbing, ashamed and emotionally worn down, desperate for a hug myself.

A hug that never comes.

Stanley avoids me for the rest of the evening. He shuts himself away in his room where I can hear him from the other side of the door matching up body parts with their corresponding capital letters.

'K is for kidneys, L is for lungs, M is for ...'

'Mummy. M is for *Mummy*,' I want to say. In fact, I'm tempted to burst through the door and bellow it in his face.

But he says 'mouth,' then moves on to 'N is for knee'.

Ed responds to the palpable tension in much the same way – by hiding in our bedroom, dusting his vintage *Star Wars* figures. Once the kids are down and I've cried my last tear, I pop my head around the door with a cold beer in hand to lure him out.

'Ed, we need to talk.'

'Okay. Let me just put my figures away first,' he says sheepishly, and off he goes to wash his hands.

I start the conversation, knowing that he is never going to take the lead. 'About before, I'm sorry. I didn't mean to lose my shit at your good news, and definitely not to shout at Stan, but everything's just got on top of me.' One tear slips out of my eye and it doesn't take long for more to follow, racing each other down my cheeks until they drip off the end of my chin. 'It was really shit when you were away. Now you're saying that you're going again, and I can't stand the thought of it right now.'

'What's happened?'

'If you bothered to charge your phone, you would know, Ed. Stan has been diagnosed. He is autistic.'

He says nothing at all.

'Yep. I found out on Friday. I called you several times and left messages.'

'I lost my charger,' he says defensively. 'I told you, I left it on the tour bus.'

'But your phone *was* ringing then, Ed, so that's a bullshit excuse. And I also called a million times before that to tell you that he had the worst meltdown I've ever seen in front of Marsha and Hugo ... and all of the kids that will be in his new class.'

Still nothing.

'Then she called to gloat and I told her that Stan was autistic, and she went all quiet and weird and now I'm in a panic that I've said the wrong thing. I've outed him, thrown him to the wolves. I should never have told her.'

'Told her?'

'That he's *autistic*, Ed.'

'But he's far cleverer than that little dipshit Hugo.'

'I know, but that's not the point is it? It's not about being clever, it's—'

'He's no different to how I was at his age,' he interrupts, then slips off the sofa on to his knees and runs his fingertips slowly across the rug. 'I can still see that blue stain. Shall I order something from eBay to shift it?'

'Ed! I'm pouring my heart out here. Why won't you listen?'

'What do you mean?' he says on autopilot, still distracted by examining the stain up close.

'What do I *mean*? God! Why do you *always* say that?' I snap. 'I *mean* that I need your support. I need you to listen and offer up an opinion about our son. I can't do it all by myself!'

'Do what?'

'All of it: the appointments, the meltdowns, the night feeds, the bum wiping, the cutting bananas into fucking circles day in and day out. And when I'm not doing those things I'm panicking about money and trying to get my career *and* our relationship back on track. It's just too hard. I have no one to talk to about any of it. No one to listen to anything I have to say.'

He sits cross-legged on the rug, his head hanging down like a naughty child being told off by his teacher. 'Do you want a beer?' he finally says.

'No, Ed. I don't want a fucking beer. I want a hug! It's not that hard, is it?'

He crawls across the floor back to the sofa and I pull him up and wrap my arms around him, crying thick, salty tears on to his shoulder.

'What do you want me to do, love?'

'You can do anything, *anything* at all.'

'Like?'

'What?' I pull away abruptly from his arms. 'You want a list?'

'Yes, that would be good.'

I look at his face and realise that he's being serious. 'Well, okay then. Brace yourself, Ed, because I've been storing these up for quite a while. One: how about you react to the fact that I just told you your son is autistic? It's a pretty big deal, isn't it? Get angry, cry, throw stuff or tell me everything's going to be okay – *anything* will do. Just react!

'Two: why don't you pick up the phone and call when you're away? I know it sounds impossible to comprehend, but maybe you can check in, talk to me, ask me how I'm coping and find out how your kids are, even.'

'But we *did* speak! You told me about Stanley playing with Spiderman.'

'Only because I called *you* – about four thousand times over three weeks.'

The words 'What do you mean?' fall out of his mouth again.

'Three: *stop* saying "What do you mean" all the time. It drives me nuts! Four: perhaps ask me how my concert went and actually listen to the answer. Remember that it's *not* just you who is an incredible musician, I am too. Or, at least, I *was*.'

'You are,' he says.

'Five: take some initiative. Maybe get up with Jack in the night every so often so I can get some sleep before I become clinically insane. Seven: pick up your dirty clothes and all of your shit off the floor and stop creating more work for me to do.'

'What about six?'

'*Fucking* number six: do something romantic for me, like you used to. Anything will do. Make me dinner again or write me another shit poem … or make an effort to seduce me, give me a kiss or a shoulder rub or something. It feels like it's always me taking the lead.'

He leans in to kiss me, but I instantly push him away.

'Eight: stop disappearing to play with your dolls all of the time.'

'They're figures,' he says defensively, 'vintage figures!'

'Ten: Stop saying "vintage figures".'

'You mean nine.'

'Are you serious? Okay, nine: stop being so pedantic about things that just don't matter, and start focusing on the things

329

that *do*! Ten: you could tell me I look nice every so often, even if it's not true. I feel like you don't fancy me any more.'

'I do fancy you!'

'Well, you should tell me that you do.'

'I just did.'

'Ugh! Eleven: control your mother – she's horrible to me all of the time. Twelve, and this one really gets to me: stop, for the love of God, *stop* undoing all of the progress that I make with Stanley.'

'I don't,' he says, 'I don't.'

'You do – all of the time, Ed. Just yesterday you said "bum germs" to him and now he'll be back to washing his hands every ten minutes. And lastly, thirteen: open your eyes and look at the mess that I've become. Ask yourself "What can I do to make things better for my wife?" Because I wasn't always like this. I used to be happy, and now I am stressed, sad and scarily overwhelmed. I can't see how it's ever going to get better if you can't support me in the way that I need.'

He sits in silence, his fingers drumming rapid rhythms on the palm of his left hand.

'Okay, wait a sec,' he says. He disappears to the kitchen and returns with a tatty brown envelope and a biro. 'Right, tell me again so I can write it all down.'

'Forget it!' I yell. Then I storm out, slamming the door behind me.

51

A Huge Weight Off

Ed left the morning after our big fight. I woke up alone in bed to find a brief note on his pillow: 'Gone to visit Mum'.

That was two days ago and I haven't seen or heard from him since. It's almost laughable to think that he was only back in the flat for twenty-four hours before running off again to hide at his mum's house. And learning that he'd rather suffer two full days of sunflower seeds and green tea over apologising to me suggests that things are pretty critical between us.

I've noticed a pattern in Ed's response to our arguments over the years. If we have a mild disagreement – or what I call a Level One dispute – Ed will usually slip off to bury his head in his Action Man collection. If a more heated Level Five goes down, he'll leave the flat and vanish to the pub for a few hours to drown his sorrows. But, on the rare occasion that a Level Ten happens, he'll totally abandon ship and run back to the arms of his mother.

In the nine years that we've been together, we've had just a couple of Level Tens, and after each one, he only came home after I gave in and waved the white flag. The man has always shied away from confrontation, and after any disagreement, he's never really known how to make amends. Sooner or later, I know that I'll have to dust off the flag once again and spell out to him what he needs to do to fix things between us. But I'm not ready to do that yet, because this time I'm not sure that we can be fixed.

My mum has made it difficult for me to have the time to sit and feel sorry for myself. Since telling her about Stan's diagnosis, I've been bombarded with calls every few hours, and although she was a bit tearful at first, declarations of love and positive thoughts about the whole thing quickly followed. Yesterday afternoon, a huge parcel loaded with treats arrived on the doorstep with a note saying 'Love you all so very much, from Nanny and Bampi'. Inside was a bottle of wine and a load of crisps for me, some bags of Haribo and a copy of Jenga to keep Stanley occupied, and a cute cuddly hedgehog for Jack. It's hard – if not impossible – to feel sad when you have such amazingly supportive parents behind you.

Rachel's reaction to the news was to distract me by yapping on the phone about the latest juicy gossip from the village. Apparently, her quiet neighbours – Dilys and Ivor – were raided at 5 a.m. on the weekend by the police, and to the astonishment of the entire community, a cannabis farm was found growing in their attic!

'Holy shit!' I said.

'I know!' she replied. 'And apparently they had more than thirty grand's worth of drugs growing up there.'

'So that's how they afforded that monstrosity of a camper van that's been clogging up most of your street, eh?'

'Yep. And that's been repossessed now for evidence, so I've got my parking space back.'

She went on to tell me that Ozzy Jones is back on the keto diet, so both the local Co-op and the Spar have been forced to introduce a strict 'only two per customer' policy on the purchase of pork scratchings. And finally came the revelation that Bungalow Baz – Tref Y Glaw's most eligible bachelor – had bagged himself a new girlfriend! The woman is sixteen years his senior and he met her waiting for a bus outside the Beacon Bingo. I mean, how is there time to fret over my son and my marriage when there's so much more drama going on in the world?

Although I've chosen to keep the truth about Ed's abandonment from my family, Charlie knows everything. She stopped by last night with a three-litre box of wine and virtually poured it directly into my mouth as she listened to me rant about Ed. Her company was welcome, but her advice wasn't particularly helpful. As much as I would like to 'dump the bozo' and 'shack up with a millionaire yacht-owner with a washboard stomach and a dick down to his knees', it wouldn't solve any of my problems.

Money, yachts and big dicks aren't what I want: Ed is. But not the Ed that came back from tour. I want the one that I met nine years ago in a TV studio: the loving, attentive man who would drop everything for me; the man who would yank acupuncture needles out of his body and wade through a city of nine million people just to give me a hug when I'm sad.

But that Ed is long gone.

It's now Wednesday, day three of no contact. With Jen busy having her wedding dress fitted, I'm taking Jack to meet Charlie at Slimmers' Weekly and straight after the weigh-in we're going for coffee to finalise details for Jen's hen do this Saturday.

When I arrive at St Peter's Church, Charlie is leaning against the wall with a Greggs carrier bag looped around her wrist. The tail end of a jam doughnut is in her hand and the rest of it is bulging out of her cheeks like a hamster.

'Doughnuts, Charls! Outside Fat Club? You're going to get lynched in there if you're not careful.'

'I'm only here for a social,' she replies nonchalantly. She wipes the sugar off her lips with the back of her hand and leans over to kiss Jack on the forehead. 'You look like shit, Luce,' she sputters, showering me and Jack in caster sugar and specks of dough. 'So, I take it that he's not back yet?'

'Course not,' I say. 'He's not even texted. Nothing.'

'The jackass! Well, he'd better get his arse home by Saturday.'

'He'll be here. If I have to, I'll message his mum to get her to send him back.'

'Or I'll drive down there and drag him out with my bare hands, Luce.'

'No! I'll handle it,' I say firmly, knowing full well that she isn't joking. 'Let's just go in here now and get this done, but for God's sake, put that cake away first.'

She rolls her eyes then delves into her carrier bag, pulls out another doughnut and takes a deliberately large bite. With her mouth full, she mumbles what sounds like 'multipack' then flashes me a gummy smile so wide I can see the jam stuck in the gaps of her teeth.

All the same faces are waiting in the queue for the weigh-in, returning to the line of shame to face the mistakes of the week just past. Once again, we are behind the same gang of slender young mums who, on account of the baking-hot weather, are all wearing denim hot pants and strappy vest tops.

'Mark ordered a Dominos last night and literally ate the whole thing right in front of me,' one of them says, 'and it was a double pepperoni with olives as well.'

'He didn't!' her friend spits, disgusted. 'He knows how hard you've been trying on your diet, doesn't he, Sadie?'

'Yep, of course he does, but that didn't stop him eating three Mars bars one after the other. Then he finished off my Pinot Blush without asking me.'

'I would have stabbed him,' Charlie interjects casually. 'The Mars bars are one thing, but you don't fuck around with a woman's Pinot. *Everyone* knows that.'

The group turn around and glare at her disapprovingly. I elbow her swiftly in the back and serve up an apologetic smile: 'Don't mind her, ladies, she hasn't had her morning coffee yet.'

They turn away and shuffle a little closer together, then carry on chatting but much quieter than before. 'Um, so where are we going for lunch?' one of them says.

'Pizza?' whispers Sadie. 'Definitely double pepperoni with olives.'

'And Pinot,' Charlie interrupts once again. 'Get yourself a pint of it, love. With a straw.'

'Hurry up, everyone, let's move it along. I have to leave a bit early today,' Pat calls out from the other side of the room, where she stands munching on a cereal bar at the makeshift shop. 'I've got a man coming to fix my washing machine at two.'

One by one, we pull off our shoes and climb on to the scales, then wait for Pat's assistant to discreetly slip the dreaded bit of paper detailing our results into our hands. Maggie, last week's Newbie Loser of the Week folds hers up and quietly slinks off to take a seat in the circle. Next up is

Sheila – the Starbucks skinny-hot-chocolate addict. After collecting hers, she hobbles over to the far end of the circle, sits down on a chair and pulls her Sainsbury's Bag for Life off the floor and on to her lap. Sadie is triumphant when she glances down at her results and lets out a brief squeal of delight, but her reaction is minor compared to Charlie's when I show her the numbers on my slip of paper.

'Four pounds off!' she shrieks extremely loudly. 'Fuck! Luce, you fucking legend!'

Naturally, I want to bolt straight out of the door and escape the disapproving looks of the pensioners, who aren't too impressed with Charlie's colourful language, but instead, I drag her and Jack over to take our seats and listen to Pat pick us apart one at a time.

Twenty tedious minutes later and Pat lifts a box of vegetables and makes her way to the middle of the circle to announce the winner of the Newbie Loser of the Week.

'And this week's winner of a delicious box of fresh fruit and vegetables is … Drum roll, please … Lucy! Four. Pounds. *Off!*' she gushes and starts to applaud.

The group join in half-heartedly and my face bursts into flames.

'So, Lucy, my honey,' says Pat once the applause has fizzled away, 'you've got to tell us all, how have you done it?'

With twenty sets of eyeballs gawping at me, waiting for me to say something profoundly inspirational, I only manage an 'um'.

'Don't be shy, honey. Speak up,' she continues. 'Did you lay off the carbs?'

'Not really.'

'Drink more water?'

'No.'

'Did you try any of our new recipes from the website? Any exercise? Come on, my darling, sharing is caring. How have you done it?'

'Actually, Pat. The truth is that my son got diagnosed with autism, then I did a giant anxiety shit and destroyed the entire sewage system of Southampton, and then I had a massive fight with my husband who has since left me. *That* is how I've done it.'

Sadie and her pack of mum friends start to applaud, then Sheila, Maggie and the woman manning the shop join in. Before I know it, I'm getting more whoops and cheers than you'd hear from a horde of teenage girls at a Justin Bieber concert.

For some unknown reason, I then stand up, plonk Jack on Charlie's lap and find myself delivering a weirdly passionate acceptance speech.

'Ladies, I'm sorry but I just cannot sit here and hold my tongue a minute longer. I just *have* to say that you are *all* gorgeous and your sense of self-worth should *not* rest upon how many pounds you weigh! Sadie,' I say, pointing at her, 'you have an *amazing* body – and you have brought life into this world. Look at your son – he's perfect, and you grew him in that amazing body of yours. So drink your Pinot and eat your pizza – God knows you've earnt it! And Sheila!' I say, swiftly redirecting my finger to the end of the circle, where she sits fiddling with the handle of her carrier bag. 'You, my lady, are beautiful! Have as many hot chocolates as you want, my love. Life is too fucking short to drink black tea!'

The applause cranks up once again and Sheila's carrier bag slips off her lap onto the floor, but she is too busy clapping to retrieve it.

'And if any of you ladies fancy a nice burger and a pint, me and my friend here are heading to the pub to celebrate our awesomeness. You're all welcome to join.'

And with that, I lift Jack and stride out of the hall.

Charlie follows, then Sheila, Maggie, Sadie and her slender friends, leaving Pat behind holding the box of vegetables, her mouth gaping open in shock.

52

The Epiphany

It has been a week of extreme highs and crippling lows and I didn't think that my heart could take much more stress, but I was wrong.

Just after breakfast, Ed finally breaks his silence with a text.

> Bought a new charger so phone working again. Home tomorrow at lunchtime. Helping Mum hang some shelves.

That's it. No apology. No acknowledgment of our fight. No declaration of undying love. No promises to change. Not even a kiss. Nothing. And worst of all, he's forgotten that I'm leaving for Jen's hen do in Edinburgh first thing in the morning.

I quickly call Amy and check that she's free tomorrow to hold the fort until he gets home, then compose an icy reply:

> I won't be here when you get back. Away until late Sunday night in Edinburgh … I DID tell you, but I guess you weren't listening. Amy free to watch boys, unless you want to come back earlier? Or are your mum's shelves more important?

I press Send, then turn my phone off for the rest of the day.

The morning flies by. There's so much to organise before leaving for Edinburgh tomorrow so I keep my head down and get it done as best I can. After picking Stanley up from nursery, I pop Jack down for a nap and set up camp on the sofa with the application form for Stan's Disability Living Allowance. I'd printed it off yesterday, all sixty-two pages of it, but only managed to reach question eleven before giving up in frustration. There are fifty-four multiple-choice questions in total, but almost every single one is followed by a blank paragraph where I'm expected to include 'additional information' about Stan's difficulties.

Writing what is essentially a dissertation about my child's problems doesn't sit well with me. Our son is amazing, and I'm not comfortable ripping him to shreds and sending it off for a stranger in a benefits office to read and pass judgement on. But, at some point, he will need financial support towards various therapies, and if this is what it takes to get it, then I have to keep going to the bitter end.

Stanley is lying on the floor in front of me in just his pants, stacking up the Jenga blocks that my mum sent him. The game has been a hit, and although it's great to see him playing with something other than body parts, the vocal interjections of rage that occur every time the wooden blocks collapse are distracting me from the arduous task at hand.

'No! No! No! NO!' he shrieks in frustration when his structure crashes to the floor.

'It's okay, Stan, just try again,' I say calmly. 'Build another one – you can do it.'

He tries again, and it collapses. Then again, and the same.

As I watch his tower rise and fall, it strikes me that Jenga is a perfect metaphor for what's happening in my life right now. Each block of my life that I've carefully added to build a soaring tower of achievement has come crashing down in one swift motion and, sadly, all that remains is rubble.

For as long as I can remember, all I've ever wanted was to make it as a musician. I sacrificed so much of my youth barricading myself indoors with just my cello for company, determined that one day I'd achieve my dream of adding the Career block to my tower. At age nineteen, my sacrifices finally paid off when I passed a fiercely competitive audition and secured a place to study at the most prestigious music college in London.

Once there, I battled another five long years trying to keep afloat in an intense environment designed to drown the weak. The competition was fierce, the bitchiness rife and the politics corrupt, and on one memorable occasion, I experienced brutal violence when I was stabbed in the hand by a concert pianist wielding a sharp HB pencil. I'd been queueing for an hour to sign up for the practice room that she wanted, so using her weapon of choice, she took it from me and I was left standing in the corridor, bleeding and in tears.

I put myself through hundreds of shitty auditions and collected a stack of rejection letters so thick that it made the Argos catalogue look like a pamphlet. But when I met Charlie and Jen in my third year, I added the Best Friends block to my tower, and with them by my side, my confidence started to soar. I learnt to keep my head down, to avoid the arseholes and to dodge the HB pencils (and thanks to Charlie's influence, I even summoned the courage to stab the piano bitch back and she never bothered me again).

After wading through all of these obstacles, the Career block was firmly secured at the top of my tower the day I was offered my first professional concert. To start with, I played for crappy choral societies in cathedrals miles out of London, but eventually, I started getting some well-paid offers with reputable orchestras.

Professional life was full of ups and downs and would flit dramatically from playing a symphony at the Royal Festival Hall one day, to teaching a twelve-year-old kid that it was unacceptable to say 'Fuck it' in a cello lesson on the next. But by the age of twenty-four, I was proud of my tower and more than satisfied with what I had built. It wasn't perfect, but it was my own. My dream career was flourishing, I had financial independence, fabulous friends and a supportive family behind me.

When I met Ed, everything changed. Aside from being the most incredible musician, he was handsome, honest, uncomplicated and possibly the kindest person I'd ever met. From the word go, we were a perfect fit and I had no reservations about adding the Boyfriend block to my tower. (Hell, even Charlie liked him, which spoke volumes because she has little time for most men.) Of course, he wasn't perfect – but neither was I. He could be jealous, impatient and clingy, and he'd get pretty upset if I had to cancel our dates to work, but these flaws were so minor compared to his many, many strengths.

After six intense months of dating, we felt ready to merge our blocks and build a new tower together. I moved in to his flat in Ealing and we filled it with furniture that we bought on 'buy now, pay later' schemes. When we weren't passing each other in the door coming and going from our respective gigs, we were out at the cinema or getting smashed at The

Lodge together with our friends. We shagged up against the fridge, spent lazy mornings watching movies in bed and, with the help of credit cards, we treated ourselves to extravagant holidays that we couldn't really afford.

We were happy, secure and in love, and a couple of years down the line, we came to the decision that we were ready to add the Baby block to our flourishing tower. It took ten months to conceive, and when I was heavily pregnant, we threw the Marriage block on to our pile and had a cheap shotgun wedding to keep my parents and Judith happy.

And just like that, we had it all: Marriage, Career, Flat, Money, Social Life, Independence and Baby on the way. But it wasn't to last, because the day that Stanley was born was the day the whole thing came tumbling down, crashing to the ground with an almighty thump.

Everything that we'd built together was lying on the floor in ruins, and neither of us had the first clue about how to start rebuilding. Overnight, I'd lost my career and my independence, which were perhaps the two parts of my life that I mourned the most. I went from travelling the country with a cello on my back – successful, admired and valued – to being stuck in the flat all hours with a new-born baby and having to rely on Ed to provide for me.

Where I found our new situation challenging, Ed just couldn't adapt to the upheaval of having a baby around. He instantly became far more impatient and overdramatic, and his anxiety was the worst it had ever been. A simple nappy change would often propel him into a state of hysteria. 'It's on the rug! There's shit on the rug!' he would yell, and then he'd prioritise cleaning the rug before tending to Stanley.

He was totally inflexible with Stan's routine and became visibly stressed when he didn't do what Ed predicted.

'But he liked carrots yesterday. Why not today?'

'He's supposed to nap for one hour and he's only had twenty minutes.'

'Why has he done another poo? He did one half an hour ago!'

'He's a baby, Ed, not a machine!' I would snap, but he simply couldn't fathom that babies had minds (and bowels) of their own.

If Stanley was crying, Ed would vanish in a flash, and hours later, I'd be furious when I found him hiding behind the wardrobe door with a Luke Skywalker in his hand. He would stay out late after work, then come home and take himself off to the bedroom, where he would sit in silence for ages. Whenever he was left alone with Stanley, he would avoid taking him out – terrified that he would cry – and would make any excuse possible to stay indoors. At the time, I thought he was selfish, that he simply wasn't prepared to put our son's needs before his own. I'd sacrificed so much, why couldn't he?

Some days, I was so fed up with Ed's behaviour that I fantasised about beating him to death with Sophie the Giraffe and burying him under a patio somewhere. But, when calm, I told myself that I had two options: sink or swim. Or rather, I could beat him to death or accept that perhaps being a parent came more naturally to me than it did to him. If I could survive being stabbed with a pencil by a piano-playing nutter, then I knew that I could survive this too.

Thankfully, as Stanley grew older, Ed was able to adjust to his role as a father and become much more hands-on. He was still wildly impatient and useless at the practicalities of parenthood, but when it came to playing with Stan, he was the master. They were like peas in a pod and spent hours lining up the alphabet together. And even though it meant that I was left to wash the shit-stained babygros, obsess over baby-led weaning and panic about neurodevelopmental milestones, I learnt to accept that he was contributing in his own way by spending quality time playing with our boy.

A couple of challenging years down the line, we stood back to admire the tower that we'd rebuilt. It was stronger and more beautiful than ever, because placed right at the heart of it was the most precious block of all: the Stanley block. Our hard work had been more than worth it, so we did what most couples do and started trying for another baby.

And now that our gorgeous Jack is here, it's clear that our tower has collapsed once again. History is repeating itself and Ed's flaws have resurfaced, only this time around, it's different. Because this time, I can finally see things clearly.

As I sit watching Stanley gradually work himself up into a rage playing Jenga, I think of Ed. I see him directly in front of me and realise that I'm not angry at him, nor do I feel frustrated or murderous any more. What I feel is guilty, the dark, stabbing pain of guilt, because after all the years that we've been together, I finally understand.

There's a reason why Ed behaves the way he does, and that reason is right in front of me, lying in plain sight amongst the metaphorical ruins.

Autism.

I've been so blind. Ed is autistic too.

53

Piecing Together

'*H*e's no different to how I was at his age ...'

Ed's words from our big fight are suddenly at the forefront of my mind, and the more I think about it, the more I realise that he has said words to this effect many times over the years.

When I told him that Stanley had memorised all of the cars on the street, his response was underwhelming. 'I used to do that when I was two or three' was all he said. And when the child read *The Very Hungry Caterpillar* from cover to cover with no assistance, I was totally flabbergasted, but Ed didn't consider it to be a big deal: 'Yeah, Mum said that I read the whole of *The Cat in the Hat* when I was a toddler.' I can't deny that I flat out dismissed this comment at the time. Judith is nothing if not a champion boaster, so I assumed that she was just full of shit as usual. But what if she was right? What if her comments about Ed's childhood hadn't been grossly exaggerated?

With Judith fresh in my thoughts, I suddenly remember the box of Ed's old schoolbooks that she'd brought down a few months ago, having hoarded them in her garage for decades. I leap off the sofa, dash to the bedroom and ransack Ed's wardrobe to find them. The box is hidden underneath dozens of carefully packaged *Star Wars* figures, and I rip it open, pull the contents out onto the floor and start flicking through piles of musty, damp exercise books.

The first book in my hands is labelled 'Edward Wright, Reception Class, Writing'. Halfway through it, I find a sweet story about Jesus written by four-year-old Ed. His handwriting and spelling are immaculate and far advanced for a child of four – exactly like Stan's.

I scroll through pages upon pages of intricate drawings and beautiful writing, rather surprised by its quality, given that Ed has always said he was shit at school and hated going. Not only was he bullied but he'd told me that he was useless at everything, except for music. He found it hard to concentrate in class and was repeatedly told by his teachers that he was naughty and lazy. Eventually, he began cutting classes and even jumped the fence and ran away on several occasions, only to be driven back to the headmaster's office by the police.

By the time he was sixteen, he'd totally given up trying and left school with a string of poor grades to work in a factory making guitar straps. Based on his stories, I'd assumed that he was a badass as a teenager – a guitar-playing wild child who challenged authority and disrespected the system.

But now I get it.

He wasn't a badass. Nor was he lazy or naughty. He was autistic, and no teacher, police officer or even his own mother would have been able to detect it over thirty years ago when such diagnoses were rarely given.

Leaving the room totally trashed, I grab my laptop and rush back to the lounge. Although I know the standard checklist of ASD traits in children off by heart, I've never quite allowed myself to imagine how Stanley will be when he's an adult, when – like his dad – he's had over forty years of experience surviving in a world that isn't designed for those who are different.

I pull open the laptop, take a quick swig of cold coffee and then Google 'autistic traits in adults'.

The results describe Ed to a tee.

- Difficulty interpreting what others are thinking or feeling
- Trouble interpreting facial expressions
- Difficulty regulating emotion
- Repetitive or ritualistic behaviours
- Fixed interests/obsessions and deep knowledge of particular topics
- Strict consistency to daily routines
- Struggles with auditory processing

Damn! Stanley is Ed.

It all makes sense. From the small things, like his obsession with vintage toys and the way he orders DVDs, to the bigger ones, like how he has been so emotionally detached from what's been going on at home lately. His daily rituals and need for structure, his inability to cope with noise and germs, his anxiety when out in busy places and the way he always disappears to the bedroom to be alone ... *all* of it has been right under my nose this whole time.

Yes, he struggles to emotionally regulate himself, and I constantly chastise him for being overdramatic. Yes, he often misinterprets my facial expressions, and he rarely responds in the way that I need when I'm craving his support or when I'm angry or sad. And a double yes to the last point about auditory processing. I think of the four irritating words that fall out of his mouth several times a day: 'What do you mean?' I always assume that he isn't listening to me, that he has no interest in what I have to say. But no. 'What do you mean' is merely a tool – a subtle phrase that he unconsciously uses to buy himself time to process my words.

From simple domestic tasks to huge life-changing decisions, he has always found it difficult to take the initiative without me having to guide him – be it mopping up a spillage or proposing marriage.

But none of this is deliberate. His brain just works differently to mine because he is autistic. It is autism.

Next, I type 'Is my husband autistic?' into the search engine and my screen floods with hundreds of articles, many of which are written by mothers who only realised that their husbands were on the spectrum after their children had been diagnosed.

One article is an excerpt from a book entitled *Asperger's Syndrome: The Essential Guide* by Hilary Hawkes and her words blow me away.

If your partner is autistic, you may be experiencing some of the following relationship issues:

- Feeling ignored or not needed
- Feeling that you are only wanted for what you do for your partner
- Being deprived of emotional support
- Lack of normal conversation due to your partner's inappropriate, pedantic or blunt responses

- Your partner may have difficulty with initiating everyday chores within the home or family. If you have a child, you may feel that the overall burden and responsibility for parenting falls on you. Your partner may feel more like an extra child than an equal in the parenting stakes.

As I read through each point, my brain yells 'Yes, Hilary!' 'YES!' and 'Holy shit! Of course!' It's like the woman has drilled into my brain, scraped out every feeling of frustration I've ever had about Ed and our marriage, then written a book about it.

The relief is tremendous, the love overwhelming, the guilt horrendous, and I start to sob on account of all three.

'Excuse me, but you are too loud,' says Stanley, who has abandoned Jenga and is now watching YouTube. 'I cannot hear my video.'

'Sorry, Stan. I can't help it. I just feel like crying.'

'Are you sad?'

'No. I'm happy. They're happy tears.'

'But you don't cry if you are happy. You smile.'

'I know,' I say, then I smile.

'Jack cries when he is sad, and he smiles when he is happy or when he is doing a poo.'

'You're right. Mummy is being silly. I'm doing it the wrong way around.'

'Okay,' he says, 'but you are too loud.'

I look down at his big blue eyes that are fixed on the singing gall-bladder on the TV and another tear drops off the end of my eyelashes. 'I'm so happy that I'm your mum,' I say.

'Excuse me. But did you know that a ghoul-bladder is shaped like a pear?'

'A *gall-bladder*, you mean. And no, I didn't, my sweetheart. I didn't know that at all.'

Then he pauses the TV and looks up at my face. 'I love ghoul-bladders,' he says, which he follows with a genuine smile. 'I love them a lot.'

I swallow my tears. 'And I love you too, Stan.'

54

Cock-a-Doodle-Do

'Right, has everyone brought their cock hair-bands?'

'Yep, Charlie, sure have,' replies Maz.

'Check,' I say casually, like it's the most normal question in the world.

It's the day of Jen's hen do and we're all standing by the check-in desk at Heathrow, waiting for her to arrive. Reluctantly, I'd left for the airport at 9 a.m. just after Amy arrived to look after the boys. Ed is due back at lunchtime, and although every fibre of my being is screaming for me to run home and wait for him, I simply can't. As one of Jen's best friends, I have a duty to stay and give her the ultimate send-off into married life. So this I will do.

Charlie turns to So Jung: 'Jungers, did you buy that cock hairbrush that I sent you the link for? And the cock chocolates?'

'The "Cock-o-lates", you mean? And yep. Got 'em.' She smiles cheekily. 'I even found some cock earrings and a matching necklace, plus a handbag with little hairy balls all over it. Where cock and balls are concerned, I think we've got it covered.'

'Good. Full marks for you, Jungers.' Charlie pats her on the back. 'Oh, here she comes!'

Jen skips up to the queue, positively beaming. 'My girls! Thanks so much for coming. I love you guys!' Tears ensue within seconds and Charlie pulls out a hair-band with two glittering pink cocks stuck to the top of it and hands it to her.

'For fuck's sake, Jen, pull yourself together and put this on, will you?'

'Really?' She wipes her tears away. 'Not sure it matches my outfit.'

'Not yet,' I say, 'but it will later, mark my words.'

Jen gives in and allows Charlie to plant the monstrosity on top of her head.

'Perfect,' she says, standing back to admire her work. 'Now get this jewellery on, Jen, and put your stuff in this hairy ball bag. Then we can check in, hit the bar and get this hen started. In fact, all of you … I believe it's time to don your cocks.'

And we do as we are told.

By the time we arrive in Edinburgh, we're all fairly merry after sharing three bottles of Prosecco at Wetherspoons in Heathrow followed by a few gins on the flight after Charlie – quite the accomplished flirt – managed to squeeze a few miniatures of Gordon's out of Scott, one of the cabin crew. She leaves the plane with his number in her pocket and absolutely no intention of ever calling him.

Just after lunchtime, our minibus pulls up outside a dingy black-bricked building which has 'The Studios' written scruffily in bright-red paint over the door.

'Oh God,' says Jen when she looks out the window, 'what is this pl—'

'Attention, ladies!' interrupts Charlie. She springs up out of her seat and makes her way to the front of the bus. 'Just to inform you that we're starting our afternoon with a little art and culture before we let rip later.'

'What ... in *there*?' Maz says. 'What is this place?'

'A sex dungeon, I think,' I say.

'Shhh! Less attitude, please, ladies. You'll just have to trust me. So, before we dismount our chariot, can we all make sure that we have our things? And that includes all cock-themed attire and empty tinnies. Thanks. Over and out.'

We unload all our bags off the bus and she ushers us into the ominous building and down a long, dark corridor, like a bossy teacher on a school trip. Upon arriving at a door marked 'Studio 54.5', she peers inside, then grabs Jen by the arm and pushes her in first.

Standing in the centre of the large, brightly lit room is an unexpected sight: a six-foot tall, tanned, muscly man with a red rose in his teeth. A man who, of course, is totally naked.

'Ladies! Welcome,' he says in a thick Spanish accent after pulling the rose out, 'I am Mateo and I will be your model this afdernoon. Dell me, ccch-oooo is Jenniver?'

'I am.' Jen waves awkwardly.

'Well, sid down and led me pour champine. Here, make yourself comfortable.'

'Mateo' fills up five flutes and slowly walks the full length of the table with a tray perched just above his love stick. Every glass removed from the tray exposes more and more of his jewels, and by the time he gets to me, I am gifted the pleasure of seeing up close everything that the man has to offer.

'Thanks so much, Mateo. What an attentive host you are,' purrs Charlie. Standing up, she clinks a pen on the side of her glass. 'Attention, ladies, here's the plan. In front of you all is a sketch-pad and some pencils. Mateo here is going to pose for us – in whatever position we choose, might I add

– and we're going to draw him. And at the end, he'll give a bottle of wine for the best portrait of the day.'

Jen's face is crimson. 'Oh gawd, I can't draw.'

'I can. I've got an A* in GCSE Art, ladies, so watch yourselves,' brags So Jung. 'That wine is mine!'

'Whatever. We'll see,' says Charlie. 'Crack on the music, Mateo, and let's get started. First, I'm thinking something with the rose, on all fours.'

'The pleasure,' he pauses to wink, 'is all mine.'

The sound of 'Sexy Thing' fills the air before the man struts out to the centre of the room and drops down on all fours, giving us a no *holes* barred view of the crack of his arse.

'Sweet Lord! I'm in my element here. Well done for getting married, Jen!' squeals Charlie as she snatches pens and pencils off the table, her eyes fixed so wide open that they're close to falling out of their sockets.

By the end of the session, we've all had the pleasure of getting to know Mateo rather well. Indeed, there isn't an inch of his body that goes unseen. The more champagne that glides down our throats, the easier it is for him to break down our inhibitions and persuade us to get more creative with our directions. What starts out as me saying, 'Mateo, can you sit on the chair with your legs folded, please?' soon turns in to Maz asking him to 'prowl like a panther'. At Jen's request, Mateo is only too happy to finish with a headstand up against the wall with the rose wedged between his butt cheeks.

Charlie is chosen as the winner, her dramatic portrayal of his love muscle having won Mateo over.

'That's so unfair,' huffs So Jung, 'you've drawn his dick all the way down to his ankles! Mine and Lucy's are much more realistic.'

'Tough luck, Jungers,' Charlie says. 'GCSE Art is all well and good, but everyone knows that it's flattery that gets you *everywhere*.'

We quickly stop off at our hotel to dump our cases and doll ourselves up to the nines, and an hour later, with arms looped, we venture out to paint the town red in short dresses, heels and, of course, our glittery cock hair-bands.

Charlie mapped out a route of all the best pubs in Edinburgh in advance and is positively militant about adhering to the schedule. But three pubs in, and what seems like hundreds of miles walked, Maz breaks. 'I'm done. My balls are burning, Charlie! Can't we just stay in one place for a bit?'

'Hell no, woman! I've got a table booked at a cool cocktail place. It's ten minutes from here. Trust me, a few piña coladas and you won't feel your feet any more.'

'I'm with Maz,' says So Jung. 'I can't take one more step in these heels!'

'Me too, Charls. My bunions are red raw. Let's sit tight for a bit to refuel, eh?' I say.

'Fine – you pussies!'

And so we set up camp in a booth in the nearest pub, aptly named The Royal Dick. Hilarious hen games follow, and once we've had our fill of traditional Scottish ales and persuaded the shy trainee barman to have his photo taken with one of our hair-bands on his head, we hobble up the street to a funky burger restaurant for a quick dinner. It's happy hour when we arrive so, naturally, we order mojitos by the pitcher and knock back as many as our livers can take, then we drag Jen to the toilets and dress her up in a battery-operated, inflatable penis costume.

Our final destination is a seventies nightclub called Disco Inferno. With VIP tickets in hand, we bypass the line of Saturday-night thrill-seekers queuing all the way down the street and venture inside. Hundreds of people wearing brightly coloured afro wigs, stick-on sideburns, flares and platform boots fill every inch of the dance floor and with 'Night Fever' being blasted out over the speakers, we don't hesitate to join right in. Jen's hideous costume immediately draws the attention of a crowd of men, and as soon as she and the girls are happily distracted by their ridiculous pelvic thrusts, I discreetly slip off to the toilets to check if Ed has called.

But he hasn't.

I've tried him several times throughout the day, but with no success. If Amy hadn't messaged earlier to let me know he had arrived safely and the handover had gone smoothly, I wouldn't know if the man was even alive. My chest aches: my heart is possibly broken. I consider trying him one more time, but a bunch of rowdy women enter the toilets and slam on the hand dryer, which puts an end to that. Sitting on a toilet in a nightclub with an audience of drunken strangers listening from behind the door is hardly the place to make this call, so I stuff my phone back in my bag and pull up my pants.

But just as I'm about to leave the cubicle, my phone starts to buzz.

I drop to my knees, turn my bag upside down and shake the entire contents out all over the tiled floor. A load of tampons and lipsticks roll away under the cubicle door, my foundation compact hits the ground and a burst of orange dust and shards of mirror explode all over the place. I grab my phone – the screen now also smashed – and carefully wipe the dust off it with the rim of my skirt.

It's not Ed, but a text from Simon Monroe, the biggest session contractor on the London music scene.

> Hi Lucy. Saw you in Southampton on
> Saturday. Well played! How are you fixed for
> three days of sessions next week? BBC Radio
> 2 live with Take That.
> Timings to follow. Let me know ASAP. I have
> other calls out. Cheers. SM

It's a text that I've waited my whole career to receive. Finally, I'm on Simon Monroe's radar, and in my hand is the precious golden ticket that could open doors to a world that most musicians never get near in their lifetime. But, weirdly, I don't care. I feel nothing. No thrills, no desire to whoop or cheer or to run out and share the news with my friends ... nothing. And what's more, I don't even bother to reply. Instead, I clean the mess off the floor, force a smile on my face and head back to the party.

Charlie has bought up most of the bar, and upon my return, she hands me a full pitcher of lager. 'That one's all for you, pal. Chin up! Tomorrow's a new day, right?'

'Right.'

I pour as much beer as I can down my throat to sedate myself from my intensifying misery, then hit the dance floor with my girls where we spend the rest of our night jiving with a beautiful Scottish man called Alasdair and his boyfriend, Joel.

Come 3 a.m. we are all danced out. Maz's feet are bleeding and my bunions might as well be broken, but, man alive, we've had fun. We drag Jen to the nearest chippy and she slumps down on a chair in the corner while I join the queue to order her a veggie burger.

With her face pressed up against the window, her skinny legs splayed open and the penis costume now rapidly deflating, it's a sight that must never be forgotten, so Charlie takes a hundred pictures of the hilarious scene and even invites the chippy owner over to pose. With a bag of complimentary food in our arms, we pull Jen up and stagger down the street in the dark to try and find our hotel.

I'm so hammered that I can't put one foot in front of the other without crashing into the wall, so being the absolute legend she is, Charlie escorts me to my room and helps me undress and flop into bed.

'You're steaming, woman! I've never seen you so shitfaced,' she says as she wrestles my skirt and tights down over my hips.

'I'm sad, Charls – about Ed,' I slur, unperturbed that my semi-naked body is splayed on the mattress in front of her. I try to sit up, but fall back onto the pillow. 'I think he's autistic. Actually, no. I *know* he is.'

'Okay.' She pauses, her expression totally blank. 'That doesn't surprise me.' She pulls my top up and over my head, then pushes my legs closer together and lays the duvet over me. 'But why are you so miserable, Luce? It doesn't change who he is.'

'But it changes *me*. Because I'm a shit wife. I've thrown all my energy and attention into Stan but I've totally neglected Ed.' My bottom lip starts to tremble, so I bite down on it firmly, wincing briefly from the sharp pain. 'I've been so hard on him ... so shit to him.'

'You're *not* shit, my friend! I won't have it. You look after Ed and those amazing boys so well. I know it's not been easy for you, but you're so patient. Damn, you're fucking extraordinary.'

'I'm ... not!' My voice cracks and, before I can stop them, the tears start to fall.

'You are. I know he hasn't been there for you in the way that you'd like, but for all his faults, he's a good man, Luce. He adores you and those kids.'

'I know he does.'

'And if you're right about Ed, then doesn't that make you feel better about Stan?'

'What do you mean?'

'Well, Ed's made a success of his life, hasn't he? Just look at what he has.' She pokes me in the chest. 'Autism hasn't stopped him, Luce – and it won't stop Stan, either.'

I wipe my soaking wet face on the duvet and sigh. 'God, you're a wise old bitch.'

'Well, duh.' She smiles cockily.

'Okay, but what now? Should I tell him that I think he's autistic? I mean, how do I do that?'

'*Definitely* tell him. Just pour him a glass of wine, sit him down and spit it out.'

'Just like that?'

'Yep. I reckon it'll probably come as a huge relief to him, Luce. And to know that you support him, that you "get" him, and that you have his back no matter what, can only be a good thing.'

My eyes fill up with tears again when I picture his face.

'Seriously, don't sweat it. It's Ed we're talking about here. Your soulmate, your knight in shining armour – your diamond in the rough! If it comes from you, he'll be cool with it.'

'He is a diamond.' I sniff. 'As men go, he's literally one in a million. Men like him – and Tom, of course.'

'Not Tom,' she frowns, 'definitely *not*.'

I look at her face and detect a hint of something unfamiliar in her eyes … sadness. 'What? What's happened?'

'Long, boring story to tell there, Luce, but not right now. Let's just say that loyalty was an issue for him.'

'Oh, Charls.' My heart sinks. I reach out to hug her and she leans into my arms. 'I'm so sorry. Want me to kick his ass?'

'You're too shitfaced to kick anything right now.'

'And you're not? Charlotte Danvers, professional violinist and champion binge drinker.'

'Actually, I'm not shitfaced at all.'

'Yeah, yeah ... whatever!' I slur.

She pulls away from my embrace, pushes her hair out of her eyes and then takes me by the hand. 'Luce. I'm pregnant.'

55

Strong

T he story takes hours to drip out.

Cosied up in my bed together, we drink our way through every complimentary sachet of tea and tub of UHT milk available, and when that runs out, we move on to the decaf coffee. Charlie tells me that the whole thing kicked off a week ago, the day after the 'l' word slipped out of Tom's lips for the first time. Not being used to hearing such affectionate words from a man, she was taken aback, and in the heat of the moment, she failed to reciprocate the sentiment. Out of guilt, she decided to make it up to him and, as a surprise, she turned up to his hospital the next day wearing nothing but a trench coat, ready to declare her love. He walked out arm in arm with another woman, and after following them to a pub on Wood Lane, she peered through the window and saw the pair snogging at the bar.

'The bastard!' I snap.

'Yep. But, on the bright side, I bet you and your roadkill fanny are a tiny bit relieved, eh?' she says, trying to make light of it. 'You'll never have to see the jackass again, Luce.'

'Stop it, Charls. It's not funny. I just can't believe you haven't told me any of this. Why didn't you call me?'

'Because you were busy. You'd your big concert and all that stuff going on with Stan and Ed to deal with. Besides, I've been putting the hen do of a lifetime together, don't forget.'

'I'm *never* too busy for you, Charls.'

She goes on to tell me that the day after catching Tom with his tongue down another woman's throat, she had to run off-stage to be sick during a camera rehearsal on the *Jonathan Ross Show*. She subsequently passed out, and when she came around, the onsite first-aider decided to err on the side of caution and sent her to A&E for a check-up. One hour and one urine sample later, she was told that she was pregnant.

'I'm ten weeks. I paid for a private scan a couple of days ago. Look.'

She pulls a photo of her scan out of her bra and shows it to me as a little tear drops out of her eye, then she makes it abundantly clear that she does not want Tom (the 'wanker') to be involved.

'You might feel like that now, Charls, but having a baby is tough. Do you really want to do it alone?'

'Yep,' she says firmly. 'My mum is the strongest woman I know, Luce. She did everything for me and my brother after my dad ditched us and—'

'I know Charls, but—'

'No. I've decided. I am *not* putting my faith in a lying twat of a man. I'm putting it in myself.'

I hug her for ages. 'You, my friend, have a hell of a steel vagina.'

'And so do you,' she replies warmly. 'Besides, I'm not doing it alone. I have you, and you have me.'

We spend the rest of the night in tears: chatting, hugging, laughing and planning our futures, whatever they are to be. Come morning, after not one second of sleep, we wipe the tears off our faces, rub some concealer under our eyes and, with big smiles on our faces, we make our way to the lobby to meet Jen and the girls for our final day of fun before heading home later.

'You're not to say anything to anyone, Luce. I'll tell Jen once she's back from her honeymoon. Promise?'

'Of course, my friend.'

One boozy brunch later, we take our glittery cock hair-bands out for one final airing. We sample the traditional delights of Edinburgh: drinking whisky in tankards, eating haggis with colcannon and dancing along the street to the bagpipers who stand on every corner. Charlie's performance is admirable. Unbeknownst to the rest of the girls, she sits in every bar with a glass of tonic water in hand, pouring every ounce of energy she has into making sure that Jen is having a ball. She leads us all in a series of humiliating games and invites strangers over to join us, and the day ends with a photo of Jen sandwiched between two topless builders, their moobs and pot bellies plastered in five different shades of our lipstick.

In the airport bar at the end of our whisky-fuelled adventure, I stare at Charlie from across the table as she flicks through the funny pictures she'd taken on her phone. She looks beautiful: so happy, so strong, so brave. The woman is a femur, and I know that she's right. She'll never allow herself to be defeated by anything, least of all 'a lying twat of a man'.

As I watch her laughing with one arm wrapped around Jen, I make the decision that I too won't let myself be defeated by anything – including autism.

56

The ABC of Love

At nearly one o'clock in the morning, I arrive home to a scene that makes me bawl instantly. The living room is filled with dozens of burning candles and on the dining table lies a spread of treats: a bunch of roses sitting in a pint glass of water, a multipack of Chilli Heatwave Doritos, Prosecco and nine bars of Toblerone, one of which has a Post-it note attached:

> One bar for each year that you have put up with me. Ed xxx

Propped up against the Prosecco is a large card which says 'To my darling wife' on the envelope. I wipe away the tears, sit down and open it.

Inside is Ed's declaration of love, delivered in a way that is so perfect, so unique and so him.

> How I feel about you can be explained in movie (and TV) quotes in alphabetical order:

> And don't forget, I'm also just a *boy*, standing in front of a *girl*, asking her to love *him*.
> *Notting Hill*, 1999

But for now, let me say ... without hope or agenda ... to me, you are perfect.
Love Actually, 2003

C'mon, guys. It's a known fact that lobsters fall in love and mate for life. You can actually see old lobster couples, walking around in their tank, you know, holding claws ... he's her lobster!
Phoebe Buffay, *Friends*, 1994–2004

Dead or alive, you are coming with me.
Robocop, 1987

Everything I have ever done, I've done for you.
Great Expectations, 1946

Frankly my dear, I [do] give a damn.
Gone with the Wind, 1939

Go ahead, make my day.
Sudden Impact, 1983

How you doin'?
Joey Tribbiani, *Friends*, 1994–2004

I'm not a smart man ... but I know what love is.
Forrest Gump, 1994

Just keep swimming [next to me]
Finding Nemo, 2003

Kan you feel the love tonight?
The Lion King, 1994

Love is passion, obsession, someone you can't live without.
Meet Joe Black, 1998

Make of our hands one hand. Make of our hearts one heart.
West Side Story, 1961

No, I like you very much. Just as you are.
Bridget Jones, 2001

Ogres are like onions [and so am I because I made you cry].
Shrek, 2001

People call those imperfections, but no, that's the good stuff.
Good Will Hunting, 1997

Once the Queen is dead, the King is useless.
Penelope, 2007

Roads? Where we're going, we don't need roads.
Back to the Future, 1985

You Should be kissed and often, and by someone who knows how.
Gone with the Wind, 1939

The greatest thing you'll ever learn is just to love,
    and be loved in return.
Moulin Rouge, 2001

U make me want to be a better man.
As Good as It Gets, 1997

May the V orce [of my love] be with you!
Star Wars: Episode IV – A New Hope, 1977

When I'm with you I don't feel so alone.
Hercules, 1997

All you need is faith, trust and a little bit of piXie
    dust.
Peter Pan, 1953

You complete me.
Jerry Maguire, 1996

Zed's dead, baby. Zed's dead.
Pulp Fiction, 1994 [Nothing starts with Z but it's still
    a great quote, right?]

Hope you had a great time with the girls. I'm so
    sorry that I have been so shit. I promise that
    I will try harder to be your perfect man. I love
    you so much. I'll wait up for you. xxxx

I sit soaking up every line of what he has written for ages,
and once I've finally stopped weeping, I go to find him. Our

bed is empty, so I wander next door to the kids' room. Jack is sleeping peacefully in his cot with his tiny thumb in his mouth, and Ed is snuggled up with Stanley in his big-boy bed, a row of mini organs lined up across his forearm.

I decide not to wake him. It's a sight that I could stare at forever.

Ed, you are perfectly imperfect, and I love you.

Just as you are.

57

I Do

I wake to the sound of Stan's infectious laughter through the bedroom wall.

'Again, Daddy! Again!'

'Okay, here we go. Five, four, three, two, one … Thunderbirds are GOOOOO!'

I tie my straggly hair up with a scrunchie, throw on my dressing-gown and hurry out to join in the merriment with my unique family.

'You look very pretty today,' Ed says animatedly the moment I step foot out into the hall. 'Coffee?'

'Thanks, love. Yes, please.' I smile, then quickly scrape off the crust of dribble that has gathered at the corners of my mouth. 'Hi, everyone. Hi, Stan, I've missed you.'

He ignores me, as expected. 'Again! Again! Daddy, again!'

'Stan, Mummy is home from her trip. Give her a big hug and tell her what you've been doing.'

He walks over and wraps his arms loosely around my waist. 'Mummy. I have four things to tell you.'

I feel my heart melt as the word 'mummy' glides down my ear canals.

'Number one, red is still my favourite colour. Number two, I drew a picture of a large intestinines for you. Number three, Jack was sick on Daddy and he said "Fuck" again. And number four, Amy took me to the park and I saw Emmanuel and he wants me to go to his house for tea. He wants to eat fish fingers and waffles and beans, but I won't eat beans because they are orange.'

'Goodness me! That's a lot of stuff to happen in one day, Stan,' I say as I look over at Ed, who is smiling sheepishly, no doubt on account of the 'fuck' revelation. 'So, when are you going to Emmanuel's house?'

My question falls on deaf ears as he wanders into the living room to watch one of his videos as scheduled. 'I would like my apricot yoghurt, my chocolate pancake and my banana *now*. In circles,' he says before closing the living room door in my face.

'Can I have it now, *please?*'

'Please,' he shouts through the door.

I head back to the boys' bedroom and lift Jack out of his cot, then make my way to the kitchen to get a coffee and start the usual breakfast routine. Ed is hovering by the kettle, drumming his fingers on the coffee canister, waiting for me to put him out of his misery.

'I'm sorry, love,' I say warmly. 'I'm sorry for being such a dick. I didn't mean it. I loved your card so much ... and all of the Toblerone.'

'Did you like the 'Zed is dead' bit?' He smiles, the relief clear on his face. 'I thought we could watch *Pulp Fiction* later. I bought steaks, and KitKats for dessert.'

'Give me a hug, you soppy jackass.'

We hug for ages before he withdraws. 'I've got to go to the shops in a minute. Do you want anything? I need duct tape for my parcel – I've sold another figure.'

'Great. How much did you get?'

'A hundred and seven quid. Plus four quid for postage. I withdrew it as cash, and I've hidden it inside *Million Dollar Baby*. It's on the third shelf down with all the Best Picture winners, between *Crash* and *The Lord of the Rings*, in case you need it.'

'Thanks, love,' I say, 'and, yes, we do need a few things. Bread, bananas, Cheetos, yoghurts, but not the tubes – it has to be in pots with no lumps.' I look across at his face and see his eyes glaze over. 'Actually, shall I just write you a list?'

'What do you mean?' he says on autopilot. Instead of snapping, I wait for him to process what I've just said and, sure enough, after a brief pause, he replies, 'A list would be great.'

Our afternoon is spent eating Cheetos and watching gall-bladder videos together in our pyjamas, and after bath-time, Ed helps Stanley to organise all his body parts in alphabetical order, which causes him to flap excitedly and insist that they do the same with his toy cars. Ed follows his lead, and with Jack in the bouncy chair observing the organised fun, the three of them are contented up until bedtime.

Once the kids are settled for the night, I open a bottle of red wine and pour two glasses all the way up to the rim. I've decided that the time is now. I'm going to take Charlie's advice and sit Ed down and tell him about my recent epiphany. There's no knowing how he will react, but for the sake of moving forward in our marriage, I'm prepared to take a chance. I glug down half a glass then kneel on the floor and set about sorting out my whites from my coloureds while I wait for him, inwardly rehearsing what I'm going to say.

Moments later, the kitchen door swings open and smacks the wall with such force that I fall back on my arse into a pile of dirty clothes. I look up to find Ed leaning in through the door, wearing nothing but a leopard-print thong with my glittery cock hair-band perched on top of his bald head. In his hand is the long reel of condoms that has been festering in the bedside drawers for weeks. He flashes me a comically seductive grin then wiggles his head to jolt the glittery cocks to life. 'Shall we?'

'Hell yes!' I laugh. 'Get that dinger out! I'll meet you in the bedroom in five – I'm just putting a wash on.'

He lingers in the doorway, watching me stuff dirty clothes into the washing machine, his fingers drumming on the kitchen counter. 'Do you still love me then?' he says quietly.

'I do,' I say. 'In fact, I do, I do, I do, I *do*.'

Acknowledgements

This book wouldn't exist without my children who are a huge inspiration for me. 'Jimmy' and 'Mr Belafonte', you are the brightest, funniest and most adorable little people who have ever walked the planet. I'm so very proud to be your mum. Thank you for being yourselves, and for showing the world that it's okay to follow your passions … no matter how unusual they might be.

You truly are my everything.

To my lush husband and soul mate, J-boy. Thank you for all the nights you cooked the beige dinners and single-handedly did 'Bed, Bath and Beyond' so that I could have peace to get the words out. I love you insanely. (Now, any chance you could unload that dishwasher, make the school lunches and take the pug out for a quick poo so I can crack on with writing these acknowledgements?)

To Sarah Hodgson, my fabulous editor, you are a genius! I can't thank you enough for your expert guidance. I've learnt so much from you and if I ever win the lottery, you're first on my list to get a cool million. It's the very least that you deserve.

To Katie Fulford, my wonderful agent and fellow lover of Hugh Jackman, thanks so much for your unrelenting support, your sage advice and for helping me get my baby out into the world. You're an absolute diamond and I've loved working with you (but hands off Hugh. He's mine!)

To Emma Dunne, Kirsty Doole, Hanna Kenne and all of the team at Corvus Books, thank you! You are all so lovely and totally brilliant at what you do! I couldn't have wished for a better team to work with. And the same goes for my proof reader, Liz Hatherell, and typesetters Ben and Ruth at Ben Studios. You're all fabulous!

Heartfelt thanks to the folks at Nescafé for producing the vital beverage needed to keep me conscious through the many nocturnal edits. Equally important are the local suppliers of Portuguese custard tarts which have helped to sustain my energy levels. A special mention goes to the inventors of the Xbox and YouTube for distracting my kids long enough for me to be able to churn out an entire book. And sincere thanks to the grape pickers in Italy. Without your Pinot Grigio, I doubt that I would have made it this far.

And now for my family who really are one in a million.

To my gorgeous mum and dad; thanks for all the laughs which never fail to happen when I'm around you both. You have supported everything that I have ever done, whether it's piercing my belly button, wearing black lipstick, learning the cello, or writing a novel. And sorry for the teenage years. I promise I'll never drink vodka ever again. Equally, I swear I'll never run up another £1500 mobile phone bill (and if I do, I'll pay for it myself). I mean it!

To my *biggest* supporter, my sister Helen; magnificent, intelligent, bossy and hilarious. Thanks for reading this novel a gazillion times, for making (brutal) suggestions, for teaching me how to use a computer and for generally being the true brains behind all of it. In short, thanks for being you. And to my brother David – your massive personality is highly contagious and vital to a writer of comedy. Thanks for being alive.

To Emma Parker, one of my best friends and a fellow autism mum, thanks for reading this book to death despite having kids hanging off your elbows at every given moment. No matter how difficult our lives get, you make me howl with laughter every day and without you, my world would be fifty shades of grey. (Um, not sure that came out as I intended, but you get my drift, right?!)

To the legendary Jessica Feaver who essentially taught me how to write a book. Thanks for your limitless encouragement, your frankness, and for making me remove the MANY passages that were just *too* crude for the public eye. You're delicious, my friend.

To Hilary Hawkes for granting me permission to use an extract from her brilliant book, *Asperger's Syndrome: The Essential Guide*.

To special friends and colleagues who have both inspired me and shared their experiences and wisdom: Lene Bausager, Amy De Sybel, Emsie, Kots, Katie Pryce, Ben Ellis, Milly, Gwenllian Hâf MacDonald, Katie Chatburn, Kevin Core, Becky Jones and Ozzy Jones. To all of the Muso Mums, Bridgend Netmums and Facebook pals who have answered ALL of my questions. And mahoosive love …

And lastly, my biggest thanks to the wonderful autistic people and parents of autistic children who have offered me and my family invaluable guidance and support over the last several years. I have learnt so much from you all and continue to do so every single day.